HUMBUG

Scrooge Before the Ghosts

HUMBUG

Scroogee Before the Ghosts

SARAH WHELAN

www.mascotbooks.com

HUMBUG

Second printing. This Mascot Books edition published in 2023.

For more information, please contact:
Mascot Books, an imprint of Amplify Publishing Group
620 Herndon Parkway, Suite 220
Herndon, VA 20170
info@amplifypublishing.com

Library of Congress Control Number: 2023907119
CPSIA Code: PRV1023B
ISBN [hardcover]: 978-1-63755-804-1
ISBN [paperback]: 979-8-89138-156-8
Printed in the United States

This book is for Catherine.

I wish she were here to read it, but sadly I must release it into a world without her. My sincere hope is that it is appreciated by others who, like Catherine, are smart, talented, and beautiful, yet feel they have nothing to look forward to in life.

To these people, I say, "You are precious, and you are loved. Humanity needs you and everything you have to offer. No matter what your critical inner voice is telling you, no matter what negative emotions fill your heart at any given moment, you are not nothing. Please stay."

I will honour Christmas in my heart, and try to keep it all the year. I will live in the Past, the Present, and the Future. The Spirits of all Three shall strive within me. I will not shut out the lessons that they teach.

—Charles Dickens, *A Christmas Carol*

CHAPTER ONE
MERCY

1850

The phantom looms over my deathbed, his skeletal form shrouded in the same hooded cloak as the first time he appeared to me, on Christmas Eve some seven years ago. He is silent, as before, but his mission is a different one. Instead of the redemption he and his fellow specters offered on their previous visit, he has come to collect and deliver me to the spirit world.

"Do not take me yet, Phantom." My voice is as shaky as my resolve.

A tear trickles down my cheek, but I lack the strength to wipe it away. It lingers there, stalled halfway through its journey, just as I remain teetering at the edge of a desolate chasm between life and death.

It is not the fear of dying that keeps me here, for I know what awaits me in the afterlife. I redeemed myself after Jacob Marley and his ghosts left me with a soul churning in regret. I embraced my penchant for compassion, loved and was loved in return, and undid some of the damage I had inflicted on the souls of others, as well as my own. It took the better part of my life to amass the courage needed to reject the moral constraints society imposed and overcome the obstacles I had embedded in my own path. True happiness came only when I gave myself completely to the person I loved most.

I earned my rightful place in eternity, and my heavenly sanctuary awaits just beyond the mortal realm. But I choose to endure, despite the agony, as spasms tear through my body and I shiver with cold, though the blankets weigh heavily upon me. I offer this suffering willingly in exchange for the opportunity to revel in the memories of my seven decades on this blessed earth.

In my final moments, I wish to honor those who walked beside me through a lifetime comprised, in turns, of misery and happiness, selfishness and altruism, isolation and kinship, bitterness and love.

On my knees, hands clasped against my chest and head bowed to the towering shadow figure, I beg, "Grant me time enough to remember. Then I will surrender my soul. I will offer no resistance. Will you have mercy on your old friend Scrooge?"

A single nod is the phantom's response.

Grateful for his gift of a temporary reprieve, I grip his bony hand. "Lead on, generous spirit. Let us journey to the past."

CHAPTER TWO

CHRISTMAS REVELRY

1810, Thirty-Three Years before the Ghosts

"Yo ho, my boys." My employer's cheerful voice announced the long-awaited end to the workday.

Abandoning my unfinished ledger, I dashed across the warehouse toward Mr. Fezziwig's office. My fellow apprentice, Nick Wilkins, approached from the opposite direction at the same speed, and our shoulders grazed as we skidded to a stop in front of the old man's desk. We steadied ourselves, backs straight and arms flush against our sides, endeavoring to hide our excitement with forced, and I suspected, unconvincing, earnest expressions.

Sitting tall in his Welsh wig, Mr. Fezziwig laid his hands upon the high desk and laughed in his characteristic head-tilting, open-mouthed, shoulder-bouncing way, which made it impossible for anyone within range of it not to reciprocate. And we did, Nick and I. We laughed along with him, our smiles as broad as his and our spirits alight with joy.

"No more work tonight. It's Christmas Eve." Mr. Fezziwig hopped down from the chair with surprising agility and fastened his waistcoat over a sizable belly. Leading us out of the office, he included the whole of the warehouse in the sweep of his hand. "Clear away, my lads, and let's have lots of room here."

Nick and I set to work, pushing crates aside, sweeping the floors, and trimming the lamps. We showed the fiddler to his chair and helped the caterer carry the food, our mouths watering as we arranged the trays of meat pies, cold roast, and sweet cakes on the tables. Our energetic operation created the desired result, and the warehouse was transformed into a ballroom fit for the merriest of celebrations.

Mrs. Fezziwig made her entrance next, her smile nearly as engaging as her husband's and her figure nearly as round. She was followed by the three Miss Fezziwigs, all beaming like their parents and dressed in fancy gowns. The youngest, Belle, tilted her head to look at me through one eye more than the other, waving a fan under her chin.

After the Fezziwig women came a steady stream of guests, each of whom played a role in the family's business or personal affairs. Soon the room filled with a joyous crowd whose liveliness raised the temperature such that there was no need for Nick and me to add more wood to the fire.

"Well done," Mr. Fezziwig cheered at the end of an especially lively round.

The fiddler beamed, his one remaining tooth interrupting an otherwise gummy smile. He hoisted a pot of ale and drank it down in its entirety, filled his lungs with air, and set his chin on the instrument to begin again. I tapped my foot and bobbed my head in time with the music, but a pang of hunger reminded me I had not eaten since breakfast. I left Nick to watch the next dance by himself while I ventured to the refreshment table.

I saw him then, for the first time.

He was leaning against a support beam, a wineglass in one hand and a cigar in the other, talking with a lad I recognized as a servant from the

Fezziwig household. He glanced my way, dismissed the boy with a nod, and turned toward me.

His lips barely parting, he grinned and tilted his head to look at me the same way Belle Fezziwig had earlier. He was older than me, I guessed, though perhaps not by much. Maybe ten years my senior? Regardless, he was a man of significance. From his meticulously styled hair to his navy tailcoat with turned-back cuffs and white cravat, everything about him supported this conclusion.

"Good evening, friend," he said.

"The like to you, sir," I replied with a bow.

The corners of his mouth curved downward. "You make me feel old. I am 'friend' or 'mate,' not 'sir.' At least I hope to be."

"Of course. My apologies, s—" I stopped myself before the irksome word fully emerged. Afraid of offending again, as I often managed to do despite my best efforts to avoid it, I asked, "Do we know each other?"

"Sadly, we do not, but I am glad to make your acquaintance." He switched his drink to the other hand, holding both it and the cigar at once. It was an impressive feat, in my opinion, and one he appeared well practiced in. With his empty hand, he shook mine. "I am Jacob Marley."

I returned his smile and offered my own introduction. "Ebenezer Scrooge."

"Well, Ebenezer, where are you heading? I fear you may be lost since the dancing is that way." He pointed over my shoulder and sipped his wine, his mustache skimming the edge of the glass and the lit end of the cigar coming precariously close to his well-oiled hair.

I had no answer for him, having forgotten my intention, but I regained my bearings and formulated a sufficiently coherent response. "I am looking for the refreshments."

"Let me be of service to you," he said, gesturing toward the table behind him, which I myself had placed in the spot.

I chose drink instead of food and swallowed it down in gulps, enjoying the warmth of the sweetened brew as it traveled the distance from my lips to my empty stomach. Ladling another serving, I drank that one down as well, all the while sensing his gaze upon me. With my glass filled for the third time, I turned to find him standing close.

"I have not seen you speaking with any of the ladies," he said. "Do they interest you?"

"They do not," I replied. Such was the truth of the matter, though I did not understand the motivation for his inquiry.

"I see." He nodded. A furrow etched in his brow, as if I had divulged a fact of great significance. "Will you dance nonetheless?"

Whether it was the drink or the unfamiliar, though not unwelcome, prickle spreading through the deepest recesses of my body, I was bold in my reply. "I shall. And you?"

He shook his head and shrugged. "I prefer to watch."

I swallowed the contents of yet another glass and started toward the crowd. Belle Fezziwig took the position across from me, and I followed along as best I could, though my clumsiness resulted in the accidental squishing of more than one lady's shoe. Amid the obligatory curtsying and spinning, my dance partner barraged me with sideways glances and eyelash flutters. I understood their meaning but was more intrigued by the attention being paid to me by another.

Jacob had assumed a perch at the perimeter of the dancing, like a hawk surveying the field for his next meal. He stared at me while alternating between sips of wine and inhales of his cigar, after which he puffed smoke in the air.

Mr. Fezziwig shouted, "'Sir Roger de Coverley' next" and held out his hand to his wife.

The fiddler struck up the song, and twenty pairs of partners gathered around the elder Fezziwigs. I joined the others in enthusiastic applause, celebrating the couple's surprising competence and agility. At the completion of the dance, they staggered away and collapsed into the nearest chairs, their chests heaving.

When the party reached its end, Mr. and Mrs. Fezziwig stood on either side of the door, shaking hands with every guest and wishing each a "Merry Christmas," while Nick and I commenced the work of returning the warehouse to its original form. I was alone in a shadowed corner, in the process of lifting a heavy box, when Jacob appeared. He did not materialize in the manner of a ghost, but the stealth of his approach startled me, and I dropped the load on my toe. Muffling a yelp, I shifted my weight to the other foot and turned to him.

"I thought you'd left," I said, my voice conveying hurt feelings I had not consciously recognized. "I searched for you."

"I know," he said, accompanying the words with a smirk, the meaning of which I was hard put to decipher. His gaze traveled from my face to my feet and back again, the way sailors ogled ladies as they strolled by the docks. "I wish you good night, my friend."

"The like to you," I said.

This should have marked the end of our farewell exchange, but he lingered, as if deliberating on the next course of action. Setting his jaw, he moved toward me, one slow step and then another, before leaning in to take my hand in his. It was more of a caress than a handshake, until his grip tightened and he pulled me closer.

I inhaled deeply, his scent an intoxicating combination of tobacco, alcohol, and cologne. Cheek to cheek now, his breath was hot against my ear. My whole body tingled, and I shivered, though I was not cold. "I will see you again soon, Ebenezer," he whispered, before releasing me and backing up to scrutinize my face.

"I am yours," I replied. It was a customary response, but at that moment it felt like an honest declaration rather than a simple formality. I cradled my right hand as he walked away, savoring the warmth that remained from his touch.

Jacob's departure left only the Fezziwigs, Nick, and me in the warehouse.

"'Twas a jolly night all around," Mr. Fezziwig said. "I venture not one person would say otherwise. Come, lads. Save me the effort. Come and bid me good night."

Nick and I did as we were told and took turns shaking his hand. Mr. Fezziwig's posture was that of an old man again, though we had witnessed his incredible, albeit temporary, transformation earlier that evening. Perhaps the drink or decadent food had fueled it, or the festive atmosphere and music. Maybe it was the Christmas spirit. Whatever its cause, the magical moment had passed, and everything was back to the way it was before.

Mrs. Fezziwig wore a sincere but tired smile and held her husband's arm for support as they walked out. Belle lagged behind, laid a kiss upon her gloved hand, and blew it to me. I bowed in return, a gesture of appropriate politeness, which also served to prevent further eye contact. When I looked up, they were gone, and I locked the door behind them. The family's departure sapped the last vestiges of celebratory energy, and Nick and I went to our beds under the counter in the back shop.

My face hurt from smiling, and my mind reeled with the promise of exciting affairs yet to come.

CHAPTER THREE

MARLEY'S SACRIFICE

1850

It is fitting the phantom transported me first to the night I met Jacob Marley, considering the paramount role he played in my life. I am grateful for a glimpse of that precious memory before the other, more troubling ones take hold.

Jacob was once my partner in business and in life. After his death, he returned to me for one night, along with the ghosts of Christmases past, present, and future, to bestow on me the truths revealed to him only after he had left this mortal realm. I was condemned, as he was, to wander for eternity, carrying a heavy chain I had forged myself link by link, yard by yard, through a lifetime of miscalculated priorities and ill-considered choices. Jacob's visit offered me the chance for redemption, one which he had been denied. He saved me from a ghastly fate, and I am forever indebted to him for his efforts.

Meeting Jacob was a significant event in my life, but it was not the first or the most momentous. I must start this journey of remembering earlier than that. While some visions will offer a blissful reprieve from my physical suffering, others will incite within me a pain more acute and abiding. Even with this knowledge, I do not wish to avoid them but to experience them fully. Looking back on my life in its totality, the joys outweighed the sorrows, and my many laudable successes outnumbered the cataclysmic failures.

"Take me to the beginning, dear Phantom. There is much to be thankful for."

CHAPTER FOUR
THE BEGINNING

1795, Forty-Eight Years before the Ghosts

I sat near the door to my family's home, covering my ears with my small hands to muffle my mother's sporadic cries. After what seemed an eternity, my nursemaid Emma returned, brushing past me as fast as her pudgy legs could carry her, and ushered the midwife upstairs. When she descended again, her breaths labored and her brow moist, she lifted me into her sturdy arms.

"There, there, Ebenezer. Your mother will be fine. Let's go outside."

She carried me to the stone wall at the edge of our property and held my hand as I walked atop it, until it disappeared into a patch of trees, and we had to turn back.

"Do you think Father will come home soon?" I asked, stopping to crane my neck and peer down the road. "Does he know Mother is ill?"

"The stable boy went to fetch him," she told me. "And your mother is not ill. She is struggling to bring you a little brother or sister, and birthing a babe takes a lot of effort."

"A lot of screaming too," I added.

Emma chuckled and heaved herself to sit on the wall. I nestled in beside her to watch the varied cast of travelers passing by on that well-trodden route to London. Grand carriages carried wealthy gentlemen and ladies, who ignored my whoops and waves, and simpler ones bearing travelers less well-off, who answered me with a smile and tip of their hat. Tradespeople with carts still full on their return trips wore dejected expressions, while those with lighter loads held their heads high and traveled faster, returning home richer than when they started. Chickens in crates flapped their wings, and pigs lounged in farmer's wagons, piled atop one another in a jumble of portly bodies, stubby legs, and coiled tails. The neighs and grunts of the glistening horses inspired me to mimic their sounds, which sent both Emma and me into fits of giggling.

As the day wore on, Emma went inside to help my mother, but I remained to act as sentry for my father's return from his office in the city. This was the purported motivation for my vigil, but in truth, I wanted to be as far away as possible from the bedlam taking place on the upper level of my home.

The sun had dipped below the horizon when I spotted him, dust swirling around the legs of his galloping horse. I ran after him, but I was not fast enough. He had left the beast in the barn and was running toward me when I saw him next. I held out my arms, but he rushed by as if he did not see me. With an urgency I had never seen in him before, he burst through the front door, leaving it swinging on its hinges, and bounded up the stairs.

I clambered to catch up with him but made it only halfway before the unmistakable sound of suffering and the most unpleasant odors hit me. I stopped, turned around, and moved deliberately in the opposite direction. Though I did not know exactly what the process of birthing a babe entailed, it was evidently a terrible and perilous deed, one I had no intention of learning more about.

Curling into one of the wingback chairs in my father's study, I pressed my ear against the cushion and covered the other side of my head with a pillow. This served to muffle the sound of my mother's wails, and my eyelids grew heavy, long blinks turning to peaceful darkness as I drifted to sleep.

Emma's voice awakened me. "Ebenezer, where are you?"

I bolted upright and stood on the seat of the chair, holding on to peer over the top. "I am here!"

She emerged through the doorway to the foyer, her copper curls poking out in all directions from under a white frilly cap. "There you are. Lord, you gave me a fright. I was about to mount a search for you."

"What happened? What's wrong? Tell me."

Emma tsked. "Nothing, silly boy. You have a sister. That is all. You are a big brother now."

She held my hand as we walked up the stairs and pushed open my mother's bedroom door. I glanced tentatively toward the bed as she led me inside. My mother was sitting with her back propped against the headboard, holding a lace-wrapped bundle in her arms. After the commotion of the day and the dreadful sounds that had originated from this very spot throughout the ordeal, I expected to find the room a disheveled mess and my mother in a sorry state. It was a confusing juxtaposition of expectation versus reality, but somehow, miraculously, everything was calm and clean.

"Her name is Francelia Abigail Scrooge," my mother told me. I stared at her, my mind as muddled as an overturned puzzle. She offered an answer to the question I should have asked. "Francelia was your grandmother's name, and Abigail is for my sister."

My father sat, stoic as ever, in a chair beside the bed, one arm across his chest, the other elbow resting on it, as he stroked his beard-covered chin.

Emma leaned over and cooed at the babe. She lifted me so I could see her too, and there she was, my little sister, her gray eyes staring back at me. She would be my confidante, the one treasured soul who loved me as much as I loved her. I was smitten.

To say my life was different after my sister entered it would be insufficient to convey the enormity of the transformation. I had been lonely before, but she provided the kinship I had longed for, a true connection and unconditional love. My life was forever changed, nay improved, by her mere existence.

I called her "Fan," having declared "Francelia" too unwieldy, and tended to her under the watchful eyes of our nursemaid, who dubbed us "two peas in a pod." Fan's first word was my name, which started as a simple long "e" sound that changed to "Nee" and finally "Neez." I gladly came each time she called it.

Our father paid precious little attention to either of us, though he managed to convey his disdain for me well enough. He had a pretty, sweet girl now in Fan, and he was at best annoyed—and at worst concerned, or perhaps embarrassed—that I was not sufficiently fulfilling the role of son. "Stand tall and put your shoulders back, Ebenezer," he would say, and "Eat more. You're too skinny." He slapped my hands when he caught me twisting them together with nervous energy. "For God's sake, be still."

As to the attention I paid my sister, he disapproved entirely.

"Go outside and play," he ordered, arm outstretched and finger pointing toward the window. "There's a group of lads running into the woods. You should be out with them, not here playing with toys meant for girls."

"Leave him be," my mother said. "He is content to stay inside with his sister."

This was one of the few times she spoke in my defense. Likely, she had only meant to ensure the stasis of the household rather than to support me, but her efforts made my chest swell with pride and sent my father stomping out of the room.

Unfortunately, the refuge of home did not extend much beyond my eleventh birthday.

Father read aloud to my mother, Fan, and me, as was our family's routine after dinner. He typically chose biblical doomsday stories, like the fiery end of Sodom and Gomorrah or when God sent the angel of death to kill firstborn sons like me, but this night he read a passage from Deuteronomy. It detailed the curses God would levy as penalties for disobedience, which ranged from plagues to blindness to exile to death, followed by disembowelment by scavenger birds and beasts. When he finished the seemingly endless list, he closed the book, fixed his stern gaze on me, and issued a punishment of his own.

"You leave for boarding school tomorrow, Ebenezer. It is a day's ride from here. A carriage will pick you up first thing in the morning. Do not bother to protest. My mind is made up. This is the best thing I can do for you as your father. You must learn to be a man."

I wilted like a flower plucked from the ground, deprived of the soil and sunlight it needed to thrive. My chin sank until it rested on my chest.

I could not muster a word of response, but my mind reeled. I had followed the Lord's commandments. Why was I being banished, instead of allowed to remain in the chosen land like the Israelites? I looked at my mother through the blur of my tears, but her gaze was on my sister. My beloved nursemaid stood in the doorway, and I spotted a trunk in the foyer behind her.

Only little Fan reacted with emotion. She gaped at me, then at our parents, one to the other and back again. "What? Neez is going away?"

Father nodded.

"Can I go too?"

"No, Francelia. He is going alone."

Fan wriggled out of her chair and charged at him. "No," she screamed, hitting his knees. Father brushed away her protests, and she gave up on him. Running to me next, she jumped into my lap and wrapped her arms around my neck so tightly I found it difficult to breathe. "You do not go away, Neez," she demanded. "You stay here with me."

Mother rushed over. "There, there, Francelia. Everything will be all right. Come now." She squeezed her hand between Fan's body and mine to pry her off, but Fan refused to let go, kicking and screaming and grasping me tighter still.

Our father's patience reached its limit, and he pushed Mother aside, wrenched Fan from me, and carried her upstairs to her room, yelling over his shoulder for Emma to follow. All the while, Fan wailed, "No. I want Neez." It was a melee of a kind never before enacted in my family's home.

Mother followed the others, chanting, "It's all right, Francelia."

I remained in the now abandoned study, my neck wet with my sister's tears and my palms wet with my own. Emma returned to fetch me some time later and put me to bed.

"Everything will turn out fine, Ebenezer." She offered the consolation my mother did not, though the doubt in her voice echoed the thoughts in my head.

When I awoke the next morning, I found my clothes laid out for me, and I dutifully readied myself, placed my folded nightshirt on my bed, and went downstairs. Peeking through the narrow window on the side of the front door, I glimpsed the carriage that would deliver me to an unfamiliar place. My mother laid her hand on my shoulder, and I looked up, silently begging her to rescue me from this terrible fate. She was still in her bedclothes, dark circles under her eyes, as powerless as I was to intervene.

"Your father thought it best for you to leave early," she said, "to save us the sadness of a lengthy goodbye." What she meant was "to avoid the drama of prying a despondent Fan from your legs."

"My trunk?"

"It is already loaded, and here is a snack for your journey." She handed me a neatly tied bundle, which Emma had no doubt prepared. She allowed me to kiss her cheek before opening the door.

Father was waiting for me near the carriage, and I was grateful he had made the effort to see me off. He said not one word, however, and I concluded his objective was to ensure that I boarded and did not attempt to escape. The horses started soon after he slammed the door, and I was on my way.

CHAPTER FIVE

SHAW'S SCHOOL

1798, Forty-Five Years before the Ghosts

I cried quite a lot during the journey that delivered me to boarding school and peeked out the carriage window very little. Shaw's School was not a great distance from home, a six-hour trip, but it was farther than I had traveled before and farther still than I wanted to be. I would not be able to return home easily or often.

"We're here, sir," the coachman yelled. His call awakened me, as was likely its intended purpose. I had tired myself out so thoroughly from sobbing that I had slept through the final part of the trip.

I peered through the window as the carriage left the high road and followed a winding lane toward an old mansion of faded brick. The sight of it made my stomach churn, and I wanted nothing more than to close my eyes and wake up to discover the last day had been a terrible dream. I licked my hand and used it to wipe the crusted lines of salt from my cheeks.

The carriage came to a stop and rolled back a bit. Perhaps the horses, like me, were instinctively fearful of the place. When they settled, the coachman opened my door, lifted me out, and set me down on the spongy ground. I glanced up at the building, close enough now to see the full extent of its disrepair. A shutter hung precariously from a second-floor window with only half of its glass panes intact. Where the foundation met the dirt, the brick on the corner was crumbling, and several slate shingles were scattered on the ground.

The coachman deposited my trunk on the porch, tipped his hat in farewell, and trotted back to giddyap the horses. Not knowing what was expected of me, I stood on the porch for some time before deciding the best course of action was to announce my arrival. I raised the door knocker and let the brass ring fall against the plate. The sound failed to elicit a response, so I did it again, wondering whether my father had made a mistake in the arrangements. Had I arrived on the wrong day, so no one was expecting me? Was I even in the right place, or had the coachman delivered me to a stranger's home?

Since knocking was proving insufficient to alert the inhabitants to my presence, I strained to open the heavy door. There were voices coming from inside, which I deemed encouraging. With significant effort, I pulled my trunk over the threshold, and the door slammed shut behind it.

The thud echoed through the sizable foyer I found myself in, and a boy's head emerged through a doorway down the hall.

"Oh, hello," he said to me and called over his shoulder. "There's a new one arrived. Get Mr. Boyd."

I remained there, my hands hidden deep within the pockets of my breeches, until Mr. Boyd waddled in. He identified himself as the headmaster of the school and hollered into the room from which the boy had appeared moments before. "Masters Enfield, Williams, and Compton, come help Master Scrooge with his trunk, and show him the dormitory."

That was the entirety of what he said to me in the way of greeting. No "welcome." No "We are glad to have you with us." His face was the ugliest I had ever seen, his skin pockmarked, eyes beady, lower jaw protruding beyond the mustache atop it. It was framed by an equally offensive ring of curly black hair bushing out from every part of his head except the top. He spun on his heel with surprising speed, considering his girth, though his short stature and resulting low center of gravity ensured he did not topple over, and heaved himself out of the foyer, shutting the office door behind him.

I followed the parade of chattering boys up the stairs. They dumped my trunk beside a cot-like bed, on which sat a set of folded sheets and blanket. Apparently, I was expected to apply this bedding to the thin, lumpy mattress, though I had never before undertaken such a task and had no insight into the methods for doing so.

Mr. Boyd had instructed the students to show me around, but they seized the opportunity to engage in what I knew to be normal behavior for adolescent boys, but in which I had never participated. They rolled on the floor in a sort of wrestling match, snorting with exertion and guffawing when one took the advantage and pinned the other. They ignored me, so I commenced a self-guided tour, peering into each of the rooms and finding them equipped with duplicates of the bed assigned to me. Some were set farther apart, tucked into the corner of the room or against the wall, and others were side by side with no space in between. The disheveled bedding on many signaled that I was not alone in my lack of homemaking skills.

A musty smell permeated the air, and I wrinkled my nose against its assault. Touching the wall, I found it cool and slippery, and I pulled my hand back and wrapped both arms around my belly. How would I sleep in these messy, mossy rooms? What had I done to deserve this fate?

My purported guides announced the end of their recreation time, lest their presence on the lower floor be missed, and flattened their tousled clothes and hair before descending the stairs. I followed them, keeping my distance as they pushed each other and rolled with laughter at one boy's joke about a sound made by a lady's body part. Though unsure of the accuracy of his claim, I knew for certain it was inappropriate to speak of such matters.

They went back to the classroom, but I lingered in the foyer to explore a bit before following them in. My purpose was to delay entering the room full of boys rather than to satisfy any sense of curiosity, so my inspection was superficial. I dragged my feet with each step, hands tucked safely in my pockets, as I shuffled from room to room. Without exception, they were sparsely furnished, damp, and cold, and I spied more than a few windows with discernible cracks, some panes missing altogether. The hollowness of the house rivaled the void in my chest where my heart had once resided.

With no rooms left to explore and no excuses left for delay, I made my way to the hall where the whole of the student population was gathered. I kept my head down and shoulders hunched to discourage their attention, but it was a futile effort, since the novelty of my presence was a diversion from the monotony of their lives. I felt their eyes upon me as I headed for an empty chair in the front row of tables facing the headmaster's vacant desk.

Shaw's School was an inhospitable place for a boy of my age and temperament. I concluded as much, if not immediately, then for certain before I had spent a full two days there. I missed my sister to a degree beyond which I could imagine and suffered from crushing homesickness that stifled my ability to breathe. Desperate to leave and clinging to a feeble hope for liberation, I devised a plan based on the belief that, if my parents understood the breadth of my melancholy, they would allow me to come home. I penned a letter describing my hopeless state and imploring my father to reconsider his decision to send me away, making what I considered a compelling argument that appealed to his Christian ideals of compassion and absolution.

I wrote hunched over my desk, surrounded by the other boys practicing their penmanship under the headmaster's supervision. I thought myself discreet as I folded the page and printed, "Mr. Abraham Scrooge, Edgware, Middlesex County," on the back side of the paper. Implementing a strategy of deception that involved concealing the letter behind my back, I approached the headmaster's desk under the pretext of needing chalk, which he kept in an open box next to the stack of envelopes he would hand over to the post boy the next day. I slipped my letter into the pile with one hand while simultaneously grabbing a well-used piece of chalk with the other. I spun around and headed back to my seat, finding myself quite out of breath, not from the exertion of the endeavor but because I had not breathed at all during its commission.

My heart was still hammering in my chest when Mr. Boyd called my name. His voice was nasally and odious, as always, and he lingered on the last syllable. "Master Scrooge."

With a gasp, I scrambled to my feet, every muscle in my body taut with panic. "Y-Yes, sir." I stared at the ceiling rather than the recipient of my words.

I lowered my gaze and searched his face for some sign of what he was thinking, of what would come next for me. Finding no clues there, I bowed my head and shuffled forward until I was standing in front of him. I had not the courage to look him in the eyes, so I focused instead on the birchwood stick on his desk, which had not been there when I deposited my letter and whose purpose was menacingly clear.

"Is there something you need to tell me?" he asked, his tone failing to provide insight into the subtext of his questioning, not that I was adept at discerning such things, even under less stressful circumstances.

"No, sir," I replied, clinging to the implausible hope that he had not discovered my transgression and was, instead, referring to an unrelated matter.

"No? Nothing . . . at all?" He pointed a chubby finger toward the stack of papers, where my illicit note now sat on top. Unfortunately, though surely not inevitably, Mr. Boyd had found my letter, thwarting my plan of escape in its earliest stage. "Then how, might I ask, did this make its way to my desk?"

"I . . . well." I clamored for an explanation to support my innocence. "I know this is where letters are kept for post, and I thought I would add my own to the pile. I am so new to this place, however. Is that not allowed?" My insides quaked with fear, coupled with a tinge of pride at my success in concocting this clever justification under duress.

The headmaster frowned and slid his hand forward to caress the branch, which was threateningly thick. He let out a melodramatic sigh and pulled his hand back. He had meant to catch me in a lie, but my explanation left room for doubt. "You are lucky you have been with us only a few days. I have to admit our rules regarding correspondences may not have been explained to you."

It was true, although I had recognized the probable criminality of my actions before I took them. I shook my head to deny the receipt of any such information.

"I shall explain them to you now, Master Scrooge. Writing your own personal notes during class time is forbidden. You were supposed to be practicing your letters, and your classmates were doing exactly that while you chose to do something else."

He was working himself into a state of anger, and I held my breath, having depleted my stockpile of cunning defenses with which to save myself.

"You must never do that again." Mr. Boyd rose and planted his hands on the desk, his bulbous stomach indenting from the weight of his body against the edge.

I nodded, cringing despite my efforts to remain calm.

"Because you will be disciplined—well disciplined, in fact—should you ever violate the rules of this school again. This is your one and only pardon. Do you understand?"

"Yes, sir," I managed, though the words came out at a higher pitch than I intended.

"Now take your seat," he ordered, plopping into his own chair with a "humph."

I complied as hastily as I could, careful not to violate the institution's rule about running in the process. The invisible weight of dread lightened on my shoulders at the prospect of escaping punishment, but the reprieve was short-lived.

"Attention, students," the headmaster said, heaving himself up and grabbing the birchwood stick, which he had begrudgingly left idle during his admonishment of me. He tapped it on the open palm of his hand, gently at first and more forcefully with each subsequent strike. The clack of the branch fell in rhythm with his feet as he waddled his way to the front of the class, one slow, methodical step at a time. When he reached his destination, he glared at his audience, one cowering boy at a time. I knew this because, in the periphery of my vision, I saw the heads of my fellow students bend forward and their shoulders drop in succession as he panned the room.

"Let me clarify our school's policy regarding the use of instructional time. As your classmates know full well, Master Scrooge, students are allotted one hour every other week to write to their families. At the completion of each session, papers are turned in to me for review before they are addressed and sealed, certainly before they are placed in the post boy's pile."

He smacked the branch against the top of his desk, emitting a loud thwack that reverberated in my ears. I winced and looked up with only my eyes to see his scowling face and penetrating eyes directed unambiguously at me.

"The proffering of misinformation and complaints in your letters is strictly prohibited. One of my many duties as headmaster is to save your families from tales of your despondency and pleas for them to retrieve you. Your parents sent you here for good reason, and it is enough for them to be reminded of your existence through the occasional note."

During his soliloquy, Mr. Boyd had meandered through the rows of desks until he was standing beside me, close enough that I could smell the sourness of his breath. He flicked the branch to make a whipping sound, but I did not startle—not because I was unafraid but because I was frozen with terror and thus unable to move.

"Now, boys," he said, turning in a slow circle to project his voice throughout the hall. "Master Scrooge is new to Shaw's School, and it is your responsibility to help him along. You have failed your classmate and disappointed me, and you will be punished for it."

Surely, he did not mean to beat all of us. I could not imagine such a scene—boys lined up to be struck, one after another. It would be a taxing endeavor, for Mr. Boyd especially, and I doubted he had the strength or endurance to accomplish it, though perhaps he had the will.

My shoulders relaxed when he traipsed back to his own desk and laid the stick upon it, but the respite was brief. With his now unburdened hand, he picked up my letter and headed for the fireplace, lifted the iron poker from its hook, and stirred the coals to encourage the meager flame. Then, quite unceremoniously, he tossed the paper inside.

Turning back to us and straightening his lapel, he continued, "Master Scrooge, since the rule violation was no fault of yours, you may take your leave while the other boys pay for your mistake. Their lines will take some time to complete, so you best eat your supper while it's hot. It will most certainly be cold by the time your classmates are done."

I left straight away, not wanting the others to see the tears seeping from my eyes, and went directly to the dormitory to hide under the covers. The pangs of my empty stomach did not keep me awake as much as the knowledge that my fellow students suffered because of me. I fidgeted in my uncomfortable bed throughout the night, alternating waves of sadness, resentment, and resignation plaguing my mind. The only morsel of pride I had for my actions was that I had been shrewd enough to look away when Mr. Boyd tossed my precious letter into the fire, so I did not have to witness it turn brown and crinkle upon itself, reducing to ashes in the flame.

CHAPTER SIX
SURVIVAL

1801, Forty-Two Years before the Ghosts

Mr. Boyd read every letter I penned after the first confiscated one—two per month, as expected and allowed. Once I wrote to my sister, Fan, rather than to my father, but he tossed that into the fire and issued several wallops with the birchwood branch to discourage any future offense.

"Your father shall be the only recipient of your letters"—whack—"not your silly sister"—whack, whack, whack.

That night, I cried myself to sleep. At the core of my heartache was a longing for home, worsened by frustration at my inability to satisfy the expectations of the headmaster and, of course, my father.

I spent the next day and every day after it endeavoring to survive my boarding school experience with as little damage as possible. I did not engage in sports of any kind, not only because I did not enjoy them, but because I possessed no athletic skill whatsoever. Fortunately, I proved adept at my studies, demonstrating an aptitude for numbers and a proficiency with vocabulary and grammar. I conducted myself in a manner proper to my station, which left me relatively invisible to Mr. Boyd, and for the most part, I avoided his attention and thus the birchwood stick he always kept within easy reach.

Each day, my classmates and I practiced our letters, used the abacus to perform calculations, read Bible verses, and sang hymns. I did not collaborate with the other boys but worked on my own, albeit in proximity to them. So went the remainder of my time at Shaw's School, with one day melding into another and years passing with relentless monotony.

There were a few noteworthy exceptions, incidents that implanted themselves permanently in my psyche.

One was receiving a letter from an unexpected source. I opened the envelope—its seal already carelessly broken by Mr. Boyd—with a mild sense of anticipation for information about the happenings in my home and the welfare of my family. I had expected it to contain a note from my parents, but instead I discovered a treasure of immeasurable value. I looked upon the single piece of parchment through a haze of welling tears. It was a letter from my little sister.

When I had left for school some three years before, Fan had been unable to read or write. During my last visit home over the Christmas holiday, she had proudly shown me her rudimentary attempts to scratch letters on her slate. This page was written with ink and quill, and I was astounded at the progress she had made.

It gladdened me to know she was thinking of me and making an effort to connect, but alongside that satisfaction came the agonizing realization that she was growing up without me there to see it. I read the letter through once and clutched the paper to my chest. A tear squeezed onto my cheek and a sob caught in my throat, but I did not want my classmates to notice, so I stiffened in my chair and wiped my face with the back of my shirtsleeve before reading it again.

"My dearest Neez," it began, and my heart filled with joy to know that she had not grown so much as to relinquish the use of the nickname she had assigned me.

"I learned to write like a proper lady. Do you see?" it said. I did see and, with the admittedly biased vision of her adoring brother, agreed wholeheartedly with this assessment of her abilities.

"Mother is well, and Father too, though he is busy. He still refuses to tell me what he does for work in the city."

Law. I wanted to shout it to her over the miles separating us. "His work is law." Damn him for belittling her this way. She was capable of understanding and did not deserve to be shielded from such matters.

"I am well also, but I miss you very much," the letter continued. "I ask Mother every day to bring you home, but she says you must stay at school for your own good. I do not agree."

Neither did I.

"I have a gift for you, but it is a surprise, so I cannot tell. You will have it at Christmas, and I will give you one hundred kisses and one hundred hugs. Your loving sister, Francelia Abigail Scrooge."

Of all the beautiful words in that letter, the last line was my favorite. At the bottom of the page, in parentheses, she had written, "Your Little Fan." Indeed she was.

Fan's first letter was followed by many more, and, while Mr. Boyd would not allow me to address my outgoing mail to her, he could do nothing to prevent her from writing to me. I figured out that he did not object to my inclusion of messages to her in my correspondences, as long as I addressed them to my father. "Please tell Fan I am impressed with her penmanship," I wrote in one, and "Give my best to Fan on her upcoming piano lesson," in another. I concluded all my subsequent letters with, "Tell my sister I love her and miss her." I hoped Father relayed my sentiments, but I had no way of knowing. Either he told her, or else she was confident enough in my devotion that she continued to write me despite my failure to respond.

The first two years after my father sent me away, he had hired a carriage to bring me home for the holidays. My dear sister and our housemaid had provided a reprieve from my loneliness, and Mother and Father offered consolation, at least, if not real affection.

He did not arrange for my trip home the third year, depriving me of the one hundred kisses and one hundred hugs Fan had promised.

Father must have informed the headmaster of his intention, but Mr. Boyd neglected to convey the information to me, and I packed my trunk in preparation for the arrival of my carriage. The other boys left, one after the other, but I clung to the hope that I would be remembered and retrieved as the last of my classmates departed. It was for naught.

Even the ugly, disagreeable Mr. Boyd had somewhere to go for the holidays and, presumably, someone to spend it with. He left me alone in the cold school with only the housekeeper to attend to me. Mrs. Simmons performed her job as custodian rather lazily, and her disregard for me and her no doubt compulsory role as my caretaker were palpable. She started the fire each morning in the melancholy hall and left a meager breakfast for me on the table.

I did not know where she went for the remainder of the day. Perhaps into town to purchase supplies or to visit family or friends, or else she returned to the warmth of her bed and spent the days cozy and idle under her blankets. Regardless, each evening she reappeared to prepare and serve my dinner, watching me eat while I made awkward attempts at conversation. That she sat with me during the meal was a small comfort at first, my only interaction with anyone for the whole of the day, but I realized she was only biding her time to retrieve my plate and return it to the kitchen as soon as I finished.

That Christmas holiday was the worst I had survived thus far, chiefly because I was unprepared for the depression that accompanied my abandonment. There was one positive consequence, however. Before my weeks-long forced isolation, I had only engaged in reading what was assigned to me through my studies. I had never read for the pleasure of it, and it had never occurred to me to do so.

Out of sheer boredom, I discovered the previously overlooked bookshelves in the library and pulled one volume down, then another. I started reading one day and did not stop. While my body shivered, crouched near the feeble fire, my mind transported me to exotic locations, and I went on myriad adventures.

Through books, I escaped into fictional worlds that were welcoming and engaging, and I discovered friends in the characters I met there. I traveled with my new confidant Robinson Crusoe to the Island of Despair, where we used our wits and ingenuity to build a home. We adopted a parrot with a green body and yellow tail and sprouts growing out the top of his head, and I adored him as much as any boy loved his first pet. I made a genuine friend in the honest and faithful servant Friday, and we fought together against the cannibals and mutineers. The book saved me, in a way, gave me hope where I had none before and new experiences where joylessness otherwise reigned.

Its last line held the promise of future exploits, and I yearned for more. I rummaged through the bookshelves but found no sequel to it and cried mournful tears at the realization that I would embark on no further adventures by Robin's side.

My disappointment did not last long, however, because I forged a new friendship with the brave and cunning Ali Baba who outmaneuvered those forty treacherous thieves.

Ali Baba was not real, of course. I knew it on a logical level, but it did not feel that way to me, a desperately lonely thirteen-year-old boy. He became my dearest friend, and we climbed the tree to spy as the thieves retrieved a bit of their treasure. I praised him with a hardy "well done" when he took for himself a modest three bags of gold. To his weak-minded brother, I scolded, "Silly foozler," and wagged my finger in disapproval at his greed, adding, "You will get what you deserve." My chest puffed with moral righteousness when his poor choices resulted in a grisly death, but I paused, guilty for taking pleasure in another's tragedy, and said a prayer for his soul, out loud, for there was no one there to overhear.

I reveled in the story's surprising plot twists and appreciated Ali Baba's love for the slave girl Morgiana, who was even more daring and quick-witted than he. What an adventure. What a tale. It lit up my heart and my imagination. I loved the story and resolved to read it again, turning from the last page to the first, and enjoying it at least as much the second time. Whenever I opened a book after that, I said—sometimes aloud and sometimes only in my mind—"Open sesame."

I discovered many new stories in that deserted library and devoured them, adding the characters' experiences and lessons to my own. Quite unexpectedly, with the help of Robinson Crusoe, Ali Baba, Aladdin and his genie, and others, I achieved a measure of happiness that Christmas holiday. My resulting obsession with books became a part of my life—nay, my soul—from that point forward.

CHAPTER SEVEN

STIRRINGS

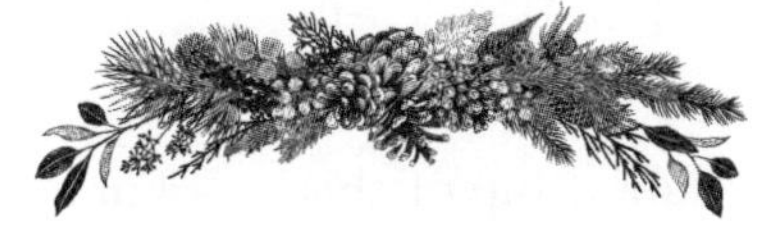

1803, Forty Years before the Ghosts

After five years away at boarding school, I still deeply missed my home and longed to be with my sister. There were only a few students with whom I conversed and no one I deemed a friend. Since I possessed little athletic talent, the boys who engaged in daily sport ignored me. Those like me, who were quiet and withdrawn, seemed uninterested in forging friendships, which, to be fair, must have been their assessment of my preference as well. I found myself in a state of hopelessness, which could no longer be described as misery or sadness but was, instead, a condition of feeling nothing at all.

That was until a new boy sat beside me in church. "I'm John," he whispered when we were supposed to be remembering our sins and apologizing to God for our weaknesses in their commission.

"Ebenezer," I said a little too loudly, eliciting vigorous shushes from the students around us. I lowered my head and pretended to read along in the missal, but I peeked out the corner of my eye at John. He was doing the same, and his lips curved into a grin. I responded with a wide, inelegant smile, pressing my chin to my chest and my shoulders toward my ears. Despite the resulting and instantaneous embarrassment at my awkwardness, it was a glorious moment—the start of something momentous, a connection with another person. It lifted the weight lodged stubbornly upon my heart and freed me from the confines of loneliness in which I had imprisoned myself.

John Davies had arrived at Shaw's School two days before, having received a welcome similar to the one I had years before. He had chosen an empty bed in the same room as me, but we had not spoken before his self-introduction in the church pew. After that initial meeting, we began a tentative journey from stranger to friend. I was unfamiliar with the process of building a relationship of this sort, but it happened despite my naïveté.

John was different than the other boys. He greeted me each day with a friendly "Good morning," and I replied in kind. After a week or so, he initiated a conversation about the content of our lessons, and another day about the ashen color and tepid temperature of the soup Mrs. Simmons had served for dinner. This sort of chitchat came naturally to others, but it was difficult for me, stressful at times. Still, I persisted, deeming John worthy of the effort. He was fifteen years old, one year my junior, and had been at a larger boarding school before coming to Shaw's.

While our friendship blossomed, John and I shared many novel experiences, both pleasant and traumatic. After supper, all students were sent to the dormitory, where we were left to our own devices, to study or talk before retiring to our beds. Not surprisingly, I spent the time reading books and organizing my thoughts from the day. The other boys spoke animatedly among themselves and played Charades, Blind Man's Bluff, and other games. Twenty Questions was my favorite. Though I was not a proper participant, I almost always guessed the answers before the others did, though they were never aware of my accomplishments.

Some of the older boys pushed the beds aside to make space for roughhousing. They demonstrated their athletic prowess, engaging in competitions, like who could lift the heaviest item or hold themselves up the longest while standing on their hands with their legs straight in the air. They also enjoyed exposing parts of their bodies, sometimes removing their shirts to compare the size and definition of their abdominal muscles or inviting their friends to squeeze their biceps to gauge whose were the firmest.

Unfortunately, there were some whose amusement necessitated the belittling and abuse of others. These unpleasant lads passed judgment on their fellow students and punished those they deemed guilty with both verbal and physical violence. They labeled the fatter boys "jollacks" and poked them hard and repeatedly in their stomachs. Those with delicate features and petite bodies the bullies dubbed "bitches" or called by female names. I learned through context that these were derogatory terms for men with feminine traits and, possibly, a preference for more masculine romantic partners.

No one addressed me by a girl's name, as I was not an attractive creature and could by no means be construed as dainty or feminine. This assessment was not born of self-loathing but simply the truth. I was not either the sort of boy to be the instigator of violence, having neither the inclination toward cruelty nor the confidence to assert dominance over others. I stayed out of everyone's way in the dormitory and, when I could not help myself, watched the events from behind an open book.

My new friend, John Davies, did not resemble me in terms of facial features or body type. My nose was pointed and long and dipped downward over my mouth, while his was small and rounded at the end, appropriately sized to match the rest of his face. While my lips were thin and dull, his were full and pink, the bottom one plumper than the top. His brown eyes and heavy lashes were nothing but perfection and would surely garner him favor with the ladies someday. In a boarding school for boys, however, his features were not an asset. Instead, they made him a target.

Being new to Shaw's School, John had no insight about which of the brawny lads were sport loving but harmless and which were mean and should be avoided altogether. One evening, he found himself surrounded by three of the nastiest students in the school. They had confronted him first in the corridor, so I assumed, as my first glimpse of the action was John stumbling into the room, off balance from the shove that had propelled him there. I was sitting on my bed, leaning against the wall, an open book in my lap.

The bullies commenced to play a game of catch, only instead of a ball they used John, and instead of throwing, they were shoving him hard, back and forth between them.

"You're pretty Jennie, aren't you?" one boy taunted.

"Who have you been kissing?" said another. "Show me how you do it."

John said nothing, struggling to keep himself upright amid the incessant pushing.

The third assailant, Doyle, unable to come up with a taunt as witty as his friends', grabbed John by the collar and slapped him across the face. The hit was brutal and hard, the sound echoing off the walls of the otherwise quiet room.

John covered his cheek with one hand and placed the other over it. The room was still. Even the three bullies paused for a moment in deference to the sudden and significant increase in the level of violence. None of the spectators, myself included, moved to intervene, lest they draw attention to themselves and be pulled into the fray. No one wanted to be John Davies at that moment. We kept our eyes fixed on the scene and did nothing except pray for it to end, which was so ineffective a strategy as to constitute no action at all.

"I'll make it better," Doyle said, forcing John's hands from his face to reveal the red puff of his cheek. Whether it was Doyle's sarcastic offer of assistance or the appearance of John's swollen, tear-stained face they found amusing, I did not know. Either way, all three of them doubled over with laughter.

John's anguished expression ignited a spark within me, and the resulting explosion filled my gut with rage that smoked and seethed and swelled. Perhaps it was fueled by the sense of fear emanating from all the other boys who, like me, were helplessly watching the events unfold before them. Maybe it was the merciless teasing that got to me, the sheer cruelty of its implied message of John's worthlessness. Likely, it was not one of these things but all of them together that tipped my limit of tolerance for the injustice of the abuse. My wrath surged to the surface with unprecedented force, unleashing within me an unexpected and powerful new ability.

I rose from my bed, and the book on my lap hit the floor with a thud, the pages folding over themselves. My movements were slow but decisive, and I stared at the trio of brutes surrounding John. Stretching my spine until it was as straight as Mr. Boyd's birchwood stick, I pushed my shoulders as far back as they would go. I advanced toward them, my whole body tense, except my head and its wild, glaring eyes pivoting from one boy to the next and back again. Doyle's laughing stopped, and he released John. He lifted his chin in my direction to alert his accomplices to the potential threat I posed, and their laughter silenced as well.

The assailants turned toward me, but I acted first, contorting my face and baring my teeth. A beastly growl emanated from my throat, the sound instinctive, not consciously made. The next one was deliberate.

"Bah," I roared, long and nasty, directing my wide-eyed glare at Doyle. The brute crossed his arms over his chest, his face transforming from amusement to alarm. I turned to the other boys next, unleashing the same on them, using both my voice and my expression to convey the ferocity of a predator, rabid and mad. The next menacing step I took prompted all three to stagger backward.

I continued to aim snarls at them and added threatening movements, biting at the air, and lunging at them with hands raised as claws. I kicked one of the boys in the gut with frenzied, hate-driven force, and he fell backward, hitting the floor with a bone-bruising thump. Turning on Doyle next, I sprang at him like a coiled snake. Stunned, the trio of now pale-lipped bullies scurried from the room.

It worked. By God, it worked. My strategy of acting the part of a vicious lunatic, however unconventional and extreme, had been effective. I had stopped an attack on an innocent person by scaring the assailants away, employing the smallest amount of violence necessary to achieve my goal.

I released the tightness in my jaw and relaxed my puckered brow and twisted lips. With a long sigh, the tension throughout my body eased, my flared nostrils shrank, and I assumed my usual stooped posture.

"Come, John," I said, as tenderly as if I were speaking to a babe.

He did not recoil when I placed my hand on his shoulder and gently nudged him away from the site of his assault. I led him to the side of my bed, urging him to sit with gentle downward pressure, and squatted in front of him, so our faces were at the same height. His eyes met mine, and he was no longer crying, though the tracks of his tears were still visible on his cheeks. His shoulders wilted, and his hands lay limp on his thighs.

"Thank you," he whispered.

I nodded my reply, and we stayed silent and still, looking into each other's eyes. Only when my crouching legs ached did I rise. I scanned the room, worried the three bullies might return, but found instead the other boys staring at us. They had witnessed the dramatic confrontation from the shelter of their beds or in the corners of the room, and now they were absorbed in watching its aftermath. Perhaps they were cowering still, though now afraid of me instead. I scanned their faces, trying to gauge their reactions to my outlandish behavior.

Their neutral expressions changed gradually, in a way that spread from one boy to the next throughout the room, their level lips turning upward at the corners. Some paired their burgeoning grins with subtle bows of their heads, and I dared to conclude these small gestures were expressions of esteem.

The pride I felt was foreign to me, but I did not dislike it. In fact, I rather enjoyed the recognition of my fellow students and was impressed with myself for accomplishing what I would have considered impossible before. I had saved my friend by intimidating his attackers and driving them away. It had not been necessary to engage in an all-out brawl with fists and weapons to achieve the deterrent effect. Eliciting fear and aversion proved a successful strategy to influence how others treated me, and over time I would perfect the use of ill-tempered rantings and intimidation to hold others at a distance.

I looked down to find John picking up the book I had dropped and flattening the crumpled pages. He stood and offered it to me, and I took hold of it in an automatic, albeit sluggish movement. He was so close that he had to arch his back and lift his chin to meet my gaze, his breath hot against my neck. We both held on for a moment until he let go and dropped back down on the bed.

When his breathing slowed and his tears dried, he slunk to his own cot and pulled the covers over his head. I slept soundly that night, my chest still warm with the memory of his touch and sated with the esteem of my fellow students.

After that incident, John and I sought each other out at mealtimes and throughout the day, walked together through the halls, and chatted at every opportunity. We stayed up late into the night, sitting on the floor with our backs against the frame of my bed, our proximity providing mutual solace and alleviating some of the loneliness we had both endured for so long.

I enjoyed his scent, the look of his petite body, and the delicate features of his face. His presence alone soothed me. I could not explain why, but he reminded me of home, of the comfort of being in the company of someone who cared about you. It was more than that, though, deeper than simple companionship.

Our conversations ranged from lighthearted jokes about Mr. Boyd and the mistakes uttered aloud by the less intelligent students to honest discussions of our families and early childhood experiences. John's family life bore little resemblance to mine, save for the blatant disapproval of our fathers, but he understood my longing for my sister, and I empathized with his plight as the youngest, oft-forgotten son with six older brothers.

John and I became constant companions and true friends, and we remained so for the next full year, avoiding the mean boys and never again threatened with harm. We matured together too. I, a late bloomer in terms of physical development, grew a full three inches during that time, my limbs stretching disproportionately longer than the rest of me, making me lanky and angular. Though John was younger than I, he had achieved his adult height by the time we met, and instead of growing taller, he developed more muscle, the outlines of which became increasingly defined. To liken our physical types to animals, his was the body of an ape, while mine resembled that of a whooping crane.

As our bodies matured, so too did our minds. Our headmaster cared little about fostering independent thought or deep analysis of ideas, his lessons mostly focused on the basics of math, Latin, and religion. On occasion, however, he led us in the reading of poetry or the works of William Shakespeare, which I thoroughly enjoyed. My favorites were the ancient Greeks, philosophers Plato and Socrates, poets Virgil and Homer, and playwrights Sophocles and Euripides.

Mr. Boyd did not encourage open discussion about the texts, and I doubted whether my classmates had the mental acuity to comprehend them anyway. But John and I did, and we discussed them at length after the lessons were finished. We sat on the soft grass outside the school, marveling at the ten-year-long siege of Troy in *The Iliad*. Our analysis continued through dinner and the evening in the dormitory, until the candles were extinguished, and we had to stop. We resumed our treatise the next day, for there was so much in the epic to discuss.

On an unusually warm October day, with our backs leaned against a tree trunk and our knees pulled up against our chests, we spoke about the mighty Achilles and his confidant Patroclus.

"I can picture Achilles's beautiful face and his strong body," John said, closing his eyes to envision it. "His muscles must have been huge."

I nodded. "And his armor. I wish I could see it—shining bronze and speckled with silver stars. But poor Patroclus," I said, adding an uncharacteristically dramatic sigh. "How tragic that he died so dreadfully after being so brave. That's the saddest part for me."

"Not me." John lowered his gaze and pulled his legs in tighter. "The worst is when Achilles finds out he is dead and goes to retrieve the body. He's so distraught he won't allow anyone to touch it. Only when Patroclus's ghost visits him and begs to be freed does he let him pass on in peace."

He paused and gave his own sigh, as exaggerated as mine, but more natural coming from him. "Would you grieve for me that way, Ebenezer?" he asked. "If I were killed, would you be as despondent as Achilles was for Patroclus? Would you cut off your hair and mourn me until your own death? Do we mean as much to each other as they did?"

The breath left my body, and it was difficult to replace. "Do not speak of such things." I managed to squeeze out the words but had to pause before speaking again. "Yes." The lump in my throat rose, but I pushed it down and placed my hand on his knee. "I am your Achilles, and you are my Patroclus."

He settled his hand over mine. Gently, slowly caressing it before reaching the openings between my fingers and stroking the length of them, giving ample attention to each before moving on to the next. A pulsing heat traveled down my spine and settled perilously in my nether regions. I did not pull away from John, but neither did I reciprocate with any movement of my own. I stared down at our hands and allowed myself to revel in the perfect sensation of his tender touch.

When he stopped and intertwined his fingers with mine, I looked down to find him staring up at me. His gaze went from my eyes to my lips and back again. He tilted his head up, and I lowered mine. I could not have prevented what was happening, even if I tried, which I did not. It seemed an inevitable progression from one step to the next.

Our lips touched, faintly at first. I was afraid to move but also afraid to stop. With conscious choice, fueled by instinct, I pressed my mouth more firmly onto his. He reciprocated, and with growing passion, we turned our heads to the side, pursing our lips and opening them again in relative synchronicity. I wondered whether we were doing it properly, but it felt right, and the thought left my head as quickly as it entered.

My hand slid downward, though I was not sure if the movement was mine alone or if John's hand pressed it in that direction. Either way, it found its way to the base of his body, between his legs. A slight sound, not a moan or a grunt or a whimper, but more of a vibration, oozed from his throat. I did not interpret it as a protest but as encouragement to continue. And I did—we did. John wrapped his arm around me and pulled me toward him. My hand lay in his lap, my fingers exploring the shape of the object underneath.

My eyes were closed, and John's must have been as well, for we were surprised by the boys' approach. Lost in each other, we failed to sense their presence until they announced it.

"Caught you!"

I jerked away from John to discover we were surrounded by four brawny boys standing in a semicircle around us. Two of them had been part of the group that assaulted John soon after he arrived at Shaw's School, and the others often joined forces with them to bully the weaker students. This gang had left us alone since my deranged behavior in the now-infamous dormitory incident, which, like all stories of this sort, had been vastly exaggerated. My reputation in the school had been enough to deter them to this point, but I doubted it would save us now.

"Whatcha doing there, nancy boys?" one of them jeered. The others laughed, and they all took a step toward us. They were closing in. Unlike the last time when I had reacted with anger to their assault on John, this time I was scared rather than incensed, stunned rather than poised to act. A year ago, righteousness had fueled my response to violence against an innocent person, but now I had none of that heroic fervor.

"Come on, you horny devils," one of them said, gesturing with a nod toward the school. "Mr. Boyd is calling us in."

The boys laughed again, shoving each other with playful camaraderie, and trotted away.

John and I shared a look of relief mixed with astonishment. We rose from our refuge under the tree and, endeavoring to hide the protrusions in our pants, followed the others.

I was relieved the four bullies had not attacked us, but their actions, or rather their failure to act as I had expected, bewildered me. The last boy who spoke, the one who alerted us to the headmaster's instruction, had offered guidance, not condemnation. They had called us names but had not responded with outrage at the discovery of John and me engaged in an unquestionably romantic embrace. It came to me in a sort of epiphany. The boys plainly recognized what we were doing, but they were not surprised or repulsed.

I had heard talk of such behavior—of love between boys—at other boarding schools, but I had seen no evidence of it happening here at

Shaw's. Perhaps I had simply not realized it before, though in hindsight I recalled several incidents that had seemed innocuous at the time but were possibly less so. For instance, one day I had returned to the dormitory to retrieve a forgotten item and found two boys together in bed. They peered wide-eyed at me from under the covers and began coughing boisterously. Since both had claimed illness and were thus excused from their studies, I had assumed they were suffering with fever and huddled for warmth and comfort. How naïve I was. What a simpleton.

On another occasion, I spotted two boys—two of the brutes who discovered John and me by the tree, in fact—emerging from the wooded area bordering one side of the schoolyard. Their faces were flushed, their hair disheveled, and they walked awkwardly, with hands in their pockets and eyes pointed downward as they kicked at the pine needles on the ground. I had guessed they were involved in a physical altercation, perhaps settling a score with their fists, but now I wondered if their appearance and behavior were attributable to something entirely different.

In reevaluating those incidents and others, I recognized a fundamental truth. What John and I felt toward each other was not unusual, and we were not alone in acting on it. Though it was immoral in the religious sense, a conundrum I intended to devote more contemplative effort to in the future, the realization of its normalcy was both comforting and intriguing.

I was in love with John Davies. I loved him the way Achilles loved Patroclus—not platonic but something more. While it gave me solace to know my feelings were neither unique nor deviant, the depth of my desire for him sat like a weight of unease in the pit of my stomach, and I worried about its repercussions for my immortal soul.

The next time I wrote home in December 1805, I did something I regretted instantly but could not undo. I told my father about John. It was the first time I identified another student by name to my father, and I reported matter-of-factly that I had at last found a true friend. I described our mutual appreciation for books, how we sat beside each other at meals and spent all our free time together. I went so far as to express hope that my family would meet him someday.

Handing the hastily penned letter to the headmaster before I could reconsider, any opportunity to take it back passed irrevocably with its transfer to the post boy's pile. Perhaps the way I worded it hinted at more, or else my father was more perceptive than I imagined. Either way, my stay at Shaw's School ended three weeks after I posted the letter.

CHAPTER EIGHT
MY SAVIOR

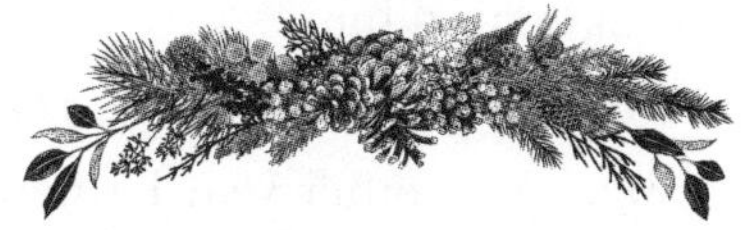

1805, Thirty-Eight Years before the Ghosts

Incessant rain and snowstorms prevented us from spending time outside, which made it difficult for John and me to steal away together. We shared only one kiss after the first one under the oak tree. It happened in the shadows of the dormitory hallway, a brief, unsatisfying touching of our lips before the housekeeper interrupted and sent us scurrying in opposite directions.

Everyone was occupied with packing their belongings in anticipation of spending the holidays at home. John and I said our goodbyes, with a handshake and a smile, in the foyer, amid the commotion of our schoolmates racing to retrieve their trunks and don their coats before venturing outside to board the carriages that awaited them.

I packed my trunk also, in the hope that a carriage would arrive for me, despite the fruitlessness of such efforts in recent years. My optimism dwindled with each passing day and extinguished completely on the morning of Christmas Eve, when I concluded I was forsaken once again.

I was seated by the small fire in the hall, my customary post, when Mr. Boyd called, "Master Scrooge, come at once."

Startled, I dropped the book I was reading and hurried to heed his command. The headmaster had been crankier than usual the past few days, berating me repeatedly for one purported infraction or another. The day before, he had struck my arm with his birchwood stick as punishment for the evidently detestable sight of my stooped shoulders as I shuffled along the hallway. That morning, I had eaten my breakfast too slowly for his liking, and he had chided me for my sloth and dimwittedness, continuing to voice his reprimands as he marched out of the room and slammed the door shut behind him.

I attributed his irritability to the fact that he remained at the school so near to Christmas, when every other year he had left long before this point to enjoy the holidays elsewhere. I theorized that this time he could not make the trip for some reason, due to money troubles perhaps, or because Mrs. Simmons was unable to stay with me. Maybe, like me, he had been abandoned by his family and would spend Christmas alone.

I rushed toward his office but found him standing in the foyer, glaring at me with an expression of annoyance.

"Sir," I said, straightening my back and raising my chin, lest my perpetually poor posture provoke his wrath a second time. The creaking of the heavy exterior door pulled my attention away from him, and I turned to watch it open an inch before closing again. I looked to Mr. Boyd for an explanation, but his lips were pressed together to form an uneven sneer. The sound came again, and the door opened wider this time, revealing the tips of four small fingers. The gap enlarged enough to allow a small figure to squeeze through. It was my beautiful little sister.

Fan snorted her admonishment at the door, as if it was at fault for being so unwieldy, and smoothed her skirt. She looked up, a smile spread across her face, and she ran to me, jumping into my arms. I held her there for a long while, her head against my shoulder and her feet dangling above the floor. Mr. Boyd released a garish sigh, and I begrudgingly set her down. Her arms remained clamped to my neck, forcing me to bend down farther than my usual slouch required.

I had no doubt that this display irked Mr. Boyd, but I did not care. I did not care about the cold permeating my body because of his miserly use of coal, nor did I care about the unfair treatment I had received at his hand over the last few days. All I cared about was the exquisite creature still clinging to me, kissing my cheeks, first one and then the other, saying "dear brother" in between pecks.

Mr. Boyd cleared his throat, but Fan ignored him. This endeared her to me even more, which was a feat I had not thought possible until that very moment, and I smiled, tears streaming down my face. When she was finished doting—and not one second before—she released me.

"I have come to bring you home, dear brother," she said, clapping her hands. "To bring you home, home, home."

"Home, little Fan?" I was slow to understand and in near disbelief at the fact of her presence there. Never before had she, or any member of my family, visited me at Shaw's School. In the past, when I was allowed to come home, I had always made the trip alone.

"Yes," Fan said, her face alight and her voice brimming with joy. "Home, for good and all."

"Truly?" I wanted desperately to believe her and shook my head to dislodge the skepticism. The possibility that this was merely wishful thinking on her part remained embedded there, until it was replaced with another of greater probability. Perhaps I was dreaming this encounter, and I would wake to find myself curled in front of the meager fire in the hall, weary and sorrowful, obliged to accept my plight of loneliness.

I blinked hard, once and again, but Fan was still there.

"Home, forever and ever," she said, nodding her head with reassuring conviction. She wrapped her arms around me and rested her cheek against my chest. "And you are never to come back to this awful place again."

"I . . . you—" My mind could not formulate a thought coherent enough to verbalize. "Oh, sweet Fan," I said, finally managing to string two words together.

She raised her head from my chest to look up at me but did not let go. "Father is so much kinder than he used to be. He spoke gently to me one night after dinner, and I asked him once more if you might come home. He said yes, Neez. And he let Emma and me come all the way here to get you."

How I loved that she still called me by the name she had invented when she was but a small child. She was ten years old now and still as sweet and delicate and perfect as the day she was born. "You are quite a woman, little Fan."

She nodded and took a backward step, so I might see the proof for myself.

"And you're to be a man," she insisted. "Father said so. But first, we'll be together for the merriest Christmas in all the world." She spread her arms to show the breadth of our promised happiness before jumping up to try to reach the top of my head. Too small yet to do so, she giggled and stood on her tiptoes, measuring her exaggerated height against mine.

"Come." She took my hand and led me toward the door.

I wanted nothing more than to leave that place and accompany Fan home, where I would stay forever and for good, but one impediment remained in the way of that heavenly goal.

Mr. Boyd addressed the coachman, who had arrived at some point during my emotional reunion with Fan. "You there, bring down Master Scrooge's trunk. Up the stairs and past the door on your right," he barked, adding, "It will be easy to identify, since it is the only one left."

My theories about the motivation for Mr. Boyd's rotten temper in recent days had been incorrect. He had known a carriage was coming for me, but the tardiness of its arrival and my continued presence at the school had hampered his own plans for the holiday. Surely, he had to concede it was no fault of mine, yet that fact had not stopped him from taking his annoyance out on me.

Though Fan and I had dispensed with the formalities of etiquette, the headmaster would not. The foyer was not an acceptable venue to receive a guest, even if it was only a young girl, so he ushered us into the parlor, where the webbed patterns of frost on the windows made it impossible to see outside.

He poured three small glasses of wine, though the term "wine" could only loosely be applied, since the liquid resembled the color of my sister's rosy cheeks rather than the dark burgundy it should have been. Fan sipped hers, crinkled her nose, and set the glass down. I was more successful at masking my disgust, though we shared a sideways glance of mutual understanding. Mr. Boyd offered her a square of cake, but she turned down the supposed treat with an upheld hand and a polite "no thank you, sir." I was not courageous enough to decline his offer and so had the misfortune of tasting the stale confection, grateful for the pink liquid to help force it down.

We suffered through an excruciating period of awkward conversation, followed by an equally uncomfortable silence, before enough time had passed for my belongings to be loaded onto the carriage. The headmaster bid us farewell, and we rushed outside.

Fan grasped my arm as we left the building, as if afraid she might lose me again if she let go. I kept my hand over hers for the same reason. Emma was standing beside the carriage, scrutinizing the fastening of my trunk atop it from her height a full yard below. I did not think it possible to be happier than I had been a moment before, but my joy grew at the prospect of reuniting with my childhood nursemaid.

Fan and I skipped down the hill, hand in hand. She reluctantly released me to allow Emma to envelop me in a hearty embrace. I reveled in her warmth and the sounds of her murmuring my name, closing my eyes to experience it fully. When I opened them again, Fan had already climbed into the carriage and was summoning me to join her. I did so eagerly and helped pull Emma in as well, with some assistance from the coachman applying pressure from the other side. She deposited herself into the seat opposite Fan and me, smiling broadly. Fan's head and mine thumped hard against the back wall as the carriage lurched forward, but we did not care in the least, giggling as we rubbed the now-tender spots.

I glanced back at the school where I had spent the last seven years of my life, relieved to watch it fade into nothingness behind us. The carriage whooshed down the garden sweep, brushing the snow off the branches of the evergreens framing its path. Fan and I held hands, and Emma stared at us with a loving, contented grin as we made our way home through a spray of white frost.

Fan and I were inseparable that Christmas after I left boarding school, and it was the happiest time in my eighteen years on this earth. I taught her to make angels in the snow, and she demonstrated her arithmetic skills by solving problems I concocted for her. Her penmanship was perfect—better than mine, in fact—and I thought her the cleverest ten-year-old in all of England.

She giggled at my clumsiness in stringing popcorn and berries for the garland on our Christmas tree. I exaggerated the expressions of concentration on my face, grimacing when I pierced my finger with the needle again and again. Mother smiled over her embroidery while Fan and I sat together on the living room floor. Even she could not contain a chuckle when we laughed so hard we toppled over.

Father was not kinder than before, as Fan had promised. He was just the same. He said nothing of the letter I had sent, and he never mentioned the name John Davies. Nor did he articulate his reason for ending my stay at Shaw's School, though I surmised that his investment had not produced the desired effect on my temperament, and so he had given up on the pursuit. All he offered in the way of explanation was that boarding school was behind me now, and I should look to the future. I tried my best to obey, resisting the urge to think about John Davies amid the excitement of the holiday.

At dinner on Christmas night, Father seated himself at the head of the table, with Fan to his left and Mother to his right. I sat beside my sister, leaving the foot of the table empty. After we ate our fill of roasted goose, potatoes, and pudding, he laid his fork against the edge of his plate and leaned back in his chair.

"You are to be a man now, Ebenezer," he announced. "I have arranged an apprenticeship for you at Fezziwig's Warehouse in London."

I had been looking forward to the forthcoming dessert of cranberry pie, but my appetite disappeared.

I said nothing, but Fan spoke in my stead. "Wait. What? No." She pushed her chair back and hopped to her feet, her napkin falling to the floor. "You can't send Neez away again!"

"Sit down, Francelia," our father said, the furrow between his eyes deepening as he glared at her. He had never punished me with hand, fist, or lash, but then I had never defied him the way Fan was doing now. I worried what he might do when he stood and lunged at her, but he only bent over to retrieve the discarded napkin and placed it on the table beside her plate. "Sit down now and listen."

Fan huffed, her chest rising and falling emphatically and her face the color of a ripened cherry, but she complied. She gathered herself into her chair and, rocking forward and back several times, skidded it to its proper position. Only once she had placed the napkin on her lap did our father continue.

"Ebenezer will not leave until spring, so you may enjoy his company until then."

"Thank you, Father," Fan said, her voice as confident as always. She turned to me and smiled.

There could be no doubt that my sister was braver than me—and stronger too, at least emotionally. I wished I could behave as she did, stand up to my father and express my opinions and desires, but alas, I did not have the capacity or the courage to accomplish it. Still, the one thing I did have control over was the way I reacted to the circumstances. Regardless of my father's disapproval, of my uncertainty about the future, and my persistent lack of self-assurance, I was determined to enjoy Christmas with my beautiful sister.

CHAPTER NINE

HINDSIGHT

1850

Denial is rather easy when one is young and smitten, as I was with Fan, but it is impossible when one is as old and shrewd as I am now, and, for certain, when the curse of hindsight refuses to concede anything but the truth. That dreadful, inescapable force is exerting its power over me now, jarring me out of my fitful sleep and into agonizing consciousness.

I stiffen as the pangs strike my old, bedridden body, and a gentle nudge guides me to roll to my side. My stomach lurches, as it has done so many times, and a hand massages my back while I wretch. There is a coolness against my lips when I finish, and a voice tells me to drink. I manage to swallow a few drops, but the rest trickles down my cheek.

The phantom looks on as I suffer, his ghostly eyes fixed upon me beneath his dusky shroud.

"I can bear the pain," I assure him. "Do not take me yet."

He touches my chest, and it is enough to transport me to where I started my reminiscing—to when I first met Jacob Marley.

CHAPTER TEN

RUMORS AND PREDICTIONS

1811, Thirty-Two Years before the Ghosts

It had been six years since I left my family home in the countryside to become an apprentice in London, and I was blossoming under Mr. Fezziwig's tutelage. The Christmas party at the warehouse was an enormous success, both in terms of its popularity with the guests and my own enjoyment of the evening. I danced with enthusiasm, drank more than I should, and engaged in conversation with acquaintances old and new. When the clock struck eleven, the festivities came to an end, and the warehouse emptied as the guests said their farewells. Jacob Marley bid me good night in a dark corner of the warehouse, and I savored the memory of his intoxicating scent and warm breath against my neck long after I retired to my cot under the counter in the back shop.

It was the greatest night of my life, and I spent the weeks after it in a stupor, my thoughts muddled by a haze of constant rumination about my interaction with Jacob Marley. I moved through sheer force of habit rather than by conscious choice. Waves of emotion overwhelmed me for short periods and long ones, too, before retreating again of their own accord. Joy followed anxiety, hope, and excitement, before they cycled back again. I had never been in such a state, and I could do nothing to wrench myself out of its clutch.

I went about my business at the warehouse well enough, regardless of my inner turmoil, and neither Mr. Fezziwig nor my fellow apprentice, Nick, seemed to notice anything was amiss.

A letter from my sister arrived the week after Christmas, and I read it over each morning before leaving my bed. Her devotion warmed my heart and gave me the strength I needed to persevere in this world, though I was frustratingly unsure of my place in it. Fan was my anchor, as always, providing a tether to family and the inspiration to succeed at work despite the outward obstacles I faced and the stress I created for myself.

A few days after the new year passed, Mr. Fezziwig called me into his office.

"Please have a seat," he instructed. "I have something important to discuss with you."

I complied, sitting on the very edge of the chair opposite him. A kaleidoscope of butterflies took residence in my stomach, making their way up my throat, and I swallowed hard to push them down, looking anxiously at him across the desk.

"There have been some developments in the state of my business," Mr. Fezziwig began. "You must know, Ebenezer, that I recognize your talents and value the many contributions you make to the success of this warehouse."

I did not know it. The thought had never occurred to me. I always performed my duties to the best of my ability and did not require or expect an overt expression of approval.

He continued, "Further, my hope is that you will assume a larger role in overseeing the affairs of it in the coming years."

I did not intentionally respond to the news, but my lips spread wide without my encouragement or consent.

"I am glad your reaction is a happy one," he said. "I have closely observed you throughout your apprenticeship, and I grow more confident in both your aptitude and trustworthiness with each passing day. My intention is to eventually pass management of Fezziwig's Warehouse on to you."

This time, my smile was intentional. "Thank you, sir."

Mr. Fezziwig nodded, but his expression contorted, his smile replaced with a tightened jaw and wrinkled brow. "I have a wife and three daughters to think about," he said, releasing a sigh. "I am not eager to leave this world and hope for many healthy years with which to enjoy their company, but I have a weighty responsibility as a husband and father. I must be prudent and plan ahead to ensure my family's welfare after I am gone. That was the only reason I considered Jacob Marley's offer and why, after considerable thought, I accepted it."

My body tightened at the mention of his name. Fortunately, Mr. Fezziwig was too focused on maintaining his own composure to note the momentary loss of mine.

"I agreed to sell him half of the business," he explained. "I will maintain control of the day-to-day operations for now, and you will take over when I am no longer able. I hope you are not too disappointed, Ebenezer." He tilted his head in what I took to be a conciliatory gesture.

I was not disappointed. Not in the least. On the contrary, I was ecstatic to learn he had chosen me to succeed him. I had been on the verge of comprehending the extent of this fortunate announcement when the subject of Jacob Marley threw my thoughts into disarray.

As I had done many times before and which had resulted in tumult nearly as often, I blurted the first thought that came into my mind. "I am confused."

"Then I shall explain," Mr. Fezziwig said, his features softening as he resumed the familiar role of mentor. "You see, I have done business with Marley before. He has provided financing for me at key junctures, and we had discussed the possibility of him purchasing a stake in the warehouse.

I went so far as to draw up a contract outlining the details of the partnership, but nothing came of it. I invited him to our Christmas party so he could meet my family and, of course, my apprentices—you and Nick. I thought he would bring his wife along, too, but alas, he did not."

Again, my words escaped before any filter of reason intervened. "Jacob Marley is married?"

I hunched my shoulders and lowered my head, so I could not see if Mr. Fezziwig's face registered suspicion or concern.

"Indeed, he is." The tone of his voice was the same as before, and I hoped he attributed my query to simple curiosity. "I wanted Marley to experience the atmosphere I cultivate for my employees and better understand the business. Though he did not join in the dancing, he seemed to get along well enough. He partook of the refreshments, I noted, and of the opportunity to talk with some of the fellows here."

Panic coursed through me, and I raised my chin from my chest to see Mr. Fezziwig's expression transform from neutral to inquisitorial. The furrows in his brow deepened, and he stared down at me through narrowed eyes. "Were you among the lads Marley engaged?"

"I was," I stammered, though my concern eased considerably with the knowledge that Mr. Fezziwig had not witnessed our encounter. I decided the best approach was to describe it as unremarkable. "He was standing near the refreshment table when I went to fill my glass, and he introduced himself. We spoke for a few moments," I said, adding, "before I excused myself to dance with the ladies."

"Ah, that is very good," Mr. Fezziwig said, the tension fading from both his voice and his face. "It is fortunate your first meeting was a pleasant one because that very evening, Marley approached me and asked if we could speak privately. I showed him to my office, and he announced his intention to invest in my business. He wanted to formalize it that very night. Can you believe it, Ebenezer? On Christmas Eve?"

I could indeed believe it, since Jacob had assured me we would meet again, but I shook my head with supposed incredulity.

"Lucky for me, I still had the draft contract in my desk drawer, so I pulled it out and handed it to him to review. I expected him to read it over and for us to engage in some negotiation, but Marley insisted we sign the agreement in its current form. He cited the quality of my employees as a major strength of the business and the driving force behind his eagerness to formalize our partnership."

Was it I who impressed him enough to warrant that investment? I was flattered by the extent of Jacob's efforts to ensure future contact with me. I felt my cheeks betraying me with their heat, but Mr. Fezziwig continued as if unaware of my guilt.

"The terms of our arrangement are favorable to both of us, Ebenezer, and the influx of capital is exactly what Fezziwig's Warehouse needs to grow. Do you understand now?"

"Yes, sir. Thank you for explaining it to me." My words sounded more confident when they reached my ears than when they left my mouth.

"I feel I must provide more insight about Marley, since I have known him for some time," he said, his expression conveying the gravity of the next bit of knowledge he was about to impart.

I was sure I had greater insight into Jacob than he did, but thankfully that thought remained confined inside my own head.

"He is a shrewd businessman. Make no mistake about it," Mr. Fezziwig explained. "His many ventures are lucrative, and his investment will give us the opportunity to substantially increase our profits. These are all positive things, but there are negatives to accompany them, as there are always two sides to the coin. For one, Marley is known for his harsh business practices, and he expects nothing less than perfection in his employees and partners. I am not put off by these qualities as they are part of what makes him successful, and you will have no trouble meeting his high standards."

I nodded my agreement. Though I had not seen this side of Jacob at the party or during our encounter afterward, I was certain I could perform my professional duties to his satisfaction. As for any other expectations he might have for me, I was less confident.

Mr. Fezziwig was not finished.

"There is another facet of Marley's character that does not pertain to the business itself but could have an impact in the future, so I feel obligated to share it with you. There are rumors he engages in immoral behaviors, that he frequents houses of ill repute, places where illicit activities occur, of a . . . sexual nature." He spat out the words as if expelling them would relieve him of their corrupting influence and accompanying discomfort.

"I am not speaking of brothels, you see. Oh, how do I explain this?" He let out a jagged breath, and this time it was his cheeks, not mine, that divulged the extent of his embarrassment. "These establishments encourage a level of deviance beyond that, with men playing both roles in the act. Do you understand?"

I had a good idea, but I did not trust my words to hide that fact, so a simple shaking of my head served as my response.

"That is fine, dear boy. How would you know of such things?" He snorted to dismiss the possibility. "The rumors about Marley are simply that, pure conjecture. He is a married man, after all, and both he and his wife are from upstanding families. Personally, I give no credence to those accusations."

Mr. Fezziwig nodded once to indicate the definitive end of the topic, having settled in his own mind any question about the righteousness of his choice to partner with him.

"On the subject of wives and families, have you considered marriage, Ebenezer?" he asked, his eyebrows raised. "My daughter Belle is quite fond of you."

My thoughts swirled around the circumstances of Jacob's marriage. Based on my limited experience with him, it seemed he had an affinity for the masculine side of the species. Was it possible he felt romantic attraction for women as well as men? I thought that unlikely, since the two were dissimilar in critical ways, but I had scant experience in the practice of physical intimacy and could by no means say so definitively. If Jacob Marley was married, perhaps I could marry as well. Indeed, perhaps I should.

"Yes. I have recently been thinking about marriage," I said. It was the simple truth.

CHAPTER ELEVEN

REPERCUSSIONS

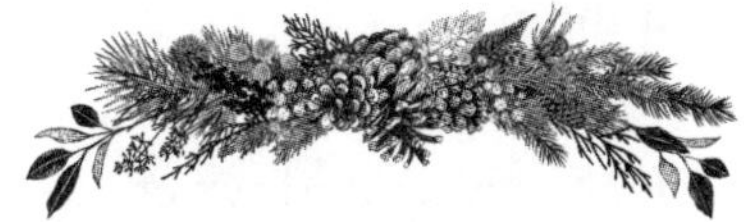

1812, Thirty-One Years before the Ghosts

I did not tell Nick about my meeting with Mr. Fezziwig, nor did I mention his intention for me to run the business one day. I did not tell him either about the encounter I had with Jacob in a secluded corner of the warehouse after the Christmas party ended. As close as we had become, I could not risk telling him—or anyone else—about that.

Nick and I had developed a genuine friendship, despite our many differences. Where I was tall and skinny, Nick was the opposite. He joked that his waist measured greater in circumference than his legs did in height, and I believed it. While my hair was blond and thin, his was dark and curled itself in all directions about his head.

Our personality differences were arguably more noticeable than the physical ones. While I struggled in social interactions, Nick flitted around the warehouse as naturally as a bee among flowers, engaging deftly with people of all types, from the laborers who lugged heavy crates in and out of the building to the finely dressed businessmen who came to meet with our employer and everyone in between. He could talk about anything with anyone and did not seem the least bit burdened at doing so. I did not possess an ounce of his conversation skills, at a loss for words even when the subject was one I knew much about.

On the matter of intelligence, the balance tipped in the opposite direction, and Nick was first to admit he was deficient in that particular asset. As different as we were, however, we found commonalities in our life experiences. Though his family lived within a thirty-minute carriage ride and mine were in the rural outskirts of the city, neither of us saw much of them. Our parents had sent us to boarding schools, and we had both loathed the time we spent there.

The most important thing we had in common was a mutual and ever-growing esteem for Mr. Fezziwig, and we endeavored to serve him to the best of our abilities. We worked well in concert, each of us applying our disparate, yet complementary, strengths to the role. Nick roamed around the warehouse throughout the day. The quickness of his footsteps exaggerated the uneven distribution of weight around his waist, reminding me of a fat mother duck hurrying her brood of ducklings through the bustling streets. He greeted visitors as they entered and addressed any complications the laborers encountered, while I sat alone in a quiet corner, performing the detailed work of tracking orders and calculating prices and profits. This arrangement suited us both.

Everything carried on as usual for a time after Mr. Fezziwig informed me of Jacob's partnership investment and his intention for me to assume an expanded role in the business. At the end of each workday, Nick and I ate dinner together, entertained each other with stories, and slept in our respective cots under the counter in the back of the building. As soon as Nick stopped talking, snores replaced his chatter, and he fell fast and soundly asleep. I was jealous of his ability to clear all thoughts and worries from his mind and appreciated the simplicity of his existence.

I cared for Nick, though not the way I had felt for John Davies at Shaw's School and nothing like the perplexing yearning I had for Jacob

Marley. My relationship with Nick was platonic, but it was real, and I cherished it.

What happened next was as much a tragedy for me as for him.

That fateful day started pleasantly enough, the birds chirping outside like a symphony playing only for me while I sat atop my own perch at the high-top desk. Mr. Fezziwig was his usual jovial self, greeting me with a hearty "good morning" as he passed by on the way to his office. Nick's "good days" and "hilly-ho's" were welcome interruptions to my concentration and brought smiles to my face.

I was content with my life as it was until Jacob Marley walked into it again.

Nick had propped open the heavy door to allow the crisp air to waft in, so Jacob entered without warning. He was standing in the middle of the warehouse, laborers bustling around him, when Nick's boisterous greeting alerted me to his presence. I looked up from my work to watch the proceedings unfold, having no control whatsoever of their progression.

"Good day to you, sir," Nick said, stretching his arms outward from the elbows and then pulling them back again to rest his open palms on his spherical stomach. "How may I be of service?"

"I am here to see Fezziwig," Jacob replied, not looking at Nick at all but instead scanning the room as if attempting to locate the man himself.

"I understand." Nick's curls bobbed with the movement of his head. I did not need to see his face to know he was smiling. "Please give me your name, and I will announce your arrival."

"Jacob Marley. I am in a hurry." The noise of the warehouse quieted, at least to my ears, though perhaps my senses were so focused on the scene playing out in front of me that I was impervious to everything else.

"Tell the old man his business partner wishes to have a discussion with him." Jacob's words were delivered with palpable annoyance.

"My apologies, sir." Nick bowed. "I will summon Mr. Fezziwig immediately. Please wait here." He turned on his heel to make his way to our boss's office. He was not smiling anymore.

I followed his progress until he disappeared from view and then turned my attention back to Jacob, who had heeded Nick's instructions and was standing in the same spot at the center of the warehouse. He turned to find me staring at him, and the corners of his lips curved upward in a surreptitious smile.

I had no awareness of whether I smiled back, since I was focusing all my concentration on keeping myself upright in my chair. I was transfixed by the sight of him standing there in crisp navy breeches, stiff-collared white shirt, and patterned cravat tucked into the neckline of his waistcoat. He held his hat in one hand and rolled the sharpened tip of his mustache with the other. He looked powerful and important, tall, svelte, and impossibly handsome. The hushed atmosphere in the warehouse was not the result of my muddled senses after all, but rather a slowing of activity that signaled a shared deference to his presence.

At the sound of hurried footsteps, he released my gaze and turned his attention to Nick.

"Mr. Fezziwig is pleased to receive you this morning, sir. Follow me," Nick said, leading the way. Jacob followed, his striding steps numbering one for every three of Nick's.

This time, it was Nick and I who shared a covert glance. His eyes widened, and the corners of his mouth turned downward, stretching his lips into a pronounced frown. I shrugged, hoping to convey the message that I was as perplexed as he was about the arrival of this man purporting to be Mr. Fezziwig's business partner. It was a lie, of course, since I knew of Jacob's involvement. With that simple gesture, I had deceived my friend, at least partially, and the guilt for doing so lodged itself firmly in my psyche.

I tried to occupy myself with work, but my eyes darted back and forth between the clock on the wall and the location where the figures of Nick and Jacob had disappeared from view. A collection of questions materialized without my conscious effort, crowding my mind and making it impossible for me to think about anything except what was happening behind the closed office door. What were they talking about? Was it business or something more personal? Would Jacob mention our first conversation by the refreshment table and the second after the Christmas party ended? I could not say for certain whether I was frightened at the prospect or stimulated, but there was nothing I could do about it either way.

Normal activity resumed after Nick returned to the warehouse floor. I continued to feign concentration on my work, holding my quill poised above the ledger, waiting impatiently for Jacob to reappear.

When Mr. Fezziwig's door slammed, I nearly fell out of my seat. If I had not had the clock for perspective, I would have guessed an hour had elapsed, but in reality, it had been less than fifteen minutes. Jacob plodded across the warehouse, headed straight for the exit. He stopped when he reached it and, grasping the door, used his foot to push aside the wooden block propping it open. He looked at me—obviously and specifically at me—then turned and walked out, the heavy door slamming shut behind him.

I hoped no one else had witnessed the intensity of Jacob's stare. Scanning the room, I searched for recognition in the faces of my coworkers but found no hint of accusation in them. Even if someone had noticed, it seemed unlikely they would guess its true meaning. I had little time to ponder this, however, because the next in a series of events arrived to change everything.

"Nick." Mr. Fezziwig's usually cheerful voice was strained. "Come here, please."

Nick placed a wine bottle back in its crate and started toward the office. He shuffled, the soles of his shoes barely leaving the floor as he made his way, his expression one of trepidation. This time, my shrug was genuine, though a leaden weight of dread settled itself on my shoulders.

The grimness of Nick's demeanor heightened my own unease, and I shivered with the chill of impending disaster. I rose from my seat and moved to a spot where I could see what was happening, peering around a tall stack of crates to spy through the windows that made up the top half of the office walls. I could not see Nick's face, but Mr. Fezziwig was standing beside his desk, his hand over his heart as he slowly shook his head.

Frozen in place, I refused to acknowledge the reality of what I was seeing. Shortly, Nick's head became visible above the half wall, and Mr. Fezziwig embraced him. He exited the office, shoulders slumped so low his hands reached his knees, and headed toward the back of the building, where we kept our belongings.

I started to follow him but stopped midstride in response to Mr. Fezziwig's strained voice calling my name.

My hiding spot was only a few yards away from his office, much closer than the desk where I was supposed to be, so I arrived too quickly. Mr. Fezziwig was waiting for me at the door. Though he did not seem vexed by my premature appearance, an aura of distress enveloped him. His face was flushed and his breathing more labored. I could not tell whether he was angry or sad or something else, but he was clearly and worryingly unwell.

The last time he had called me into his office, he had delivered encouraging news about my future. This time, I was certain it would be the opposite.

He ushered me in with a touch of my arm. "Please sit, Ebenezer," he said and, to my relief, took his own seat, or rather collapsed into it, behind his desk. He breathed a melancholy sigh and melted into his chair, the fat roll under his chin resting on his chest. "I must make some staffing changes related to the ownership arrangement we spoke of before." He paused, closing his eyes in a blink that lasted a second longer than normal.

My thoughts launched in a hundred different directions, most of them leading to failure and financial ruin. Was I being dismissed? First Nick and now me? Would Mr. Fezziwig provide me a favorable reference, so I might find another position? Or would I be forced to slink back to my family home, confirming once and for all the validity of my father's dismal assessment of my worth? How could this be happening when I had thought the partnership would bring advancement for me? Apparently, I had been wrong about that—and about Jacob too.

"Your apprenticeship is over," Mr. Fezziwig said, confirming my most dire prediction. "You are a manager now." He raised his eyes to meet my gaze for a moment, before lowering them again.

This bewildering exchange sent me first into a bleak subterranean pit of despair before lifting me back to the earthly level and into the heavens. This was good news, not bad, so why was his expression somber, even apologetic? It took me longer than it should have, but with the reassurance that my situation was secure, I turned my concern toward my colleague and friend.

"And Nick?" I asked, though I suspected what his answer would be.

"That is the thing, dear boy." Mr. Fezziwig paused, his pronounced frown telling me what I needed to know before he spoke the words. "Regrettably, I had to let Nick go."

A thought entered my mind, and I was powerless to stop myself from speaking it aloud. "Did Jacob Marley demand this?"

The muscles of his jaw tightened, evident despite the layer of fat around them, and he pursed his lips so tightly that the color faded, leaving them the pallid gray of the city sky. I worried sincerely that he might keel over for lack of air, but he composed himself with several exaggerated breaths, in through flaring nostrils and out through his mouth widened by the protrusion of his lower lip. Finally, his features loosened, and he donned the grave yet resigned expression of a man accepting his inevitable fate.

"Yes, this was Marley's doing. But, as much as it hurts me, I acknowledge it is the right decision for the business. Nick is a wonderful, good-humored boy, but he is deficient in skills that are crucial to his role. Proficiency with numbers, for instance, and careful recordkeeping are not among his strengths. Sadly, he cannot contribute to our success. You, Ebenezer, are the future of Fezziwig's Warehouse."

I opened my mouth to champion Nick's cause, but I could not formulate a valid or persuasive defense.

"I must also tell you that, in exchange for enacting Marley's demands, I made some of my own." He smiled weakly and placed both hands on the desk before continuing. "You and I shall be left alone to run the business, without his interference. Neither of us will see or hear from Jacob Marley for some time."

I was speechless again.

"I must tell you that his resistance to that idea was surprisingly forceful," Mr. Fezziwig said. "He went so far as to threaten dissolution of our partnership because of it, but the contract is signed and secure. I did this for you, Ebenezer, so you may learn and grow as a manager under my guidance."

I nodded, but my eyes remained focused on the floor, stubbornly refusing to meet his.

"Do not be sad," Mr. Fezziwig said, correctly interpreting my unintended, yet apparently obvious, expression of disappointment. "This is good news for you. It brings you one step closer to managing the warehouse on your own."

His words were meant to console me, but they did not have the desired effect. Nick and Jacob had to be set aside to make room for me to prosper. How could I feel anything besides guilt for the repercussions of my good fortune?

CHAPTER TWELVE

NEW NORMAL

1813, Thirty Years before the Ghosts

Nick left Fezziwig's Warehouse the day after the decision to dismiss him was made.

I helped him pack his belongings, and Mr. Fezziwig hired a carriage to take him home. I entreated him to write me when he found a new post, and he asked me to send him updates about the business and the people he had interacted with in the performance of his duties. He wanted to know when Robert's wife had her baby and what they decided to name the lad or lassie, whether Mr. Harris, the tailor who received a delivery of fabrics every few weeks, succeeded in arranging the engagement of his eldest daughter, and on and on. I had no idea who Robert was, and I had only seen Mr. Harris's name on my ledger, so all I knew about him was that he owed us money from his last shipment. Still, I agreed to everything Nick requested out of sympathy and for the sake of kindness. We shook hands and said our farewells, my heart heavy with regret for our mutual loss.

The transition from Nick's departure to my promotion was seamless. There were no papers to transfer, no information for him to convey. Nick's contribution to the business had been limited to his cheerfulness and goodwill. Regardless, he would be missed by everyone associated with the warehouse, myself foremost among them.

The only tangible repercussion of Nick's departure was its negative impact on my well-being, as I had become accustomed to his constant presence. With his seat empty beside mine at dinner and viscous silence in the warehouse during the evening hours, I begged for sleep to rescue me from my solitude. I had not felt such extreme isolation since boarding school, and I missed the sound of Nick's persistent chattering until he tired himself out and fell asleep. I even missed his snoring. The only noises left to keep me company were the skittering of mouse feet and the clatter of the occasional hackney coach passing by on the street outside.

I gave up on the notion of sleep that first night after Nick left and instead lit a candle to write to my sister Fan. All my previous letters had centered on descriptions of my work as an apprentice and the mundane details of my life. They must have been mind-numbingly boring, though my dear sister never said so. The letter I penned that first night alone in the warehouse was different, composed in the darkest recesses of my soul. It confessed my loneliness without my coworker to share in my daily activities and guilt about the circumstances by which my success was achieved. I told her about Jacob Marley—not everything, of course—but about his looks and his wealth, his partnership investment, and his role in the decision to fire Nick. I portrayed him not as a villain but as a source of apprehension, which accurately reflected my current state of mind.

I hoped Fan was mature enough to understand the breadth and complexity of my emotions. She was, after all, nearly eighteen years old and had often written to me of her own inner thoughts and struggles. The truth was I needed her. I was desperate to feel a connection, to share my hopes, fears, insecurities, and perceptions of the world. I yearned to be loved and understood.

I left the candle burning after I finished writing and laid my head on the pillow. It was wasteful, a squandering of resources, but I could not bear to face the darkness alone. When I awoke to the sunlight and the sounds of people on the move outside, the flame had long since snuffed itself out, leaving behind a small lumpy mound of wax.

In Nick's absence, the atmosphere in the warehouse was palpably less cheerful. I moved my desk out of the back corner, where I preferred it, and closer to the front door, so I could acknowledge visitors as they entered, while still completing my bookkeeping work. I did not greet them with anything close to the enthusiastic hospitality Nick had provided. When I heard someone enter, whether by the door slamming shut behind them or their cheery "hello," I did not look up right away but instead completed the letter or number I was writing, then set down my quill and waved them over. I found it unsettling and distracting to be disrupted in this way. Each time I addressed a visitor's needs, I had to locate the place on the page where I had left off and refocus my concentration. It took more time for me to complete my work under these circumstances, and I stayed up late into the night to accomplish it.

Beyond these inconvenient consequences of shifting from apprentice to employee, there was another for which I was wholly unprepared.

Mr. Fezziwig explained it to me in matter-of-fact terms. "It is not proper for the future manager of this business to reside here in the warehouse. It is time you found a place to live."

I had been unaware of the impropriety of my situation. Apprentices did not earn wages enough to sustain a life outside of work and so resided at their place of business, and I was perfectly comfortable sleeping under the counter in the back of the warehouse. As an employee now, I would have to live elsewhere and pay for my own lodging and board. How was I supposed to find new accommodations?

Predicting my question before I spoke it, Mr. Fezziwig said, "We can help you secure a suitable arrangement and provide a reference for you, should you need it."

I was not sure which "we" he was referring to, but I did not have the luxury of choosing among a sizable collection of willing assistants. I needed their help, whoever they were, because I had no idea how to go about finding a flat to rent, nor even where to begin. I accepted Mr. Fezziwig's offer, quite graciously, I thought, with a bow and an expression of gratitude. His kind smile in undertaking this responsibility reinforced my assessment of this performance.

"We will find you a nice place, Ebenezer," he said, patting me on the shoulder as he followed me out of his office. "Mrs. Fezziwig has connections throughout the city and will find out what is available, both advertised and not. She is wonderful at this sort of thing. I dare say she enjoys it and will pursue the endeavor with enthusiasm."

Mr. Fezziwig was correct on this last point in particular. Each morning following his offer, he had a new update for me on his wife's quest. First, she heard of a suite of rooms available on a quiet street near the Tower of London, but it was unfurnished and far too large for me. When he told me the cost—twenty-two shillings per week, plus the price of furnishings—I gasped and had to steady myself against his desk to keep from falling over. I could not fathom spending so much.

Next, Mrs. Fezziwig's friend's sister-in-law told her about a flat available near Regent's Park. It was clean and fully furnished, but she deemed it too far away from the warehouse and did not want me trekking back and forth in the heat of the summer or the blistering cold of winter. I rather enjoyed walking, even considerable distances, since it gave my mind a reprieve from the toll social interactions took on it. I expressed a version of this to Mr. Fezziwig, but the feedback I provided either never made it to his wife's ears, or else it arrived successfully but did not penetrate deeply enough, because she rejected the possibility outright.

From a lady she spoke with in the park, Mrs. Fezziwig learned of a room for rent, with shared common areas, which was less expensive than the other two options presented thus far and closer to the warehouse. This one was to my liking, and I said as much, but it became clear that my opinion did not matter. In this case, she concluded it was not good enough.

The process continued for several weeks, and while I did not experience a fraction of the enjoyment as my emissary, I did enjoy speaking with Mr. Fezziwig about it each morning, noting his amusement and the tenderness in his voice as he described his wife's latest discovery. One day, he reported that she had found a place she wanted to show me. I thought a visit was a waste of time, since she was the one deciding anyway, but I wisely did not say so.

Mrs. Fezziwig arrived at the warehouse that same afternoon. The laborers bowed and held open the heavy door as she and her youngest daughter made an entrance as grand as if they were arriving at a ball. Normally, I paid little heed to ladies' attire, but the boldness of their dresses demanded attention. Belle wore a gown of deep red, and her mother a burnt orange one, complete with a matching bonnet adorned with a garish gold flower. They reminded me of the trees changing shades as autumn progressed, and if I was not so surprised to see them, I might have chuckled at the sight.

As it was, I nearly toppled my chair as I scampered over to greet them. I was midbow when Mr. Fezziwig appeared.

"My loves," he called out, his short legs working overtime to propel him. "What a lovely surprise."

I doubted their arrival was unexpected, but I excused him from culpability for the falsehood, since his devotion to family superseded all else.

The old man embraced his wife and daughter, planting kisses on their cheeks. "What brings you here this day?"

"We have come to fetch Master Scrooge," Mrs. Fezziwig announced. "I want to show him a flat I think will suit him perfectly."

"How wonderful," Mr. Fezziwig said, smiling widely at the ladies first and then at me.

"But my work," I protested. "I must log the new sales, and we have another shipment coming today."

Mrs. Fezziwig would have none of it. "Nonsense," she said in a tone so sweet that it almost made up for her utter dismissal of my objection. She turned to her husband. "Surely you can spare him for one hour."

"Please, Father," Belle added, accompanying her whining request with a pronounced frown.

"Of course, my dearest," he said, kissing his daughter's hand. "You may have him for the entire afternoon if you like."

She smiled and tilted her head to look at me through fluttering eyelashes. "Will you join us, Ebenezer?"

Mr. Fezziwig nodded, and I assumed, correctly in this case, that I had no choice in the matter.

"I would be most grateful for the pleasure," I agreed, bowing for them and trying to sound sincere, even forcing a smile. I looked to Mr. Fezziwig and then to his wife and back again. I thought I had done and said enough, but their expressions told me they expected something more.

"Get your hat and coat," Mr. Fezziwig said, rescuing me from my awkward inaction. "The carriage is waiting for you outside."

"Yes, of course." I bowed again and hurried to retrieve my belongings. We loaded into the carriage, ladies first. Mr. Fezziwig waved vigorously as the driver giddyapped the horses.

"The weather is changing," I offered in a weak attempt to start a conversation. "Winter is only weeks away."

"I think autumn is the most wonderful time of year. Don't you, Ebenezer?" Belle asked, though she did not wait for me to reply. "I love the cool air in the morning and the way the sun warms everything by afternoon. And the colors are glorious as well. Don't you agree?"

I nodded, but I was beginning to understand that she did not need—or even want—me to respond. This realization brought unexpected relief.

"Yes, dear, you are right," her mother said. "Autumn is the most beautiful."

They carried on this discussion, comparing the seasons to one another and agreeing wholeheartedly on the preeminence of autumn. Luckily for me, they did not oblige me to make additional contributions to the conversation.

"We are here," Mrs. Fezziwig announced, peering out the window.

Already? It had been ten minutes, maybe less. How wasteful to hire a carriage for this short distance. We could have walked and enjoyed the beauty of the autumn season outright rather than paying for the luxury of talking about it from the confines of the cab. I supposed the ladies did not wish to exert themselves, or else they were trying to save their dresses from being sullied in the city streets. Either way, it was an extravagance that could have been avoided.

Despite my lack of skill in understanding what was expected of me in such situations, this one was neither subtle nor complex, and I wisely kept my thoughts to myself.

I disembarked first, and the coachman and I helped Mrs. Fezziwig out. It was a strenuous task to take on the burden of her weight before her feet reached the ground, but I managed to repress any signs of exertion. The coachman did not grant her the same courtesy, however, and let out a loud groan. She glowered at him and huffed as she patted flat her dress and stepped away from the carriage. Belle was next, and I appreciated the relative ease of aiding her descent.

The coachman might have been rude, but he was competent, having delivered us to the correct location, directly in front of the house we were to visit. A woman waited for us in the doorway atop a flight of stone steps, her gray hair pinned in a bun and her mourning dress unembellished. It took a significant amount of effort for Mrs. Fezziwig to make it up, evidenced by the sluggishness with which she ascended and the gasping breaths she took along the way. When she made it, she wiped her brow with her handkerchief and greeted our hostess with a polite embrace. She introduced us, and the woman, Mrs. King, invited us inside.

The foyer was simple and clean. She beckoned us to follow her up another flight of stairs, explaining on the way that she had lived in the house for many years and raised her family there. Her husband had died a decade before, and her children had homes and families of their own, so she had converted the second level to a separate living space.

Mrs. King resided on the first floor and rented out the upstairs rooms, which had until recently been inhabited by an older man whose life story was much the same as hers. She did not offer a reason for the previous tenant's departure, and I did not ask, assuming he had passed away rather than chosen to leave. I hoped his life had been satisfying and his soul was at rest, leaving no unresolved issues to tether his spirit there.

The door at the top of the stairs served as a separation between the leased space and the main house, but it did not include a lock, so the barrier was superficial instead of secure. Mrs. King and I waited patiently for Mrs. Fezziwig to climb up, but Belle sighed dramatically, saying, "Do hurry, Mother." Her exasperation did not speed the woman's ascent, serving only to add stress to her efforts. When Mrs. Fezziwig reached the second floor and recovered her breath, she apologized to her daughter, who sighed again and turned away.

Mrs. King encouraged us to explore the flat, and the Fezziwig women took full advantage of the invitation, flitting about and pointing out various features and amenities. The main room contained a faded green sofa and two cushioned high-back chairs facing the fireplace. There were also two small bedrooms. "One for sleeping and the other for your belongings," Mrs. Fezziwig said. I could not imagine having an entire room for storage, but all three ladies agreed to its necessity.

"Look at these windows," Belle said, parting the curtains. "They will let in light and fresh air when the weather is fine."

Mrs. Fezziwig turned to me and clasped her hands in front of her chest, fingers intertwined. "Do you like it?"

"Indeed." It had everything I needed in a residence. I thought it a rather larger space than necessary, having been comfortable sleeping under the counter in the warehouse until then, but the price of twenty shillings per month was reasonable, especially when compared with the more expensive options presented to me over the last several weeks.

Mrs. Fezziwig maintained a prayerful pose, and the three women appeared to be holding their breath, staring expectantly at me. I had assumed my response was adequate, but their reactions told me otherwise.

"I like it very much," I offered.

Thankfully, Mrs. Fezziwig started breathing again.

"I am grateful for your help," I added with a smile that, I hoped, supported my verbal assurances.

Belle let out a high-pitched squeal, and I scanned the floor to identify what type of vermin had startled her. Finding nothing, I turned my eyes upward instead, expecting to see a spider hovering above my head. Neither of these threats appeared. The only impending attack came from Belle herself, who rushed over, grabbed my arms, and planted a kiss on my cheek.

"How wonderful," she said. "We live only a short distance from here, Ebenezer. Did you know that? You will be able to come for dinner and visit me—I mean, us—often." She covered her mouth with her fingertips and giggled.

"And you will walk to work with my husband each day," Mrs. Fezziwig added.

"That is fine indeed," I said, agreeing to the terms of the arrangement.

"He'll take it," Mrs. Fezziwig said. "We will deliver his belongings this very day."

"But," I started to protest. I had far too much work waiting for me and could not pack and move that same day. It was simply not possible.

"I do not want to hear a word about how much you have left to do," Mrs. Fezziwig said, anticipating my objection. "My husband gave you leave for the entire afternoon. I heard it myself. Let's go pack your things, and our coachman will help you carry them up. You can finish your work tomorrow."

Resigned to my fate, I was silent throughout the trip back to the warehouse. The Fezziwig ladies spoke enough for all of us, and I did my best to nod during momentary pauses in their conversation. They remained in the carriage while I went inside. I packed the entirety of my possessions within minutes and returned to my seat for yet another ride made wearisome by the unrelenting chatter of my companions.

My new proprietor, Mrs. King, appeared in the doorway when we arrived, and the ladies stood by as the coachman and I lugged my trunk up the stairs, into the house, and to the second floor. The flat was mine for a period of one year and renewable after that, according to the agreement Mrs. Fezziwig negotiated and I signed.

I unpacked my belongings without assistance while the ladies enjoyed tea in Mrs. King's sitting room. Tucking my clothing and a few grooming items in the bureau, I reserved the top drawer for my precious letters from Fan, which I kept wrapped in canvas and tied with the red satin ribbon she had used to wrap my Christmas gift the year I returned home from boarding school. I resolved to utilize one of the bedrooms only, leaving the door to the spare one closed to save the cost of coal in the winter. It was the perfect arrangement for me, and I gave credit to Mrs. Fezziwig for a job well done.

In the proceeding months, I spent little time in my flat since my growing responsibilities at the warehouse kept me occupied well into the evenings. I walked to the Fezziwig home each morning, which was a greater distance than I had expected based on Belle's initial description, but I did not mind. Mr. Fezziwig met me at the door, and we strolled to work together, albeit at a much slower pace than I would have taken on my own.

I enjoyed the time alone with him. We discussed business and family and other topics, ranging from the state of government affairs to our projections about which commodities would be most sought after in the coming years. Our relationship grew to be more than that of employer and subordinate. Mr. Fezziwig became my mentor, the only authority figure who ever showed me both love and respect. He was everything I wished my father would be.

At the end of each day, I helped him into the carriage that took him home for supper, and I stayed to finish my remaining tasks. Mr. Fezziwig's workday became shorter each week, which I attributed to a deliberate and strategic reassignment of his duties to me. He had certainly earned the indulgence of spending more time with his family through years of hard work. Plus, he had named me his successor, so by stepping back now, he could act as advisor while I learned to become an effective manager.

That was how I rationalized it rather than admit the truth that he was slowing down, weakening physically and mentally. Mr. Fezziwig's condition deteriorated, despite my denial, and I knew the real reason he went home early was because he was too tired or too sick to work the long hours he once did.

I dined with the Fezziwigs once per week, as Belle had suggested during the tour of my flat and which Mr. Fezziwig formally requested the next morning. The other days, I saved half of my lunch for dinner, having learned through the suffering of hunger pangs that the street vendors were closed by late evening when I left the warehouse to walk home. Occasionally I treated myself to a hot meal at a tavern along the Thames. If

I had any energy remaining when I arrived home, I wrote to my sister or read a book until I blew out the candle and went to sleep.

I became accustomed to this life, living on my own, achieving success in the workplace, and socializing with the Fezziwigs. I was content.

CHAPTER THIRTEEN

TOLERABLE

1813, Thirty Years before the Ghosts

My weekly visits to the Fezziwig home included hearty meals and pleasurable conversation. Mr. Fezziwig and I discussed business—the latest shipments of wine from France, grains from the countryside, and small furniture items with origins around the world. We considered developments in the chain of supply, speculated about future demand, and strategized about engaging new clients.

In Mrs. Fezziwig, I found a source of nurturing I had only received before from my childhood nursemaid, and I reveled in her kind attention. She inquired about my health and encouraged me to take a second portion of food at dinner. I believed she treated me the way she would her own son, if she had one.

Belle was more complicated and her personality flaws so dramatic that I recognized them easily, despite my ineptitude at distinguishing such things. The youngest of three sisters and the only one still living at home, she took every advantage her doting parents allowed. If Belle wanted something—a new dress, for instance—she only had to say so, and her parents commissioned a seamstress to make one immediately in her choice of style and fabric. Despite the best efforts of all parties involved in its procurement, the garment could not be handed over quickly enough to satisfy her. She did not make requests but rather demands for what she desired in any given moment, and she never utilized the word "please" unless it was delivered in a protracted, high-pitched whine. "Thank you" was not part of her vocabulary.

I could not have imagined the intensity with which the Fezziwigs pandered to Belle if I had not witnessed it with my own eyes. Their deference to her was the exact opposite of the disregard I had experienced during my own childhood. If character flaws were caused by a deficiency in parental devotion, as in my case, and by an overabundance of it, as in Belle's, I concluded that neither extreme produced an optimal outcome.

More than once, I found myself staring in disbelief as Belle engaged in tantrums that involved screaming, stomping of feet, and crying by both the perpetrator and her victims. One such occasion started as a fine day, warm and sunny with a breeze that spread the fresh scent of springtime blossoms through the air. Mr. Fezziwig felt strong enough to walk home, so we closed the warehouse together and enjoyed the sun on our faces, surrounded by others doing the same, along the bustling city streets.

When we sat down to dinner, everyone seemed in high spirits, and I was content and comfortable in their familiar company. The soup arrived first, and the maid set down a round loaf of sourdough bread to be sliced and shared among us. For the next course, she delivered four small plates, each holding a plover's egg suspended in aspic jelly, shaped in a perfect shell and garnished with sprigs of green to form a starburst on top.

The maid backed away to make room for the butler to present the featured dish, which he set before Mr. Fezziwig. It was a tray of roast saddle of mutton, the oblong cut of meat glistening and surrounded by chunks of roasted potatoes, carrots, and beets, all marinating in the drippings. Steam delivered the delectable smell to our noses, and I marveled at the cook's skill in providing a dish so meticulously prepared and timed to arrive at the table fresh from the oven. My mouth watered, eager to enjoy the flavors promised by its presentation.

Promptly after the butler left the room, Belle slammed her napkin on the table with force enough to rattle the silverware and cause the jelly-encased egg to jiggle.

"I hate mutton," she said, crossing her arms and extending her bottom lip beyond its counterpart above. It resulted in an unattractive expression that overpowered her otherwise pleasant features.

"Please, Belle," Mr. Fezziwig said, holding his hands out as if trying to calm a wild animal.

"You know I hate it. I said so last time."

"But it is your father's favorite, dear." Mrs. Fezziwig used the same soothing tone as her husband.

"I don't care!" Belle's face flushed, and she sprang to her feet, sending her chair toppling over behind her.

The servants, who had left before the outburst started, came running back in at the sounds of commotion.

"Take it away," Belle demanded.

The butler looked to Mr. Fezziwig for instructions, and the old man nodded, issuing a backhanded wave.

"Please bring us something else," Mrs. Fezziwig said. "My daughter is not fond of mutton."

The butler removed the offending dish and carried it into the kitchen. The maid righted the fallen chair, guided Belle to sit with a tentative touch of her arm, and tucked it beneath her.

There was silence for a time as Mr. Fezziwig stared down at the empty space where his favorite meal had sat moments before. His wife kept her eyes closed, but her posture—heavy head and wilting shoulders—mirrored that of her husband. Only Belle looked about, her chin held high in defiance. She pulled the small plate closer, dug into the plover's egg jelly, and shoveled a spoonful into her mouth. Unsure what to do, I followed the lead of the person in charge and took a bite of what should have been a side dish but was now the main course. I kept my gaze focused downward, however, as the elder Fezziwigs continued to do.

The servants returned and placed a soup crock in front of each of us. I could not fathom how the cook had managed to prepare an alternate meal so quickly, but when I peered into the newly delivered bowl, I understood. It held the same type of broth served as the first course of the evening's meal, only now it contained small chunks of meat and slices of carrot and potato. I grinned, despite my immense effort not to, and buried my chin in my chest to hide my amusement. It was obvious to me, as it must have been to my dinner companions, that the cook had simply sliced the components of the rejected meal and added them to the left-over soup to produce a "new" dish. I suppressed a chuckle before it made its way out of my throat.

"Spoons?" Mrs. Fezziwig said, as if the maid could have foreseen the omission and included two soup spoons when she had set the table.

"Oh," the woman gasped. "I'm sorry. I will fetch them now."

"Delicious," Belle said when the proper utensils arrived, and she took her first sample of the dish. I had to agree with her evaluation, despite her overdramatized "mm."

Mr. Fezziwig ate his soup in silence, and I ventured to guess the poor man would never again enjoy the taste of roast saddle of mutton at his dinner table.

While I knew their relationship was rooted in love, I did not think the elder Fezziwigs' coddling of their daughter was healthy. In fact, it seemed to weigh them down emotionally, draining their already dwindling energy. As for Belle, though she always received exactly what she wanted, she was never truly satisfied.

Regardless of the ill treatment they received and my growing doubts about embarking on a romantic relationship with the source of their abuse, the Fezziwigs encouraged us to spend time together. Mrs. Fezziwig instructed me to take Belle on outings, and I complied, walking with her by the Thames before dinner. Belle's behavior improved significantly when we were alone, and she laced her arm through mine and chattered throughout the duration of our strolls. Increasingly, she spoke of the future, of her desire to marry and have a house of her own apart from her bothersome parents. I did not understand her haste for independence, nor her complaints, since it appeared she had everything she could ever want already.

Mrs. Fezziwig counseled us to keep our walks short because we were unsupervised, and it was improper to remain so for long, lest we were tempted to indecency or else became the subject of rumors. She had no cause to worry. There was no chance I would shower too much, or perhaps improper, attention on her daughter. I spent the entirety of my time with Belle longing to return to the house and distracted myself from her incessant babbling by thinking of other things.

Belle possessed exactly two redeeming qualities, as far as I could tell. The first was that she was a member of the Fezziwig family. In order to enjoy the company of the elder two members, I had to engage with her as well. The second was her resemblance to my sister, albeit a superficial one. Since Belle was seventeen years old—almost eighteen, as she corrected me each time I said it—she was the same age as my sister, whom I missed immensely. The two had little in common in terms of personality. While Fan was sweet and loving in disposition and as smart as anyone I knew, Belle was, well, she was none of those things. The two shared similarities in appearance, however, both being attractive, light complexioned, and petite. Belle's voice, when she was not yelling or whining, reminded me of Fan's. She smelled like her, too, and if I closed my eyes and focused on the faint rose scent of her perfume, I felt a bit of the calm that my beloved sister's presence instilled in me. That was true, of course, until Belle opened her mouth to utter a complaint or another frustratingly frivolous observation. Still, those small moments of peace made the time I spent with her, if not enjoyable, then tolerable.

CHAPTER FOURTEEN

ENGAGEMENTS

1814, Twenty-Nine Years before the Ghosts

It should have been obvious to me that my involvement with the Fezziwigs was heading in a definitive direction, but alas, I did not enjoy the gift of insight. It became clear, despite my ineptitude for discerning such things, one November evening I spent with the family. Dinner had been unsullied by complaints from its youngest participant, and we engaged in conversation about the unfortunate, though accidental, beer flood the previous month in the area of St. Giles rookery, which had destroyed buildings and killed eight people. Mrs. Fezziwig lamented the deaths of several innocent children and hoped the Horse Shoe Brewery would be held liable to compensate the victims' families.

After dinner, Mr. Fezziwig invited me to join him in the study. Normally after a meal, all four of us went to the parlor, where we played games or took turns reading passages from their collection of books. It was not the first time we had separated ourselves from the ladies to discuss business, but I thought it strange that Belle had not protested her exclusion, as she had every time before.

Mr. Fezziwig directed me to sit in one of the fine leather chairs in front of the fireplace, which burned hot, having been lit sometime before. He handed me a glass of port, which had been set out on a small tray table prior to our arrival, and eased himself into the chair beside mine. The motion caused the crimson liquid to slosh in his glass, and some escaped, dripping down the side and landing on his fingers. He clicked his tongue in disapproval and raised his hand to his lips to recover the rogue drop.

Seated comfortably and warmed by the fire, I took a hearty sip and swirled the thick liquid in my mouth, savoring the plum flavor and sweet aroma. It stung slightly as it made its way down my throat, but I judged it an exceptional cordial to be served without cause or as part of a special celebration.

"Mrs. Fezziwig and I have enjoyed spending time with you, Ebenezer. My dear Belle has grown quite fond of you as well," he said. "Do you feel the same?"

"I do," I replied. It was a response to his first statement about himself and his wife rather than to the second about his daughter, but I failed to make this distinction.

"I am glad to hear it." His eyes welled with tears, and I worried the drink was too strong for his oft-troublesome digestion, but he continued. "I have a proposition for you, dear boy—one I hope you will accept."

He drank deeply and wiped away the tear inching its way down his cheek. "I think you are a good match for my Belle."

I did not agree, having previously concluded we were not compatible in any way.

"I wish to propose a marriage agreement," he said, anticipation brimming in his eyes.

My mouth was as dry as sand, and I could not form a word of response, but my mind mounted a vigorous examination of the evidence I should have noticed before. I began to process the clues and assemble them into a pattern of behavior that had led to this moment—the fire prelit for us, the atypical lack of complaints from Belle, a fine port in our glasses. It struck me that every member of the Fezziwig household—family and servants alike—had known this was coming before I did.

"Please give this fair consideration." Panic resonated in his voice. "You will be a good husband for Belle, and it will give me a great deal of comfort to know she will be supported through the business I built and which you will continue after I am gone." He spoke quickly, as if to ensure he could complete his argument before I had a chance to interrupt. His efforts were unnecessary, however, since I was still preoccupied with understanding his proposal and had not yet begun to consider its merits. I had no coherent thoughts to share, nor did I expect any to be forthcoming.

"My Belle is not perfect, I know that," he said. "I admit I have doted on her too much and perhaps made her more self-indulgent than is preferable for a wife. But she will become more reasonable over time, and you are patient and forgiving enough to teach her."

I agreed with him about the magnitude of his daughter's self-centeredness, and his explanation helped me understand what he meant by saying we were a "good match." It was not that we were similar, but the opposite—that my passivity was a direct contrast to her demanding personality. The options were slim for a girl so thoroughly spoiled by her parents and impossible to please. My tolerance for Belle, despite her extreme behavior, made me the ideal choice of husband.

"She will be a fine wife to you someday," Mr. Fezziwig assured me. He placed his empty glass on the tray table and straightened himself against his chair, his speech reverting to its typical explanatory tone. "But, my proposal comes with a significant stipulation. If you accept, you must agree to a lengthy engagement. You see, I am growing old, and I fear I may not have many healthy years ahead of me. Belle's presence is what keeps my heart beating each day, and I wish to keep her home with me a while longer. Do you understand?"

I nodded, recognizing his desire to keep his youngest child close to him, but struggling to grasp the rest.

Mr. Fezziwig continued, "At twenty-seven years old, Ebenezer, you still have many years left in which to marry. I myself married at thirty-two.

Belle is only nineteen, and for a woman in her situation—from a family of means, such as ours—there is no urgency for her to leave home. While it is my responsibility as her father to ensure she is well positioned for a comfortable life, I am not ready to part with her. I can do my duty and also have more time to enjoy her company if you agree to a marriage in the future, maybe a year or two—three at the most."

He paused, searching my face for clues about my reaction to his proposal. Any insights he garnered were as good as mine at that point, since I could not coalesce my thoughts into any meaningful semblance of order. I said nothing, staring down at the hands twitching in my lap.

Mr. Fezziwig spoke again, filling the increasingly uncomfortable void. "To clarify, you will not have to wait until I am dead. I want to be there for her wedding, to witness the ceremony and her face glowing with happiness. A few years is all I ask. Can you wait to marry my Belle?"

I nodded again. That was the one thing I was sure of. I could wait a few years—two or three or even ten—to marry Belle. Waiting was no problem at all.

"You bring me much joy, Ebenezer." A smile spread across the old man's face. "We must tell the ladies right away. This is marvelous news." He beckoned his wife and daughter to join us in the study. They appeared immediately—too quickly to have been anywhere but directly outside the door—when he called them.

My heart beat fast and hard in my chest, and I struggled to catch my breath, despite not having exerted any physical effort. What had I done? By answering in the affirmative to the question of waiting, I had also agreed to the marriage itself. I had not meant to do so, but I could not take it back, not since it had brought Mr. Fezziwig so much relief.

There was no way around it. I was engaged to be married.

Mr. Fezziwig announced the happy news, which elicited squeals from my new fiancée. She hugged her mother and father in turn, both of whom turned to me with tears welling in their eyes. Before Belle turned her attention to me, her father interjected to clarify the terms.

"Unfortunately, my dear," he said, as if he could do nothing to change it, "you will have to wait a year or two before marrying."

At this, Belle stomped a foot and pushed out her lower lip, but she did not protest further. I thought Mr. Fezziwig's choice to deliver the unfavorable news while she was still celebrating an ingenious tactic to avoid the full brunt of her wrath.

Her mother laid a hand on her arm while he explained the necessity of allowing time for me to settle into my new position at the warehouse and for her to reach a respectable age to marry. Blaming the delay on societal norms, instead of Mr. Fezziwig's preference, was also a wise choice.

"Besides," her mother said, "a long engagement has its advantages— think of the courting activities and parties. We will have plenty of time to plan a lavish wedding celebration."

I expected Belle to complain, but she accepted the caveat easily enough. Surely, her parents would not escape future tantrums when the initial excitement over the engagement waned, but for now she was content.

"I am engaged," she squealed again. "Can you believe it, Mother? I am to be married soon."

"Not too soon," her father corrected.

"We are so happy for you." Mrs. Fezziwig clasped her hands under her chin. "Congratulations to you both."

This was the first time either of the ladies acknowledged me, and it had the effect of drawing attention to the importance of my role in the affair. Belle sauntered over, moving her hips in an exaggerated way, such that I could see them swaying despite the layers of fabric in her dress.

"Shall we seal our engagement with a kiss?" she asked, fluttering her eyelashes the way she did so often when looking at me.

I did not answer but hunched over to maneuver my cheek within reach. She was aiming for another target, however, and she launched herself on her tiptoes, holding my arms for support, and planted a kiss directly on my lips.

Rather than solidifying our engagement as it was supposed to do, this show of affection made me question my resolve. Belle's kiss was neither welcome nor enjoyable, but I submitted, recognizing that most men in my position would jump at the chance.

The ladies insisted we celebrate with a toast, which Mr. Fezziwig delivered with his usual eloquence. My second glass of port went down as easily as the first, and the third tasted like sweet nectar. I gorged myself as a hummingbird in a flower garden and did not protest the filling of my cup a fourth time.

I could scarcely focus my eyes when I left the Fezziwig home hours later, holding the railing to keep from falling down the stairs. The glow of the streetlamps provided the light I needed to navigate, since the moon and stars were hidden behind the clouds and smog that perpetually clogged the air.

I found my way home by habit rather than conscious thought, and fumbled with my key, dropping it more than once as I endeavored to unlock the front door. Once inside, I scuttled up the stairs, hoping to make it to my bed before I lost my momentum and collapsed wherever it ran out. Three steps into my ascent, I noticed an envelope on the endcap of the railing and leaned back to grab it, catching myself before I toppled over. Squinting to decipher the words written on it, I was delighted to discover it was a letter from Fan.

Suddenly, I had energy to spare, and I bounded up the stairs. My elation did not curb the mind-altering effects of the alcohol I had consumed, however, and I tripped over the lip of the top step and splatted on the floor like a toad run over by a carriage wheel. I lay there for a moment, assessing my condition.

"Are you all right, Master Scrooge?" Mrs. King called to me from the bottom of the stairs.

I righted myself, first on hands and knees, then crawled backward to use the door for support to stand up. My head was spinning, but a patdown of my body confirmed I was free from serious injury. I grasped the railing and peered down at her. The candle she held aloft illuminated her concerned expression—and also her dressing gown, which she held bunched together at the neckline. I could see the lace ruffles at the collar and sleeves, and I muffled a chuckle somewhat less successfully than I had hoped.

"I am fine, Mrs. King," I assured her. "Sorry to disturb you."

The woman shook her head, with disgust or worry I could not tell.

"Good night, then."

I watched until the candle's flame disappeared and shut the door, shushing myself when the sound of it echoed through the otherwise silent house. I fumbled to light a candle of my own and set it down without incident on the small table in front of the unlit fireplace. Collapsing into one of the wingback chairs, I tore open the envelope and read the letter inside. The words made little sense, so I forced myself to slow down and tried again.

I spied larger print and an exclamation point further down the page and wanted to reach that part as quickly as possible, so I skimmed through the initial greeting and first two paragraphs with news about my parents and the monotony of life at home in Edgware, vowing to give those sections more attention later.

The fourth paragraph started, "I have news for you, dear brother, such wonderful news!" I inhaled deeply and pulled the paper to my chest to enjoy a moment of anticipation before continuing. "I told you in my last letter that I have a suitor, Mr. Samuel Wright, who lives in London like you. He is coming to visit this Christmas. Father does not know it yet, but he will ask for his blessing to marry me. After the wedding, I will move to London. Won't it be lovely, Neez? We will finally be close to each other. We can be together all the time."

My little Fan was to be engaged, and I learned of it the very night I myself entered into the same arrangement. I never imagined I would share this milestone with my sister. How delightfully queer life was.

CHAPTER FIFTEEN
FRESH START

1814, Twenty-Nine Years before the Ghosts

I woke in a state of confusion, my head resting against the inside of the cushioned wingback chair in front of the fireplace in my flat. The events of the last evening came back to me in spurts of recollections bafflingly detached from one another. Was I engaged to be married, or was that only a dream? I closed my eyes to concentrate, hoping to seize upon a solid piece of evidence to confirm or refute my memory.

I opened them again to scan the room instead of my own chaotic mind. The candle on the table beside me had a bit of wick left, so I'd had the wherewithal to extinguish it before falling asleep. I was gratified that, even in my drunken state, I had acted to conserve my resources. What was less impressive, however, was that I was still dressed in my daytime clothing, and my hat, scarf, and coat were lying in crumpled piles on the floor, first one and then the other in a line from the top of the stairs to my current position. How careless of me. My outer garments were now a wrinkled mess.

I stood to retrieve my discarded belongings but immediately slumped back down. Legions waged war inside my head, and a wave of nausea accompanied their raucous incursion. I placed my hands on the seat to steady myself, and my fingers brushed against paper—Fan's letter, which had slipped between the cushion and the arm of the chair.

I lifted it and attempted to read, but the soldiers in my head stepped up their attacks, making it difficult to puzzle out the words. Surrendering to the invading army, I closed my eyes and concentrated as intently as my pounding head would allow, questioning which of the myriad memories of the last night were genuine. I recalled the conversation with Mr. Fezziwig that had sealed my engagement and the unwelcome kiss Belle had pressed on my lips. Was Fan's engagement true, or had I contrived the story to make my own reality easier to bear?

I rested my head against the soft padding of the chair. An hour or more must have passed because when I woke again, sunlight was forcing its way through my eyelids. Late for work already, I washed and dressed, tasks made more difficult because I had to pause repeatedly to counteract the dizziness. I vomited more than once but managed it in the end, retrieving my outerwear from the floor before venturing outside.

I tipped the brim of my hat to shield my eyes from the sun, but the morning air was refreshing, and I arrived at the warehouse feeling healthier than when I started the journey.

A full sixty minutes late, the laborers' expressions told me they were worried, or at least vexed, by this unprecedented anomaly in my behavior. My boss—and future father-in-law—arrived via carriage an hour later. He tipped his hat to me as he lumbered to his office, his face ashen and his skin glistening with sickly sweat. I fretted about his health, though I guessed I looked no better than he.

As the day progressed, the constant pounding in my head abated, but my body ached, and I discovered bruises on my elbows and knees, no doubt the result of my ridiculous fall the night before. It appeared I had been injured after all, though not severely.

When the clock struck five, I dismissed the laborers and closed out my ledger for the day. I had accomplished little, my ailments making it difficult to concentrate, but had survived the day without collapsing, and I supposed that was an achievement in itself.

Mr. Fezziwig had not reemerged since his arrival that morning. I knocked lightly on his office door and interpreted the muffled sound from inside as an invitation to enter. He was struggling to fit his arms into his coat sleeves.

"You look about as well as I do, Ebenezer." He started to chuckle but cut it short, squeezing his eyes closed.

"It was an eventful evening," I said, considering that an accurate appraisal, and helped him with his coat.

"Indeed, it was." His grin brought a trace of pink to his otherwise pallid face. "Walk me out, dear boy. Let us lock up together and call it a day. Tomorrow we will have a fresh start."

I did as the old man instructed, though I declined his offer of a carriage ride home, hoping the exercise would aid in my recovery. It did, and I purchased a biscuit and cheese from a street vendor to nibble along the way. The soreness of my body eased a bit, and the food sat well in my stomach. Climbing the stairs to my apartment was exhausting, but I accomplished it without the same clumsy result as the night before. This time, I hung my hat and coat in their proper places before retiring to my bedroom.

I was grateful my landlady was nowhere in sight, as I did not have the energy to face her. I would apologize for my drunken behavior at a future time. She deserved at least as much, along with a promise that it would not happen again.

My sole objective for the night was to reread Fan's letter and pen a response. I covered my shoulders with a blanket and sat down at the little writing desk. My recollection of the letter's contents was correct. Fan was to be engaged to Mr. Samuel Wright, a businessman of reputed success. The letter continued with pleas for me to travel home for the Christmas holiday and to write back as soon as possible with details of my impending visit.

The prospect of my sister living in London was beyond wonderful, and I told her as much in my response. I advised her not to rush the marriage process, however, since she was still so young. She should insist on a long engagement, like the one I was promised with Belle, and in a few years, we would both live in London with our respective spouses and could be together as much as we wanted.

I informed her, with much regret, that it would not be possible for me to visit home for Christmas, since I could not abandon my duties at the warehouse for even one day. Besides, I expected Belle to insist I spend the holidays with her family. I ended my letter with an appeal for Fan to write again soon to provide additional details about her suitor and their future plans.

I considered asking Fan to deliver the news of my engagement to our parents but decided against it. I had not corresponded with them for some time, relying on Fan to transmit any pertinent news. If Mother or Father had written to me, I would certainly have replied, but they had not, and so I did not either. I composed a separate letter to them, telling them of my engagement and my promotion as well.

Planning to put the letters to post the next day, I went to bed, determined to have a decent night's sleep. As Mr. Fezziwig had said, tomorrow would be a fresh start.

CHAPTER SIXTEEN

GROWTH

1814, Twenty-Nine Years before the Ghosts

I recovered fully after a night of rest, but Mr. Fezziwig did not. His skin warmed from pallid beige to a shade resembling the inside of a peach, but it retained a sickly yellow undertone. He reported feeling tired, but he protested vehemently against any suggestion of enlisting a doctor to evaluate him.

In the weeks after the engagement, we carried on as always, though the demands of the business were increasing at the same time as our social obligations.

Mrs. Fezziwig arranged a dinner to announce the news to their immediate family. Both of Belle's sisters, whom I had met before but whose names I could not recollect, were in attendance, as were their husbands and a gaggle of children of varying ages. Elated, Belle's sisters embraced us both in turn. Their husbands' congratulations, on the other hand, were more restrained. Mrs. Fezziwig beamed throughout the evening, seeming to enjoy the chaos surrounding her, and Mr. Fezziwig donned a wide grin as he accepted hugs from his children and grandchildren and handshakes from his sons-in-law.

After dinner, the gentlemen retired to the study. I settled Mr. Fezziwig into a comfortable chair, ensuring both his pipe and his glass were within arm's reach. Philip, the elder sister's husband, touched my elbow and gestured for me to join him in a corner of the room.

He leaned conspiratorially toward me and whispered, "How long have you known Belle?" I paused to do the calculation and arrived at the answer of six years and two months, but he did not wait for my reply before adding, "I mean, how well do you know her?"

"Well enough," I said. "I dine with the Fezziwigs every week."

"Then you know that Belle is—" He crinkled his nose and pulled at his already-pointy beard. "She is accustomed to getting what she wants. I do not want you to be surprised by her behavior after you are married. I mean, I do not think it fair for you to enter into a marriage without a full understanding of her . . . temperament."

Mr. Fezziwig called to me then, before I had a chance to reply to Philip's somber inquiry. This must have been how the servants felt, beckoned from one side of the room to the other and back again to meet the demands of their employers. I did not care for it, but I excused myself and went to Mr. Fezziwig, who motioned for me to lean in.

"What did he say? It looked like you were discussing a topic of some seriousness." Mr. Fezziwig was properly concerned about the subject of our discussion. Philip had been warning me about Belle's sense of entitlement and her penchant for drama, but I had the good sense not to convey this to her worried father.

"It was nothing, sir," I assured him. "Just casual conversation."

My response assuaged him, and the evening proceeded pleasantly enough. After we finished our drinks, we joined the ladies in the parlor for games and music. The eldest daughter played piano, and the other two sang. Their voices mixed brilliantly, though Belle always performed the lead while her sister harmonized.

The sisters had informed us earlier that the festivities would have to end early due to the children's bedtime schedules. Still, Belle protested loudly at the first mention of this, insisting on one more song and then another. A fit of crying by one of the smaller children forced the harmonizing sister to abandon her post, but the music continued until another child began to wail, pulling the eldest away from the piano.

The families packed up their children and their belongings while Belle sat pouting on the stool. She nodded to each family member as they bid her farewell. The sisters embraced me, and their husbands shook my hand, delivering a final round of congratulations. Philip held his handshake longer and, balancing his youngest child against his chest, said, "I hope you are sure of your decision, Ebenezer. I wish you luck."

The next day, Belle and her mother set to work announcing the engagement to their extended family, friends, friends of those friends, and acquaintances of all degrees of familiarity. It seemed their objective was to inform the entirety of London.

Letters of congratulations began to arrive soon after. According to Mr. Fezziwig's daily reports, his wife and daughter opened them without me, for which he begged my forgiveness. His apology was unnecessary, however, since I would derive no pleasure from reading them, and the ladies purportedly loved it. I was relieved, not insulted, to be excluded from the process of opening, logging, reading, and responding to the correspondences. It sounded tedious to me.

Belle insisted on showing me the many letters and small gifts that she—we—received. I indulged her with my attention once each week after we dined at her parents' table. The notes were many, I observed with sincere awe, and the gifts generous. Belle's eldest sister gave her a pewter jewelry box with her name engraved on the cover, and the middle sister presented an ivory-colored kerchief with delicate, hand-embroidered flowers and Belle's initials on each corner.

From her dearest friend, she received a teacup and saucer. I commented that the teacup was a most useful gift and asked her to extend my gratitude to the giver. Mrs. Fezziwig giggled when I said this, and Belle explained, amid the rolling of her eyes, that since tea was a comforting drink for old unmarried women, the gift of a teacup would only be given by a friend in playful recognition that, having secured a fiancé, she would not suffer a spinster's fate. I was unfamiliar with this custom, and Mr. Fezziwig's shrug told me he was similarly uninformed. The complexities of social expectations, particularly those of women, never ceased to confound me.

"I almost forgot," Belle said, pulling an envelope from the bottom of the pile. "This one is addressed to you. Mother insisted I let you open it."

This was an oddity, to be sure. Even my own mother had addressed her letter to my fiancée. I examined the envelope, but the penmanship did not look familiar, and there was no indication of its source on the outside. I looked up to find Belle waving a letter opener impatiently.

Obeying her implicit command, I tore it open and read the message inside—a simple expression of congratulations on the occasion of my engagement. What made this note different, besides that it was addressed to me, was the signature at the bottom and the last line, "I am yours, Jacob Marley."

"Well?" Belle's tone conveyed her exasperation. "Who is it from?"

When I answered, Mr. Fezziwig choked on his drink. "What? Let me see that." He started to lift himself out of his chair, but I rushed over to save him the effort.

He read through the note, frowned, shook his head, and handed it back to me.

I tried to give it to Belle, but she waved it away.

"It is yours. You keep it," she said.

It was mine, and according to the closing line, so was Jacob Marley. I folded it and placed it in the front pocket of my breeches, intent on adding it to the drawer that held my precious bundle of letters from Fan.

Belle insisted on having a ring to show off to her family, friends, and strangers she passed on the street. She chastised me for failing to present one at the time of our engagement, but in my defense, the circumstances were such that I could not have prepared in advance. A worse offense was that I had not alleviated the oversight in a timely way. She accompanied her admonishment with a fair amount of tears and whining, and I was obliged to issue multiple apologies before the discussion could move forward.

"Do not be angry with him." Mrs. Fezziwig spoke for me. "He has been occupied with work at your father's company."

Belle answered with a "humph" and a pronounced scowl, aggressively crossing her arms.

"This is a blessing, dear, because now you can choose your own ring," her mother said. "He will take you this very day. Won't you, Ebenezer?"

I shook my head. No. I could not take Belle to purchase a ring. To begin with, I had no inkling where to procure jewelry of any kind. More importantly, I could not afford to do so.

Mrs. Fezziwig ignored my silent protest, insisting we leave right away. She knew precisely which shop we should visit and instructed me to tell the owner she had sent us. How opportune that she had set my arrival time that day an hour earlier than normal, so the shops were still open. How fortunate that she had a jeweler recommendation at the ready, so Belle could have her wish granted immediately. I suspected luck had nothing to do with it.

The shop owner acknowledged me by name when we entered, and any question I had about the surreptitious planning of this endeavor vanished. He beckoned us to peruse the variety of rings he offered, though of course Belle already knew what she wanted—a single large stone set with silver prongs upon a ring made of gold. The current trend, apparently, was for the engagement ring to feature the bride's birthstone. Since Belle had been born in March, that was aquamarine, which the shop owner informed me was one of the least expensive of the gemstones.

Belle pointed out that had she been born a mere seven days later, her birthstone would have been diamond and cost many times more. I was grateful for that auspicious happenstance. As it was, with the salary I received as managing employee of the warehouse, I would have to go without food some evenings to pay for it.

I used my savings to buy the ring the next day, sweat dripping from my brow as I counted out the coins. Belle squealed when I placed it on her finger, and she showed it off to passersby, whether they cared to see it or not, throughout our Sunday walk along the Thames.

Despite my initial skepticism about the suitability of our match, I became accustomed to Belle. Most of our time alone was spent walking, a pastime I enjoyed, though her arm entwined with mine and her perpetual chattering detracted from the pleasure. Fortunately, since she was talking to me, rather than with me, I did not have to listen carefully. My feedback was not required, except for the occasional "hm" and "that's interesting," which it never was. I learned to block out her voice and turned my mind to other pursuits, like work and investment ideas, so our walks were not a complete waste of time.

When the arrival of gifts at the Fezziwig home slowed, Belle informed me that the annual Christmas party at the warehouse would double as an engagement celebration. She insisted I procure a proper outfit for the occasion and commanded her parents to commission a new dress for her.

As always, Belle's demands were granted expeditiously. I managed to find acceptable attire at a tailor's shop on the edge of Camden Town, which was no small feat because it had to be navy in color to match the ribbon on Belle's gown. The suit was used, of course, since I could not afford a custom-made piece. I had to pay an additional sum to have it tailored, as its original owner must have weighed a hundred pounds more than me. I could not find the tall boots I needed to complete the ensemble at a discounted price and was obliged to purchase a new pair from a cobbler on the south side of the river.

My role, as Mrs. Fezziwig described it, was to remain by my fiancée's side throughout the evening while she flitted from one group to another, accepting endless congratulatory sentiments meant for both of us. I did as instructed, shaking hands when required and expressing gratitude when appropriate. There was no merriment for me, as there had been in years past. I scanned the warehouse repeatedly, but there was no Jacob Marley either.

Mr. Fezziwig spent the entirety of the evening sitting in the chair I had placed for him close enough to watch the dancing but far enough from the fiddler that he could engage in conversation. He was jolly enough, laughing and cheering and enjoying the refreshments I brought him.

Throughout that long winter, Mr. Fezziwig took a carriage to the warehouse each morning, instead of walking. He cited a sapping of his energy by the many social events he was required to attend, compounded by freezing temperatures and almost daily precipitation, which were impacting him more that year than any other. I accepted these explanations eagerly, content to dismiss the nagging fear that his symptoms were attributable to something other than simple cold and fatigue. He grew a scraggly beard of gray and white, which underscored the blanching of his once-rosy skin.

When the weather warmed in spring and the engagement activities dwindled, he complained of swollen feet and soreness of joints and continued to ride to work. On more days than not, he left the warehouse early to rest at home before dinner.

As Mr. Fezziwig's contributions waned, the business grew more profitable under my focused efforts. I used the influx of money provided by our silent partner to diversify the merchandise and appeal to wealthier, more discerning customers, shifting our focus to finer items that brought in more income and were easier to transport. Rugs from the Orient were much desired by London's elite, and paintings from artists in Italy, Spain, and France demanded hefty prices.

Fezziwig's Warehouse was thriving and promised even greater gains in the future. What was more difficult to quantify but was progressing steadily nonetheless was my own personal and emotional growth. In sustaining a romantic relationship of sorts with Belle and through interactions with her family, I was becoming better at judging others' intentions and reacting appropriately in response. I also took on the role of caretaker to Mr. Fezziwig, devoting myself to him in a way that had once been reserved only for my sister.

My self-confidence grew with these new responsibilities, though I continued to question my perceptions of Jacob Marley, and he remained absent from my life. My body matured along with my mind. Though I was still thin, my shoulders widened, and I became thicker, less scrawny. Fan had promised I would become a man when I left home for my apprenticeship. More than a decade later, I finally proved her right.

CHAPTER SEVENTEEN

LOSS

1819, Twenty-Four Years before the Ghosts

Monday, July 12, Mr. Fezziwig failed to appear for work at the warehouse. I glanced at the clock several times in the first hour but continued with my day, as I had two meetings on my schedule and a pile of paperwork awaiting my attention. By ten o'clock, however, my eyes darted between the pages and the door, which I expected him to walk through at any moment. Where was he?

When I looked back at my ledger, after glancing at the door for the tenth time in an hour, I noted a mistake in my calculations. Crossing out the figure with no small amount of consternation, I decided it would be a better use of my time to solve the mystery of my employer's tardiness than to continue and risk making additional mistakes.

I forgot my summer hat in my rush to leave the warehouse, but I darted back inside to retrieve it. Shouting to the workers to carry on in my absence, I took off toward the Fezziwig home.

As I turned the corner onto their street, I was relieved to find no doctor's carriage outside, no constable's horse, only a few ladies strolling with parasols held aloft. Had I made the trip here unnecessarily? Were my worries unfounded? Perhaps Mr. Fezziwig had slept in, or he was taking the day off, enjoying the leisure he had earned through many years of exacting work. The normalcy of the scene calmed my churning stomach.

I bounded up the steps, pausing to wipe the sweat from my brow before knocking. The door opened, and the butler's angst-ridden face was the first solid piece of evidence that something was wrong. The second was the horrific sound assailing my ears. A woman was screaming, and my first thought was there had been an accident; maybe the cook had burned her hand, or someone had fallen and broken a bone.

I stepped inside, despite my trepidation, and shut the door behind me, since the butler had left me there without saying a word. A housemaid sat in the foyer, in the embroidered chair so fancy as to warrant placement where all visitors would see it but too expensive to sit on. The woman's elbows rested on her knees, and she glanced up at me before covering her face with her hands. If she had meant to hide her emotions, the action came too late because I had already seen her red, splotchy face and sodden cheeks.

The screams turned to wails, and I was unable to take a single step forward. My stomach lurched, and I squeezed my lips together to stop the rising contents from forcing their way out. I swallowed hard, wincing as the acid burned my throat, and looked down at my paralyzed legs, willing them to animate. When that did not work, I reached down and lifted my pant leg to compel my foot one pace forward. This served to remind my body of its duty to respond to my commands, and my legs functioned normally after that first step, propelling me through the foyer and up the stairs.

The dreadful sound, which grew louder with every step, guided me to its source, and I pushed open the bedroom door.

The scene struck me with as much force as a punch to the face. Mrs. Fezziwig sat in a chair next to the bed, her arm outstretched, hand resting on the blanket. Her eyes were closed, but her mouth hung open, allowing her anguished cries to escape. Belle was seated on the opposite side of the bed, loud lamentations emanating from her as well. In the center was Mr. Fezziwig, his head on a pillow, eyes shut, hands stacked on his chest.

I took two steps into the room before my legs failed me again. It did not happen all at once, and I did not drop to the floor as if my feet had been swiped from beneath me. Rather, the strength drained from them, one ounce at a time, starting at my waist and continuing downward until there was nothing left to support me. My knees bent without my permission, and I crumpled to the floor, kneeling with my backside propped against my feet, my forehead resting on the rug and arms lying flat beside me.

I would choose to stay in that position forever, since I could not acknowledge the reality before me with my face hidden and my eyes clenched shut. It was a desperate attempt at denial, but I remained there, unable to do anything but breathe.

The wailing stopped, and the room was silent for a moment. It was enough of a reprieve for me to regain a modicum of control, and I lifted my head and wiped my eyes with the back of my hand. With enormous effort, I rose, and the ladies became visible again as my vantage point ascended over the obstruction of the bed. They rushed at me, Belle reaching me first and wrapping her arms around my neck. Mrs. Fezziwig joined her, hugging me from the side, arms encompassing both her daughter and me.

"He is gone," Belle said between sobs.

Though Mr. Fezziwig's decline had been prolonged, the end came unexpectedly. He had been my employer, my mentor, my future father-in-law, and more. He had guided me through workplace and social challenges, taught me everything he knew about business, and set me on a path to success. He had welcomed me into his home, made me a part of his family, and showed me through his example how to behave as a respectable man. He was the father figure that had been missing from my life for so many years. And now he was dead.

The women explained the events of the day while I stared down at the body laid out on the bed. Mrs. Fezziwig had awoken before her husband, which was not the normal order of things but also not the first time it had happened. She heard him stirring but left the room quietly, so as not to wake him.

Later, when Belle had joined her for breakfast, they noted his absence. Not wanting him to miss the hot morning meal, Mrs. Fezziwig had gone to him, but despite shaking him and yelling his name, he would not wake. She sent a servant to fetch the doctor, and it was not long at all, she assured me, before the man arrived and declared him deceased. They had dispatched a messenger to inform the other two daughters, which was when I entered the scene.

The messenger must have completed his task because Belle's sisters arrived soon after, bringing new waves of sobbing. The grief in the house compounded with each new visitor. I remained with the family until I could no longer delay my return to the warehouse, lest the workday end and the building be left empty and unsecured.

The time alone walking calmed my mind and allowed my heart to resume its normal rhythm. When I arrived, I discovered the laborers had carried on in my absence, and I was grateful for their loyalty. I informed them of Mr. Fezziwig's death, dismissed them for the day, and promised to keep them apprised of arrangements for his funeral services.

I shuttered the windows and locked the doors and, for the first time since I started there as an apprentice a decade before, left for the day without permission.

At the Fezziwig home, the two brothers-in-law and I carried the body down the stairs and into the parlor, where his wife and daughters arranged him for viewing. The task of announcing his death was assigned to the middle daughter's husband, who did so through visits to close friends in the city, messengers sent to extended family, and written notices to the various authorities who documented such events.

The oldest daughter's husband, Philip, accepted the responsibility of procuring a coffin and hiring men to dig the grave. Since I was not an official member of the family, my assigned duties were limited to stopping the clocks in the house, covering the mirrors, and draping black crepe over the front door to signal this was a household in mourning.

The next few days passed with a tedium that bordered on torture. I went through the motions, doing everything expected of me, but none of it helped me accept the loss or manage my grief. Mrs. Fezziwig and her daughters received mourners during the day, while I oversaw business at the warehouse. At five o'clock, I left and returned to the Fezziwig home to sit beside Belle while they continued to accept condolences from friends and acquaintances, who left flower arrangements on the floor surrounding the coffin. After the family went to bed, I kept vigil late into the night, until another relative relieved me.

On the third and final evening of the wake, Jacob Marley walked into the parlor, accompanied by a woman with her arm wrapped around his. She was his wife, I assumed, for who else would he bring to this morbid affair? She was beautiful—stunning, in fact—with long, wavy copper hair, its vibrancy made more prominent by its contrast with her emerald dress. Though I had mostly ignored her existence in my ponderings about Jacob, this gorgeous creature was nothing like what I had expected.

Though her attractiveness was undeniable, I thought Jacob her equal, polished and sophisticated in a reserved, though still fashionable, black suit. His dark hair was parted in the middle, sculpted so it resembled waves that started at his temples and ended behind his ears. His mustache was different than the last time I saw him, blunter at the edges. He was, I dared admit, a bit thicker around the waist, but the extra weight amplified the aura of masculinity about him.

The handsome couple greeted Mrs. Fezziwig, who nodded slowly as Jacob spoke. I could not hear his words from across the room, only the resonance of his voice, low and melodic.

There was a third person in their party, a woman shorter than Mrs. Marley, who wore a dress of the same color. She stood behind them, as if tethered by an invisible leash, trailing the couple as they spoke with the two older Fezziwig daughters and their husbands, bowed solemnly in front of the body, and made their way to where Belle and I sat.

Belle rose to greet them, and I followed suit. She accepted the condolences Jacob offered and nodded as Mrs. Marley cradled her hand and assured her that she, too, lamented the loss of Mr. Fezziwig, whom she had known as a man of character.

Though I was standing beside my fiancée, I could not help but stare at Jacob, recalling the banter we had exchanged at the Christmas party years before. I shook my head to expel those recollections, which were especially inappropriate during this time of grief. Endeavoring to look anywhere but in Jacob's eyes, I scrutinized the furtive woman standing behind his wife. Her hair was red like Mrs. Marley's, but it was less radiant, and her face was pleasant but plain. She reminded me of a farm girl, the freckles on her nose and cheeks evidence of ample time spent in the sun.

She looked away as soon as our eyes met, and I wondered what role she played in their household. Perhaps she was Mrs. Marley's lady's maid, or a younger cousin. She could also be a ward they had taken in as an act of charity. The possibilities were many, and pondering them served to divert my attention. I avoided looking at Jacob until Belle obliged it.

"You know my fiancé," she said, patting my arm.

"Indeed." Jacob shook my hand. "I am sorry for your loss, my friend."

"Thank you," I replied. Despite my extreme efforts to suppress my emotions, my voice broke.

Jacob was the first and only person to acknowledge my grief at Mr. Fezziwig's death. His words, simple yet poignant, dislodged the tenuous hold I had on my emotions. I focused all my strength on holding back the sobs clamoring to escape my throat and covered my eyes with my palms to prevent the tears from falling on my cheeks. When I composed myself, I looked up to find that Jacob was gone. If I had any capacity left for heartache, I would have mourned him as well, but as it was, my soul was overcome with sadness for the loss of my mentor.

When the wake and funeral were over and Mr. Fezziwig's body was in the ground, I turned my energies toward the business of the warehouse. Everything there reminded me of him, and I struggled to fill, or at least cover, the chasm left by his death. Challenging as it was, I carried on as he would have expected me to.

CHAPTER EIGHTEEN

BALANCE

1850

I consider giving up now, exhausted as I am from the strain of my battle to forestall death's arrival. The pain comes in excruciating waves that drag me out of sleep for brief periods of lucidity. The phantom grabs hold of my dressing gown, but I flail against him, unwilling yet to retreat to the afterlife. I am determined to honor the memories of those I loved.

Losing Mr. Fezziwig was a sorrowful experience, and I grieved for him throughout the remainder of my life. Mankind was weakened by the loss of his extraordinary presence, of the joy that radiated from him at every opportunity for merriment, his loyalty to family, evenhandedness with his employees, and his commitment to fairness in every transaction.

I should have modeled my life on his.

Alas, I did not, and I bear the weight of that failure still. Despite the guilt and regret of this period, there were times when I was content—

happy, even—and those memories deserve the same consideration as the wretched ones. There is a balance to these things, a synchronicity the world imposes on itself. While the low points of my life were miserable indeed, there were highlights as well, and those are equally significant.

Thankful for this truth and resigned to complete this pilgrimage of remembrance, I retreat to unconsciousness, and the phantom grants me mercy once again.

CHAPTER NINETEEN

OPTIMISM

1819, Twenty-Four Years before the Ghosts

I spent the remainder of the summer after Mr. Fezziwig's death learning to manage the warehouse on my own. Though I had believed I was doing most of the work while he was alive, I realized the significance of his contribution only after he was gone.

Face-to-face interactions were a challenge for me, in terms of the time they consumed and the energy they demanded. Meetings with suppliers, large-volume customers, and individual tradesmen required me to engage in casual conversation apart from details of the business. I had to work hard to accomplish them with any degree of success, and it was exhausting. Finding that some conversations were best conducted in private, I begrudgingly shifted my workspace into Mr. Fezziwig's office.

I pretended to be fine, but on the inside, I was suffering. Though my stomach growled in protest, food brought little comfort. Belle and Mrs.

Fezziwig noticed the resulting change in my appearance, as my breeches were sliding down below my waist, and the top edges of my coat protruded an inch beyond the breadth of my shoulders. Belle complained that I looked too thin, and her mother sobbed at the prospect that my weight loss was a sign of sickness. She worried aloud that I would die like her husband, so I forced myself to clean my plate when I joined them for dinner. If satisfying the Fezziwig women and meeting my body's basic needs were not enough justification, I ate because, if I continued to shrink, I would need to purchase new clothes. If eating would save me that expense, then by God I would do it.

I endeavored to hide my unrelenting grief. Belle and her mother, on the other hand, embraced their role as mourners, flaunting their status through their behavior as well as their appearance. They commissioned new dresses to commemorate the mourning period.

"Mine shall be made of pure paramatta silk," Belle said, declaring it preferable to the bombazine alternative. I could not discern a difference, apart from the price, and the amount of lace on the final product distracted from the quality of the fabric. She accessorized it with her mother's jet jewelry, saying, "She refuses to wear it, so why should I let it sit idle in a drawer?"

Mrs. Fezziwig's dress was more traditional than Belle's, with crepe bustled heavily around her neck. She wore a weeping black veil whenever she left the house, which those days was only to attend church. Even the household servants endeavored to memorialize their employer, who had always treated them with kindness and respect. The women wore their darkest clothing, and the men affixed black armbands over their jacket sleeves.

I maintained my obligations to Belle, which was made easier because the family's state of mourning severely curtailed her activities. I was able to eliminate most social events from my schedule, a relief since I was so exhausted at the end of each workday that I barely made it up the stairs to my flat before passing out on my bed and waking up the next morning to do the same.

Several weeks after the death, I received an invitation to join Belle and her mother for dinner. There was no option to decline, since the messenger left immediately after placing the paper in my hand. I ran after him after I read it, but he was already gone.

I arrived at the Fezziwig home a few minutes early, but I was not eager to go inside. I waited at the top of the steps until the church bells completed their chimes, and I had no choice but to announce my presence, lest I be late. Bracing myself, I lifted the knocker, dreading the sadness I would feel when Mr. Fezziwig did not greet me and, worse, when his chair sat empty throughout the meal.

I survived the ordeal well enough, as did Belle, but Mrs. Fezziwig made up for our relative composure. She cried and held me in a constricting embrace upon my arrival and sobbed again while we sat in the parlor, reminiscing about how her husband used to say this and do that. She came wholly undone during dinner, insisting she was unable to enjoy the occasion with her husband "dead in the ground."

"Please, Mother," Belle pleaded. What a turn of the tides that she was the one appealing for decorum when she had always been the culprit before. As was the case when the petition was directed at her, it had no effect, and the housemaid guided Mrs. Fezziwig upstairs to bed.

Belle huffed. She was, in fact, grieving the death of her father, but the consideration being paid to her mother was vexing and, I guessed, unnerving. Throughout her life, she had been spoiled by her parents' fervent attention, and suddenly she found herself wanting. Her shoulders slumped, but for the moment at least, she was resigned to this new reality.

I used her silence as an opportunity to tell her about the wedding.

"Do you remember my sister Fan is to be married?" I started.

"Of course. She is engaged, just as we are."

I took a deep breath as I would need all of it to get through the next part without interruption. "Her wedding is two weeks away. On September twentieth. At the church in my hometown. I am traveling there for the day, but you cannot go with me since you are in mourning." I ran out of air, and Belle took full advantage.

"What? No! Why is this happening to me, on top of everything else?"

Belle could not attend an out-of-town wedding, and she knew it as well as I did. First, it was improper to participate in a joyous event so soon after her father's passing. Second, a young, unmarried woman could not travel alone with her fiancé. She would require a chaperone to accompany her, but her mother was not available, and the rest of her family was in mourning as well, so there was no one qualified to serve in that role.

Belle was quiet, and her downturned eyes told me she recognized the impossibility of her attending the event. Still, I had expected the realization of it to be accompanied by no small amount of pouting and foot-stomping protestations. Belle's reaction was delayed, but she did not disappoint.

"But I want to go." She slammed her fist on the table. "This is so unfair."

She was right, for once. It was unfair, and sad as well since this disappointment would add to her already weighty grief. I had not yet introduced her to my parents, which I should have done long before. It was traditional for the fiancée to meet her betrothed's family soon after the engagement, but I had managed to avoid it thus far, citing my demanding work schedule and the distance between our families' homes. I harbored well-justified guilt for neglecting my duty, but Belle had not protested the oversight, content to ignore the reality of my family's meager means and their simple home in the country. Until now.

"I will go to the wedding with you. I will find a way," she insisted. "Father?"

She looked around the room, but it was to no avail. Belle's father had always found a way to give her what she wanted, but he was no longer there—and never would be. This reminder pushed her over the precipice of emotional restraint. She ran from the room, her hands covering her face, and did not return, though I sat at the dining table for some time, waiting for her.

Eventually, I concluded that neither of the Fezziwig women would bid me good night, and I fetched my hat from the hook in the foyer and left.

The two weeks before Fan's wedding passed so slowly I would have sworn it was a full month. I saw Belle once during that time, visiting with her in the parlor of her home with her mother sitting between us. She spoke exclusively of my sister's wedding and how she hated me for going without her. She hated her father for dying, and the world as well, for forcing her to suffer in this way. Lamenting her boredom, she complained incessantly about the injustice of my sister marrying while she had to wait. The two were the same age, so why was Fan allowed to marry when she was not? I had no answer for this except to point out that her father's death necessitated a pause in our wedding plans. In truth, we had not made any progress in that regard, since her father had wanted to delay it as long as possible. I did not mention that, however, fearing she would release another expression of animosity toward the man.

I was in no rush to marry Belle, but I looked forward to Fan's wedding, optimistic for the first time in a long while.

CHAPTER TWENTY

BACK TO LIFE

1819, Twenty-Four Years before the Ghosts

The wedding brought me back to life.

When the day arrived, I dressed in my finest attire, which consisted of the navy suit I had purchased to match Belle's dress for our engagement party, and started my journey to Edgware before sunrise.

"Married in golden September's glow, smooth and serene your life will go" was the saying Fan cited in choosing her wedding date. September 20 turned out to be a perfect day, cool before the sun rose fully and warming to a comfortable temperature by midday. There was not a single cloud in the sky.

The church bells announced Fan's arrival for the ceremony at ten thirty in the morning. I served as an usher for the event, along with two of the groom's friends. The bridesmaids were girls Fan had grown up with, none of whom I recalled meeting before.

My parents sat in the front pew, and the groom's elderly aunt sat alone on the opposite side of the aisle. Many people from town attended, though I could not name them and paid them no mind. I focused all my attention on my sister, though I would not have noticed the particulars of her dress if she had not described it to me in a recent letter. She had declared it ivory in color, but it looked pale yellow to me, illuminated by the sunlight filtering in through the church windows. It was made of silk, with a shell motif on the hem and cream-colored satin trim. The same piping decorated the bodice and sash, which accentuated her tiny waist. The sleeves were puffy and small, covering her shoulders and ending before they reached her elbows. The neckline was rounded, making her pearl necklace—the same one my mother had worn at her wedding—a focal point.

She was glorious.

The ceremony itself was formal yet quaint. I paid no heed to the minister's words but listened intently to every one of Fan's. When the service ended, she walked hand in hand with her husband out of the church and rode back to our family home in a coach pulled by a gray horse.

I marveled at the expenditure our father, a solicitor by trade, had committed to this occasion, though I did not envy my sister for it. I wished her nothing but the best, and I was pleasantly surprised to find Father willing and able to provide it.

The reception took place in our family home. Fan had spent the entirety of her life in that house, but I had lived there for only the first eleven years of mine. I had called it "home" throughout my time at boarding school and in the early years of my apprenticeship, but I no longer considered it so.

I, along with the wedding party and guests, traveled on foot from the church to the house. The coach was empty when we arrived, and the footman was watering the horse to keep it ready to carry the newlyweds away at the reception's end.

Fan and her husband were seated inside at a small table set just for them. I was astonished at the transformation of the house to accommodate the event and the large number of people that fit in it. My parents had rented chairs, plates, and utensils to serve the many guests. They had hired extra servants for the day to prepare the meal and keep everyone's beverages refreshed.

The food was spread across a series of long tables in the center of the living room—ham and eggs, roasted pheasant, and other hearty dishes, as well as an assortment of fruits and pastries of myriad shapes and varieties. Everyone served themselves from the massive display and ate standing or seated in chairs positioned along the walls of the living room, foyer, and even my father's study. The guests took turns greeting the couple, congratulating the groom and wishing Fan good fortune.

The crowded house became less so as people left, clutching tiny boxes of fruitcake to enjoy at home. My mother, who I was glad to see in good spirits, had maintained a post close to Fan for the entirety of the event. When she stepped away for a moment, I seized the opportunity to address the couple. As I approached their table, my sister sprang from her chair, ran to me, and jumped into my arms, leaving her husband scrambling to his feet.

"Oh, Neez," she crooned. "Where have you been all day?"

"I am here for you, as always, dear sister," I said, before lowering her gently to the floor and kissing her head.

Fan's new husband made a sound like the clearing of his throat, but he was unable to escape the confines of the couple's table, his path blocked on one side by a wooden support beam and on the other by a large servant who was hovering over Fan's vacated chair to tidy her place setting.

"Silly me." Fan giggled. "I forgot to introduce you to my husband. Can you believe it, Neez? *My husband*?" She waved her arm toward him as if showing off a prize. "This is Samuel Wright."

I reached over the table and offered my hand in greeting, finding I had to lean at a steep angle, since the gentleman was shorter than me by eight inches, maybe more. He had me beat in terms of age, however. I guessed he must be more than ten years my senior, though I did not have a talent for judging such things. Still, if my estimation was correct, that would make him nearly twenty years older than his bride. Fan had not mentioned an age difference when she described him in her letters, saying only how kind he was and how successful. It was too late for me to express concern about it now that they were married.

His smile seemed genuine, and he shook my hand with both of his.

Fan spoke again, preventing us from issuing a proper greeting to one another. "Samuel, this is Ebenezer Scrooge, my dear brother and the very best man I know."

"With that introduction," he said with a chuckle, "I dare say I am fortunate to make your acquaintance."

My cheeks warmed. "My sincerest congratulations to you on this blessed day."

Mother reappeared, this time with our father in tow.

"It is time to go, Francelia," she said. "Your bags are loaded on the carriage."

Fan gasped. "Already? Oh my, let me prepare myself. Excuse me." She fluttered away, leaving me alone with our parents and the still-trapped Samuel Wright.

Father shook my hand. "I trust you are well and finding success at Fezziwig's Warehouse. I hope—"

Mother interrupted before he could complete the sentence. "You're too skinny," she declared as a matter of fact. "You must take better care of yourself, Ebenezer. When will you bring your fiancée to meet us? You have kept us waiting too long."

I accepted responsibility for failing to introduce my parents to Belle, but neither had they taken it upon themselves to travel to London for this purpose. I offered the excuse that her father had recently died and that she could not leave her poor mother with their loss so raw. Of course, we had been engaged for five years, and Mr. Fezziwig had died only two months before, but my explanation assuaged her for the time being, and she asked me to convey her condolences to the family.

"Soon then," she said, then gasped and mumbled about some detail she had overlooked, finishing the thought on her way to attend to the forgotten task.

My father remained, stoic as ever. "We shall meet Miss Belle Fezziwig when we are in London."

I nodded and offered a weak smile. I did not relish a visit from my parents, knowing they would judge me harshly for the meager accommodations of my rented flat and my sparse wardrobe and amenities. Their faces would assuredly reveal their disapproval when—not if—Belle revealed her true personality. More than any of these other reasons, however, I could not rejoice in the prospect of their visit because they would not be coming for me. If they made the trip to London, they would do so for the purpose of visiting Fan. I was only an afterthought.

"I look forward to meeting your fiancée as well," Samuel chimed in, providing a welcome respite from the uncomfortable silence. "It will be my pleasure to host you at my home for the occasion."

"A kind invitation," my father said with a nod. "Pardon me while I collect my daughter."

I excused myself as well and made a plate of food from what remained of the buffet. When I finished my last morsel of meat, but before I started on the sweets, my father announced that the newlyweds were taking their leave. I, along with the remaining guests, gathered outside to wave our farewells.

Fan, her hand tucked into the crook of Samuel's arm, walked the length of the pathway from the house to the awaiting carriage. I stood near the rock wall where I had spent so many hours as a boy watching carts and horses and people pass by. That day, it was my sister who provided the entertainment as she embarked on the next exciting phase of her life. To my delighted surprise, she turned back after she was lifted into the carriage and called out, "Farewell, Neez. I will see you in London."

I smiled widely, despite myself, as I watched her wedding coach depart, taking her away from this small, constricting town and moving her forward to a life more suited to her intelligence and personality. I wiped the tears from my cheeks before issuing my own goodbyes and returned to London straightaway.

CHAPTER TWENTY-ONE

BLESSED

1820, Twenty-Three Years before the Ghosts

The next time I saw Fan was in London, as she had promised. She sent a messenger to Fezziwig's Warehouse to summon me to dinner that very night.

Scarcely able to contain my excitement, I managed to complete only the highest priority tasks on my list. At exactly five o'clock, I dismissed the laborers for the day, locked the doors, and started on my way. Pulling the collar of my coat upward to shield my neck from the wind and vowing to wear a scarf the next day, I set myself on a fast and steady pace.

I found myself in a fine neighborhood with sidewalks as wide as the street itself and trees lining either side in brilliant autumn colors. I retrieved the letter from my pocket to confirm the address before climbing the stairs.

A doorbell rather than a simple knocker was the method employed to summon the residents of this house, and I could hear its ring from the other side of the carved wooden door. The butler, a man almost as tall as me but dressed in finer attire, welcomed me to the Wright home. He took my coat and hat and led me through the foyer to an extravagant living room, where my dear sister was waiting for me.

She sat primly on a rose-colored settee, her tiny frame resembling a child's doll within the grandness of the room and its furnishings. A large wingback chair faced the opposite direction, its occupant revealing itself after the servant announced my presence and Samuel's face appeared around the side.

"You're just in time, Neez!" Fan said, clapping her hands. "I told you to arrive by six o'clock, and here you are."

Dinner was served straightaway in the formal dining room, starting with turtle soup and a tray of cured meats, cheeses, and bread. The main dish of roasted duckling was so moist that the meat fell off the bone at the touch of my fork, each bite as delicious as the last. I protested the appearance of dessert, deeming my stomach too full to accommodate another bite, but I could not resist the array of confections—Turkish delights, according to Samuel. I enjoyed every one of them equally, unable to choose a favorite flavor.

We spent a most wonderful evening together, entertaining each other with stories of our pasts and plans for the future. Fan described their honeymoon in the countryside, and Samuel asked about my work at the warehouse. He relayed anecdotes about their courtship, and I found it amusing to hear his vastly different versions of the events my sister had described to me in her letters.

Fan recounted how our father had tripped over his own front step the first time Samuel visited. We laughed out loud as she acted out his clambering, unsuccessful attempt to pretend the gaffe had not occurred. Samuel told of his arrival one full day late for a scheduled visit. He pointed out, between chuckles, that he had been a half hour early, according to the clock, but very late indeed as judged by the calendar. The retelling of this blunder brought a blush of embarrassment to Samuel's cheeks, and when he expressed relief for Fan's immediate forgiveness of his mistake and her equally eager acceptance of his marriage proposal, my sister's cheeks ripened to match his.

It was after ten o'clock when I said my goodbyes and promised to dine with them again the next weekend. Though the sun had long since set and it was undoubtedly colder than when I had traveled the reverse journey, I barely registered it, as the warmth in my chest counteracted the blistering wind.

That winter and throughout the next full year and beyond, I managed to make sufficient time for each of the various elements of my life—my work, my sister, and my fiancée. I spent as much of it as possible with Fan, and we came to know one another well after having been kept apart, at least geographically, for so long.

Fan's husband was a merchant and traveled frequently, so she was alone for days, sometimes weeks at a time. She did not complain and always spoke of him fondly, calling him "my Sammie." She had always been one for nicknames.

Her portrayal of Samuel's financial position had not been entirely accurate. His parents had amassed significant wealth, his father through a successful trading business and his mother through inheritance, but both had died years before, leaving the house, money, and business to their only surviving son.

Samuel had continued his father's enterprise, but he made poor choices in buying products, selling them, and negotiating deals, which were essential skills for success as a merchant. Based on my calculations and in spite of Samuel's best efforts, the Wright family fortune was decreasing at an exponential rate.

For now, Fan was safe and secure, and I enjoyed having her all to myself when her husband was away. We went ice-skating in the winter months and for long strolls in the spring and fall. We sat on her front porch on the hottest of summer evenings, fanning ourselves and sipping cold drinks delivered to us by the servants.

"Yes, Mrs. Wright. Can I get you anything else, Mrs. Wright?" I was surprised every time I heard them addressing my sister this way.

She was indeed Mrs. Wright now, but she had been "my little Fan" first, and I would always be her "Neez."

After a year of marriage, and despite Samuel's nearly constant absence, Fan informed me she was pregnant. I thought she was teasing, as her stomach was flat and her waist as thin as it had always been, but a physician had confirmed it. She was fatigued and nauseous, but she assured me these were common ailments for a woman in her condition.

I worried regardless and kept her company as often as I could. As her stomach grew larger, we left the house less frequently and instead sat in her elegant living room. Her favorite spot was the pink settee, where she had been the first time I visited her in London. When autumn turned to winter, she reclined there, her hand over her distended belly and the servants flitting about to attend to her every need.

Fan spoke endlessly of her plans for the child she was carrying. If it was a girl, she would call it Martha, after our mother, and a boy would be named for her husband's father. She listed the schools the child might attend and reported that Samuel was already interviewing candidates for a nursemaid.

Still, there was only so much one could speak about a babe not yet born, even for an expectant young mother. Fan was bored with being cooped up in the house for those many months, and she begged me for stories of the outside world. I told her about the strategies I was using to increase the clientele at Fezziwig's Warehouse. She listened patiently, but what she really wanted were accounts of the diverse people I interacted with in my life and work.

When I described Belle's misbehaviors, Fan pressed me to recite her words exactly as she had spoken them. I did so to the best of my ability, endeavoring to produce the same high-pitched intonations. Fan laughed, clutching her stomach as she did so. "Do it again," she pleaded, and my repeat performance elicited open-mouthed guffaws that left her gasping for air.

Each week, I had a new story of Belle's precocious demands and rude conduct. Fan took to calling her "Bratty Belle," and I could not protest because she was 100 percent correct in her characterization. In more serious moments, Fan expressed concern about what my life would be like as the husband of such a spoiled woman, how I would have to deal with her complaints every single day and address each of her demands in one way or another. Could I be happy in this life? The answer to that question was no, but there was nothing I could do about it since I had promised to marry her.

I tucked that concern away, as my highest priority was to ensure my sister's continued health and happiness. After a time, even my stories about Belle became monotonous, and Fan pressed me for information about Belle's friends' lives as well. Apparently, when one was confined to her home with no other source of entertainment, gossip about anyone, even perfect strangers, was a welcome diversion. I endeavored to provide as many details as I could recollect, but I had limited resources in this regard.

Since Fan's love of books rivaled mine, we took turns reading aloud, me from books I borrowed from Mr. Fezziwig's study and Fan from books her husband gave her, along with chocolates and other treats he brought home from his business travels. She was an excellent orator, and I reveled in the confident sound of her voice when she read from *Pride and Prejudice*, a novel written by a woman named Jane Austen. Fan and I found it easy to relate to the rural lifestyle it described, having grown up under similar circumstances, and delighted in acquainting ourselves with a new style of hero in the main character, Elizabeth Bennet. We cheered when she overcame her predispositions, and again when Mr. Darcy suppressed his ego and they surrendered to love for each other.

At Christmastime, the servants decorated the Wright house with an intensity I had never seen before. There were fresh cut evergreens in the living room and foyer, each ornamented in a distinct color scheme with beads, tinsel, paper trimmings, and shiny baubles. Boughs of pine and holly framed every doorway, fireplace mantel, and even the staircase railings. Each door had its own wreath, spiked emerald leaves contrasting with bright red berries.

Fan longed for fresh air and to admire the festive streets with her own eyes. Since she was unable to venture outside in her condition, I described for her in detail the decorations I observed on my walks through the city, the storefront displays of toys and clothing, and bakery windows filled with sweet treats.

On each of the twelve days of Christmas, I brought Fan a gift. Most were small, like roasted chestnuts, still warm, which I purchased from a vendor at Leadenhall Market; scented soaps; and a hand-painted card featuring a fluffy yellow chick recently freed from its eggshell and prancing in a bed of wildflowers. The last gift was her favorite, as well as mine. I spent one pound, two shillings on it, which was all I had left after purchasing the bracelet Belle had demanded. Fan cried when she opened it, and I worried about the soundness of my choice, but she assured me that being overcome with emotion was a common occurrence for pregnant women.

"I love it, Ebenezer. Thank you." She held it to her chest. It was a book titled *Emma*, another of Jane Austen's novels published before the author's recent death.

It was I who should have thanked her. The gifts she bestowed on me—her affection and companionship and the bond of family—were far more valuable than any material item I could procure. I loved her beyond what words could describe. I was truly blessed.

CHAPTER TWENTY-TWO

MIRACLE

1821, Twenty-Two Years before the Ghosts

My world changed again on Saturday, February 17, 1821. Samuel Wright's footman arrived at the warehouse with news that Fan was in labor. Her pains had started the day before, the man explained, after I shook him by the shoulders in an effort to extract more information. The delivery was imminent.

I was fortunate they had sent a messenger for me. My mother, who had traveled to London for the last weeks of Fan's confinement, had told me childbirth was an endeavor reserved solely to the realm of women. There was no role for me to play, and my presence was neither required nor welcome. I wanted to be nearby, despite these prohibitions, if only so Fan would know I was there to support her.

I hailed a hackney coach. Damn the cost. Twisting my hands together the way I had as a nervous child, I silently begged the horse to trot faster.

How was Fan faring? Would she survive the ordeal? What of the babe? I could not help but recall the trauma of my sister's birth when I had been left alone, confused and frightened, listening to my mother's screams. I was just as terrified now as I had been that day.

The streets were slippery and wet, making the ride from the warehouse to Fan's home frustratingly longer than it should have been. When I arrived, I hopped out of the carriage, bounded up the steps and let myself into the house. I collided with the butler in the foyer and shoved a coin in his hand, barking at him to pay the coachman. He looked back at me with wide eyes, but he bowed and proceeded to do as I instructed.

There was none of the commotion I had expected, based on my admittedly limited experience with childbirth. I stiffened, the sound of sleet pounding from the open door behind me and silence looming in front of me. I was unable to move from the spot, unwilling to face the certain heartbreak of what I feared most.

After what felt like an eternity, one of the maidservants appeared at the top of the stairs carrying an armful of fabric flickering with crimson wetness. She was smiling, and my mind struggled to process these contradictory signals. Fan could not have survived the loss of so much blood. I was certain of it. But, if she was dead, why did the maid's face register joy?

The woman took pity on me, thank God, since I was frozen with terror turning decisively toward grief. "She is fine, sir. Mrs. Wright is quite well. And so is the babe."

I heard a sound—not the cry of a woman in pain but the whimpering of an infant.

Whereas I could not have forced my body to move one second before, now I could not stop my legs from jerking into action. They propelled me, without any conscious effort, up the stairs, through the partly open door, and into Fan's bedroom.

"Neez!" my sister said. Her smile was as reassuring a sign as I could hope for, evidence that all was right in the world.

What a sight I must have been, dripping wet and heaving breaths of exertion. The maidservant appeared behind me and removed my coat and hat. Another woman—this one I did not recognize—rushed over, tsking her disapproval and coughing into the rags she was using to wipe the floor. Her hacking sounded as wet as I was, and I questioned why a person so obviously ill was allowed in the birthing room. The babe's whimper interrupted my semiformed thought, and I summarily abandoned it.

"Come meet your nephew," Fan bade me.

My nephew? A boy!

I made my way to her bedside, trying to appear a calm and sane uncle instead of a man who belonged in Bedlam asylum. I peered down into the small white bundle she cradled in her arms and saw his face, round and chubby with rosy cheeks and a tiny button of a nose. His eyes were closed, and his little lips puckered on and off as if sucking an imaginary nipple. Fan smiled up at me.

"He is perfect," I told her. It was the undeniable truth.

Samuel looked the part of a proud father, watching over his wife and baby from the opposite side of the bed. "His name is Frederick," he said.

"But we will call him Freddie," Fan added.

I smiled at my little sister. Of course her child would have a nickname. Freddie. I loved it.

"He will share his middle name with you, Neez. And we want you to be his godfather."

Frederick Joseph Wright. My mouth hung open, and I stumbled backward as a wave of profound emotion overtook me. My sister had survived the ordeal of childbirth, and I had a nephew, a beautiful baby boy who shared my middle name. I would be his godfather, his protector, his family. I would love him always and provide for him in whatever ways he needed. He would be the most significant responsibility of my life—this boy, this miracle.

CHAPTER TWENTY-THREE

REGRET

1822, Twenty-One Years before the Ghosts

Fan's presence in London and the birth of my precious nephew were gifts to me, but my sister needed me more than ever, and my relationship with Belle dwindled to near insignificance. I did not abandon her or her mother, but rather stopped making any effort to play the part of devoted and loving fiancé. I had never been particularly skilled at it anyway, so I doubted my abysmal performance alerted anyone to my disinterest in the marriage.

Mrs. Fezziwig continued to dress in mourning clothes, but after a time Belle and her sisters replaced their simple black dresses with dark purples and blues. Sadly, just as they started to reengage with society, the eldest sister's child fell ill. The boy, once so full of energy and vitality, wasted away in a matter of days and was buried beside his grandfather. I hoped they both found peace and comfort in the afterlife.

Another tragedy followed soon after when Mrs. Fezziwig's sister died suddenly, her body discovered by her husband when he returned home from work. The woman had a reputation for melodrama and was prone to bouts of depression, so there were murmurings she had caused the death herself, making the situation more difficult for the family to bear. The Fezziwigs were in mourning for the better part of four years.

I continued the obligatory courtship activities, nothing more, though the hours I trifled away at the house were far less enjoyable than when Mr. Fezziwig had been alive. Every interaction with Belle was as tedious as the next, and I dreaded Sundays, when I had to accompany her and her mother to church and lunch with them afterward.

Belle hounded me with demands and complaints. The delivery of her new dress was delayed, which she blamed on my ineptitude in running her father's business, though I would have assured her, if she had let me, that I was experiencing a good deal of success at it. She was distraught at not being able to attend her friends' parties, but there was nothing I could do about that since her family's state of mourning prevented it. Most of all, she complained about the length of our engagement, shedding tears over the injustice of having to wait and threatening to lock herself away should our marriage be delayed further. This was a dramatic response, as was typical of Belle, and I did not consider it a valid threat.

It would take time for me to save the money needed to pay for the lavishness Belle would demand of the wedding itself. She did not realize—or simply did not care—that her continual demands for jewelry and gloves and capes and other expensive items were hindering progress toward our marriage. The standing excuse I used for my absence was my work at the warehouse, for I could always truthfully claim to have an order waiting to be filled or important paperwork left to complete.

I was busy, so busy, too busy for her. What happened next should have been no surprise.

Seated at my desk, as usual, I noted a quieting of the customary bustle in the warehouse. My curiosity piqued, I peered through the open office door to identify the cause of the disturbance, knocking over an inkwell in the process. Vainly patting the black blots on the paper, I cursed under my breath, exasperated that my perpetual clumsiness would necessitate the copying of a full page of figures.

A soft knock pulled my attention away from the ruined document, and I looked up to find my fiancée staring back at me with an expression of disgust that likely topped my own.

"What are you doing here?" The words came out nastier than I intended, but my annoyance was quickly displaced by concern, for it was unusual for Belle to venture out unaccompanied. I stood, the feet of my chair grinding against the floor as I pushed it roughly backward. "Is something wrong? Is your mother ill?"

"No. Everyone is fine." Her answer was succinct, and the terror gripping me shifted to unease when she added, "I am here to discuss our future."

I helped remove her coat and hung it on the rack next to mine before guiding her to one of the chairs opposite my desk. Once seated, she grabbed my arm with more strength than I gave her credit for and pulled me into the chair beside her.

I dreaded what I expected to come next—a demand that our marriage take place straightaway. Cringing on the inside, I hoped it did not show on the outside. I was a man of my word, and I would not break the vow I had made to her father. I had done everything in my power to postpone this conversation and the marriage itself for as long as possible, but it seemed my efforts to delay had reached the end of their fruitfulness. I steeled myself against the inevitable.

"Our engagement has lasted seven years," she started, "and I feel we are farther apart than when we began. Do you even want to marry me anymore?"

I could not tell her the truth, which was an emphatic no. Instead, I replied with the reality of the predicament in which I was ensnared. "I have promised to do so, so it does not matter whether I want to or not."

She made a sort of sobbing noise and turned away from me to stare at a point on the floor. "It matters little. To you, very little. But to me it matters a great deal. I aspire to have a marriage of love and affection. I deserve that. In fact, I demand it."

Belle was proficient at making demands, and she usually received whatever she wanted. But love could not be compelled, and I lacked the ability to feign its existence. No matter how much Belle whined or pleaded, it was not possible for me to give her what she required.

"Another idol has displaced me," she said. "And if it can comfort you, as I would have tried to, then I have no just cause to grieve. There is nothing I can do to make you love me instead."

Panic swelled in my chest. How could she know I harbored feelings for someone else?

"What idol has displaced you?" I said, looking at the floor, as she did, and endeavoring to conceal my distress that she might have guessed my gravest secret.

"A golden one."

Then I understood, to my immense relief, and smiled, though fortunately she could not see my face. Belle did not suspect that I yearned for another, but that money was my vice. My reliance on work as an excuse had convinced her that I valued profit over all else. Though I did indeed place a high priority on business, I did not treasure it more than the people who were important to me. How would she know? She was not included in that category.

I could have corrected her logic, but I did not, since allowing it to persist would benefit us both. Belle's assumption was an act of self-preservation, which made severing our relationship easier. If I were a cold and unsympathetic man, as she asserted, consumed with wealth over love, then she would be justified in breaking our engagement. Moreover, she would bear no responsibility since it was my character flaw and not hers that necessitated it.

I was the villain in the scenario Belle imagined, but the opinions of others did not bother me as they did her. It would be a crushing embarrassment for her to admit that I had chosen not to love her. It was far easier to say the decision was hers, that she did not want me because of my inadequacies as a partner. This narrative would save her reputation. For me, it provided a means of escape from the promise I had made, a dissolution she demanded and I could not prevent.

I resolved to embrace her story, regardless of its falsehood.

"This is the way of the world, Belle. You do not want to live in poverty, do you? There is no plight so cruel in life as being poor." I paused before adding, "There is nothing wrong with the pursuit of wealth."

"All your other hopes have merged into the one desire," she said, shaking her head at the floor. "I have watched as your nobler aspirations fell off one by one until one singular passion—greed—has taken over."

Certainly, she did not believe I was motivated by my own personal gain. This could not be further from the truth. I had not increased my salary one shilling since her father died. Though I managed the warehouse alone and had grown the business threefold, I gave all the profits to Mrs. Fezziwig. Belle and her family, it seemed, were unaware of my generosity. I could correct this misunderstanding. Indeed, perhaps I should, and earn a bit of gratitude and respect for it, but that would only serve my own selfish purpose. It was better to let Belle think what she wanted about me, if it eased her suffering.

"What then?" I asked. "Even if I have grown wiser, I am not changed toward you."

"Our contract is an old one," she said. "It was made when neither of us worried about money, and life was full of possibilities. You are changed, Ebenezer. You know it as well as I do. When we made our promise, you were a different man."

"I was a boy." My face grew warm, but I swallowed down the welling resentment. "Your father had plans for me, and so did you, for a future I did not choose for myself. Now my responsibilities weigh heavily upon my shoulders, which were once free from such burdens."

"But I want to be married, to start my life," Belle said in her familiar whining tone. "I have been through so much."

It was true that she had suffered at her father's death, but so had I. It was unjust that she was unable to live the life she wanted, but yet again, that same circumstance applied to me.

"I had hoped for happiness for us, but there is only misery now. Regretfully, I must accept that you are not available for marriage since your true partner is found elsewhere. I can release you from your commitment."

The stitch in my side was either relief at being set free or panic that my life was changing forever. I could not discern which.

"Have I ever sought release?"

"In words? No. Never," she conceded.

"In what, then?"

Belle's eyes met mine. "In a changed nature, in an altered spirit, in everything that gave my love any value in your sight. If my father had not arranged our engagement, if we had not been linked by him, tell me, would you seek me out and try to win me now? The answer is clearly no."

She was right, of course. I had not desired her when she had shown interest in me so many years before, and I certainly did not want to marry her now. If not for the love I had for her father, I never would have agreed to the engagement in the first place. Still, dissolving our contract would fundamentally alter the trajectories of our lives, and I had not given consideration to those possibilities.

"You think I would not choose you?" I offered a half-hearted protest. "How are you so sure?"

"I would gladly think otherwise if I could," she said. "Heaven knows I would. What a scandal this will be—me, forced to find a new match when all of my friends are engaged or married already. I can only hope my suitors understand I had no option but to make this choice. If you were free today, tomorrow, yesterday, you would not choose to marry me—or anyone for that matter. You prefer the pleasures of money over anything a woman can provide. Even if, for a moment, you allowed yourself to embrace the love I offer, I fear you would still find me inadequate to what you truly adore."

She was correct on this point. She could never be the person I loved.

"I release you, Ebenezer, with a full heart and love for the man you once were."

I was the same person I had always been, never more or less than I was now. She had never truly known me, nor had she devoted an ounce of effort to doing so.

Belle stood, and I looked up sheepishly as she spoke. "You may regret this someday in the future, but you will dismiss the recollection of it as an unprofitable dream, from which you thankfully awoke. It is done now, Ebenezer. Our connection is severed. I hope you are happy in the life you have chosen." She took her coat and walked out.

I yelled after her as she made her way across the warehouse and out of my life. "I wish you well, Belle Fezziwig."

I did not mourn her loss or regret my choice. The only distress it caused was knowing that I was breaking the promise I had made to her father, that his well-orchestrated plans for his family's future would not be fulfilled.

My sincere hope was that Mr. Fezziwig was in an eternity free from worry about the goings-on in the world below. He had been righteous in life, kind and forgiving, and had earned the gift of peace. Whether in heaven, as I suspected, or roaming the earth as a tortured soul, for his sake I would not allow his family to descend into poverty.

CHAPTER TWENTY-FOUR
REVELATIONS

1823, Twenty Years before the Ghosts

It had been over an hour since the laborers left, and I was seated at my desk in the room I continued to refer to as "Mr. Fezziwig's office," though he had vacated it forever years before. The creaking of the front door's hinges roused me from my concentrated focus, and a rush of air followed closely behind, cooling my cheeks. I was sure I had remembered to lock up, but someone had managed to gain entry nonetheless. I held my breath and listened.

A thud told me the heavy door had been shut again, and the unmistakable sound of footsteps meant someone was inside. They were heading in my direction.

I placed my quill in its well and tiptoed to the corner where Mr. Fezziwig's cane remained propped against the wall. It scraped against the floor as I picked it up, and, with my presence exposed, I had no choice but to continue a hastily conceived plan of defense. I raised it over my head, both hands grasping firmly, and prepared to strike.

"Ebenezer Scrooge, are you here?" A voice called to me, and I rummaged among a vast assortment of memory fragments in an effort to identify it.

I was in a ridiculous position—legs wide, wooden cane held high, and my head cocked to the side, trapped somewhere between confusion and terror—when Jacob Marley peeked around the corner.

"Ho there," he shouted, holding his hands out in front of him but still advancing. "Stand down, friend. It is only me."

My heart leapt to my throat, and the displaced organ prevented me from issuing a reply. *Only me*? As if I should have been expecting him. As if he had not disappeared from my life more than a decade before. How could "only me" be his means of reintroduction? I lowered the cane until its tip rested on the floor.

"Are you not pleased to see me?" Jacob asked, offense in his tone and a furrowed brow contaminating his otherwise handsome face.

My emotions swayed wildly from elation to consternation. There was a fluttering in my stomach, not nausea but rather a rekindling of a long-ago neglected yearning. At the same time, I was angry—no, irate—at him for ignoring me all these years. He had held the keys to the warehouse since the night he signed the contract with Mr. Fezziwig, yet he had not used them until now. His absence had made me question the meaning of his actions and mine, and I had convinced myself that the connection I thought possible between us was not real.

"Where have you been?" I asked, though I knew full well he had been here in London the whole time. "Why are you here?" This was the question I wanted him to answer first.

"To see you, of course," he said. "I have met my obligation to the Fezziwigs, and you have met yours. We are free to continue where we left off."

"What obligations?" I shook my head, though it did nothing to help the words make sense. "I don't understand."

He started toward me, but I took a step backward, and he stopped.

"Then I shall explain," he said solemnly. "As you recall, my friend, after we met at that very merry Christmas party, I purchased a stake in the warehouse and met with Fezziwig some time later in this very office."

I did remember the meeting. It had been early spring, the day bright, and the sound of chirping birds filtering in through the open windows. I did not verbally acknowledge it, though I may have nodded. Either way, Jacob continued.

"I insisted on a reduction in the workforce and a focus on the most valuable employee. Do you know what I am speaking of?"

This time, my nod was intentional. After Jacob's visit, Mr. Fezziwig had released my fellow apprentice from service, and I assumed the management role.

"As you can imagine, Fezziwig opposed my demands and exacted his own conditions." Anger flashed across his face. "In exchange for implementing my reforms, I had to step away and allow him to run the business without my interference. He wanted to train you himself, to teach you his management methods, and guide you as you matured as a businessman. He forbade me to see you or interact with you. It was not what I wanted, but I had no choice."

My mind was reeling. "I thought you had forgotten me," I confessed, unable to control either the content or tone of my response. Only the truth escaped, with no filters applied to conceal my own feelings, or to protect his. "I assumed I was not good enough for you."

"Forgotten you? Never. Not good enough? Bah." He held his hands out, palms up, as if pleading for forgiveness, before pulling them back again to rest on his head. He grabbed his hair with his fists and then let his arms fall to his sides, his now disheveled tresses giving him a wayward look that made my body quiver, and I could not repress a gasp.

"You must understand that I honor my promises. Only at Fezziwig's wake did I lay eyes upon you, though it could not have been avoided, given the necessity of your presence there as a friend of the family and mine as a business associate."

I thought back to the circumstances of his visit to the Fezziwig home, noting that he had arrived in the evening hours, after the warehouse closed, which increased the likelihood that I would be present.

"And after that, I mean, after Fezziwig died, well, then you were promised in marriage to his daughter, and I would not tempt you to violate that agreement. I am a decent man, Ebenezer, and I sense you are as well. We must always be true to our word and protect our reputations, always strive to be worthy of esteem. But now your engagement has been annulled. We are both relieved of our commitments, free to pursue our desires without restriction."

He reached for my hand, and this time I did not pull away. Mr. Fezziwig's cane slipped from my hand, bouncing once before it settled to the floor.

CHAPTER TWENTY-FIVE

GAIN

1825, Eighteen Years before the Ghosts

Jacob returned to the warehouse the week after his surprise visit and every few days after that. There was little for him to do, since Fezziwig's Warehouse was thriving under my management, but he checked in on the latest developments and offered suggestions to improve operations.

I hired an apprentice to assist with the workload and, knowing how isolated it could feel to labor and live alone in the expansive warehouse, convinced Jacob to concede to two. The first was from the countryside, a tall, lean chap with a cheerful personality. The second had grown up in the city and was more serious in demeanor, though still pleasant enough. They complemented one another, as Nick and I had years before, but unlike us, both were sufficiently capable in writing and arithmetic and possessed social skills adequate to the job. They moved seamlessly between the duties required of the position.

I was content with my life and satisfied with my accomplishments. The new business venture was Jacob's idea.

"I have a surprise for you."

I had been concentrating on my work and was so startled by Jacob's sudden appearance that I nearly fell from my seat.

"How do I frighten you so?" he said, his hand on his chest, feigning indignance. "It is only me, your loyal friend and business partner. Gather your hat and coat, Ebenezer, and come with me."

I offered a weak protest but did as he commanded. Jacob refused to divulge the projected length of our excursion, so I instructed the apprentices to dismiss the laborers and lock the doors if I did not return by five o'clock.

Jacob and I walked, largely in silence, along the Thames, over London Bridge, and through the winding streets of the city center. It was hot and dry, as it had been for each of the seven days since July began. Smoke from an infinite number of coal-fueled chimneys clogged the air, making it difficult to breathe, let alone talk. A series of hackney coaches passed by, filled with people who had chosen comfort over economy, and it occurred to me that one positive side effect of the arid weather was the absence of puddles whose contents would have been sprayed on us by the carriage wheels. Plus, I had Jacob by my side, so it was not so bad after all.

That moment of appreciation for everything good in my life elicited a grin, which due to its transience, went unrecognized by anyone else. It disappeared at the appearance of beggars at the outskirts of Leadenhall Market. Witnessing the plight of the poor always tugged my spirits downward, as it reminded me of the fragility of success and the responsibilities it demanded. For all the merchants who earned a decent living selling their wares, there were at least as many prostitutes selling their bodies to keep their children fed and drunkards trading their souls to fuel their vice. Lives that were once happy and secure could crumble due to sickness or misfortune. This was the simple reality of life, and I knew that my own prosperity, though hard won, was as precarious as that of any man of humble beginnings.

"Where are we going?" I asked, partly to prevent myself from sinking deeper into an empathetic abyss and partly because my legs were aching.

"You will see," he said over his shoulder. I loved that we were the same height, and I did not have to look down to meet his eyes as I did with almost everyone else. Though beads of sweat were running down his reddened temple, he gave me a wry smile and turned forward again. I wished he would continue looking at me but acknowledged the prudence of watching carefully where one stepped, since horse dung and uneven terrain were constant threats.

We arrived at the epicenter of finance for the city, near the Royal Exchange and Bank of England, surrounded by merchants hurrying up and down the street, chinking the money in their pockets and flaunting their great gold seals. Jacob tipped his hat to one man and again to a group of four who acknowledged him by name.

Were these men business associates? Did he have partnerships with them, as he had with Mr. Fezziwig? Did he know them well, or were they merely acquaintances? I had so many questions and scant few clues to the answers. It struck me how little I knew of Jacob's life outside of the tiny sphere that encompassed me, Fezziwig's Warehouse, and our undefined, yet budding, relationship.

I had no secrets, no outside business investments, no mysterious liaisons. Jacob was more enigmatic. How much of his life did he keep hidden from me? How much always would be?

These questions consumed my thoughts, such that I only noticed we had entered a narrow side street when the closeness of the buildings shaded me, providing a respite from the sun's burning rays. Jacob was no longer in front of me. I had lost sight of my guide.

"Ho there," he called out. "We are here."

I turned on my heel and doubled back. We were on the north side of Cornhill, having traveled through a series of alleyways and courtyards to reach the spot. Each little area of the city center had its own personality, in terms of architecture as well as its resident characters. This one was dark but not unpleasant, and there was a constant flow of businessmen passing through. We were in Newman's Court, or so the sign said, but I had no idea why "here" was significant.

Jacob reached into his pocket and held out a key. He tipped his head toward one of the buildings and motioned for me to follow before bounding up the stairs. After a significant amount of jiggling the rusty lock, he succeeded in the task, as evidenced by the thud of a bolt and the creak of hinges. He pushed open the door, and I followed him inside.

"What do you think?" He grinned widely and waved his hand, palm up, in a half circle, directing me to admire the dingy room.

"What do I think of what? What is this place?"

"Our new office," he said. "If you like it, that is. I already signed the papers, but we can find a way out of the contract if you do not approve."

"I already have an office," I said. "Mr. Fezziwig's. In the warehouse. Why would I need another?"

"For our counting house business, of course," Jacob said, planting his fists on either side of his waist.

Confounded, the best response I could muster was an incoherent "Uh," followed by, "I don't . . . You? What?"

My reaction had no deterrent effect on his excitement, and he proceeded to offer a full explanation of his plans. We would be partners, he and I, with equal stakes in a counting house, which offered bookkeeping and moneylending services. The business would require the merging of our strengths. My talent with calculations and attention to detail would be crucial to our success in managing the accounts of a variety of clients, from individual merchants to larger firms and factories. Jacob's professional connections and wealth would give us credibility and provide critical lending capital, which we would grow by collecting interest on loans. Since I had Fezziwig's Warehouse operating smoothly and apprentices to handle some of the workload, we would devote the bulk of our time and energy to this new venture.

Jacob went on for some time, detailing his ideas for building our client base and how we would organize our priorities. He justified his choice of this office location as its proximity to the Royal Exchange and to his own home, which was a few blocks away. I nodded slowly throughout, too busy taking in the information to muster a response.

He was endeavoring to persuade me of the wisdom of his plan, but his efforts were unnecessary. I was already convinced. It sounded grand to me. I found this type of work fulfilling, plus it meant that he and I would spend our days working side by side to build the business.

When he finished, his breaths were quick from the exertion of verbalizing his proposal in one long soliloquy. His forehead furrowed, and his eyes searched mine.

I did not let him squirm for long. "Wonderful," I said, my smile broadening until I could see the outline of my cheeks in the periphery of my vision.

Jacob's expression transformed to match mine, relief and joy evident in his handsome face. Two long steps brought him mere inches from me, and he opened his arms and leaned in for an embrace. His warmth soaked through my shirt and onto my chest, but he stopped suddenly and pulled away, straightened, and took a backward step. Had I done something wrong?

I followed his gaze to the bay window and to the heads of people—businessmen like us—passing by on the street outside. We had almost forgotten where we were, almost made a mistake that could have cost us dearly. Our behavior, the mere perception of it, mattered now more than ever. If we were to be successful in the counting house business, we had to be seen as moral and trustworthy, beyond reproach. Our future prosperity was at stake—that and so much more.

Instead of giving me the hug I desperately wanted, he shook my hand. "Congratulations, Ebenezer Scrooge," he said, his voice deep and genteel.

"The same to you, Jacob Marley." We held our handshake for a moment longer than was customary, which was as much as we could prudently accomplish and better than no touch at all.

He led me on a tour of the office then, starting in the room where our conversation had taken place, where the window offered a view of the ancient tower of Saint Michael's Cornhill, whose tolling bell would mark the hours we spent there together.

"We will need a proper curtain for that window," Jacob observed, citing the benefits of preserving warmth in the winter and preventing us from overheating in the summer. He neglected to mention the obvious justification of it as a shield against prying eyes.

The room was spacious enough to serve as our shared office, where we could collaborate and hold meetings with clients and prospective borrowers. Beyond it was another chamber, either a large closet or a tiny room, depending on one's perspective. It had no windows to let in light or air, though it did have a small stove for heat. We agreed to utilize it as storage for documents and supplies. The whole place needed to be scrubbed and polished, and we would have to purchase furnishings, but its size and location suited our needs. I relished the prospect of spending hours there with Jacob each day.

"Our first task as partners is to choose a name for our business," he said, pulling a chair, or rather a stool, since the back pieces had been broken off, into the center of the room and plopping down on it. I found a small crate and did the same, though mine was much shorter, which resulted in my knees being higher than my bottom. I propped my elbows at the highest point, my chin resting in my hands, and we snickered at the absurdity of my position.

I let Jacob speak first. Since he had been planning this for some time, he surely had an idea at the ready.

"I was thinking some combination of our names would be appropriate. Marley and Scrooge, perhaps? Or Scrooge and Marley? That one has a ring to it. What do you think?"

I did not care whether his name came first or mine. Simply stringing them together brought me pleasure.

"You decide," I said. "I like them both."

"Scrooge and Marley it is then. I will commission a sign maker this very day."

Over the ensuing months and years, we toiled to establish the business and built our client list, securing prominence in London's financial industry. My schedule was daunting, but I could not have been happier. I allocated my mornings to the warehouse and left at noon to make my way along the south bank of the Thames, over London Bridge, and through a cacophony of streets to our little courtyard. Each day, I found Jacob waiting for me in the counting house, and we spent the afternoon together engrossed in our work. This schedule repeated itself six days a week, but every morning I woke with renewed energy and hope for the future.

Jacob was the salesman, tasked to persuade his many business and social contacts of our firm's superiority over others. He engaged in conversations on the street or met them for lunch, spreading the news that Scrooge and Marley's counting house had capital available for investment. Those interactions led to meetings, and those meetings led to clients. Those clients, satisfied with the services they received, made referrals that resulted in still more contracts and new connections. Before long, our accounts numbered in the dozens, and I had as much work as I could handle.

I participated in select interviews with prospective borrowers, but my most significant contributions were the detailed computations that buttressed our operations. I kept careful records for those who contracted with us for accounting, and Jacob reviewed them to ensure their accuracy, not once discovering an error or oversight.

We considered loan applications together, evaluating their merits and analyzing the liabilities. He was more skilled than I was at judging people's character and came to conclusions about their likelihood for default rather easily. I, on the other hand, deliberated at length, weighing the risks against the prospect of helping the less fortunate.

Jacob was more pessimistic in his projections about the reliability of loan applicants, while I tended to give people the benefit of the doubt. On occasion, our contradictory opinions led to prolonged discussions, with each of us explaining our rationale and hoping to sway the other. In one instance, I supported the application of a struggling businessman, citing his upstanding reputation in the community, his past record of success, and his family's need. Jacob argued that the man's business would fail because new merchants had entered the market and were selling their goods at lower prices. He predicted the man would default on the loan, leaving only devalued products and no way for us to recoup our investment.

I acquiesced to Jacob's judgments more often than not, acknowledging that strict standards were crucial to our success, but I suffered terrible guilt for failing to help people who clearly needed it.

Jacob made the official notifications on loan acceptances and denials, and I was thankful for it. His willingness to be the bearer of bad news spared me the anguish of witnessing the disappointment in the faces of those whose applications we rejected. He drew up the paperwork, delineating the stringent terms and penalties for delinquency, obtained the necessary signatures, and filed the contracts as required by law. I calculated the interest and repayment schedules and logged the monies we received. We made an excellent team and, through our combined strengths, achieved significant success.

CHAPTER TWENTY-SIX

RELATIONSHIPS AND LEARNING

1827, Sixteen Years before the Ghosts

I learned much in the years Scrooge and Marley's counting house began its exponential growth. As a forty-year-old man, I was juggling many roles, each with its own title, obligations, challenges, and rewards. I endeavored to fulfill each of them adequately, though I might have served all parties better if I had allocated my time differently, concentrated on one over the others.

The role that consumed most of my time and energy was that of businessman. I had been practicing at it since I was an eighteen-year-old apprentice to Mr. Fezziwig, though I could never have imagined the complexities and demands it entailed. As sole manager of the warehouse, I oversaw a dozen laborers, some of whom had been there for many years, and others who had recently joined the ranks. Their jobs were simple enough—moving boxes from one place to the other, according to the well-defined list of incoming inventory and outgoing orders, but they came to me with questions, for specific instructions, and to resolve discrepancies and conflicts.

I also had two apprentices who required attention beyond simple supervision. An apprentice invested significant time and effort in exchange for the imparted wisdom of a wise, experienced leader. I felt like an impostor, unqualified to fulfill my end of the agreement, but I did my best to pass on my knowledge and expertise, such as they were. This required that I know each of them well enough to identify their strengths and weaknesses, so I might guide them in developing the skills they would need to achieve future success.

I tried to be as supportive and encouraging as Mr. Fezziwig had been to me, but I struggled to create bonds with them and feared I was falling far short of that goal. I would never have the desire or ability to host festive holiday parties or provoke joy through my laughter alone, as Mr. Fezziwig had done so effortlessly. Still, I endeavored to be the best mentor I could, and I dared say I achieved a modicum of success.

My professional life also included the role of partner in the firm of Scrooge and Marley. Being a partner was different from being the boss—easier in some ways, but harder in others. Our counting house was an equal partnership between Jacob and me, but the two of us were unequal in terms of ability. To be sure, neither of us was more skilled nor more important, but rather, our contributions were disparate, and we had to learn how to collaborate. Fortunately, our personalities were compatible and our talents complementary, and over time our interactions in the business realm became seamless. The end result did not come without a fair amount of compromise, but it was worth the effort.

My other roles consumed far less time but were no less important.

"Brother" was not a new title for me, nor was I unfamiliar with its responsibilities and benefits. After all, I had served in that capacity for the majority of my life and for all of my sister's. I spent every Sunday afternoon with Fan, going for walks when the weather was favorable, with little

Freddie toddling along beside us.

We made up stories about the lives of the strangers we passed, speculating about the reasons for their idiosyncratic behaviors and choices of attire. For the skinny woman bundled in a fur shawl in the middle of summer, we surmised that she had burglarized a home and was attempting to escape without detection by wearing the stolen item rather than concealing it. For the gorgeous, immaculately dressed man walking arm in arm with a woman wearing what would best be described as rags, we guessed that he was a theater director and she an actor in costume, on break from rehearsal.

When it was raining, too hot, or uncomfortably cold to venture outside, we sat on Fan's porch or in her living room talking for hours on end. We spoke of her activities the previous week, of the pleasures and challenges of parenting, and her interactions, oftentimes frustrating, with her husband, Samuel. She relayed the gossip spread by the ladies in her social circle, and I told her of the news I had read or overheard during my walks through the city.

Each Sunday ended with discussion about our plans for the week ahead—mine always to work on this or that and hers to take Freddie on an outing of some sort or engage the servants in a project at the house. We hugged and bid our farewells until we would meet again the next week for more of the same. I showed Fan unconditional love as I always had, through my words and deeds, and I was confident I was adequately fulfilling the role of her brother.

Being a brother *and* a friend was something quite different, however. Until the obligation was bestowed on me, I had not realized there was a distinction. Fan was an adult now, my peer, not just my adoring little sister. She was a wife and a mother, and, though I would always be older, I was no longer the more experienced, knowledgeable, or mature. She had surpassed me on many of these measures.

Fan looked to me for friendship now rather than guidance or protection. She wanted me to share my troubles and self-doubts with her, the way she did with me. I had to learn to see her as a confidante, but the process of doing so was an unexpected challenge.

When Fan asked about my life, I answered with details about the products that had arrived in the warehouse and the orders to be filled. I told her about the new firms Jacob and I had added as clients and the recipients and purposes of the loans we had made. Fan listened politely, but she prodded me for more personal information, like the people I met, where I took my suppers, and my thoughts on various subjects. I did my best to give her what she asked of me, telling her about my apprentice's relationship with a local girl, which had progressed from letter writing to an in-person meeting, throughout which the girl's nursemaid had not removed her gaze from the boy for a second longer than it took to blink her eyes. I reported that one of the laborer's wives had delivered twin baby girls and named them Emma and Ella, which I thought an unfortunate choice since it practically ensured confusion in the years to come.

My stories entertained Fan, but I had been doing that for as long as I could remember, and it was not enough anymore. She wanted to hear about me—my opinions, my emotions, my reactions to certain events. How did I feel about the news of Belle's engagement to another man, for instance? What did I hope for my future? Who would I choose for a wife since work could not be my only source of passion?

Fan sought to understand who I was in my heart and soul. By holding back, by not sharing all of myself with her, I was depriving her of this opportunity. The last thing I wanted was to deprive her of anything, so I worked harder at it.

I did not fully understand my own inner sentiments and was equally incapable of deciphering the emotions of others, which resulted in me bungling my way through many social situations. When I replayed them again in my mind, approached them analytically as I did with the numbers in my ledger, I recognized where I had gone wrong and identified my mistakes. Regrettably, these insights came too late to be useful, and I was destined to commit the same blunders over again.

Fan beamed as I explained this conundrum to her. Apparently, this was what she had been looking for all along. I had assumed I needed to sort things out in my own mind before sharing them with her, but the processing of my thoughts was what I was supposed to be discussing. I wished I had realized this sooner because it proved not so difficult after all. I grew progressively better at it over time, and we engaged in deep conversations about morality and life's mysteries. We discussed the issue of poverty, for example, agreeing on the cosmic injustice of a world in which some found themselves with extravagances while others led lives of scarcity.

To some of Fan's questions—the ones about Belle and a future wife—I did not have insightful answers, but to other things, like denying a loan to a family in need, I had plenty to say. I shared with her my most unorganized thoughts, and she added her own interpretations to help me make sense of them. This process of self-reflection offered us both a glimpse into my psyche, which had until then been inaccessible to anyone, including myself.

To my surprise, I found it cathartic to delve into my deepest insecurities and guilts. Expressing my thoughts aloud to a sympathetic ear freed me temporarily from a pervasive sense of inadequacy.

Confiding in Fan, as she did in me, intensified our bond. It surprised me to learn she had felt abandoned when I went to boarding school. This revelation saddened me to my core, but it provided the opportunity to tell her about our early years together.

I told her everything I remembered about her birth and how I loved her the very moment I saw her perfect cherub face. When she was a babe, I had selected her outfits, wrestled her wriggling limbs into them, and when I succeeded, praised her for how lovely she looked. She had gawked at me as I made silly faces and danced to the songs our nursemaid, Emma, had sung for us.

Later, I had introduced a game to our repertoire of amusements, covering my face with my hands and quickly removing them to reveal that I was still there. It surprised her every time. When she tired of that, I had stepped up my efforts, hiding below her line of sight and popping up from under the table or behind her chair. Her giggles had been so contagious that even the most sober of men could not have contained a chuckle in response. Eventually, I increased the level of sophistication and left the room entirely, varying the length of time I waited to heighten the suspense. Fan had celebrated my return with waving arms and shrieks of delight.

I had taught her to clap, a skill she mastered with a minimal amount of instruction, and shown her how to crawl, getting on my own hands and knees and urging her forward. At first, she had dragged herself across the floor using only her arms, but I lifted her hips to position her legs beneath her, and before long she had learned the proper form. She had used her newfound mobility to follow me throughout the house, which she did all day, every day. Once she had succeeded in hoisting herself upright while hanging on to the seat of my chair for leverage, I decided walking would be her next lesson. She had wrapped her little fingers around my larger ones, and we had toddled around the house in this way until she developed enough strength and balance to do so without my assistance.

Fan wept at these recollections, as did I, but unlike the sad tears we shed for our mutual suffering, these were tears of celebration for the precious connection we shared.

It was like she opened a floodgate with her questions, and memories of my time at boarding school came pouring out in a steady stream. Father had announced my imminent departure with no input from me, and I had not left by choice. The headmaster of the school had restricted to whom I could write, and every moment I spent in that terrible place, I had wished I was with her instead. I, too, had felt abandoned, particularly when our father failed to retrieve me at Christmastime, and I had spent the holiday in a cold, empty schoolhouse.

I held back, though, wrestling with whether to tell Fan about my secret romantic desires. Though I did not believe she would reject me outright—we were too devoted to each other for that—she might admonish me for them, pointing out their immorality. Would she forbid me to act on them? Or would she encourage me to pursue happiness, regardless of what form it took? I was not sure which of these two options I preferred.

For Fan to truly know me, she needed to understand the longings I buried deepest. Our relationship was strong enough to survive anything—

at least I hoped it was—and I owed it to both of us to share them with her, no matter how difficult it was, no matter the risks.

The ideal opportunity presented itself one sunny spring day while we lounged on her porch. Her husband was away, as usual, and the nursemaid had taken Freddie for a walk. I mustered the courage to tell her about my last few months at Shaw's School and how, at age seventeen, I had developed a relationship with a boy named John Davies, which went beyond the platonic. Our actions had encompassed romance, both emotional and physical.

With tongue-tied awkwardness, I stumbled my way through explaining even the simplest elements of my story, trying desperately—and I feared futilely—to describe my behaviors in a way that would soften the jolt of their disclosure. My efforts resulted in a narrative that lasted far too long and was unnecessarily cumbersome in its delivery. While I stammered and restarted and corrected myself, Fan listened patiently. She did not interrupt, except to help me along by offering a word or phrase I could not seem to find on my own.

When I finished, she sat quietly for a moment, her expression revealing no signs I could interpret as either revulsion or approval. I fiddled self-consciously with my fingers as fear crept into my throat.

Finally, the corners of her mouth turned up in a tender smile. "You are my brother, Neez, and I adore you. I will leave the judgment of your sins to God. You choose for yourself who to love, and so long as that list includes me, I do not object."

Tears welled in my eyes, and my chest filled with appreciation for her. I was about to tell her as much, but I noted that her expression, brow furrowed and eyes downcast, did not match her words.

She spoke again before I did. "Do you feel this way about Jacob Marley?"

How could she know? Were my romantic feelings for him that obvious? If they were so to her, they might be to others also. Perhaps only my sister could guess because she knew me so well, and I had spoken of him many times before. She might have detected emotion in my voice that I had not consciously imparted. Maybe Fan was more intuitive than most people. I hoped so.

I could not deny it and replied with a simple yes.

She bade me to tell her more, and I did. I told her about the attention Jacob had paid me at Fezziwig's Christmas party many years before and the stirrings he kindled in me still. I described my reaction upon meeting his wife at Mr. Fezziwig's wake and his reentry into my life after his agreement was fulfilled and my engagement annulled. I told her how my stomach fluttered every time he smiled or called me by name, how my body tingled when we touched, even if it was an accidental brushing of our hands while we were reviewing figures on a ledger or shaking hands when we met on the street.

"You are in love," she said.

I was not certain if my attraction to Jacob reached that level, but Fan's words were not a question and therefore did not necessitate a reply.

"Have you acted on your feelings?" Fan's grin was painted on, forced instead of natural.

"I have done nothing more than what I told you," I assured her.

"I want you to be happy, brother," she said. "You cannot change who you are, and I love you without condition. But there is one favor I must ask."

I braced myself for the inevitable demand for censure.

The brightness drained from her face. "Please be careful. The path you are on is a dangerous one. If you are discovered, your reputation will be ruined and your businesses shuttered. Or worse, you could be arrested and hanged. Promise me you will be discreet."

"Oh, my sweet Fan, I promise." I leaned over the table to embrace her, knocking over the tray of refreshments in the process. She giggled as I scrambled to right the glasses and pitcher and pick up the tiny plates and their former contents, which were now splayed on the floor. I sat back down in my chair and reached for her, this time being careful not to upset the dishes, and held her hands in mine. "You are the best sister and friend anyone could ask for."

"I had an excellent teacher," she said.

Fan was the best human being I knew, and I was honored to be worthy of her devotion. Our relationship was central to my life, yet there was one other I considered more important.

Only the titles "uncle" and "godfather" superseded those of "brother" and "friend." With preeminence over all others, the part I played in the life of my nephew, Freddie, was the easiest of all to fulfill. It came naturally to me—loving and caring for this precious child. I held him when he was a babe, bouncing gently up and down to stop him from crying. I was often successful at quieting his wails, even when Fan herself could not accomplish it.

When Freddie was a bit heartier, I tossed him in the air, eliciting giggles from him and equally emphatic admonishments from his nursemaid. The rate of his growth astounded me. One day, I was crawling with him on the floor, the next he was toddling along on his own, and before long, he was running faster than me. He was a sturdy, healthy, loving boy. I read him books, taught him the basics of arithmetic, and took him on excursions to the park, circuses, and fairs.

I doted on him, thoroughly and incessantly, and I had no qualms about doing so. He seemed no worse off for it, blossoming under the devoted attention of his mother and me. I could not imagine loving any person more than I loved Freddie. Being his family was the most important thing I had ever done.

While I had achieved a measure of success in merging my many responsibilities as mentor, boss, business partner, brother, friend, uncle, and godfather, there was another role I had yet to embrace. I was slowly, and ineptly, learning to be a man in love. Not the kind of familial love I shared with Fan and Freddie, and not the affection I'd had for Mr. Fezziwig either. Not even the tenderness I had felt for John Davies so many years before. This was something special and new. I was journeying toward a relationship that was more than companionship, more than friendship, more than physical attraction. I was advancing toward the ultimate connection, one that combined all these things into a single person and would require me to assume a new role with its own set of challenges, obligations, and benefits.

I was not a lover yet, but I was inching tentatively closer to that goal.

CHAPTER TWENTY-SEVEN

LOVE

1827, Sixteen Years before the Ghosts

Fan's approval gave me the permission I needed to consider a relationship with Jacob that included romance as well as friendship. Jacob reached that conclusion as well, albeit of his own accord.

Perhaps the Christmas spirit had something to do with it.

I remained at the counting house on Christmas Eve, hours after Jacob had left, wanting to finish any remaining tasks, so my mind would be unencumbered, and I could thoroughly enjoy the holiday with my sister and her precious child. I had fallen asleep at my desk, but the slamming of the door awakened me with a jolt. I wiped the drool from my chin and shook my head to dislodge the fog muffling my senses.

A whisper came from a location only a yard or so away, raspy and ethereal. "Ebenezer."

Was this a spirit come to haunt me? I squinted in a futile attempt to see through the viscous darkness, my heart pounding with terror for the source of this intrusion.

"I can't see a damn thing in here. Where are you?"

I knew then that this was not a ghost but a man—the one man whose presence warmed my heart and whose touch incited a smoldering desire that superseded every one of my body's needs. Jacob Marley.

"At my desk, of course. Where else would I be?" I whispered back. "I guess I fell asleep."

"Come to me, Ebenezer."

I complied with his command and stepped hesitantly forward, my hands held out in front of me. An invisible current radiated from him, beckoning me closer. He must have been standing with his arms by his side rather than groping at the air as I was, because both of my hands made contact with his chest at the same time.

"You found me," he said, and his hands covered mine. "Light a candle, so we can see each other."

Since the candle on my desk had extinguished itself, I would need to find another. Having a general idea of the direction I should proceed, I pivoted toward the back of the office. Jacob's hand rested on my shoulder as I shuffled across the room until I located—or rather collided with—the table I was searching for. As I probed the surface, Jacob's hand slid down to the small of my back. My body tingled at his touch, and I was thankful for the darkness, so he could not see the flush of my face.

With fumbling fingers, I gathered the candle and tinderbox, which, for some reason, had been left on opposite ends of the table, and managed to start the flame. My breath almost extinguished it, but it held fast, and I lifted the candleholder and turned toward him. He did not move away, and I was forced to hold it to the side to avoid setting either one of us on fire. We were as close as possible without touching, our faces mere inches apart.

I had no choice but to look into his eyes, which stared back at me with an intensity that rendered me as helpless as an animal caught in a snare. Until now, I had thought Jacob's eyes only blue, but in the flicker of candlelight, I realized they were many colors at once. The shades did not combine, but rather each existed on its own beside the others—blue as brilliant as the summer sky, speckled with tan, navy, and emerald green.

"Are you familiar with the tradition of kissing under mistletoe?" he asked, cocking his head to one side.

I nodded. Of course I knew of it. Why would he ask such a question?

He broke the lock of our gaze to glance at the candle I held aloft, and I understood that he meant for me to set it down. I did so, and he took hold of my hand. "You see, dear friend. I have neglected my duty to uphold that tradition, and I do not wish to let the season pass without observing it. Since I will not see you on Christmas Day itself, I thought we might observe the custom together, tonight."

Did he mean to kiss me? Or was I misunderstanding? I could think of no other explanation for what was happening, nor could I say, even in my befuddled state, that I was opposed to it. The thought of sharing a romantic kiss with Jacob ignited its own fire within me, which started in the deepest recesses of my body and traveled throughout of its own accord. I could not contain the shudder it produced.

Not knowing how else to respond, I stated the obvious. "There is no mistletoe here."

"Ah, but you underestimate me." He drew out the words and accompanied them with a lopsided grin. "I brought my own."

Indeed, he had. Jacob removed a sprig of pointy emerald leaves from his jacket pocket and raised it above my head. With my backside against the table, he pressed his mouth to mine. His eyes closed while he kissed me, but I kept mine open, reveling in the warmth and supple strength of his lips. He pulled back slightly and leaned in again, sliding his arm around my waist.

This was not my first kiss, but its passion far surpassed that of the one I had shared with John Davies at boarding school, and it was nothing like the frigid pecks I had been obliged to bestow on Belle Fezziwig during our engagement. Eventually, he released me and took a backward step, leaving me unsteady on weakened legs.

"I do believe we have done justice to the tradition," he said. "Thank you, Ebenezer."

I gave no reply, since standing and breathing were the only actions I was capable of at that moment.

"I bid you good night, dear friend," Jacob said. "I wish you much joy in the celebrations with your sister tomorrow."

I lost sight of him when he stepped beyond the candlelight's reach. I endeavored to say something—anything—before he left, but I struggled not only to decide which words to use but to produce them aloud. Finally, I succeeded with "Merry Christmas," shouted just before he closed the door behind him.

I fell in love with Jacob Marley that night beneath the mistletoe. Truly and completely and forever in love.

CHAPTER TWENTY-EIGHT

SMALL STEPS

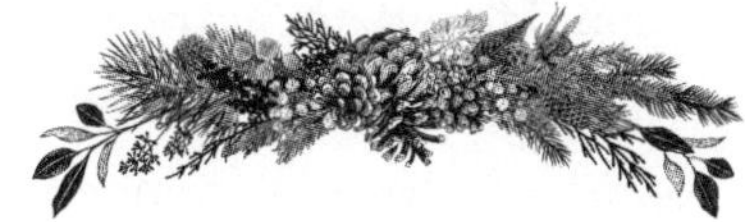

1829, Fourteen Years before the Ghosts

Jacob had always been the initiator of physical contact between us, whether it was his hand on my back as he scrutinized the papers on my desk or the occasional embrace in celebration at the landing of a new contract. All of it had led to our passionate kiss under the mistletoe, to which I had submitted and reciprocated.

He had made his intentions clear, and now it was up to me to move us forward toward intimacy. But before I invited his affection and gave it to him in return, I had to believe I deserved it. I needed to overcome the self-doubt that told me I was not good enough for him, not attractive or charming enough to warrant his affection. My conversations with Fan helped me do this, coupled with my own internal struggle to vanquish my haunting insecurities. Ultimately, I broke free from my self-imposed constraints and resolved to show Jacob how much I wanted him.

My first attempt was a feeble one. Cowardice almost stinted it, but I persevered. We were working late at the counting house, the sun having set and the streets empty. I feigned a shiver, though my insides seared with nervous anticipation, and I walked over to the window to pull the curtain closed. Instead of returning to my desk, I went to Jacob's and leaned over his shoulder the way he had done to me many times before. I wanted to touch him, and my hand hovered over his back while the deliberating voices in my head offered a range of competing warnings and commands. "Do not do this, Ebenezer," one said. "Now is the time," said another. "He will reject you, and you will lose him," the first one countered. And finally, "You must show him you love him."

I heeded the last voice's advice, lowered my hand, and started rubbing his back in a circular motion. He did not acknowledge me but continued to stare down at his papers. I worried that the other voice had been the shrewder one, but I held my breath and continued, pushing a bit harder and broadening my strokes until it was clear that my movements were a form of massage rather than a pat on the back from a friend. Still, he ignored me, and I panicked, fearing I had gambled unwisely and made a terrible mistake—one I would not be able to fix. Only when I took my hand away did Jacob turn toward me.

"Please don't stop," he said.

I smiled back at him and resumed, using both hands and pressing harder, feeling the muscles of his back and giving attention to each one in turn. The more I tried to indulge him, the more pleasure I reaped. The panic rose again, though this time it was not out of concern for Jacob's reaction but because my own was rapidly escalating beyond my control.

I removed my hand and stepped away. "Will you have dinner with me? I am starving." It was a clumsy attempt at diversion, though not untrue.

He agreed, and we headed to Simpson's Tavern, which was bustling as usual on a Friday evening, filled with people who had already drunk more than they should. The environment provided an opportunity for me to step back for a moment, to breathe through the intensity of my yearnings. Perhaps Jacob felt the same, since we ate our meals amid scant conversation. It was not unpleasant, at least not for me, for I enjoyed his quiet company.

With the bill paid, we found ourselves outside again. "I wish you good night, dear friend," he said, but the faint illumination of the streetlamp made it impossible for me to discern his expression.

"I am yours," was my reply, the same words I had used when we had parted company the first night we met. It was a common way of bidding farewell, but it was also an undeniable truth. We went our separate ways, as we had that first Christmas Eve so many years before.

The next day, we resumed our normal routine as if nothing out of the ordinary had happened. I worried that the boldness of my actions might have made it uncomfortable between us, but he acted no differently. In the ensuing weeks, I made up reasons to be close to him, asking for his help to lift a box, though I was more than capable of doing so myself, and requesting he review my calculations or reread a letter I had drafted, so I could feel the warmth of his body as he bent over my shoulder. I continued with these subtle tactics, not sure of their fruitfulness or whether they were appreciated.

Jacob made the next move.

After a full day of work at the counting house, I went to retrieve my coat and hat from the back room, but Jacob rushed to get there before me.

"Allow me," he said, helping me into my coat one sleeve at a time. He had never done this before, but I welcomed the attention. He took me by the shoulders and turned me toward him. We were close enough that I could smell the cigar smoke on his clothes and the oil he used to keep his hair and mustache neat. He started fastening the buttons, the top one first before moving to the second and the third, feeling the contours of each before pushing it through the opening. He grinned at me, desire brimming in his eyes, before he dropped to his knees. The shift in position was necessary for him to continue with the lower buttons, but it made my breath catch in my throat, and I held it while he finished his work. With my coat properly secured, he rose and planted a kiss on my cheek. His movements slow and deliberate, he kissed my other cheek next and then my lips. We stayed in that position, our mouths pressed against each other until he pulled away, leaving me breathless and wanting more.

"There. You are ready to brave the cold," he said, patting my chest. "You go, and I will lock up. I will see you tomorrow."

I managed a weak "good night" and did as he instructed. On the long walk back to my flat, in a daze of disbelief and heightened stimulation, I could think of nothing but him.

We went back and forth like this, Jacob and I taking turns at initiating intimacy. It was my move next and then his. With each encounter, passions swelled, and our embraces lasted longer. I would inevitably lose my nerve at some point and go home alone, but I continued to muse over him, fantasizing about what the next one would entail.

Most nights we took our suppers together at Simpson's, but one Saturday evening Jacob suggested a tavern farther away from the counting house. The new place was much the same as the old one, not worth the extra effort to get there, in my opinion, but it was pleasant enough. When we finished our meals, he ordered another round of drinks, and another after that. I exceeded my limit after the fourth pint, tipsy in both mental acuity and physical coordination.

"It is a long way home for you, Ebenezer, and my house is so much closer," he said, paying the bill for both of us. "Why don't you come for a short visit before you make the trek?"

I had never been to Jacob's house before, but the prospect of walking to my own flat was not a welcome one in my current state. I agreed, and we headed east, past the Royal Exchange and the entrance to Newman's Court, which was home to Scrooge and Marley's. The houses grew grander as we went. Even the streetlamps shone brighter in this section of the city, or at least it seemed that way to me, though perhaps the stars were unobscured by the clouds that night, so they were responsible. I craned my neck to check the sky, which caused me to stumble.

"Steady there, friend," Jacob warned, catching me by the elbow and supporting me until I stabilized. He repositioned me at an appropriate distance away from him, and we continued on.

It was not long before he announced, "We are here."

"Here" was somewhere between Fenchurch and Leadenhall, though I was unsure of the exact street. I followed Jacob's gaze and could not believe my eyes. The house was huge, and though I was unable to discern the exact colors, multiple shades were represented on the main fascia and moldings. I looked up at the grandiose front door to the ornate windows of the second floor, and higher still. There was a third floor above it, maybe even a fourth, though I could not tell for certain because the light from the streetlamps did not reach that high, and the house disappeared into the darkness.

For a second time that evening, my attempt to look skyward made me lose my footing. I stumbled, and Jacob caught me again. He settled me at his side, holding me against him with an arm wrapped around my back. His touch, even through the thick fabric of my coat, sent a surge of desire through me.

"Come." His voice was husky and low. He guided me up the stairs, unlocked the richly carved wooden door, and pushed it open.

I had expected it to be dark inside, since the hour was late, but the candles were burning, and the gold inlaid wallpaper sparkled in their glow. Jacob hung our coats on the wrought iron rack while I stared in awe at the width of the staircase, which could easily accommodate five men walking abreast. He led me past the immense foyer, through a formal parlor, and into a dining room with a table set for eight. We continued through another doorway, near the back of the house by this point, I guessed, since we had traveled such a long way already. We arrived in the living room, which was also fully lit and, to my surprise, occupied.

Two women were seated on one of the couches, each with an embroidery piece in her lap. I recognized them from Mr. Fezziwig's wake, though until that moment, I had forgotten they existed.

"Good evening, husband," the taller woman said. Her copper hair fell in waves around her shoulders, and she issued an enchanting smile. The other woman looked up briefly before lowering her head again to continue her needlework.

"Good evening, Rebecca," Jacob said, bowing to her before turning me around to leave the room the same way we had entered. The strangeness of this interaction confounded me. Jacob had not greeted the woman seated beside his wife, had not even acknowledged her presence. Neither had his wife addressed me, nor had Jacob introduced me, as he should have done as a matter of politeness.

He took me by the hand and led me back through the dining room, parlor, and foyer to yet another room. This one had a grand piano in one corner and seats of various colors and styles. Shelves built into the walls held a collection of books, as well as boxes labeled as one game or another. There was a door at the far end, which I assumed led to the kitchen because I had not seen that room yet, and it was necessary to support the others.

This sort of room did not exist in most houses. It was not the formal parlor, not a living room, not a sitting room or study, but a space designed exclusively for entertaining. I stood in the doorway, noting the double pocket doors tucked away in the walls and gawking at the grandeur of it all. Jacob continued inside, beckoning me to join him. He opened the glass doors of a cabinet and pulled out a small wooden shelf, which until that point had been hidden within it.

"It is just as well that my wife is occupying the living room," he said, pouring a ruby liquor into two small glasses. "This room is more suitable for two gentlemen like us. Don't you agree?"

I accepted the glass he handed me but did not answer his question. Instead, I blurted out the first thoughts that congealed themselves enough in my head to force their way out of my mouth.

"Does your wife mind you staying out so late? Why did you not introduce me? Who is the other woman?" I had so many questions.

"Sit, Ebenezer. I will explain." Jacob directed me to one of the matching leather chairs facing the fireplace. He bent over to light it, which required minimal effort since the kindling and wood had been previously arranged to facilitate it. Even starting fires was easier for the rich. He poked at the logs to ensure the flames took hold and sat beside me.

"Rebecca and I have an arrangement," he said. "She does as she pleases, and I do the same. We are married, and we fulfill the formal roles of husband and wife, jointly attending funerals and other such events, but we have our own . . . how should I say it? Friendships." He nodded heartily, pleased with his choice of vocabulary. "Part of our agreement is to avoid interacting with each other's romantic partners. As for the lady, her name is Grace, and she stays by my wife's side always. She is her closest friend." He paused over the last word before adding, "As you are mine."

I had never considered the possibility of marriage under such terms, though Jacob insisted it happened with some frequency. In most cases, it was only the husband who engaged in romantic behaviors outside the marriage, while the wife's part of the agreement was to ignore it. In the case of Jacob and his wife, it suited them both equally.

I wondered if I could have accomplished that sort of arrangement with Belle. If I had married her, despite my feelings for Jacob, I might have managed to have it all—a family, a prosperous career, and a separate romantic relationship—simultaneously. How different my life would be. The prospect of it intrigued me, though I doubted it would have worked, since Belle could never have set aside her own wants for me. By her nature, she could not have ignored my activities outside our marriage bed or suppressed her resentment enough to feign a normal spousal relationship in public.

My mind was spinning, a situation not helped in the least by the additional drink Jacob offered me, and which, whether out of habit or poor judgment, I drank down as quickly as the first.

"I am yours, Jacob," I said, setting my emptied glass on the table between us.

He stood before me, took my hands in his, and pulled me to my feet. Wrapping his arms around me, he kissed me. We stood there for a long while, the fire warming us from the outside and desire burning us from within. I could have stayed there, secure and happy in Jacob's embrace, for eternity, but my irksome conscience clamored its way to the surface, and apprehension replaced pleasure. I reluctantly pulled away, head turned toward the floor, the quickness of my breaths betraying my moral weakness.

The pace of Jacob's breathing matched mine. "What are you thinking, Ebenezer?"

"I think I should go home," I whispered. This was not what I wanted, but I was encumbered by a yoke of shame that prevented me from pursuing the life I coveted.

"Then that is what you must do." He sighed, and I could not discern whether it was an expression of disappointment or resignation because I was looking at the floor instead of his face. I immediately regretted my choice, frustrated with myself for lacking the courage to do what would make me truly happy and fulfilled. I followed Jacob to the foyer, assuming he would bid me good night and send me on my way, but he stopped, opened a small cabinet set into the wall, and reached inside.

I gave him a quizzical look, and one side of his mouth turned up in amusement. "This is how we summon the servants," he explained. "See? Pulling this rope rings a bell in their quarters on the fourth floor. My footman will bring you home."

I protested the disturbance of the footman's rest as unnecessary, but Jacob insisted. When the carriage was ready and my coat donned, this time fastened solely through my own efforts, I turned to him. "I am sorry," I said, though I offered no justification for my actions.

"There is no cause for apology. I will do nothing to make you uncomfortable. We will move forward only when you are ready, no matter how slow the process or how small the steps. I will see you Monday."

CHAPTER TWENTY-NINE

ABOVE ALL OTHERS

1830, Thirteen Years before the Ghosts

Alone in bed in my cold, dismal flat, I wished I had stayed with Jacob in his grand home, where I would have been warm and loved.

Jacob, for his part, did not begrudge my temporary lapse of courage, and he invited me to his home many times after that. Our embraces in front of the fireplace became more desperate, our kissing more intense. He never pressured me to do more than I was ready for, and ultimately, I joined him in his bed.

With Jacob, I experienced pleasure I had never dreamed possible. He was patient and gentle, until I craved something more, and he gave me that as well. For the first time in my life, after decades of frustrating ignorance, I became a sexual being, unafraid of intimacy, open to new experiences, satisfied.

I spent at least one evening a week in Jacob's bed, though I never stayed overnight. The footman delivered me to my rented flat in the early morning hours, since it was important that I was home when my landlady woke up and she would witness me leaving for work. I had to be cautious and avoid suspicion because Mrs. King would not tolerate the implication of immorality from a single man living in her home.

I did not need to shield myself from the curious eyes of Jacob's wife for I rarely saw her. The second floor of the house was his, while Rebecca kept her bedroom on the third. Her friend Grace also lived in the house, purportedly serving as her maidservant, though there was another woman on staff who performed the duties required of that position. I wondered about the nature of their relationship, certain it went beyond the platonic, though I could not imagine what sort of pleasure two women could give each other. Was it possible for them to satisfy one another sexually? What methods might be deployed to achieve the desired result? I had not the slightest clue. Regardless, the fact that Rebecca was content with the marital arrangement made me feel less guilty about the erotic activities Jacob and I engaged in while under the same roof.

Our relationship was advancing and evolving, but it did not follow a straight, ordered path, and it was not always a course I fancied.

Jacob confessed he had not gone home after dinner the evening I had made my first clumsy attempts at intimacy. Neither had he stayed home the nights after we kissed in front of the fireplace. When I had returned to my flat and gone to bed, unable to sleep and longing for his touch, he had set out to find satisfaction at other places, with other men. He had visited such seedy, hedonistic establishments as I had only heard about in lore, where men of similar tastes offered him the opportunity for romantic encounters that continued where we had left off.

It was unfair of me to expect him to suffer the frustrating tension I put us both through, but I struggled with feelings of betrayal and jealousy.

How deep was his love for me if he continued engaging with other men? I was a fool to think I could be enough for him.

Jacob was the man I loved, and his illicit behaviors outside our relationship did not change that fact. I desired no one but him, but he had a lust for experiences that I alone could not fulfill. He had spent many years indulging in those pleasures before I came along, and it was selfish of me to ask him to deny himself simply to placate me.

Once I experienced his proficiency in the mechanisms of manly love and the breadth of his appetite for it, I could not help but be flattered at his self-control when it came to me. He had never pressured me to do more than I was ready for. He had taken his time, moved us slowly from one level of intimacy to the next, making sure I consented fully before we tried anything new.

He was careful with me, gentle. He valued and respected me. He loved me even though he was a handsome man, and I was not, even though he was skilled in various sexual techniques, while I was only a novice. Jacob could have had any man he wanted, yet he chose me above all others.

CHAPTER THIRTY
ANOTHER WORLD

1830, Thirteen Years before the Ghosts

At forty-three years old, I added a new role to the many I already fulfilled. I was Jacob Marley's lover.

To be sure, I was not the only one. There were many others, in fact, though it gave me solace to know that I was the only man he invited into his home and his bed. I struggled against my own insecurities and to keep my jealousy at bay. After all, I reasoned, Jacob had engaged with men this way throughout his life, while I had become a part of it a relatively short time ago.

I asked him about the other men sometimes, while we lay in bed together late at night. I shouldn't have, but I could not stop myself. He generally dismissed my inquiries, saying, "Do not concern yourself, Ebenezer. It means nothing," and "You are the only man I love."

I could not fathom why he loved me, and I begged him to explain it, to make me understand why he chose to build a life with me, a man indisputably less attractive than him, less interesting and experienced. He promised to tell me the truth, with the agreement that I would accept and cease to question his devotion.

When he first met me at the warehouse Christmas party, I had been a novelty, just another in a sizable collection of young men to whom he was attracted. Mr. Fezziwig's insistence on keeping us apart had served to spark more intense interest, as I became a forbidden fruit. He had quelled his cravings with the many other men he engaged with in mostly fleeting but sometimes long-term affairs. He had forgotten about me, he admitted, until he had seen me again at the Fezziwig home, and his desire reignited.

When my engagement to Belle ended, he had returned to claim me, his patience finally rewarded. But, he realized I was not just another silly boy—I had never been that, after all—with whom he would have another meaningless tryst. He had felt a genuine connection and vowed to take his time, to explore the depth of our compatibility. With me, he had found a true partner to share his life and was steadfast in his commitment.

I believed him, but I wanted to know more and pressured him to tell me about the places he went and the men he met there. He refused, insisting there was nothing to be gained by discussing such things. "Why do you worry yourself so?"

But I did worry. I feared Jacob might be arrested inside one of those immoral establishments and jailed, or even executed for his crimes. I worried he could be sickened with one of the diseases that ran rampant among men who sold their bodies and those who purchased them. Worst of all, I worried he would find someone else he desired more than me.

I was satisfied with our relationship overall, despite my concerns, but my sister had taught me that to genuinely understand someone, you must know their secrets, the parts of their life they kept hidden from everyone else. I wanted that with Jacob, and I told him so.

"If you insist, dear friend, I will show you that part of my life," he conceded, "though I hope you are not sorry for it afterward."

"I look forward to a new adventure with you," I said.

He winced and shook his head. "I promise it will be that."

Jacob's hesitance made me question my resolve. Did he think I could not handle witnessing what went on in the places he visited? I was certain I could. Did he think I would disapprove and forbid him from going in the future? I would never tell him what he could or could not do. Did he want to keep that part of his life from me? This was the likeliest rationale, and to this, I objected wholeheartedly. The segmenting of his existence, holding me at a distance by excluding me from an integral part of it, was the only thing in this world I would deprive him of.

It was difficult to concentrate on my work in the days leading up to the one when I would accompany Jacob to a place that was familiar to him but a mystery to me. When that Saturday arrived, I was so flustered with nervous anticipation that I forgot my coat in my flat and then my hat, and I had to make two extra trips up the stairs before starting off for work. I completed my morning at Fezziwig's Warehouse and hurried to the counting house, defeating my own personal record for the trip—twenty-six minutes. My heart was racing faster than my legs as I turned the final corner and spotted the "Scrooge and Marley" sign swaying in the breeze.

Inside, I found Jacob seated at his desk, as professional and stoic—and handsome—as always. He wished me good day, and I responded likewise, taking my seat across the room and opening my ledger. I did not make any progress that day, however, merely feigning concentration.

My mind was otherwise occupied with thoughts about the last romantic night we had spent together, relishing memories of the pleasure he had given me, which I had returned in spades, and by fantasies about the new experiences awaiting me once the seemingly interminable afternoon hours passed. I held the quill too long in one spot, and the ink pooled on the page, forcing me to tear it out and copy it over. It was a task I was grateful to undertake, since it was mindless work, and my musings did not pose a hindrance. By the time we broke for the day, I had accomplished almost nothing of value.

We went to Simpson's Tavern, where Jacob ate his dinner and I pushed my food around the plate, the fluttering in my stomach leaving no room for food. I yelled over the noise of the other patrons, rowdy with drink and merriment. "Now, will you tell me where we are going tonight?"

Jacob's brow furrowed, and he shook his head. "Not here." He mouthed the words, which was the most prudent method of communication considering the sensitivity of the subject matter. I had forgotten the necessity of discretion and mentally berated myself for my folly. This was my first gaffe of the night, but it would assuredly not be the last.

When we left the tavern and were far enough away from our fellow pedestrians that we would not be overheard, I asked again.

"We are going to a molly-house," Jacob said. "Do you know what that is?"

I had heard about molly-houses—brothels of a sort that catered exclusively to men—and had read about one such establishment, "Mother Clap's," which had closed some years before when its owner was convicted of encouraging sodomy, sentenced to stand in the pillory, and imprisoned. Rumors and innuendo were the only other source of information I had to draw on, but my understanding was that men and boys sold their bodies in those places, submitting to or committing deviant acts in exchange for money.

"It is different than you think," Jacob said, accurately guessing the nature of my ill-informed preconceptions. "It is not prostitution, or at least not only prostitution, that happens there. We go there to be among others like us. It is a place—the only place, in fact—where we can socialize freely and find partners to share affections in whatever ways we prefer. Everything is done with the consent of all parties involved, and no one is taken advantage of or made to feel uncomfortable. It is a place for men like us, Ebenezer. We are safe there, free to act as we choose."

It sounded wonderful to me.

We continued walking, all the while remaining an appropriate distance from one another and acting the part of businessmen heading to a tavern for a drink before going home to our wives.

"We are here," he announced.

Already? I had assumed molly-houses were located in the seedier sections of the city, but we were still in the business district, blocks away from the Royal Exchange. Jacob pointed to a building that looked like any of the hundred other taverns in London. I had walked by it countless times before, having had no inkling of its true purpose, ignorant of the happenings underway at the precise moment I passed it by.

The sign above the door read, "Fiddler's Green." I knew that reference from somewhere, and I probed my brain to identify it.

"Are you all right?" There was alarm in Jacob's voice. "Maybe we should not go inside."

My expressions often betrayed my inner musings, but this time he was misinterpreting my reflection as distress or apprehension.

"I am fine—excited actually," I said as we crossed the street. "I am only thinking where I have heard 'Fiddler's Green' before." It came to me then. "I remember. One of the workmen at the warehouse, who takes whatever jobs are available when he finds himself ashore for a time, sang of it. Fiddler's Green is heaven for sailors who die at sea, with a fiddle that never stops playing, dancers who never tire, and a boundless supply of tobacco and grog."

"I never knew that, but it is clever, I think," Jacob said. "Are you ready to go in?"

I was ready to experience this part of his life—to understand him better than before, the way only a true partner can. I nodded, and he opened the door for me, ushering me in with a downward wave.

I did not know what I had expected to find, but it was not the scene before me. The inside of Fiddler's Green looked the same as the outside, like any other tavern. A few men sat on stools at the tiny bar, partially drained mugs set before them. An old man wiping down a table nodded to us, though his blank expression remained unchanged. Where was the excitement? Where were the interesting characters enjoying the freedom this place provided? Where was the endless music and dancing promised in its name? How disappointing.

Jacob kept walking, and I followed, past the old man behind the bar and the ones seated across from him, toward the back of the room. When we got there, I discovered it was not one flat wall, as it appeared. Only when we were directly in front did it become clear that there were two walls, one the true end of the room, and the second, about a yard in front of it, painted the same dull black, which did not reach all the way across. This created a corridor, and Jacob led me into it. There was a door at the end, partly obscured by the hulking figure of a man.

"Hello, Hugo." Jacob addressed the giant by name. His bald head reached almost to the ceiling, and his shoulders spanned the width of the hallway. His nose had a discernible crook, evidence of a previous break, perhaps more than one. He would have to duck down and turn sideways to fit through the door he was guarding.

"Good evening, Jacob." The man's voice was the lowest I had ever heard. It reverberated like the gong of a metal bowl dropped on a brick hearth. He opened the door and pushed himself against the wall to make room for us to pass.

The door shut behind us, and I heard muffled voices but could see nothing. I clung to Jacob's arm, grateful for his steadiness. He parted two thick curtains and pulled me through the opening, out of the darkness and into an exciting new world. The light temporarily blinded me, but the sound of laughter brought relief, and I blinked to acclimate my eyes. Here was the molly-house I expected. Here was the freedom I had been promised.

"Jacob!" A man seated in a high-back chair called out, opening his arms wide, his smile welcoming and his voice jovial. His body was as thickly cushioned as the seat he sat on, maybe more so, and his head was bald on top, outlined with a horseshoe of dark hair around the sides. He wore no jacket over his shirt, which was unfastened from the collar to his navel, revealing a thick carpet of hair that matched the ring on his head. Another man, this one much skinnier, emerged through a curtain-covered doorway and smiled at us before plopping down on the fat one's lap.

Jacob waved his greeting and, holding my hand, opened another curtain to lead me into a new room. This one had a bar, and he went straight to it, ordering us both a sherry. I reached into my pocket to pay for my share, but Jacob shook his head. He did not pay either, and I realized I had committed my second blunder of the night. Payment, I deduced, came at a later time and perhaps at a different location. Thanking the barkeep, he handed me a glass and took a sip of his own.

"Let's sit for a while," he said, motioning to an empty table with two stools tucked underneath.

We were surrounded by the most interesting cast of characters, all talking, laughing, and drinking. At a table beside us, a curious-looking woman sat on a chair, her legs draped across the lap of a young man. She was quite large, not fat, but broad and tall, and I worried the man beneath her might be crushed under her weight. He appeared comfortable, though, smiling broadly and running his hand up and down her stockinged tree trunk leg.

"What do you say, dear?" he asked. I could not help but overhear.

"I would never do such a thing," the woman responded, her voice strained, unnaturally high in pitch.

The man nudged her skirt higher up her thigh and tickled the inside of her knee. She responded with a giggle, which turned to a genuine fit of laughter, but instead of the forced falsetto she had spoken in before, the laugh was lower in tone—much lower. She twisted away from him to stop the tickling, giving me a brief but enlightening look at her, and I realized she was not a woman at all, but a man. Her dress was open in front, in keeping with the current fashions worn by ladies to display the feminine roundness of their cleavage. What this dress revealed, however, was the broad chest of a man, devoid of hair and coated with white powder. Her face was similarly smooth and dusted white, though the thick lines of her jaw and prominent Adam's apple left no room for debate about her true sex. Not a woman, but not a man either.

"A mollie," Jacob said, answering the question I had asked only in my mind. "Over there too," he said, pointing to several ladies chatting in the center of the room. Their skirts swayed side to side, and they waved fans under their chins.

"Do not stare," he chided, and I pried my eyes away from them, silently scolding myself for committing yet another faux pas and vowing not to perpetrate another.

Unfortunately, I committed the same transgression almost immediately after I had sworn against it. I spied over Jacob's shoulder a most peculiar sight—a person unlike any I had seen before. I thought he was a child at first, based on size alone, but I craned my neck to scrutinize further and noted his face was that of an adult. A scraggly beard made that fact clear enough. His arms and legs were shorter than the average man's, and his head, by comparison, was large, his forehead more so than the rest. He sat atop a table, smiling as he chatted with the full-sized admirers gathered around him. He swung his feet back and forth, seeming to enjoy the attention being paid him. Here in this place where men were free to indulge their true, if unconventional, desires, this man's oddities were an asset.

Jacob followed my gaze over his shoulder and turned back toward me, eyes wide. He nodded, acknowledging a shared astonishment at the spectacle.

"There is more yet to see," he said, holding his hand out for mine. "Come with me."

I had seen plenty already. What more could there be?

Returning our empty glasses to the bar, Jacob led me deeper into the room. In the corner, two men sat across from one another. They were businessmen like us, dressed the same as we were and sipping from metal mugs. They could have been in any tavern in London, possibly discussing a business deal or catching up on news of family and friends. The only difference was that they were holding hands.

Both men greeted Jacob by name and rose from their seats, releasing their hold on each other to shake his hand. Jacob dropped mine only long enough to return their greeting and introduce us. He told me their names, but I could not remember them a moment past their articulation, my mind too overwhelmed with the happenings around me to allow space for information that was trivial in comparison.

"Is this the virgin you told us about?" one of them said.

Jacob responded with a slight nod, peeking at me out of the corner of his eye but not turning his head. I knew what a virgin was, at least in the conventional sense, and I certainly qualified under that definition. In this context, however, it likely had a more nuanced meaning, implying a purity in experience I had not possessed before I started sharing his bed.

"He is lovely," the man said.

"Yes, he is," Jacob agreed, kissing my cheek and pulling me against him, his thumb tucked into the waistband of my breeches.

I ought to have been offended by this exchange that relegated me to an object rather than a human being. But I was not. I felt pride at being deemed desirable and attractive, worthy of their admiration.

Jacob bid farewell to the couple and turned us back in the direction we had been heading before the encounter had diverted us. He crooked his head toward mine and said, "Those two are married."

"Married?" I said, much louder than I should have. This was another misstep, but in my defense, how could I not be taken aback by such a statement? I had never heard of such a thing. "How?" I asked in an appropriately softer volume.

"It is a marriage only within these walls," he explained. "They held a ceremony and everything. I was there. Of course, they are not a couple in society and may even have real marriages—and children perhaps—though I do not know for sure. Likely they do not see each other outside of this place, but here, they are bound together by vows."

I nodded, only pretending to understand.

The men's behaviors intrigued me, but Jacob's were perplexing. He kept his hands on me throughout the evening, entwining his fingers in mine or resting his hand on my back while we walked. Otherwise, he had his arm around me, hand grasping my opposite shoulder or my hip. He touched my bottom once, cupping my buttocks and leaving his hand there for all to see. The norms of behavior we followed strictly in public did not apply here, and I loved it.

Jacob introduced me to several acquaintances, though he only approached those who made eye contact with him first, respecting the privacy of the ones who preferred to keep to themselves. The men engaged in a variety of ways, some talking, their coats buttoned fully and their interactions formal, as if they were meeting for the first time. It occurred to me that perhaps they had been strangers before this evening and were courting one another in a somewhat traditional way.

Others were quite familiar already. One such couple stood in a corner, their bodies pressed against each other, arms wrapped around, engrossed in a passionate kiss. Another pair walked hand in hand, approaching and conversing with an uncoupled man before moving on to do the same with another. Two others sat, one on a chair and the other on the floor nestled between his legs to receive a shoulder massage. We passed two men cuddling, their eyes locked, talking softly on a rose-colored settee, and I had to swallow down my discomfort at witnessing the intimacy of their connection.

Jacob promenaded us through the place like I was his prize. I found this more bewildering than anything else. I had never considered myself attractive, which was not unfairly self-deprecating since it was a fact as true as any other. My nose and chin were too pointy, and I was skinny as a light post. I did not possess a smidgen of athleticism or grace, and my gait was stiff, qualities my former fiancé had criticized many times.

Being tall was my only positive physical trait, but Jacob was equal to me in height and broader in the shoulders. He was handsome, too, his jawline well defined and his thick lips parting to reveal impossibly straight teeth. His dark brown hair had become speckled with gray in recent years, which somehow made it more alluring. Standing beside him underscored my own deficiencies.

I was nothing compared to Jacob in terms of attractiveness, yet he seemed content—proud, even—to have me on his arm. That he valued me so, especially here in the molly-house where we were surrounded by men of similar appetites, warmed my heart and bolstered my precarious ego. I straightened my slumped shoulders and smiled as charmingly as I could manage, endeavoring as always to be worthy of his love.

The couple that had been conversing with single men, one after another, at last recruited a third, and the threesome walked, hand in hand in hand through a doorway covered by the same thick curtain we had passed through to enter the bar room, which muted the sounds and sights of what lay beyond.

I raised my eyebrows and pointed with my eyes toward the newly revealed exit. Jacob nodded, and we followed them through the curtain and up a flight of stairs. The trio was nowhere in sight, but we found ourselves in a conspicuously ordinary hallway, the type one might find on the second level of any home. There were doors on either side—I counted four in all. Three were closed, but Jacob took my hand and led me to the open one.

He stopped and turned to me, his eyes searching mine for answers. Did I want to see what was inside? Honestly, I was not sure. The sights and sounds I had experienced thus far had not offended me. On the contrary, they enthused me, adding coal to the fire of my own lustful cravings. What I felt was not disgust but pleasure, not fear but excitement.

I smiled and stroked his arm in what I hoped was a reassuring gesture. This time, I led the way, pulling him gently toward the open door. He rewarded me with an impish grin, and I peeked inside, discovering a fully furnished bedroom, complete with side tables, four-poster bed, and paisley-patterned fainting sofa. The sofa was empty, but the bed was not. The bed-curtains were pinned to the posts, revealing two men in a state of embrace. Their bare chests were visible, but their bottom halves were covered. On one side of the bed, a set of men's clothes—pants, shirt, jacket, and shoes—lay in a heap. On the other, a pooled dress and a feminine wig cast off on the floor.

I turned away, not wanting to commit the same mistake as before, but Jacob held my chin between his fingers and turned my face toward the scene.

"It is all right to watch," he whispered. "In fact, that is what they want us to do. If they preferred privacy, they would have closed the door. An open room is an invitation."

We gave the couple the attention they sought, Jacob leaning against the doorway and me leaning against him. My breaths quickened as I fought to quell the desire welling within me, precariously close to emerging from its lair. One of the men, to this point lost in the pleasure of the other's embrace, turned toward us. He made eye contact with me and smiled before turning back to his partner and issuing a wheezy groan.

"This room is called the chapel," Jacob explained.

Suddenly, it was all too much for me. While I quite enjoyed watching their performance, I was uncomfortable at being drawn in as part of it. Plus, Jacob's mention of the chapel and its reference to religion reminded me of my utter failure to adhere to my moral obligations, and guilt asserted its hold. I tugged Jacob's arm, and we stepped away from the source of my discomfort.

"Are you ready to go?"

I nodded. I had seen enough—more than I could have imagined.

He led me down the stairs, through the main space with bar and tables, and back to where we had started, in the room that marked the beginning of the molly-house. The fat man and his skinny companion were gone, but the padded chair remained, available to host a new couple.

Jacob pushed aside the heavy curtain to where Hugo stood guard. Bidding farewell to the ugly giant, he pressed a coin into his hand, which the man accepted with a nod and swiftly deposited into his pocket. In the tavern area, Jacob handed money to the old man behind the bar as payment for our drinks as well as our admission to the establishment.

Outside, he waited until we crossed the street before asking, "What did you think?"

My thoughts were an incoherent jumble, and any words I might string together would be more of the same. I owed him a response, but telling him I liked it seemed trivial. I could say I found it interesting, but that, too, was an understatement. I could declare it overwhelming, which was accurate, though he might interpret that as a negative.

I settled on, "It is another world."

I was not sure whether I wanted to be part of it, or if I preferred to go back to the way life was before. As we walked along the desolate streets, we fell back into our default, public-facing conduct, staying an appropriate distance apart and pretending we were merely business partners, at most old friends. I missed the closeness of him and mourned the loss of his hands upon me. Despite its strangeness and the risks it presented, I understood Jacob's preference for this world over the one in which we were forced to reside.

CHAPTER THIRTY-ONE

END OF MY WORLD

1832, Eleven Years before the Ghosts

I told Fan about my visit to the molly-house, though I left out some of the more lascivious details. In this case, I thought it wise to hold back, if only to save her from the moral complications of knowing precisely what went on in the upstairs rooms, both behind closed doors and in full view of willing spectators. Though we had vowed to confide in each other about every aspect of our lives, I felt justified in this omission because I had only observed the behaviors but did not participate. This was a tenuous line to draw, but I heeded it nonetheless.

What Jacob and I did together did not qualify under that exemption, and I was obliged by my promise as brother and friend to tell Fan everything. At times, I could not bring myself to look at her as I struggled to accurately describe the intricacies of our romantic activities. I explained the methodologies as if I were an authority on the subject, while in truth I had only recently learned them and was a novice compared to my partner.

I apologized for corrupting her in this way, but Fan assured me I was doing nothing of the sort, asserting she was strong enough in her own convictions that knowing the full truth of my sexual life would not lead her to partake in similar activities herself. She smiled wryly as she said this, and I acknowledged the validity of her argument, given her romantic inclinations were more conventional than mine.

Fan showed immense interest in the arrangement between Jacob and his wife, prodding me to explain in minute detail the workings of their relationship agreement and its benefits to them both. She surmised, as I did, that Rebecca and her companion were more than platonic friends, and we wondered aloud about the types of carnal activities in which two ladies might engage. I had nothing to contribute to the discussion, but Fan offered tangible insights into the mechanisms by which women experienced sexual pleasure. She whispered them in my ear, though no one was near enough to hear us. I had no way of knowing if her theories were correct, but we enjoyed the exercise of considering them, blushing simultaneously as we shocked ourselves with our candor.

As the years passed, I became Fan's primary connection to the outside world, since Samuel was frequently away on business, and she was too tired to venture outdoors. She opted out of strolls through the park, which we had delighted in before, and we spent most of our time together sitting in her living room or on her porch.

I asked Fan pointedly the reason for this change, citing our mutual pact to share our truths. I feared she was falling into a depression, feeling isolated and abandoned by her husband, but she assured me her spirits were high. It was not that she preferred to stay indoors, but rather that the exertion required to engage with society was not worth the minuscule benefits it provided. She was content with her life as it was, watching her son grow larger and smarter and reveling in the connection we shared. I was delighted to fulfill her need for friendship and entertainment, but I worried about her persistent paleness and occasional coughing spells.

She dismissed my concerns outright, attributing her exhaustion to the demands of motherhood and managing a household. I conceded these points and indulged her rationalizations, regardless of their insufficiency to account for her symptoms. I told myself that she had always been a delicate creature, and her current frailty did not constitute a change significant enough to warrant continuous fretting.

Fan did not have another child after the first, though she desperately wanted one. Since the inner workings of a woman's body were well outside my own sphere of knowledge, I did not attempt even a cursory speculation of what her problems might be in that area.

Freddie had to be enough. And by God he was. My little nephew had an endless supply of energy, running and jumping into my arms every time I visited, begging me to take him outside and watch him perform a somersault, cartwheel, or some other physical feat.

I oftentimes relieved Fan and the obviously weary nursemaid of their responsibilities for the boy by taking him out on excursions. At the park a short distance from the house, I told him, "Run to that tree and back. I will count how long it takes you." Perhaps I was too generous in calculating his pace, but he seemed to grow faster each week, and no matter how many times he ran back and forth, he never tired.

Once, I took him to a springtime fair where actors played the roles of women and men on wooden platforms. We watched jugglers perform, in awe at their physical dexterity, which far surpassed my own. On the opposite end of the talent spectrum, artists sat quietly beside their canvases, vying for the attention of prospective buyers through standoffish behavior, which conveyed their superiority over the amateurs who beckoned passersby to turn their way.

The food was miraculous. I could not choose between the oyster stands, stalls of oranges, and cloth-covered tables harboring both delicacies and classic dishes that made my mouth water. Most amazing were the gilt gingerbread houses with glimmering decorations and ornate designs.

I looked down to direct Freddie's attention to one particularly impressive structure and discovered he was gone. I called to him, but it was to no avail as the volume of the noises surrounding me drowned out my voice.

Pushing people aside as I hurled myself through the crowd, I did not care one bit about the curses they flung at me in return. It seemed an hour went by before my frantic search succeeded, and I found Freddie behind the line of booths, racing back and forth between two carts as he had done many times before between trees. This day, he had enlisted several other boys to join him.

I scooped him up, hugging him tightly and admonishing him for wandering away from me. Freddie shook off my distress, embarrassed by my dramatic display in front of his new friends, but I was so relieved to find him safe that I ignored his protests. How upset would Fan be if I returned home without her only child? I could not imagine it. After that day, I gave him my full attention on our excursions, an ever-vigilant watchman whenever he was in my charge.

Freddie was growing in size and strength with each passing day, while his mother's health progressed in the opposite direction. Fan was withering, as a plant deprived of water, and she was tired—so very tired—all the time.

One Sunday, I let myself in, as had become my custom. Since I was a regular fixture in the house, I deemed it unnecessary to pull the servants away from their duties to greet me at the door. All was quiet, and my sister was missing from her usual spot on the settee in the living room.

"Fan?" I called out, turning in a full circle as if I might have missed someone on my first glance around the room. "Hello?" Surely she had been expecting me. I had visited her every Sunday for more than a decade. I returned to the foyer and, standing at the bottom of the stairs with one hand on the railing and the other cupped around my mouth, directed my voice upward. "Fan, are you here?"

The housemaid appeared, balancing a tray with a teapot and biscuits piled atop it. She was moving faster than I had ever seen her before, and she pushed by me to access the stairs.

"Mrs. Wright is unwell, sir," she said, her voice strained with urgency.

I followed her up, but a sense of foreboding made me stop at the threshold of the bedroom, my body unwilling to proceed farther. The woman set the tray down on the bedside table before lifting Fan with one arm and arranging the pillows to prop her up. She filled a teacup and offered it to her, but my sister spotted me lurking in the doorway and raised her hand to refuse the steaming cup.

"Leave us, please," she told the servant. Her voice was barely audible, despite the heavy silence in the house. The woman obeyed, shaking her head as she left the room, and closed the door behind her.

I rushed to my sister's bedside, recalling the last time I had been this worried for her health, in this very room, on the day of Freddie's birth. She had been happy and strong, her skin glowing and her expression content. She looked so different now, frail and ashen, nestled into the fluff of the blankets.

"What is wrong? Are you ill?"

"I am," she started, but I cut her off before she had a chance to elaborate.

"I will fetch the doctor," I said, intent to solve the problem with immediate action, but Fan's next statement stopped me in my tracks.

"He has already come and gone." She patted the bed beside her. "Sit with me."

I complied silently for I had no words, and slowly for I could sense the impending heartbreak and was in no hurry to receive confirmation of its approach. I took her hand in mine. It was warm and pallid, and it fit neatly in my upturned palm. I stroked the top of it, more to comfort myself than her.

"I have consumption, or so the doctor says," she explained. "I have known for some time, but it has taken a stronger hold of me in recent days."

I raised my gaze from her hand to her face, noting the dark circles ringing her eyes and her skin flush with fever. Taking a steep breath, I blurted, "What do you mean 'you have known for some time'?" I stopped stroking her hand and instead held it firmly between mine, as if to keep her from slipping away.

She closed her eyes for a long moment, and when she opened them again, they betrayed the weight of her guilt. "It has been several years."

"Wait." I let go of her hand, which fell limp on the bed, and stood up, arms pinned to my sides. "You have been ill for *years*? And you did not tell me? You said you were tired from the burdens of managing the household." My mind clamored to make sense of the information, with only limited success. "What about our promise?" I was shouting now, coming undone before her, my arms flailing with every word that brought me closer to grasping the truth. "We are supposed to tell each other everything."

"I am sorry, Neez," she said. "Sit, please, and I will explain."

I did as she bade me, struck silent and weary. This time, Fan took my hand in hers.

"At first, I believed exactly what I told you, that I was worn out by my responsibilities. I thought I might be pregnant again, and you remember how tired I was then. Sadly, that was not the case, and it grew worse with time, not better. Eventually I summoned a physician who gave me a definitive diagnosis, but I did not want to believe it, Neez. I did not want to say it out loud because that would make it real. That is why I didn't tell you." She sighed before continuing. "But it seems my denial has done nothing to change the truth—and nothing to delay its progression. The end is inescapable."

"No. I do not accept that," I protested. "I will bring you to the country. Fresh air is a treatment for consumption, and there are medicines as well. I do not care what they cost. You will rest and regain your strength."

"There is nothing you can do," Fan said, "except forgive me for not telling you sooner."

How had I not seen this before? I cursed myself for missing the signs that had been there all along but were only visible to me in hindsight. I was angry at Fan as well, as much as I did not want to be. How could she have deceived me for so long? Why did she break our most solemn vow to each other? Worst of all, how could she deny me the opportunity to comfort her in her suffering?

My sister had endured the effects of disease, as well as the burden of its reality—alone. If she had told me, I could have offered her sympathy and support. I could have mitigated the loneliness she must have felt at facing her own mortality. Not only had she punished herself by keeping this secret, but she had denied me the honor of standing by her side throughout it, as her confidant and friend. Now, she was begging for forgiveness, and I did not know if I could grant it.

As the implications of her confession continued to unfold in my mind, I remembered the one person whose life would be impacted most by this revelation.

"Where is Freddie?"

To this, Fan's face brightened, for neither she nor I could resist smiling at the mere mention of his name. "He is at the park with his nursemaid. He insisted on going, so he could practice running and surprise you with how fast he is the next time you take him."

She laughed, which brought on a bout of coughing. This had occurred many times before, but it held a new significance now. When it was over, she rested her head against the pillow.

The inevitable happened too quickly after that.

Samuel returned home the day after her illness had forced her to bed and called for a physician straightaway, despite Fan's protests of its futility. I sympathized with his desire to take action, to believe he had some power over the outcome.

I went back to Fan's bedside after the examination was complete and remained there while the doctor spoke with Samuel at the threshold of the room. They used hushed voices, though the doctor's advanced age and apparent hearing deficiencies necessitated a volume loud enough to reach my ears. This doctor gave the same diagnosis and treatment advice as the previous one, so his efforts were, as my sister had predicted, pointless. The discussion ended with Samuel's promise to pay the bill at a later date, along with the dubious explanation that in his rush to be home with his wife, he had neglected to ensure he had a sufficient amount of cash on hand.

I had long ago deduced the precariousness of Samuel's financial situation, but this was evidence it was worse than I had feared. My theory was further bolstered by his insistence, only two days later, that he must leave yet again to attend to business obligations outside the city. He had a deal in progress, he insisted, which involved an enormous sum of money, and his presence was vital to the negotiations.

His departure left Freddie and me to tend to Fan, an arrangement I considered entirely appropriate, since we were the two who loved her most.

Jacob assumed my workload at both the warehouse and our counting house, which allowed me time to care for Fan. I took up residence in the chair beside her bed, listening to her labored breathing as she slept and speaking softly to her when she was awake. I read to her from the Jane Austen novel I had given her for her birthday. At one point, thinking she was asleep, since her eyes were closed and her breathing slow, I marked the page and shut the book.

"Please don't stop," Fan whispered. I opened the book and started again, trepidation settling itself into the pit of my stomach.

Part of my contribution to her care was to entertain Freddie, a task which I embraced. I took him outdoors as often as possible, for the boy had boundless energy, and keeping him cooped up in the house was not preferable for anyone. Fan rested most of the day, but she perked up whenever her son visited her room, endeavoring to appear healthy and energetic as a show for him. I propped her up with pillows, so she could look into his precious face, and she gifted us her sweet, beautiful smile when he kissed her on the cheek, a gesture that comforted all three of us.

Freddie and I spent many hours together, sometimes at play but other times seated beside Fan's bed. He no longer sat on my lap as he had when he was a toddler. At eleven years old, he asserted, he was too mature for such things. We took turns reading aloud to his mother and talked and reminisced and even laughed once or twice. I was careful not to disrupt Fan's rest and ready at a moment's notice to give her water or pat her back, as the doctor had instructed, when a coughing fit overtook her.

Her demise was steady and undramatic. She simply wasted away, her head sinking deeper into the pillow as each day passed, her body shrinking under the blankets.

The end itself was mercifully peaceful and calm.

It happened in the darkest, quietest part of the night. Freddie had eaten his dinner and sat with me beside his mother's bed for hours until finally his head drooped, and he rested against my shoulder to sleep. The atmosphere was serene, though I was the only one awake to appreciate it.

Fan's breaths were shallow and raspy, the time between them lengthening as the night progressed. I counted the seconds between them—one and two and three, before the next breath came, reaching five and six and then eight counts near the end. Finally, she released a long, jagged breath, and another did not replace it.

I held my own breath along with her, counting higher and higher, willing the next one to arrive. Eventually my body forced me to submit, and I filled my lungs with air. Fan's did not compel another breath, having at long last surrendered to the illness that had gorged itself on her, until there was not enough left to sustain her. She was still now, her face placid.

The heaving of my shoulders jostled Freddie awake, and he sat upright, rubbing the sleep from his eyes. He looked up at me, searching my face for an explanation. I was powerless to stop my tears. He knew it then, but I told him anyway. "She is gone."

Freddie did not go to his mother to confirm. He believed me. He trusted me. I wrapped my arms around him, and he curled himself in my lap. In that moment, in the first groundswell of grief, he was not too old for such things. I cradled him and rocked him back and forth while he cried.

Poor, sweet Freddie. He faced a life changed irreparably by the tragedy of death. With his father away intermittently and his mother gone forever, I was all he had left. I hoped I was enough.

Samuel arrived the day after next, but by then I had already made the funeral arrangements. He displayed all the signs of mourning expected of a widower, but I resented him for his absence during Fan's final days. He had not only abandoned his wife but left his only child to experience that devastating heartbreak without a parent's support. My precious nephew deserved better than him.

I went about the next few days as if the smoke and fog of the city concentrated around me like a cloud and followed me wherever I went, leaving me without the means to orient myself in the world. Jacob's appearance at the wake brought a brief respite from the enormity of my grief. His wife accompanied him, funerals being one of the events they attended together. He shook my hand and offered his sincerest condolences, as did Rebecca. Her companion stood silently behind them, her eyes pointed at the floor.

He addressed Freddie next. He did not kneel when he spoke to him, as others had, and did not employ a condescending tone. Instead, he shook Freddie's hand as he would any other man's, calling him "Master Wright" rather than "child" and relating for him a story that emphasized his mother's strength of character. My young nephew stood tall and puffed out his chest, proud to be acknowledged as mature and deserving of respect.

I could not bear to leave the house where my sister's body lay in wake, and Samuel graciously offered to let me stay in the guest room. I remained with Freddie throughout the week, making sure he ate his meals, though neither of us was hungry, and that he went to bed early, since sleep was the only activity, besides crying, either of us was capable of doing well. When the day of burial came, I held Freddie's hand as we walked behind the carriage in the funeral procession, and I laid my hand on Fan's coffin one last time before it was lowered into the ground.

I paid the interment expenses since my brother-in-law did not have the necessary funds on hand. Though I wished I could remain there with my nephew, when the services were complete, it was time for me to return to my flat. Freddie clung to me when I said my goodbyes, but I assured him I would visit often. I looked over my shoulder as I walked away, and my heart broke a second time at the sight of his father holding him back while he reached for me and cried out, begging me not to leave.

My parents did not attend Fan's funeral services since their own health was failing, and the winter weather made the journey impossible for them. News of their deaths, first Father's and then Mother's, days apart due to fever, came two months later. Their passing did not sadden me, numb as I was after my sister's tragic death. My parents had lived long enough to see their children grow to adulthood. That was not the case for Fan. She deserved more time with her son, and Freddie deserved to have his mother with him as he grew to adulthood. How unfair for her life to be cut short, when she had brought love and light to this world. Her death left a crushing weight upon my chest, and my heart was forever weakened by this wound that would never fully heal.

CHAPTER THIRTY-TWO
BROKEN

1850

My own death is not progressing as peacefully as Fan's. I open my eyes, but there is only darkness, and it takes me a moment to remember that I am here in my bed and not at the site of my sister's grave. Her death was the worst thing that ever happened to me. I can say that with absolute certainty. The wound it left on my heart continued to ooze and fester, and my sorrow remained perilously close to the surface, threatening to reemerge unexpectedly and drag me back into the abyss of despair. It is doing so now as I teeter on the edge of life and death.

My body reacts on its own, my mind powerless to control it, as I writhe and thrash against the cramping in my gut. I reach out, grasping futilely for help, but a gentle pressure on my shoulders calms my frantic movements. These are not the phantom's skeletal hands but those of a human being. Their settling warmth brings comfort, and the inner forces within me start to give way. The gates to the afterlife are creaking open.

Panic thrusts itself to the forefront of my senses. I cannot die now, not with the memories of my sister's death as my final thoughts.

The phantom pulls me toward him, but I resist with every fragment of strength that remains in my withering body. I must continue my journey of remembering, as I found the will to live on after my sister died. I fought to survive the destruction that tragedy inflicted on my soul, and I beg the phantom to honor my fortitude, to grant his continued generosity and patience. So that the last moments of my life on earth are not defined by heartache, so that grief is not my sole companion when I enter the spirit world, I must persevere.

CHAPTER THIRTY-THREE

COLD COMFORT

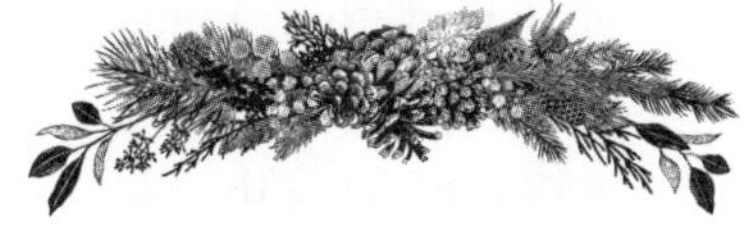

1832, Eleven Years before the Ghosts

To say Fan's death devastated me would not begin to convey the extent of its impact. I felt as if I had died with her. At times, I wished I had. With my sister's body in the ground and my nephew with his father, I returned to my flat to wallow in my grief. I went unwashed and unfed for days, my curtains drawn against the sunlight and the fireplace unlit. I did not read or eat or sleep. I cried off and on, but mostly I did nothing.

I spent Christmas alone, and the next day was the same. There was no telling how long I might have gone on like that if Jacob had not come to rescue me.

"Ebenezer," he called to me from the bottom of the stairs. Mrs. King must have admitted him, though I had not heard the door. "It is Jacob Marley. I am coming up."

He let himself in and called to me again. I tried to speak, though

I could not project my voice loudly enough for him to hear. I had not uttered a sound, other than the anemic gasps of my sobbing, in days.

He called again before entering my bedroom.

"There you are," he said at a volume far louder than I preferred.

I opened my eyes and found him peering down at me. The next thing I knew, I was blinded by the light Jacob invited in by opening the window curtains. I squeezed my eyes shut against the assault and pulled the blanket over my head.

He pressed on my chest and shook me, and a meager moan released itself from my throat.

"Are you ill, man?" he asked, pushing me again. My body remained limp, moving only in response to the force of his touch. His attempt to rouse me unsuccessful, he gave up rather quickly and left the room, only to return a few moments later.

"Here, drink," he instructed, removing the blanket from my face, lifting my head, and holding a mug to my lips.

I blinked, acclimating my eyes, and complied with his instructions, taking a small sip. The effort was exhausting, and I rested my head on the pillow once again. That first taste awakened a thirst I had subjugated for too long, and I lifted my head on my own accord and gulped down the remainder of the liquid.

Jacob touched my forehead. "You do not feel hot. How long have you been like this?"

Clearing my throat, I managed a gravelly "What day is it?"

"It is Sunday," he said. I needed more information than that to answer his question. "December thirtieth," he offered, concern in his voice.

Almost a week had passed since Fan's burial, and I had been here, like this, since then.

Jacob left the room and returned with the mug filled again. "Why isn't the fire lit? It is as cold in here as it is outside."

What did I care how cold it was? I was shivering, yes, but the discomfort was strangely consoling. It was better to suffer than to feel nothing at all.

I did not offer a reply, so Jacob continued. "I hoped you would come to work tomorrow. The apprentices at the warehouse have gone home for the holiday, and the paperwork is piling up. You have been away so long."

"Ten days," I said, propping myself up on one elbow and accepting the mug he handed me. He sat beside me while I drank down the contents and gave it back to him before collapsing once again.

"Ten days since Fan died, but you have been absent longer than that."

He was right. I had been at my sister's bedside for the weeks preceding her death, and Jacob must have been working long hours to handle my responsibilities in addition to his own.

"I am sorry," I said. "I promise to return soon and catch up on everything."

"It is more than that," he said. "You have been gone in other ways as well."

The sadness in his voice deposited the weight of guilt upon my already overburdened soul, and I sank further into despair. I had neglected him as well as my work, focusing my attention on my sister and nephew, ignoring him entirely. We had not shared his bed since Fan was confined to hers. Poor Jacob. It was wrong of me to abandon him. I was a failure in so many ways.

It dawned on me that perhaps he had finally realized my inadequacy, a fact of which I had always been aware. Had he lost his desire for me? Found someone new to replace me?

"I am sorry," I said, this time in a whisper. I had no other words.

"Apologies are not warranted," Jacob said, "but the time for grieving is over." He set the empty mug on the table with a thud. "It is time for healing. I will get the fire going, and you will rise from this bed, wash, and dress. We are going out."

Going out? The idea was ludicrous. How could I step outside when the prospect of leaving my bed seemed impossible? I honestly did not know if I could manage the feat, or even how to begin. I listened to Jacob fiddling with the fireplace, cursing the meager amount of coal he found in the bin, while I devised a strategy to comply with his demands.

I took one deep breath and then another, the air forcing my chest to expand. This helped immensely, spurring confidence that I might succeed in the endeavor. I swung my legs over the edge of the bed and sat up in one fluid movement, but the resulting dizziness forced me to collapse back down. Now, I was right where I had started, which was a setback to be sure, but the blankets were pushed aside, so that was some progress at least. My second attempt was more successful, and I managed to stand and wash at the basin Mrs. King's maid refreshed for me each day. I brushed my hair and changed out of my rank nightshirt and into relatively clean clothes. Patting every article of clothing to ensure I had remembered all the required components, I left my room for the first time in days.

Jacob was stoking the fire. "Come and sit," he said. "We will have a drink before we go." I did as he instructed, and the heat from the fire hit my face with the force of a slap. He handed me a cup, and I drank it down, noting that he must have brought a bottle with him because I did not have liquor as fine as this in my flat.

It warmed me from the inside as it made the journey from my mouth to my stomach. I experienced pleasure for the briefest moment before the guilt of it choked me, and I crumpled into the chair.

"You must not let the sadness overtake you."

Jacob was unrelenting. He did not understand my pain. How could he? My beloved sister's death had left a gaping hole in my chest, and I could not imagine feeling true happiness again. I was incomplete, a shell of the man I had once been, my insides hollow. I had nothing left to contribute to this world with my heart broken in pieces and my soul incapacitated.

As if reading my thoughts, he said, "I know you miss your sister, but you must find a way to move beyond the pain. You have life left in you, Ebenezer, so much yet to offer. Fezziwig's Warehouse is floundering, and your apprentices need your guidance. You are the foundation on which that business thrives, and Scrooge and Marley is only successful because of our collaboration. I cannot do any of it without you."

I believed everything he said, but my grief had forced me to forget who I was and what I had achieved. There were people counting on me, and my success made it possible for them to work and support their families. It was selfish of me to neglect my responsibilities, to disregard their needs.

Jacob's words were breaking through the wall I had built around myself.

"There are things even more important than our businesses, and your withdrawal from life is putting those at risk too. What about little Freddie? With his mother gone, he needs you more than ever."

The mention of my precious nephew pierced my heart with shame, but it left in its wake a tiny wisp of hope. I had a responsibility to Freddie, one that had passed from my sister to me. Besides his father, I was his only living family, his only source of support and moral counsel. I had an obligation to make sure his needs were met and his potential realized.

His father was not disciplined enough to save for his future, not intelligent enough to manage his finances. What if Samuel's next business venture failed, and he lost what remained of his family's fortune? What would happen to Freddie then? Even if Samuel earned enough to sustain the household, his work took him away from home often. I would not allow him to send Freddie away to boarding school, so I had to step up and ensure his continued security.

This realization was the first step toward resurrecting myself, recommitting to my life and my work. I had become lost in my own misery and failed to recognize the self-indulgence of doing so. It took Jacob's encouragement to bring me back, and I resolved to set aside my grief, even if it meant burying it deep within me, to be the man I needed to be.

"And there is me," Jacob said. "I miss you."

The lines under his eyes and his wounded expression told me he was hurting. I had left him alone for weeks, to do my work and his, with no one to keep him company. While I was wallowing, he had been suffering heartache of his own because of me. My negligence might have caused irreparable harm to our relationship, but in my shattered state, I did not think I was capable of fixing it.

"I do not know if I can be the partner you deserve, Jacob. I am nothing without my sister. Don't you see? Even before this, I was unworthy of your love. Now, I am broken and have neither the skill nor the strength to satisfy you. I am sorry." This was the second or third or perhaps the tenth time I had said those words, but it was the one thing I knew for certain. I was sorry for Fan and for Freddie, for my apprentices and my employees, and for Jacob. Mostly, if I was honest, I was sorry for myself.

He lowered his eyes and slowly shook his head. Perhaps he had misunderstood. I was not refusing him, but simply pointing out that it was he who should have been rejecting me. I endeavored to explain. "I want you more than anything, but my sister was my rock, my confidante, my one constant in this life. She took a piece of me with her when she died, and I fear there is not enough left of me to offer you. You deserve better."

He let out a sigh. "I could be your confidant, Ebenezer. I could be your one constant in this life, holding you close for all time. Am I not enough for you?"

I trapped the sob before it escaped my throat and nodded my response. Yes. Jacob could be the rope that tethered me to this world. He could be my everything. The issue was whether I could be the same for him.

Courage did not drive my next inquiry, but rather desperation. I had so little left, I could not bear another loss. "I want to ask you something, and you must promise to be honest in your reply," I said, though I did not give him the opportunity to answer before I continued. "With all I have told you of my broken heart and wounded soul, with my many shortcomings, both the ones you already know and those that will reveal themselves over time, do you still want me?"

"How can you ask such a thing?" he said. "Of course I want you."

I shrugged my shoulders. I was not sure of anything, but the swiftness and clarity of his reply gave me hope.

"There is only one thing that gives me pause," he said.

At that, my tenuous return to the world unraveled. There was an exception to his devotion, a flaw in me that could nullify his love. I slumped forward, my head suddenly too heavy for my neck to support, wanting nothing more than to slink back to the shelter of my bed.

Jacob reached over and lifted my chin from my chest. His playful grin and the sparkle of the fire's reflection in his eyes hinted that his caveat was something less dire than I assumed.

"It is your beard, Ebenezer. It will be too scratchy, I think."

He winked, and I laughed out loud, a belly laugh so thunderous and full that my shoulders shook. I could not control it any more than I could control the malaise that had paralyzed me for over a week. A quarter hour before, trapped in my despair, I would not have thought it possible to laugh this way. I wiped away the tears drizzling down my cheeks.

"You do not like it?" I asked, stroking the coarse hairs on my chin, which I had forgotten to shave off as part of my recent grooming efforts.

He shook his head solemnly. "It has to go."

"Then it shall," I said, intent on undertaking the task immediately, but Jacob stood and placed a hand on my shoulder.

"It can wait until tomorrow morning, before you leave for work," he said. "My first priority is to get you some sustenance. A hearty meal is what you need to build up your strength and fatten you up, so I am not the only one with some extra padding here." He pointed to his midsection, which I noticed for the first time was puffier than it had been in years past. "Are you ready to join me in the world again?"

"No," I said, but I would do it if he wanted me to.

"Get your coat."

It was freezing outside, and there was a fresh layer of snow on the ground, but I inhaled deeply, filling my lungs with the frigid air. I coughed and pulled my collar up over my neck, though I welcomed the discomfort of the cold since it was a reminder that I was alive and capable of feeling something other than grief.

Jacob and I dined together at a nearby tavern and said our goodbyes from a respectable distance apart. I went to bed with a determination to rise in the morning and continue living. My sister was gone, but I was not alone.

CHAPTER THIRTY-FOUR
REAWAKENING

1833, Ten Years before the Ghosts

I shaved my scraggly beard, as promised, and returned to work the day after Jacob coaxed me back to life. Exhausted after spending the morning at Fezziwig's Warehouse and my workday not half over yet, I trudged through the streets littered with dirty snow to Scrooge and Marley's counting house.

Jacob greeted me with a cheerful "Good day, friend."

"Bah," I replied, hanging up my coat. Ordinarily, I addressed my partner with a cheerful "hello," followed by inquiries about his well-being, the state of the business, and meetings scheduled for the afternoon. That day, I had neither the energy nor the desire to do so.

I took my seat, noting the stack of papers on my desk. Though it was not nearly as tall as the pile I had found at the warehouse, it would take me weeks to sort through it all.

I put my head in my hands to restore my equilibrium and readied myself to confront the tasks awaiting me. I startled when I felt Jacob's hands on my shoulders but softened when he began to knead the muscles of my back and neck. Reveling in that glorious sensation, I resolved to remain in that position for as long as he continued.

"There, there, Ebenezer," he said. They were words used to console a child, but they were precisely what I needed to hear. I melted, the tension dissipating under the pressure of his touch. His hands traveled down my back and, when they reached the place where my backside met the chair, reversed direction and made their way upward again. When he finished, he stood beside me, but I remained hunched, my elbows on the desk, head resting in my hands.

I reluctantly raised my eyes. "Thank you. I needed that," I told him. "Sorry I was brusque with you. I am so very tired."

"I know, but you will heal, Ebenezer. It will get easier."

He took my hand and kissed it, but instead of looking back at him, I glanced toward the door. It was a reflex over which I had no control, as I was afflicted with constant worry that someone might enter unannounced, find us in a too-familiar position, and discover the truth of what we meant to each other.

"We have no meetings scheduled today," Jacob assured me but retreated to his desk anyway.

I went straight home after the workday ended and did the same the next day and the one after it, but I grew stronger, and my endurance increased. Eventually, I returned to my routine of long hours at my desk and suppers with Jacob, but it was some time before I felt ready to be intimate with him. I struggled with the guilt of being alive while my sister was dead, to believe that I deserved to experience pleasure when she could not.

Jacob never pressured me, but after a time, I found my desire for intimacy returning. I planned to accompany him home one Saturday evening, but when the time came, I could not follow through. Sundays had always been reserved for visiting Fan, and the eve of that day brought dismay that I would not see her again.

Jacob and I parted ways after supper, as had become our custom, and I went home to my dreary flat, where I spent the next day in my bed with the curtains drawn and the fire unlit. On Monday morning, I pulled myself out of that depression without any prodding, which was a noteworthy accomplishment in itself.

I tried again the next week, this time on Friday.

"I am not the least bit tired this evening," I said when we finished our meal at Simpson's Tavern. "Perhaps we could walk for a while, or go to your house."

Jacob raised an eyebrow and smiled at me over the rim of his mug before gulping down the last drops of ale.

"I, too, have energy to spare," he said. "Will you join me for a drink?"

I accepted the invitation, which I myself had elicited, and we walked through the yard of Saint Michael's Cornhill, along the familiar alleyways, and in between the empty booths of Leadenhall Market. The air was crisp, but the wind did not bite at our faces. It felt like we were the only people awake in the city, with the streets vacant and not a single beggar in sight. I had the ideal companion in Jacob, and we walked together in comfortable silence, the moon lighting our way.

His house was dark and quiet. Jacob lit the lamps and opened the bar cabinet to pour our drinks, neglecting our visit to the living room to perform the obligatory, if awkward, greeting of his wife and her companion. Perhaps the ladies had already retired to their accommodations on the third floor. Jacob instructed me to light the fire, though I thought it wasteful since we would not remain in that room long enough to justify the expense. At least I hoped not.

We sat beside each other, staring at the dancing flames and sipping port from cordial glasses. Conversation, which usually came effortlessly, was not forthcoming. I was certainly not contributing my part, my mind preoccupied with thoughts about what would happen in his bedroom after we finished our drinks. I drank mine down quickly, and he filled my glass again. I settled into my seat then, resigned to wait until Jacob was ready to move forward, as he had done for me.

"I am happy you are here with me," he said. "I have something important to discuss with you."

I could not imagine what sort of conversation would take precedence over the intimate pleasures awaiting us upstairs, but patience was in order, and I gave him my full attention.

"Are you feeling well, Ebenezer? I mean, are you recovered, do you think, healed from your loss?"

Why would he bring this up now, when I was finally ready to resume our physical connection? What purpose did he have in reminding me? The wound of my sister's death was still raw, and I struggled every day to keep my spirits aloft, always just one insensitive comment away from sinking back into the depths of my latent grief. I would never fully recover, and he knew it. Why was he forcing me to acknowledge that trauma now, when I had hoped to experience pleasure again for one blessed night?

"I am better," I said, deciding on a strategy of brevity, if not complete honesty, and willing him to abandon the subject.

"I do not mean to call your sadness to the surface," Jacob said. "Please forgive me. I have news to share with you, but I want to be sure you are prepared to hear it."

My thoughts turned immediately to the worst possibility I could imagine—he did not want me anymore. That was the only sort of news that would require me to be healed from my loss. My absence from his bed for these many weeks had driven him away, and he had found a replacement. He needed me to recuperate enough so that his rejection would not push me beyond what I could bear.

I wanted to cover my ears, but I held my breath and steeled myself for the impending cataclysm. The room was starting to spin when he set down his emptied glass.

"Are you?" he prodded.

I could not recall his question. My mind had considered so many possibilities in the moments since he had asked it. Did my grief remain precariously close to the surface? Yes. Was I prepared to hear bad news? No. Was I ready for our relationship to end? Certainly not. Instead of saying any of this, I simply shrugged.

He knelt in front of me, taking my hands in his.

"I love you, Ebenezer, and I want us to be together always, not only at work and one night each week, but every day and every night. Will you live here with me?"

My head shook briskly and involuntarily. It was not an answer but rather an attempt to free myself from the saturating confusion. My body twitched, and I nearly jerked my hands out of his, but he held them securely.

Of course I wanted to be with Jacob, to live together as a true and committed couple, but it was a fantasy I dreamed of, not reality. It was not possible for men like us to build a life as romantic partners, not in a respectable society—not anywhere.

I shook my head again, incapable of producing even a single word of response.

"We will be safe. I promise." He was tugging my hands to accentuate his words, as if the jostling would help me understand. "We will tell people we are saving money this way, that you will live on the third floor and have an office there, so we can continue working into the night. We will present it as a shrewd business decision. It will not be suspicious at all."

"I-I don't—" All my thoughts were fighting to come forward at once, and I could not choose between them.

"Please do not say no," he pleaded. "You must hear me out first. I know you are afraid of being discovered, but we can do this. We command respect in the business community and are well known for being frugal and reserved. We are outgrowing the space in the counting house. You were saying so just the other day. And this house is large enough to serve multiple tenants and provide storage space for our files."

His speech was passionate, and my head bobbled at the end of each sentence as he tugged my hands. "People will not suspect our motives are anything but monetary. They will say we are miserly creatures who cannot bear to spend money to rent a flat when we could invest it instead. My household staff is loyal and discreet, as you well know, and my family's wealth and reputation will shield us from scrutiny."

I stopped my head from shaking and took a deep breath, which helped clarify the fuzziness of his features and ceased the flickering of stars clouding my vision.

With renewed composure, I asked, "What about your wife, Jacob? What does she say about this?" Obviously, I was afraid of the dire consequences we might face if I conceded to his proposition, but also I could not imagine living under the same roof as Rebecca and her doting, ever-silent companion.

"My apologies," Jacob said, sitting back on his knees. "In my excitement, I have gotten ahead of myself. You see, Rebecca's father passed away this winter."

I gasped, instantly remorseful that I had been too consumed by my own grief to comfort him in his loss. Jacob shook his head, as always, anticipating my thoughts.

"I was fine—am fine—and did not want to burden you with the news. Since he had no heirs besides Rebecca, his estate passed to me. She railed at the unfairness of it, of course, that her family's wealth would be added to mine, and she neared a state of hysterics at my assertion that it was simply the way of the world. After much discussion, we came to an agreement that is beneficial to us both."

Jacob and his wife already had an arrangement where they coexisted as legal spouses while maintaining their own lives and romantic relationships apart from each other. What could be more beneficial than that?

"The largest portion of her father's estate is the family home," he continued, "which is free of debt and managed with a small staff. I agreed to grant ownership of the house to Rebecca, and she has relinquished any claim to this property. She and Grace will live in her family home—they moved weeks ago, in fact—and I will remain here. I will pay her expenses, but she will not interfere in my life, nor will I dictate how she conducts hers. We will attend events together, as necessary for appearances, but our lives will be our own."

Though shocked, I comprehended the situation clearly. "You have this all figured out."

"I do." Jacob puffed his chest with pride. "And everything will be perfect if you agree. Will you live here with me, Ebenezer?"

Thoughts whirled in the chaos of my mind, colliding with each other before disappearing in turn, only to reemerge in a different form before undergoing the same transformative process. Questions, fears, hopes, and worries compounded, but I gathered them all and tucked them away. I would worry more later, analyze again, and make sense of it all, but my answer was simple.

"Yes."

Jacob rose and pulled me to my feet, embracing me and then leading me upstairs to his bedroom, which would soon become *our* bedroom. We enjoyed each other with the fervor of desire long delayed and the promise of a blissful future. Before this, our relationship had been genuine, but it was informal and undefined. Once we were living together, sharing our work, our recreation, and our bed, it became something more. With Jacob as my true partner, my soul was renewed and my spirit reawakened.

CHAPTER THIRTY-FIVE

HOME

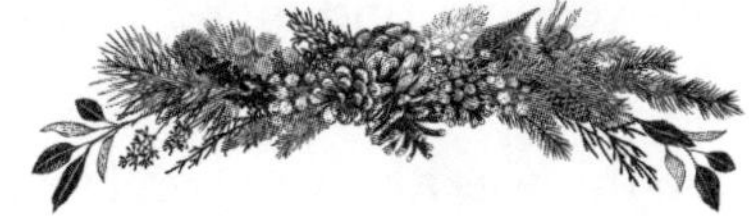

1833, Ten Years before the Ghosts

I moved into Jacob's house as the winter of my forty-sixth year receded to make room for a spring of new beginnings. It was five months after Fan died and only a week after he asked me.

I paid an extra month's rent to Mrs. King. Though not required, it was a gesture of kindness, as well as an incentive to discourage any disparaging comments she might make about me to her friends. I had something to hide and needed to do everything in my power to avoid becoming the subject of gossip. Along with the extra payment, I offered a thorough explanation of the motives for my change in living situation.

Jacob worried that I might accidentally reveal details that would stoke suspicions or raise questions about my character. So did I. Whether it was the result of nervousness or my perpetual awkwardness, it was a risk to be avoided, so I practiced the speech several times before delivering it. It was persuasive in delineating the money-saving aspect of my new arrangement, the benefits to the business, and the increased efficiency offered by the proximity of Jacob's house to the counting house, which would mean a shorter walk for me each day.

It was vital to disseminate our version of the story before speculations arose and rumors took hold. Mrs. King was the ideal conduit for our narrative, since she was well connected in society, with the ladies in particular, who were most often the source of such chatter.

Our plan was to employ her to disseminate our carefully fabricated story throughout the city. She would unwittingly accomplish this over tea with her friends; on strolls in the park, where she did more talking than walking; and in her everyday activities, where she conversed with storekeepers, the butcher, fruit vendors, and more. Word of our altered living arrangement would have spread swiftly in certain circles anyway, whether we wanted it to or not, so this was a way to regulate the message. I hoped it would work.

The moving process itself was simple, as compared to the rumor-control strategy we concocted, since I had little in the way of belongings. Jacob's servants packed my clothing, which did not fill an entire box, and my books, which required several. By noon, I was organizing my volumes on the living room shelves where Rebecca's had once resided. Jacob purchased a new armoire for me, placing it beside his in the bedroom, but it had far more space than I required. My clothing fit into one drawer, and since I owned exactly two pairs of shoes—heavy boots for winter and short ones for the rest of the year—I needed storage for only one pair at a time.

My prized possessions were my letters from Fan, and those I placed in the top drawer of the table next to the bed. I had reread them many times in the previous months, careful not to let my tears fall on the pages.

I continued to call it "Jacob's house," and each time I walked through the front door, I was struck by the grandness of it. The ornately carved banisters on the staircase would not be out of place in the palace itself, and there were eight fireplaces in all, dispersed among the first three floors—eight! Even the servants were of the highest quality, managing to clean and cook and attend to us while remaining nearly invisible.

How far I had come from such humble beginnings. The unfavored son of a solicitor sent to a second-rate boarding school, I had progressed from apprentice to employee to manager and finally to co-owner of the warehouse and partner in a prosperous firm. More than the material wealth I had amassed, however, my most significant accomplishment was achieving happiness at living the life of my choosing with the man I loved. Though I continued to struggle with the loss of my sister, I considered myself the luckiest man in London. What had I done to deserve such joy?

Jacob encouraged me to make my own additions to the décor. I might have done so if I thought it would be an improvement, but Rebecca had expertly furnished every room, and I found nothing lacking in either the style or quality of the furnishings. Moreover, I had no sense of fashion whatsoever, so I had nothing of value to offer.

Despite my objections, Jacob insisted I contribute one item at least. Since everything in the house coordinated so well and I dared not alter it, we settled on an exterior element. He took me to a blacksmith shop on the outskirts of the city, far enough away that we required his carriage to transport us. We could have gone to a store near the counting house or to one of the blacksmiths close to Fezziwig's Warehouse, but the endeavor seemed an intimate one, and he preferred a place where no one knew us by name.

Jacob held the door for me as we entered the shop, so the heat and smell of molten metal reached me first. I did not find it unpleasant, but Jacob blew out a long breath and ran the back of his hand across his forehead. The blacksmith's wife, a small woman whose features were clustered together in the center of her face, greeted us with a cheery "welcome, gentlemen." After inquiring about the reason for our visit, she showed us a diverse assortment of items, including a simple wrought iron boot scraper, a weathervane shaped like a rooster, and a small garden sculpture of a sleeping fairy lying in a leaf.

I asked for Jacob's input, but he insisted the choice was mine alone, so I perused the options while he propped open the outside door and swabbed his face with his handkerchief. As soon as I saw it, I knew which one was my favorite—a pewter door knocker twice the size of my fist. It was oblong and smooth, with black highlighting the grooves of the border and the connection between the swinging part and the rest. Jacob agreed with my assessment of the item's preeminence, though I did not know for sure whether he genuinely liked it or simply wanted to leave the sweltering shop. Either way, I purchased the door knocker, and we installed it together, with assistance from his coachman since neither of us possessed the skills needed to accomplish the task on our own. Jacob had been correct about the significance of my contribution to the house, for it had the intended effect of solidifying my position in his home and his life.

Our new arrangement was perfect, except for the inconvenience of the third-floor location for our office and storage space. The desk and chairs were added easily enough, hauled upstairs by several burly men who carried the heavy wooden pieces with minimal signs of exertion. The boxes of documents, however, were our responsibility. Jacob and I moved them from the counting house in one large batch at first, and piecemeal after that as the cabinets overflowed and we needed additional space. Some were so heavy I had to take breaks as I climbed the stairs from the first floor to the third, setting them down on each landing and shaking my arms to restore circulation before proceeding farther.

Only once did Jacob attempt to do the same. Grunting, he ascended a handful of steps before dropping the box onto the stair above. He rested it there, breathing heavily and grumbling about the excessive weight I had packed into it. With considerable effort, he lifted it again and ascended a few more stairs before depositing it on the first landing, having made it only halfway to the second floor. He abandoned it there, holding a hand to his chest and struggling to catch his breath, and assured me he would complete the task later. After he went to bed, I picked it up, finding it no heavier than the others, and carried it up myself.

Jacob and I never spoke of his difficulty breathing or the pains in his chest. Neither did we mention the transformation of his once-trim body to a softer one that was markedly expanding. It became an unspoken rule that I was the designated laborer for the two of us whenever strenuous activity was required.

We adopted a fair number of unspoken rules, in fact, besides that one. The most significant had to do with Jacob's romantic activities outside our home and my obligation to ignore them. For months after I moved in, we spent every moment together, or nearly so, working, dining, and sleeping beside each other. It was glorious. This was the life I had only dreamed of before, which had miraculously become my reality.

But it was not enough for Jacob. One Saturday, after we finished our dinner and started our walk, he announced, "I will not be accompanying you home this evening, Ebenezer. I am going out, but I will return to you later tonight."

He turned then and walked in the opposite direction, leaving me standing alone on the street, my mouth hanging open in disbelief. I did not run after him or call out his name. Such a scene could draw attention to us, rouse suspicion, and put us in danger. Instead, I snapped my lips shut, clenched my teeth, and resumed the journey home, focusing my eyes on the ground in front of my feet throughout the entirety of the trek.

When I arrived, I poured myself a drink and sat staring at the unlit fireplace in the drawing room. I was uneasy sitting there alone and decided the living room was a better venue. I headed in that direction, glancing at the front door as I passed through the foyer, willing it to open and for Jacob to walk through. Alas, it did not, and I navigated through the dark dining room to my destination, where I lit a candle to illuminate the bookshelves. Reading had always provided solace, and I chose one of my old favorites, *Robinson Crusoe*, as my medicine. The words were so familiar that I might have recited them without referring to the text, but I was distracted, and my imagination resisted entry into the fictional world.

With my usual means of escape ineffectual, sleep was the only viable solution. I returned the book to the shelf and made my way upstairs, glaring again at the front door as I passed by. It remained frustratingly inert.

Sleep did not save me either, as the empty bed was a reminder of my abandonment. I stewed and fretted and agonized about my predicament, knowing where Jacob was, though he had not told me so. He was in a molly-house, maybe the same one he had brought me to, with other men like us. Was he hoping to find a compatible partner for the night, or else to reconnect with someone he had been intimate with before? Perhaps, at that very moment, he was in one of the chapel rooms upstairs, bedding a young, slender man—the type that had always attracted his attention. The thought made my stomach constrict, and I jumped out of bed and retched, losing my dinner into the chamber pot and leaving me emptier than before.

How could Jacob tell me he loved me and be unfaithful? I tossed and turned in our bed, apprehension gnawing away at my insides. Finally—I had no idea how long—I heard his footsteps, and I sat up and lit a candle. I had planned exactly what I would say when he returned, but my well-thought-out arguments vanished from my mind when he walked through the bedroom door. Instead of calmly inquiring as to his whereabouts and expressing my distress for his safety, I raged at him.

"Where have you been? I have been sick with worry."

"I told you I was going out," he said, his tone matter of fact. "I have been to a familiar place. You have no cause for concern."

"Oh, I know where you went," I scolded, though I could not bring myself to name it. "How could you do this to me?"

"I have done nothing to you, Ebenezer."

"You betrayed me." I was shouting still, but I could not help it. "You told me everything would be perfect if I came to live with you, yet you continue to be with other men besides me. That is not perfect, Jacob." I did not intend to cry, nor had I consciously allowed it, but the tears flowed nonetheless.

Jacob sat on the edge of the bed and placed his hand on mine.

"Who were you with?" I demanded, pulling my hand from under his. "What did you do?"

He let out a long breath that ended in a groan. "Do not ask me this," he said softly. "You do not want to know. Suffice it to say it was nothing I have not done before."

He was correct. I did not want to know the specifics, so I abandoned that line of questioning and turned to another.

"Why must you seek out others?" I asked, wiping the wetness from my cheek with the sleeve of my nightshirt. Then I asked the question that had lodged itself in my throat. "Am I not enough for you?"

He reached for me, and I did not pull away this time. Cupping my chin, he gave my tired, weepy eyes no choice but to look at him. "You are more than enough for me. I could not ask for a better partner in life, nor could I love any man more than I love you. It is I who am not enough."

He paused, and I sensed the struggle inside him. "I have needs that can only be fulfilled through variety and the excitement of the unknown. It has nothing to do with you. I am flawed, to be sure, but this is part of who I am."

I had no words. I sank into the bed, turned away from him, and pulled the covers over my head. I was incensed, but it was entangled with sorrow and resignation. Jacob had taken pleasure in other—maybe even many—men before me, but I had expected his cravings to disappear after we committed to each other. Unfortunately, despite everything we had together, he needed more than I could provide. I could not deny him what he needed to be happy.

Jacob extinguished the candle and slipped under the blankets. He did not reach for me or kiss me good night but whispered, "I will always come home to you, Ebenezer. I promise. No matter what."

I pretended to sleep, and the next morning pretended it had not happened at all.

This was how we handled all of Jacob's subsequent dalliances. On Saturday nights, he went out and did what he wanted while I stayed home and busied myself with work or lay awake in bed fretting about his safety and the strength of our relationship. In the morning, I would rise before he awoke to attend church and visit my nephew. The next day, we went back to our daily routines, as if the hours between Saturday's supper and Monday morning did not matter.

Jacob restricted his illicit activities to one night each week and kept the details to himself. For my part, I tried not to be hurt by them. He was my everything, even if I could not be his. I had found my home.

CHAPTER THIRTY-SIX

OUTINGS

1835, Eight Years before the Ghosts

Jacob and I went to work each day, to the tavern for our suppers and home again, only to wake up and start over the next morning. We engaged little with society outside of our business obligations. The primary reason for this detachment was that we simply did not have time left for recreation. Fezziwig's Warehouse ran smoothly enough, but it required my daily presence and oversight. Scrooge and Marley's counting house was growing in both volume and profitability, and it took our combined efforts to sustain it. There was no time in the day and precious little energy left within us to participate in nonessential distractions.

Another motive for our hermitage was that we could not act in public the way we did in the privacy of our home. We had to be careful not to stand too close, lest we raise suspicions or provoke gossip about the true nature of our relationship. We could not hold hands or touch one another, aside from the occasional handshake or sturdy pat on the back. Equally dangerous were more subtle expressions, such as sharing a look or a smile that might be interpreted, correctly, as a sign of intimacy.

Outside our home and office, we restricted our conversations to topics of business and politics to avoid being overheard discussing our shared bedroom or any other behavior deemed deviant by the larger society. We chose to spend our precious free time at home rather than under the stifling scrutiny of the outside world.

There were two occasions for which we made exceptions to this policy. The first was a Saturday in November 1835. Jacob had organized the outing, telling me only that we needed to rise early to make it in time and to wear my warmest coat and hat. I did as he instructed, excited to discover what adventure he had planned for us. We took the carriage, though we traveled only a short distance before he announced our arrival at the still-undisclosed destination.

We disembarked, and I followed him through the streets and alleys until we rounded a corner to where a crowd of people were gathered. At seven thirty in the morning, this was a surprising sight indeed. They were a diverse group, young and old, men and women, rich and poor, but all were facing the same direction—toward Newgate Prison—and there for the same reason—to witness the hangings of two men.

I had read a newspaper article about the trial and convictions, but I had not noted the execution date, nor had I any desire to watch it. Why Jacob would choose to do so, I could not understand.

The condemned had not yet emerged from the prison, and the spectators were vying for the best viewing positions. They looked up at the raised platform, moved to one side or the other, a half step backward or two steps to the side, to improve their angle for viewing the gallows. Some pushed their way forward, only to discover their progress hindered by a border of wooden rail around the base of the scaffold, with guards stationed behind it to keep any would-be interlopers at bay.

Jacob led me into the mass of people, stopping near a small group of men. There was something about the way they stood, leaning so their shoulders were touching and tilting their heads toward each other. I recognized two of them immediately, though I had seen them only once before. These were the men from the molly-house, the ones who were married inside the walls of that establishment.

I scanned the crowd again, this time looking at the faces and discerning the different subgroups within it. Some were eager to savor the violence, their voices loud and enthusiastic. I could not comprehend how a hanging was considered a form of entertainment, but it was clear the spectacle fulfilled that need for some.

Others, small groups of men, such as the one Jacob and I were now part of, were there for a different reason. They wore troubled expressions and spoke in whispers, standing closer together than the social norms dictated, though the density of the crowd shielded them from accusing eyes.

I looked to Jacob for reassurance, but he kept his gaze pointed at the tall platform in front of us. Beyond what I had read in the newspaper, which was not much at all, and what Jacob had told me, which was even less, I garnered everything I needed to know by listening to the conversations taking place around me. Two men would be hanged that day for the crime of buggery. John Smith and James Pratt, both in their thirties, had been caught in the act, arrested, and charged for the crime. They had denied their guilt, but the testimony of a landlord and his wife, who had witnessed the unnatural acts through the keyhole of their door, were enough to convict and condemn them to death.

The executioner appeared on the scaffold, drawing hoots from the crowd and sparking a renewed jostling for position, which likely negated their earlier efforts at the same objective. At the eight o'clock hour, the governor of Newgate Prison ascended the stairs to the platform ahead of the two condemned men, flanked by guards.

Their appearance elicited more hollering. "Sodomites!" someone shouted. "Inverts!" said another. These jeers, accompanied by hisses and grumbles, continued unabated. I was struck by how small the men looked standing there on the platform and how haggard, being held upright by the guards as they faced the dangling ropes that would convey their final sentence.

Smith was first to be led to the appropriate spot, where the hangman positioned the noose around his neck and the hood over his head. Pratt wailed throughout the process, dissolving into sobs when it was his turn to be dragged into position. He said, "Oh God," and alternately, "This is horrible. This is indeed horrible."

I had to agree and turned away as the bolt was drawn to release the floor beneath them. I heard them fall, which I thought preferable to watching it, but what I saw instead was probably worse. The faces of the men around us turned to anguish, as the punishment of two men caused the suffering of many more. The couple standing next to us held hands, and others shook their heads, wiping tears from their eyes. Thankfully, everyone else was too engrossed in the macabre scene to notice.

The spectators, who had quieted while the men struggled to die, broke their silence when the jerking of their limbs ceased, and the movement of the ropes slowed to a gentle sway. Instead of hissing and shouting, now they laughed and whistled, celebrating the deaths.

With the bodies still hanging, the crowd started to disperse, boasting as they went about the righteousness of the punishment and the swift delivery of justice. The men in our small group skulked away, their heads lowered and their proximity to each other resuming its proper proportions. Jacob and I did the same.

Such an experience should have left me speechless, but I could not contain my emotions. "Why did you bring me here?" The words came out louder than I had intended, and I realized at the same time as Jacob that I was angry rather than sad.

"I wanted to show my respect," he said. "They are men like us."

"I know. That is precisely why we should not be here." I shook my head. How could a man as intelligent as he was ignore reality in this way? Did he not understand the obvious danger we were in or the need for us to remain hidden? I tried my best to enlighten him. "That could have been us hanging from those ropes. We have to be cautious, Jacob. You, especially."

He stopped then and turned to me, his hands planted firmly on his hips.

"That will never be us." Now he was angry as well. "We are men of standing. We have money enough to hide our actions and repel, if necessary, any attempt to indict us. The gallows are for poor men without the means to bribe a would-be accuser or pay the authorities to look the other way."

I did not possess a fraction of his confidence in our immunity and intended to argue this point, but another thought superseded it.

"Have you ever had to pay someone off?" I asked, holding my breath while awaiting his answer.

"We are perfectly safe, and I will not speak of it further." Jacob turned away from me, but I remained frozen in place, struggling to process his reaction to the morning's events, as well as my own. How could he witness an execution of "men like us" and dismiss the risk we faced? Perhaps wealth and standing could indeed insulate us from punishment, but even if our necks were safe from the hangman's noose, that protection did not extend to our reputations. There was more at stake than Jacob was willing to admit, despite the recently demonstrated proof that terrible consequences could result from our exposure. He doggedly minimized my concerns, and I concluded that my efforts to caution him into restraint were pointless. If a hanging did not deter him, nothing would.

I followed him to the carriage waiting for us a few streets away, and for once, I was glad to ride rather than walk. I was exhausted, though it was still early in the day, and my legs were weak, though I normally had the strength to travel great distances on foot. We rode in silence until the coachman stopped to let me off at Fezziwig's Warehouse. I assumed Jacob would proceed to the counting house, though I did not know for certain, and neither did I ask.

I could not understand his motivation to attend that miserable event, and even less his choice to bring me along with him. The next time he suggested an outing, I would be sure to inquire about the destination before agreeing to join him.

Thankfully, our next excursion was less traumatic.

A posting for the Zoological Gardens' new exhibit had piqued Jacob's interest, and he wanted to go, deeming the prospect of viewing wild animals we had never seen before worth the cost of admission. I agreed with his line of reasoning, including his plan to visit on a Monday when the price was half what it was every other day of the week.

We left Scrooge and Marley's early and made our way to Regent's Park while the afternoon sun was high. The attraction would close at dusk, giving us several hours to enjoy the sights.

London Zoo, as most people called it, had opened seven years before, according to the sign we read by the entrance. Inside the gates, we found a delightful assemblage of structures and a menagerie of creatures. The oval cattle shed was home to all manner of bovine: bison, camels, and zebra among them. The Gothic House was one of the most beautiful buildings I had ever seen, and the llamas in it were curious animals, their constantly chewing jaws moving side to side instead of the usual up and down.

Another impressive feature was a glass building, round and three hundred feet in diameter, occupied by two pairs of lions, as well as tigers, leopards, and hyenas. The smells were the only negative part of the experience, the trapped air in the building making it unpleasant to remain inside for too long.

There were elephants in pens outside, polar bears, and a wedge-tailed eagle, but the newest acquisition was what had driven Jacob's quest. The crowd was thick, but fortunately Jacob and I were tall enough to peer over the others' heads to see the small herd of giraffes, which were similarly blessed with height. We gawked at the creatures before moving on to the rhinoceros exhibit. I was in awe of its rarity, as well as its titanic cost. The Zoological Society had paid over £1,000 to acquire it.

The gardens themselves were worthy of note, with trees and flowers of all kinds, including an ominous-looking cactus that only grew in the hottest, driest places on earth. A full 2,447 ornamental plants thrived in the gardens' soils. Jacob chuckled at my retention of this bit of information, but this was normal for me, as numbers were what I understood best.

The architecture, the animals, the flora, and yes, even the statistics of the place fascinated me. Jacob smiled widely throughout our visit, his eyes conveying the innocent wonder of a child, and there was a liveliness in his step that had been absent for some time. When dusk arrived, we reluctantly left the zoo. It had been a satisfying and enjoyable day, my favorite outing with my love.

CHAPTER THIRTY-SEVEN

CONSEQUENCES

1836, Seven Years before the Ghosts

My nephew outgrew the practice of racing back and forth between trees, and I had to find new ways to entertain him. We visited shops and fairs and walked in the park, just as I had with his mother. Freddie reminded me so much of Fan, especially when I looked into his gray-blue eyes and could pretend for a moment that she was still with me. He had grown so tall he would have towered over her by now, and he was as clever as his mother had been at that age, excelling under the tutors I provided.

My nephew was perceptive in a way I was not. He had the ability to read people, understanding their emotions through their facial expressions and guessing their motivations after hearing them speak only a few words. This trait was thanks to his mother.

From his father, Freddie inherited a laissez-faire attitude. He did what he wanted without regard for the long-term implications of his actions, without knowing what he might do with a prize once he took it. His path seemed perilous to me, and I urged him to consider all possible consequences before taking an action he could not rescind. I hoped my influence would prevent him from replicating his father's poor business practices, which featured ill-advised ventures driven by instinct instead of logic.

I was devoted to the boy, regardless of his father's attributes and his growing propensity for rash decision-making. I loved him despite it and because of it. I loved him as if he were my own son, which made what happened that summer day all the more unbearable.

My nephew and I returned from an afternoon at the fair to find Samuel waiting for us on the porch. When Freddie saw him, his smile fell away, and he bid me farewell, stomping past his father into the house without a word of greeting. It was normal for a boy of Freddie's age to be in a state of contention with his parent, though I would speak to him about the importance of respect for his elders when I saw him the next Sunday. For now, he had taken his leave, and I was forced to engage with Samuel.

I ascended the porch stairs and shook his hand.

"Good afternoon, brother," he said.

My jaw tightened at those words. Samuel only called me "brother" when he wanted something, and I braced for the request I knew would come next.

"I have a business proposition for you."

There it was, just as I had suspected. For a moment, I was proud of myself for having insight enough to predict it, but the satisfaction was fleeting, and dread replaced it. He did not invite me to sit down, and I was glad for it, for Fan and I had sat on that porch more times than I could count, back in the days when we talked and laughed together for hours, back when my sister was my best friend. Though I had reached the point in my mourning where those memories brought comfort rather than sadness, I did not want them tainted by Samuel's forthcoming appeal.

He started on a lengthy explanation of a business prospect with a guaranteed return on investment. It had to do with a ship and its cargo of valuable goods, but I did not pay attention to the details, focusing instead on which words I would use to turn him down. This was an "excellent opportunity," he assured me, "one of a kind," and it would earn us both significant rewards. All he needed to secure the deal was money from me—a large sum of it.

When he finished, I told him, "I must decline. I am not interested in any new business ventures at this time."

"But you cannot let this pass you by. Take my word for it, brother, this one is going to make us a fortune."

He had said this before, and I had always given in, providing partial, if not all, of the funding he requested. Without exception, all the promising deals he proposed turned into failures. He continued to drone on about how this wager was different from the others, while I nodded and feigned interest. His persistence, despite my clear rejection of his offer, was insulting. I had enjoyed my day with Freddie, and he was ruining it with this annoying plea for charity, disguised as an investment opportunity. My face burned and my breath quickened as the indignance rose to the surface. Had I not done enough for him over the years? Would I allow him to take advantage of me again and again? I thought not.

"Humbug," I said, interrupting him before he recited another meaningless assurance. "The answer is no, Samuel. I will not invest in any more of your schemes. You have already taken enough of my hard-earned money."

His deference turned to rage in an instant.

"You have plenty to spare. Do not pretend you are penniless." He glared at me, his neck turning a deep, splotchy red. "If you do not wish to build your own fortune, then consider it a loan to me, and I will repay you when the goods are sold."

"But you won't," I said, "as you have not repaid any of the previous ones. This venture will fail as all of them have, leaving you bankrupt once again. As it is, I pay for Freddie's tutors."

"That is your choice. I never asked for it, did I?"

"You did not," I conceded, though he might have expressed some gratitude nonetheless.

His reddened face wrinkled with anger. "But I *am* asking you now. I will make this investment whether you choose to support me or not. Will you force me to mortgage my house to do it, when you could simply loan me the money instead?"

I was reaching a state of ferocity I had experienced only once before, in boarding school when I had defended my friend against his attackers. This time, I was protecting my nephew, and I was ready to strike. I shouted back at him. "Smarten up, Samuel, and stop squandering your money. Honestly, you have no business sense at all. Think about Freddie's future and what will become of him if you lose everything. I forbid you to leverage this house to pursue another imbecilic venture."

"You forbid me? What a ridiculous notion," he said with a nasty chuckle. I detected something new in his expression now, something more than anger—malice, maybe. Regardless of the vehemence of his protests, I refused to enable his foolishness any longer. I turned and descended the stairs.

"It is I who forbid you." He spoke to my back, but his voice reached my ears well enough. "Frederick is my son, and I can no longer ignore your depravity or allow your immoral influence."

His words stopped me in my tracks before my feet touched the sidewalk.

"My depravity?" I spun around and started back up the steps. My heart lodged in my throat, restricting the flow of air to my lungs.

"You think I do not know? Then you are a fool, Ebenezer Scrooge." He spat the words at me. "You and your business partner. What is his name? Marley. That's it. Your perversion sickens me."

My anger drained away and was instantly replaced by earth-shattering, breath-stealing panic. I shook my head. "It is not . . . we do not . . ."

"Denying it is pointless," Samuel said. "Your sister told me something of it when she was alive, and I have spoken about you with the bankers in the city. You share a residence with this Marley of yours, do you not?"

"It saves us money," I countered. "And we maintain separate quarters within the house." Our campaign to spread a justification for our arrangement was supposed to have prevented such allegations. How could this be happening?

"That is what I call 'humbug,'" he continued. "You are a sodomite. There is no doubt about it. Until now, I have looked the other way because of our relation, but since you see fit to insult me on my own porch, I will tolerate you no longer."

The volume of his voice ensured his words were traveling farther than my own ears. I had to stop him, lest the neighbors or passersby overhear. My reputation and my very life were at stake. My response was no more than a whisper. "What will you do?"

"I will report you to the authorities. It is my duty as a God-fearing man."

"And if I give you the money you ask for?" I said, acknowledging that he held all the power in this situation. My only choice was to submit to his extortion.

"In that case, I will reconsider." A grin akin to that of the devil himself spread across his face. "Out of respect for my late wife, of course, and with your gift an indication of your commitment to improving your moral character, I will protect your secret."

My head heavy with the burden of submission and my voice betraying the severity of the wound to my soul, I agreed. What choice did I have?

His lip curled up to one side, revealing a predator tooth. "I will not report your crimes, but I cannot allow you to corrupt my Frederick. I denounce you, Scrooge. You are no longer a member of my family, no longer an uncle to my son."

"Do not do this, Samuel, please," I begged. "Think of Freddie for once. He enjoys the time we spend together each week. He will be devastated if you steal our connection away from him."

"I am thinking of him," he insisted. "I am protecting his immortal soul. This is not my doing but yours. Remember that. It is your sinfulness that necessitated this action. Under penalty of exposure, you shall not see the boy again."

A sob escaped my throat, and my shoulders curled as if I had been struck in the stomach. My reaction had no impact on Samuel as he was motivated by revenge and bent on destruction. I had no choice but to surrender.

Freddie emerged from the house then. His sudden appearance, unpreceded by the sound of footsteps on the stairs, meant he had been listening to every word of our conversation from a perch on the other side of the door.

He flung his arms around me, but he spoke to his father.

"You will not take him from me," he said. "I am alone here when you are away, and his visits are the one thing I have to look forward to. Uncle Scrooge is the only person who truly loves me."

"That is not true," Samuel said, though his tone lacked conviction, at least to my ears.

"It is true," Freddie said. "If you forbid him to see me, then I will run away. You won't even miss me because you are never here. I will take my things and go live with him instead."

"You will do nothing of the sort." Samuel's face turned the same crimson shade as before. Freddie squeezed me tighter, but it was to no avail. "You will never see your uncle again. Not as long as I am alive. The warning I gave him applies to you as well. Should you defy me, he will pay the price. He will be arrested and hanged, and it will be your fault."

"No."

"Yes."

"Enough!" I had to stop this vicious exchange before it inflicted further trauma on my nephew, who was sobbing and distraught.

I hunched over and spoke softly, only to him. "Hush, my dear boy," I said, struggling to keep my voice steady. "You will be all right. Continue to be the fine person I know you are and live a good life. Your mother wanted more than anything for you to be happy, so you must do that in remembrance of her. Promise me, Freddie."

His father did not give him the opportunity to do so. "Leave now," he told me, taking Freddie's arm and pulling him away from me with increasingly forceful tugs.

"Don't leave me, Uncle," Freddie begged, further tightening his grip.

My heart broke to be the cause of his pain. Leaving him was the last thing I wanted to do, but I had no other choice. There was no use prolonging his misery since the end result would be the same, and I could no longer hold my own tears at bay.

"We must say goodbye now," I said, pushing him gently away while his father jerked roughly from the other side. "Remember I love you always, Freddie. Be well."

I walked away then, down the porch stairs and onto the street, farther from my sister's precious child with every step.

"Do not forget my words, Scrooge," Samuel called after me, turning the knife he had plunged into my stomach. I could never forget them.

I sent him the money he demanded and continued to pay the salaries of Freddie's tutors and caregivers. Samuel continued to passively accept my financial support while failing to acknowledge it. The gleaming hypocrisy of his stance could blind any observer. In his eyes a sodomite's influence and companionship were unacceptable, but his money was welcome.

Samuel did mortgage the house in subsequent years, confirming my prediction that his wealth would steadily disappear into the void of his poor business choices. He did not inform me of this development, nor did he come to me for the loan. Jacob learned of it through conversations with the owner of another counting house. I bought Samuel's mortgage debt, a fact of which he was not informed. That way, when he defaulted, which he would eventually do, I could ensure my nephew was not turned out on the streets. I refused to allow Freddie to suffer as the result of his father's idiocy.

It was torturous to be in the same city as my nephew but unable to spend time with him. His father had forbidden us to see each other, but he said nothing of other forms of communication. So I wrote to Freddie, and he wrote back, and we maintained our relationship via letters, the way his mother and I had when I was away at boarding school. For Fan and me, our father was the cause of our separation, and it was the same for Freddie. Letters were an inadequate substitute for being in each other's company, but it was better than having no contact at all.

On Sundays, when I would have visited him, I sat at my desk on the third floor and wrote to him instead. I told him about my work, describing in detail my methods for assessing risks at Scrooge and Marley and the strategies I used for managing my employees at the warehouse. I hoped to provide insights he could draw upon when he became a businessman himself. The one subject I did not broach was Jacob. Freddie had heard his father's accusations, but he never asked me about them, and I interpreted his silence on the subject to mean he did not wish to discuss it.

I received a return letter from Freddie every week, and I tore open the envelope promptly upon its arrival, devouring the words over again whenever I needed to lift my spirits. My nephew was becoming a talented writer, and his descriptive and entertaining stories were so vivid that I felt I was watching him grow up through my mind's eye. He reported achievements in his studies and how he was excelling in Latin and literature. Arithmetic was not his favorite subject, and he struggled to grasp the more advanced concepts, but he persevered.

I wished for the chance to tutor him myself, certain I could have instilled in him the same affinity for numbers I had learned at his age. He missed my weekly visits and was lonely in the house with only the servants to keep him company. This confession widened the chasm in my chest, but I urged him to be strong and assured him he was loved beyond what words could describe.

Though Samuel had stripped me of the privilege to spend time with my nephew, it was still in my power to alleviate his loneliness, or at least distract him from it. Since I was paying for his education, I instructed his tutors to include outings as part of his studies—to bookstores to enhance his exploration of literature, on nature walks as part of the science curriculum, and to lectures and organized sporting events.

Freddie found success in a variety of athletic pursuits, being far more coordinated and agile than his awkward uncle ever was. He practiced a new sport, which I had not heard of before. It was similar to football, though it involved carrying the object rather than kicking it, and quite a bit more physical contact than I preferred. I watched a match one day—not Freddie's team, of course, since I could not risk having either him or his father see me there. The level of physicality bordered on outright violence, and the possibility of Freddie being seriously injured during this dangerous game added one more worry to the many that plagued me. In my next letter, I cautioned him to be careful and reminded him how valued he was.

Before my expulsion from my nephew's life, I had lectured Freddie about the importance of considering the repercussions of his actions. I should have heeded my own advice. The choice to love Jacob, however happy it made me, resulted in estrangement from Freddie, my only living relative and the last connection I had to my sister. The pain of it added weight to my already-burdened shoulders, but it did not crush me. My life was hollow without my precious nephew, but Jacob gave me a reason to live.

CHAPTER THIRTY-EIGHT

SLOWING

1836, Seven Years before the Ghosts

My sister was gone and my nephew beyond my reach, but I still had Jacob, and I thanked God for him every morning when I awoke and again before I went to sleep at night. We started reading together in the evenings, cuddling in our bed with candles on both side tables providing enough light for us to see. I read aloud most of the time, as Jacob preferred, though I was not sure if it was because he enjoyed hearing my voice, or if it was vanity, since he now needed spectacles to see the text.

I had dabbled in Greek literature when I was younger, but Jacob and I delved deeper. We found in the ancient prose instances of romantic love between men, which were sometimes subtle and other times overt. This was particularly true of Plato's work.

In one piece, Socrates and young Phaedrus sit together under a chaste tree that suppresses carnal desires, but even under the tree's quelling influence, their conversations are rife with sexual innuendos. Socrates notes a bulge under Phaedrus's cloak and asks him what he is hiding there, and the boy delays his departure from the spot because it is "straight-up, as they say." I stopped reading at this point, and Jacob and I looked at each other in wide-eyed disbelief at the audacity of the prose. "Carry on, then," he told me, and I did, grateful for the dimness of the candlelight to hide the flush in my cheeks.

Plato's *Symposium* portrayed love between men as a normal, if forbidden, facet of society. In it, a group at a banquet engage in a contest of speeches and, with food and liquor lessening their inhibitions, tell outrageous stories. One is of the origin of humans, where every person was once a four-legged creature until Zeus cut them in two. Searching to be whole, each half tries to reunite with its mate, but it is more complicated than one might think. Men whose original form was androgynous seek out their womanly half and become lovers of women. Those who were double men in their four-legged state direct their affections solely at other men, and they are the most masculine of all.

These stories served as an aphrodisiac for Jacob, stirring his cravings for physical intimacy. They stimulated me as well, but more importantly, they confirmed what I had long suspected—that our generation of men was not the first to harbor romantic inclinations for members of our own sex. Men like us had existed for centuries before, maybe millennia. If our sexual preferences were unnatural, then why had they persisted for so long? Why would God create men this way only to scorn and punish them for the desires he himself placed within?

The writings of Plutarch, the procurement of which required a monthslong search of booksellers' collections throughout the city, provided the most stunning revelations for me. They did the same for Jacob as well, or so he said, though he preferred Plato's erotic passages to Plutarch's historical accounts. We were inspired by the triumphs of the Sacred Band of Thebes, the elite troop of Theban warriors in the fourth century BC. It was composed exclusively of male lovers, 150 pairs to be exact, who fought bravely in numerous battles, including the one that ended Spartan rule. The superiority of the force was evidence that masculine love was not unmanly or dishonorable, that those who practiced it could be virtuous and strong.

The stories gave me hope that I might be a good and righteous man in God's eyes, as well as my own. They soothed the persistent self-loathing that had taken root in childhood and remained, despite my choice to embrace my true self and live with the man I loved.

I was doubtful they did as much for Jacob since he did not grapple with the immorality of our relationship the way I did. Though I could not peer into his soul, he seemed unbothered by the ethical quandaries our lifestyle presented and the negative judgments of others.

Jacob's immunity from moral dilemmas extended beyond his sexual proclivities to everyday life and our business dealings. Where I was inclined to give people the benefit of doubt, Jacob assumed the worst. Where I apologized for an accidental collision with a person on the street, he immediately and vociferously assigned blame to the other. Where I expressed pity for the poor, he had disdain.

It assuaged me to believe that our differing views balanced each other, making us ideal business partners and helping us achieve success. This might have been true at times, but Jacob's personality was stronger, and it overpowered mine. His wrath was often unprovoked, his spitefulness unwarranted, and his cruelty excessive. It was the sole source of conflict between us as we grew older.

On one occasion, a blacksmith stood before us, his face stained at the edges with soot from his work, his wife beside him. He had completed the loan application to the best of his ability, which, based on the grammar and penmanship, was not extensive. Still, he had made a concerted effort and had a solid reputation as a trustworthy and skilled craftsman.

He had fallen ill and been forced to shutter his shop for the winter, during which both of his children had died, and his wife, having to care for them, had lost her own job laundering clothes. They had used their savings during those months without income and were in debt to their landlord and others. The blacksmith was back to work now, and business was steady, but he needed money to resolve his debts and bring his shop to full productivity. He required a small loan, and the repayment schedule would span only a year or two. I thought it a reasonable venture, but

Jacob did not agree.

"Bah." The abruptness of his outburst startled me, and the young couple standing before us reacted similarly, their eyes opened wide and lips pressed shut. "You are a failure," Jacob said. "Inadequate as a craftsman, father, and husband as well. Why should I help you?"

The man pushed his shoulders back and, letting go of his wife's hand, replied in a steady tone, devoid of anger but rife with shame. "I aren't asking for charity, sir. I'll pay ye back in full. My work is good, and my shop was busy before. Sickness was the reason for my failure. It wasn't my choosing."

I thought the man's argument a strong one, but Jacob shook his head. "But you see, it was not beyond your control. Every one of your past decisions brought you to this place, teetering on the edge of poverty. It is not my responsibility to rescue you or subsidize your foolish choices with money I earned making sound ones. You must pick yourself up by your bootstraps with your very own hands."

"Please, sir," the woman started, but her husband placed a hand on her arm, and she fell silent.

It was too late. Jacob turned on her next.

"Your pleas, dear woman, do not find compassion in my ears. Your children's deaths are the result of their parents' failures. And, I see you are with child again."

This was a detail I had not noticed, though the evidence was there in the bulge of her stomach and the way she rested her hand atop it.

Jacob held back nothing of his contempt. "You choose to bring more children into this world you cannot afford to feed and clothe. These filthy wretches, if they are lucky enough to survive, will be burdens on society."

The woman cried openly, and it was all I could do to prevent my own sympathetic tears from falling along with hers. I wished I could reach out and lay my hand on Jacob's arm to silence him, the way the blacksmith had done with his wife. Alas, we were too far away from each other, seated in our respective desks with the width of the room between us.

Jacob continued his attack on the innocent couple. "You have chosen your lot in life, and now you must endure it. It is not the obligation of an honorable man like myself to enable you. The answer to your loan request is an unequivocal no. Please leave."

The man put an arm around his wife, her tears completing their journey down her face and dropping, one by one, on the floor of our purportedly respectable business. The blacksmith did not rail against Jacob or argue his point further. Rather, he swallowed down the humiliation and anger he must have felt and maintained his composure. The two silently left the counting house, and I never saw them again.

After the door slammed shut, I turned to Jacob, who was staring at me with a defiance that made me shiver.

He spoke first. "Do not give me grief about this, Ebenezer. You know I am right."

Though I knew my disapproval would change nothing, I felt compelled to speak out. "I do not agree with your assessment, but that is a matter of opinion, one we should have discussed before you made a final determination. What I object to is your treatment of those people. You humiliated that man in front of his wife and spoke callously of his children's deaths. It was beyond cruel, and you know it."

"I was being honest," he said. "Giving them a loan is too great a risk, and I will not apologize for executing a sound business decision."

Growing frustrated, I tried again to explain. "Even if their application was substandard, even if it revealed an unacceptable risk of default, they did not deserve to be treated with contempt. Everyone, no matter their station in life, deserves a modicum of respect. I insist that those who come into this office be addressed with proper deference, that their basic dignity be acknowledged."

Jacob never apologized, nor did he express an ounce of regret for his malicious behavior. Rather, he justified it as "for their own good and for ours" and insisted the government already had protections in place for people like them in union workhouses and, if those failed, prisons. Our charity was unnecessary.

The blacksmith and his wife had paid the price for Jacob's sour mood. It was unfair, but I could do nothing except communicate my sincere disapproval.

Jacob's ill temper showed itself with increasing frequency as the years passed. I intervened when I could, but my words did nothing to quell his outright disdain for the poor or mitigate his nastiness toward them. From an off-putting comment to a beggar on the street to his spitefulness in denying loans based on his judgments about their life choices and his refusal to pay a halfpenny more than he deemed an item to be worth, he grew more miserly and cantankerous with each passing day.

We curtailed our already limited social activities, trading dinners at the tavern for meals cooked and served by the servants. We retired to our bedroom early most nights, and Jacob stayed home with me on Saturdays rather than going out to meet other men.

Six days a week, I worked at Fezziwig's Warehouse for several hours before joining him at Scrooge and Marley. Jacob started sleeping late, instead of going to the counting house when I left in the morning. Sometimes I beat him there, having already put in a half day of work, and he strolled in at lunchtime, complaining of fatigue.

He was aging, and it was happening quicker than I had imagined it could. One minute, he was svelte, and the next his middle section was round and protruding. His salt-and-pepper hair became more salt than pepper, and he lost his breath after walking a short distance on a flat course. He had to stop and rest more than once as he ascended the stairs to the upper floors of our home.

I compensated for Jacob's absenteeism by working longer and harder myself, and I handled his irritability with as much patience as I could muster. He grew fatter and crankier still, but I did not complain. He was mine, and I would pay any price for the privilege of living with him as partners, lovers, and friends.

CHAPTER THIRTY-NINE

ENDURE

1850

I am on my knees, clinging to the phantom's heavy robes as I face down another of my life's tragic losses. I could spare myself the agony of remembering what came next in the sordid chronicle of my life if I concede to his directive and take my place among the dead.

How much torment can one man endure?

The question is moot. I survived it once, and I will do so again—to memorialize my beloved and the life we shared.

CHAPTER FORTY

NO REPRIEVE

1836, Seven Years before the Ghosts

I was not ready. Not for the holiday, not for the long list of errands awaiting me, and not for the tragedy unfolding without my noticing it. Unfortunately, being unprepared for something did not prevent it from happening.

Jacob relaxed into his chair in our living room while I fluttered from one task to the next.

"Take a break, Ebenezer," he said. "Have a drink with me. It is Christmas Eve, for God's sake."

I had so many gifts yet to wrap and decorations to hang. I insisted that we celebrate the holiday fully, every aspect of it, a goal that required both preparation and commitment to accomplish. The house needed to be decorated in a way that reflected my joy at spending Christmas with Jacob.

"That is why I have to finish this tonight," I explained. "I want to be ready to go first thing in the morning, so I can make my deliveries early and devote the rest of the day to you."

I set a pot of kernels on the fire and dropped to the floor to continue wrapping the gifts, exasperated at the size of the pile in front of me, which had not diminished significantly, despite my concerted, though admittedly inept, efforts.

Jacob grunted, rubbing his temples. It was the first time all evening that he did not have a drink in his hand. "My head hurts, and watching you is making me tired. Why don't you just stop?"

I glared at him with a mixture of resentment and annoyance. Since I had never been skilled at masking my emotions, I was sure my expression revealed the breadth of them. Before I said anything, a burning smell reached my nose, and a second later it registered in my mind. I had forgotten the corn! I jumped to my feet and ran to the fireplace, where the pot sat unshaken, smoke emanating from the partially opened lid. On top of everything else I had left to do, now I would have to begin the process again. We had to have stringed popcorn to decorate our evergreen tree—the necessity of this festive tradition was nonnegotiable.

"You could help me." I fumed along with the pot. "Instead of sitting there doing nothing, as usual." It was not like me to lash out at him this way, but I was overwhelmed with the many tasks before me and frustrated by my incompetence at completing them.

I disposed of the burned corn and returned to find Jacob leaning forward in his chair, his head in his hands. Regretting my sternness with him, especially on Christmas Eve, I placed a hand on his shoulder and squeezed. "I am sorry. I did not mean it."

He grunted and lifted his head, though the movement was slow, as if the effort to accomplish it was substantial. His eyes were watering, and his whole face was flushed, not just his cheeks. He must have had more wine than I thought.

"I am sorry too," he said. "I wish I could help you, but my head is pounding."

I smiled down at him, and he grinned back at me, his discomfort clear in the pronounced crease between his eyes. One side of his mouth drooped a bit lower than the other, a sheepish plea for my forgiveness. I could never remain angry at him for long, and this was no exception. "You have had too much to drink, that is all," I told him. "Let's get you to bed, and I will finish everything myself."

I helped Jacob up the stairs. It was a process, I thought, which he treated far more melodramatically than was necessary. He requested several breaks along the way, during which he rubbed his temples to ease his throbbing head. His complexion was deep red by the time we reached the bedroom, and I settled him into bed.

I should have comforted him more, but I was intent on returning to the tasks awaiting me, and instead, I pressed a wet cloth to his head, securing it with a clumsily tied bandage. He thanked me for my efforts, saying the coolness made him feel better, and assured me he would be completely recovered by Christmas morning.

I kissed him on the forehead and left him to sleep off what I thought were the effects of an excess of liquor. After quietly shutting the door behind me, I rushed downstairs and back to the living room, which was a mess of sloppily wrapped gifts and a pile of boxes awaiting the same fate. I stopped in the doorway and sighed, but I set to work, as I always did, and finished the task before the candles extinguished themselves.

I slept for a few hours beside Jacob and arose early the next morning. I moved about as quietly as possible while readying myself for the day, so as not to wake him. When I returned, I hoped he would be well rested, cheery, and eager to celebrate the holiday.

Bundled in my coat, hat, and scarf, I lifted the satchel of packages over my shoulder and tucked a larger item under my arm before setting out on my Christmas errands. My first stop was my late sister's home, where I left Freddie's gifts on the porch. In our correspondences, my nephew had mentioned watching other boys race on snow sleds down a nearby hill and wished he could join in the fun. His gift was a sled made of wood and shiny metal, which I had adorned with the nicest bow I could concoct out of packaging materials from the warehouse. As I leaned the sled against the house, I said a silent prayer that he would not hurt himself while using it. Beside it, I left another package, this one wrapped in paper and tied with string. On the tag, I had written, "Open sesame." Now my nephew could read about Ali Baba's adventures with his own copy of the book.

I did not sign my name to the tags. Freddie would know they were from me, and his father could pretend they were not. I touched the door before leaving, indulging a momentary pang of sorrow for my little sister. I did not linger, however, as I had more stops left to make before I could go home to Jacob.

My load lightened by my first delivery, I slung the bag over my shoulder and continued on. The Fezziwig home was next. Every year since Mr. Fezziwig had died, I brought his widow a gift on Christmas morning. It was the least I could do for the man who had set me on the path to financial success. I knocked on the door and handed Mrs. Fezziwig the gift—scented soaps I had purchased from a shop in Covent Garden. As always, I accepted her thanks but not her invitation to come in, wished her a merry Christmas, and went on my way.

I crossed back over London Bridge and headed to the two orphanages I supported, leaving at each a large box of hard candies to satisfy the children's hunger and thick socks in an assortment of sizes to keep them warm. By this time, I was tired, having walked several miles already, and grateful to finally sit down for the service at Saint Michael's Cornhill, resting my tired back against the pew. I went home as soon as I and the rest of my fellow worshippers filed out of the church. Clouds covered the sun and a jolting, frigid wind stung my skin, but the weather did not dampen my spirits. It was Christmas Day after all.

Glancing at Mansion House as I passed, I imagined the cooks, butlers, and maids—some said there were fifty or more—preparing an extravagant feast. I did not envy the mayor, though, as my destination was grander than his, the home I shared with my love. I could not wait to give Jacob his gift and start our day of celebration. I did not know what I had done to deserve this happy life, but I was undoubtedly blessed.

"Merry Christmas!" I called out when I entered the house, slamming the door shut behind me to seal out the cold. I had expected to be met with a cheerful greeting from one of the servants or from Jacob himself, but silence was my only welcome. The chandelier was not lit either, though on a dark day such as this, it should have been. I hung up my coat and peeked into the drawing room, where we enjoyed our cocktails in the evenings, but no one was there. Switching direction, I passed through the parlor and dining room to the living room, where the evergreen tree I had decorated with baubles and a popped corn garland stood companionless.

Jacob's absence was disconcerting, but I surmised that he was still suffering the aftereffects of the alcohol he had consumed the night before and was waiting until I returned to muster the energy to rise from bed. The servants' disappearance was a more serious concern, as they had neglected their duties entirely. They were not in the kitchen, where they should have been busy preparing our Christmas feast, and the fireplaces were cold, the cinders remaining as a relic from the previous night's fires.

Where was everyone? My mind clamored for an explanation. Perhaps Jacob had given the servants leave for the holiday, though it would have been the first time he had done so, and I thought it unlikely. The possibility of violent intruders entering the house came to the forefront of my thoughts, sparking panic within me, and I raced to the foyer and bounded up the stairs.

Our bedroom door was open, and it was as quiet and dark inside as it was in the rest of the house.

"Jacob, are you still sleeping?" I went to the windows and spread the drapes apart. The sunlight, diffused by the thickness of the clouds, gave the room a ghostly glow, but it was illumination enough for me to realize there was something amiss.

The bed-curtains were missing. I could not make any logical sense of this fact. Was I in the wrong house? No. The rooms downstairs held our furniture, not someone else's. This was our house, and this was our bedroom. The bed-curtains had been there when I left that morning. I was certain of it. And Jacob had been sleeping soundly, snuggled beneath our blankets.

What blankets? Those, too, were gone. I blinked hard, but when I opened my eyes again, they did not reappear. What was this trickery? No bed-curtains, no warm quilt, but the bed itself was not empty. There was a lump of a familiar size and shape, covered by a sheet. It was deathly still.

I inched closer, the contours becoming clearer with each step. The shoulders were the highest part, but the bulge of the middle section vied for the honor. At the other end, the legs, skinny by comparison, were stacked one atop the other, crossed over at the knees. The sheet covered everything except the tuft of hair visible at the top. I lifted the thin shroud to confirm the identity of the form.

It was my beloved Jacob. And he was dead. I knew this in the way one accepted a fact in a textbook. His eyes were closed, and the expression on his pallid face was tranquil. His hair stuck out in all directions in a way he never would have allowed while he was alive, and I smoothed it down as best I could.

I pulled the sheet back further to find him still dressed in the dressing gown I had helped him into the night before. There was no sign of trauma, so I shrouded him again, making sure to cover his head, and left him there alone.

I felt nothing—no emotion, no pain. The beating of my heart was fast but inefficient, and my breaths reached only a superficial depth, as if my body was fighting to keep reality from entering. In a daze, I roamed through the house, checking every room on the second floor but finding nothing out of place. Holding the railing, I ascended the stairs to the third level, where the files from our business and our desks sat, the same as always. The condition of the servants' quarters on the top floor offered the first clue. The rooms had been emptied of their clothing, candles, and personal items. Even the bedsheets and blankets were gone.

I knew then what had happened.

Jacob had passed on to the next world. Perhaps it was while I slept beside him during the night, or this morning while I was delivering gifts or praying in the church pew. The timing mattered not. He was dead nonetheless.

Unfortunately, I had not been the first to know it, as that gruesome discovery had fallen to his servants. I envisioned the events as they might have proceeded. The housemaid had knocked on the bedroom door to deliver Jacob's breakfast, perhaps cursing him under her breath for failing to give her even an hour of leave to celebrate the holiday. When no answer came, she had let herself in and found him silent and still. The other servants rushed in when they heard her screams, or else she summoned them to come see for themselves. Together, they had devised a plan that was both heartless and macabre and enacted it straightaway.

They had capitalized on Jacob's death and the opportunity my absence provided to steal from us. Rather than summon the coroner or send the coachman to fetch me, they had ignored Jacob's lifeless body and embarked upon the vilest of missions, taking advantage of our tragedy to line their pockets—and likely bags, boxes, and whatever else they could easily assemble—with the loot of our belongings.

I explored the house again, but instead of looking for people, this time I searched for missing items. Sadly, there were many. Not only had they taken the bed-curtains and blankets from our bed and theirs, but they had also pilfered two seals from our desks and the pewter pencil case Jacob had given me for my birthday. His dresser drawers were open, their contents rifled through. I did not know what he kept there, but I guessed it had contained items of some worth: cufflinks, buttons, and watches.

They would have found no such valuables in my armoire, though the prospect that they had gone through my nightstand hit me with the force of a blow, and I rushed across the room to inspect the top drawer. To my immense relief, the stack of letters from my sister was undisturbed, still bound in its red satin ribbon. I released the terror in a long sigh and held my hand to my chest to calm the frantic beating of my heart.

Some of Jacob's clothes were missing, as were several pairs of his shoes and my only pair of boots besides the ones currently on my feet. The silverware and crystal stored in the dining room, I assumed, were among the most sought-after items, but I cared little about those things. I was more concerned about the objects with sentimental value—the gifts we had given each other and trinkets that inspired memories of happy times.

Jacob had compensated his household staff fairly for both their work and their discretion, but this precarious arrangement had given them the opportunity to enrich themselves through our betrayal. It also left me without the means to seek justice. I could not report their crimes because they would report mine in return. Their offense was simple theft, which could result in imprisonment or restitution, but mine was moral depravity, which carried punishments far worse in severity.

I would have to shoulder the truth of their treachery in silence and find a way to continue on in spite of it. There would be no recourse for me and no justice for Jacob.

I collapsed onto the bed beside my beloved, placed my hand on his sheet-covered arm, and allowed the grief to engulf me. My heartbreak was not pure but tinged with rage and resentment that blackened my soul. I seethed against the miscreants who had preyed upon my partner as he lay defenseless and exposed. Like vultures tearing into a carcass, they had circled his body, pinching and prodding before flitting away with pieces of him in their talons. At this very moment, the scavengers were probably selling their spoils to a pawnbroker in some filthy alley reeking of misery and malevolence. The scene played out in my mind with more details added each time it repeated. They were bartering for more money and arguing about the value of this item or that, caring nothing for the man from whom they had pilfered it and neither for the man left to mourn him.

The bile in my stomach churned, but I swallowed it down.

I hated those traitors, but I reserved some of my contempt for Jacob himself. He had brought this tragedy upon us by causing his own premature death. While he had once been particular about his appearance and taken care to stay healthy and spry, in recent years, he had surrendered to age and sloth. By neglecting his health, by drinking too much and eating too much and loafing about, he had shortened his life one imprudent choice at a time.

I had moved into Jacob's house just three short years before he abandoned me with an early death. Our time together was brief, and it was his fault it ended so soon after we had finally found happiness. Now, I was alone—and I detested him for it.

More than Jacob, more than the servants even, I leveled hatred at myself, for I bore the blame for countless oversights and mistakes. The first was my failure to recognize the gravity of my partner's overall state of health and the severity of his recent symptoms. I had ignored his headache, the redness of his face, and his labored breathing. I had put him to bed so I could selfishly tend to my own interests. I should have called the doctor, should have insisted he take better care of himself all along. His death was as much my fault as it was his.

What haunted me more than my negligence, however, was the dire and chronic miscalculation of my priorities. The night Jacob died, or the morning, whichever it was, I had chosen to devote myself to activities that did not involve him. Those tasks—the gift giving and decorating and even my churchgoing—to which I had assigned such importance before, meant nothing now. I had allocated hours to charitable causes at the expense of time spent with him, had snapped at him and accused him of sloth when all he wanted was my attention. He had died alone while I was engaging in frivolous tasks.

I should have been lying beside him as he left this world, loving him the way he deserved. I had been on a fool's errand, delivering donations to the poor, while Jacob's body was being desecrated and our possessions looted.

I arrived at the simple, undeniable conclusion that I had made the wrong choices.

This had been a failure of mine long before that Christmas, long before Jacob's death. For years, I had maintained a platonic relationship with him, more concerned about my principles than my feelings and his. I had held myself back from physical intimacy, kept him an arm's length away when I should have been holding him close to my breast. I had treated him as a mere business partner and friend, when I should have invited him into my heart.

True fulfillment came only when I had allowed him to take me as his own, but it was a triumph much delayed due to my cowardice. We could have had more happy years together, if only I had not been such a fool.

There was not enough generosity within me to forgive myself. Jacob was gone forever, and there was nothing I could do to recapture the time I had wasted. The rage inside me grew by the minute, bubbling and frothing and burrowing its way deeper until it settled into the very core of my being.

I chose anger over grief. I embraced bitterness rather than contend with the overwhelming nature of my loss. Doing so denied me the opportunity to heal and Jacob the honor of being properly mourned. There could be no comfort for me, no forgiveness, and no reprieve.

CHAPTER FORTY-ONE

EMPTY

1837, Six Years before the Ghosts

I passed the days after Jacob's death in a state best described as semi-consciousness. The sounds of the world were muffled in my ears, my vision clouded at the edges. My mind bore the worst of this numbing condition, and I went about the business of life with a tenuous grasp on reality.

I called the undertaker to take him, since I had no one to help me lay his body out for viewing, as I had done for Mr. Fezziwig and my sister. I dressed him in a suit before he was carted away and purchased a coffin to hold him. My most important responsibility, beyond the funeral arrangements, was to announce his death to those who knew him. Regretfully, I did not do a thorough, or even adequate, job of it. The efforts I made were at best half-hearted and at worst utterly negligent.

At Fezziwig's Warehouse, I did not say a word. Jacob had rarely visited, and I presumed our employees were not likely to miss him. They were decent people, to be sure, and I had no doubt they would have been generous and sincere in acknowledging my loss, but I did not give them the opportunity.

In truth, I did not want others to share in my grief. It was mine alone to bear. Moreover, it was dangerous for me to do so since the breadth of it might reveal the intimacy of our relationship. I might lose control of my emotions, might cry or sob or wail while accepting their expressions of sympathy. Perilously close to doing just that every second of the day, I did not trust myself to effectively hide my love for Jacob, so I suppressed my sorrow and avoided the danger altogether by simply neglecting to tell people he was gone.

I did not tell our clients at Scrooge and Marley either. We served as moneylenders on one end and collectors on the other, and such positions did not engender meaningful connections. As to the businessmen Jacob had greeted on the street, I did not know their names, nor whether they would appreciate receiving news of his passing. If anyone noticed his absence, they did not say so.

I thought about telling the men at the molly-house, but I did not. Sending a messenger to deliver a funeral invitation was impossible because the back part of the building was not supposed to exist. I should have gone there and delivered the news personally, but I could not bring myself to do so. Who would I tell anyway? I did not know the identities of the men Jacob had fraternized with, or if they even knew his. Perhaps no one would care.

There was only one person I told, as I felt it my duty to do so. To his wife, I wrote, "Jacob is dead." That was all. If she wanted to mourn him, I at least gave her the opportunity.

The morning of the funeral, I roamed aimlessly around the house, finding myself in the living room, where the evergreen tree sat, still adorned with the garland I had placed on it so late on Christmas Eve. Now it was dry as tinder, its fallen brown needles forming a halo on the floor around it. I did not care. It brought me no joy, and I loathed the prospect of removing it. To do so would require me to attend to the package sitting beneath it—Jacob's gift, which I had devoted considerable effort to procuring. He would never open it, and I would never see his smile, never revel in his surprise or accept his gratitude for my thoughtfulness.

I stared down at the present, inexpertly wrapped with newsprint and twine and covered with a layer of fallen needles. I knelt and tore the paper gently, reluctantly, a little at a time, as if drawing out the process could delay its finality. It took only a few movements to reveal the item it contained.

The brass grip of the cane I had commissioned for him sat atop a shaft of hand-carved walnut wood. I allowed myself a moment to admire its quality and the craftsmanship that had gone into its manufacture. The fact that Jacob would never use it sent a painful spasm through my chest, but I caught my breath and rose to my feet. I had no choice but to endure, as this was my lot in life, but I would take this treasure with me wherever I went from that point on.

As the sole mourner at Jacob's funeral, I sat alone in the empty church, staring at the casket in the middle of the aisle, and walked unaccompanied in the procession to the graveyard. I was the only witness as they lowered his body into the ground.

I felt more alone—nay, I was more alone—than I had ever been. As a child, deserted at boarding school during the holidays, I had known my sister loved and supported me, and I was bolstered by her devotion. When Mr. Fezziwig had passed away, Fan had been there to bring me back to life, and when poor Fan died as well, I still had Jacob and Freddie. Now, I was forbidden to see my nephew, and Jacob was gone forever. There was no one to mourn with me, no one to console me in my grief.

After the funeral, I went home and slept fitfully in an empty bed.

CHAPTER FORTY-TWO

OUR BED

1850

I am crying, though no tears wet my cheeks, as there is not enough liquid left in my body to produce them. Weak whimpering sounds are the whole of what I can accomplish as mourning for the loss of my love. As much as I try, my eyes will not open, though I am still alive, still lying here in my bed.

It was our bed once—Jacob's and mine—but only for a time cut brutally short by tragedy. Still, the knowledge that I will die in the same bed as he did brings me consolation.

The phantom is resigned, as I am, to complete this journey of remembrance. I need not beg for his leniency any longer.

Jacob's death was not the end of my story. There was more to come after I lost him, experiences that spanned the spectrum of emotions, from fulfillment to frustration, from contentment to fear, from joy to heartbreak. Nothing could ever be worse than that which I already experienced. With this simple truth as my buttress, my silent companion and I retreat once again to the past.

CHAPTER FORTY-THREE
ACCIDENT

1837, Six Years before the Ghosts

My life continued without Jacob. At times I was not certain how I managed it, and at others I did not want to, but I had no choice in the matter. I replaced the stolen blankets and bed-curtains with substitutes inferior in quality to the originals, but I did not light the fireplaces to warm the house. I preferred the discomfort of the cold to the emptiness that would take its place in its absence.

Work was all that was left to distract me from the agony of my losses. With no joy in my heart, I spent the mornings at Fezziwig's Warehouse and headed to the counting house at midday to do the job of two men in the afternoon.

The trek between businesses each day became a chore rather than the respite it had once been. With the knowledge that Jacob would not be there waiting for me, my perceptions muddied, and the negative aspects of every experience displaced the positive. The sights, sounds, and smells I encountered, which I had formerly considered part of London's charm, became intolerable. Filth soiled my shoes, and smoke from the chimney tops mixed with various foul odors, making my eyes water and my chest heave as the air burned its way from my nose to my lungs. Even in pleasant weather, the streets reeked of the waste of livestock and people. Passing by Leadenhall Market on hot days was the worst, and I pushed my way through, dodging sheep and oxen who unknowingly trudged toward their grisly fates, past people of all shapes, sizes, colors, and creeds.

Their endless numbers and diversity confounded me. Women and children walked alongside businessmen like myself, surrounded by merchants and hawkers and accosted by pickpockets, vagabonds, and prostitutes. They talked and gestured and moved about in maddening chaos, all rushing to reach some destination, clamoring to satisfy their own disparate needs. I acknowledged no one, shutting myself off from the possibility of human connection.

The only thing that sparked emotion in me, that I looked forward to each day, was rounding the final corner of my trip and catching sight of the sign hanging from the building, the carved letters reading "Scrooge and Marley." For a fraction of a second, I allowed myself to believe Jacob was still alive, that we would spend the afternoon at our desks, working together until we tired and returned to our shared home. It was a small deception, and only fleetingly effective, but it provided me a brief moment of comfort before I saw his empty chair and was forced to acknowledge the truth.

With my eyes pointed perpetually downward, I walked with the cane that was meant to be Jacob's Christmas gift. I did not need it, of course, as my legs were sufficiently strong to propel me despite the weakness of my spirit, but I carried it with me nonetheless as a reminder of him, leaning on it as I went to make my attachment to it more convincing.

I dreaded the prospect of engaging in the courtesies society demanded. I spoke to no one, nor did they speak to me—not the businessmen who had once greeted Jacob amiably and not the ladies shopping for food and fabrics, not even the merchants or beggars. I might have had cause to be insulted by this, except that I actively discouraged any attempts they made to engage with me, my expression and behavior conveying clearly the message of my disinterest.

When I neared a group of bankers gathered at the corner, I turned my face sharply away. If a beggar, newly recruited to the profession, approached me, I sneered at him, using the deep-seated rage conveyed in my wild blue eyes to repel him, a strategy I had learned when I saved my friend at boarding school. To anyone senseless enough to ignore my overt warnings and offer a smile or jovial "good day," I replied with a gruff and succinct "bah."

Unfortunately, my efforts to discourage interactions were not effective when it came to certain elements of the population bent on harassing the innocent. One afternoon, a Cornhill boy accosted me in one of the many alleyways I traversed on my way to the counting house. He stood in my path, stance wide and arms crossed.

"Where you goin', old man?"

"Keep your distance," I said, turning left and then right to discover there were more of them encircling me. I was trapped.

"Why should we?"

They laughed in unison, a menacing sound that reverberated off the walls of the buildings and continued through me, causing my heart to beat violently in my chest. I sensed instead of saw them move a half step closer. They were closing in.

Instead of freezing in place as helpless prey, I reacted with force in defense of myself. Raising my cane above my head, I yelled, "Leave me alone."

"What? You gonna kiss us?" A boy behind me spoke this time, and I spun around to face him. What kind of taunt was this? Why in God's name would I kiss them?

"Bugger," he jeered.

Suddenly, I understood.

I had assumed the boys' intention was to hassle me, since I had a well-established reputation as a cantankerous old man. These were the sort of adolescents who derived pleasure from such degeneracy. This boy's accusation was evidence that I had severely miscalculated their motives, which were more sinister and dangerous. They were not harassing a random old man but rather mustering a targeted, righteous attack against a deviant. They were confronting me because of who I was, but how could they know? I thought I had hidden it so well. Was it my mannerisms that gave me away? When I was a child, my father had beseeched me to clench my hands by my sides when I spoke and keep my gestures understated. Perhaps I had not been as successful as I thought in projecting my masculinity.

"Invert," said one boy. "Disgusting," said another. They laughed in unison once again.

The image of men like me hanging from the gallows flashed through my mind, and my eyes darted back and forth between their threatening faces. This time, I witnessed the predators circle closer. I peered past them toward the end of the alley, to the well-traveled street beyond, hoping a fellow pedestrian would notice my predicament and intervene to save me. Without exception, the passersby kept their heads lowered against the rain, their belongings stashed under their arms, and their chins tucked into their coats. They hurried along, unaware of the attack happening a few yards away, or else ignoring it.

No one was coming to my aid, and I was desperate to escape. I swung the cane like an axe as I pivoted side to side, until it found its mark on the shoulder of one of the boys. He cried out in pain, but I did not let my sympathy for him deter me from further action. I was fighting for my life. I struck out at them again, this time whirling my weapon horizontally. My attackers backed up to avoid it, and the circle around me widened.

I lunged toward the one who seemed to be the leader of the pack and saw genuine fear in his eyes. He took a halting step backward and slipped on the wet cobblestones. On hands and knees, he scrambled away, while the others hollered, "Let's get out of here. Run!"

This advice was equally applicable to me, and I took off in the opposite direction. Focused only on escape, I darted into the street, pushing people aside to clear my path. I glanced over my shoulder to confirm they were not in pursuit and ran straight into someone. Propelled by the inertia of my frenzied retreat, the force of the collision sent them violently to the ground, and the full weight of my body landed on top. The heap beneath me released a screech of shock mixed with pain, and I rolled off.

To my horror, sprawled in the mud beside me, lay a woman, her chest rising and falling at a disconcerting pace and her hands clutching her bulging belly. In my scramble to flee, I had razed and crushed a pregnant lady.

I pleaded for her to speak to me. She moaned but did not heed my request. Raindrops fell in steady streams, and she squeezed her eyes shut against the flood. People were gathering around us now. Apparently, the sight of a man leaning over a woman's body was cause enough to justify the discomfort of extended exposure to the frigid rain.

One such bystander, an elderly, well-dressed woman, shooed me away and bent over the victim, issuing the same command as I had moments before. She must have achieved more compliance than I did because her next words were a reassuring, "Good, good. That's it." At least a dozen people gathered around them, blocking my view. I was unable to assess the damage for myself and powerless to offer assistance.

The impact had caused the woman to lose hold of her packages, and they were strewn across the street. I fetched them and tethered them together as best I could. The injured woman was standing now, and I offered the parcels to one of the ladies attending to her.

"Here are her things," I said. "Is she all right?"

"No thanks to you, beast." The old woman pointed a scraggy finger at me. "Get out of here before I call the constable."

I had forgotten the danger I was in, but this new threat brought the panic rushing back. The boys who had attacked me were nowhere in sight and would likely remain so, since the last thing they would want was to be caught up in a gathering of concerned adults. The imminent risk of violence was gone, but the underlying reason for their attack replaced it as an equally dangerous outcome. I thought it prudent for me to leave before the authorities arrived and started asking questions.

I slithered away from the scene of the accident, exhausted and defeated, and walked home in the driving rain. Unsteady on my feet, I leaned on Jacob's cane for support. Once home, I bolted the door behind me, placed my dripping coat on the rack, and went directly upstairs. With an empty stomach and a freshly wounded soul, I collapsed into bed. I left the shabby bed-curtains open and lay atop the blankets to spend the night sleepless, shivering, and alone.

CHAPTER FORTY-FOUR

RESPONSIBILITY

1839, Four Years before the Ghosts

My behavior on the street that day earned me a reputation. Evidently, defending myself against a group of attackers before running away and knocking over a pregnant woman qualified me as violent and mad. No one bothered me after that, and I went about my daily travels with a degree of immunity that insulated me from future threats.

It was not that I became invisible but quite the opposite. Whereas I had once been the one to step out of the way and avert my eyes, now others avoided me. My eyes were most often pointed toward the ground, so I saw their feet stop as I approached and then sidestep to give me a wide berth. On the occasion that I lifted my gaze, it was they who turned away. This by-product of my unfortunate encounter relieved me of any responsibility to acknowledge people I had no desire to engage with anyway.

It was by chance and several years later that I discovered the unintended consequences of my actions. A crowd was gathered not far from the place where the incident had occurred, impeding my progress toward the counting house. I found myself trapped in a mass of people pushing one another and craning their necks to get a better view of whatever spectacle was playing out in front of them. Being taller than almost everyone else, I could see well enough. A body lay in the street, that of a vagrant, I concluded, since the feet were bare and the clothing tattered. He had been trampled by a lone horseman who had sped by at a reckless pace and continued on after his victim was felled.

Wedged between two ladies who were intent to carry on a conversation despite the impediment my body created, I could not help but overhear.

"The poor soul," one said, shaking her head.

"Reminds me of that woman a few years ago. Remember?" prompted the other. "The one mowed over by some brute. He knocked her flat on her back, and she was heavy with child. Can you imagine?"

"Some rich banker did it, or so I heard. Thinks he's better than us regular folk." They simultaneously shook their heads and clucked their tongues in disgust.

I cringed. I did not consider myself a brute, nor did I think I was superior to anyone else, but their story sounded remarkably similar to the accident in which I had been involved.

"The monster didn't have the decency to see if she was all right. Just continued on his merry way like nothing happened."

This part of the narrative did not resemble mine. I had stopped to inquire about the woman's welfare. I had even picked up her packages but was shooed away by ladies just like the two of them. Still, how many pregnant women were knocked to the ground by a banker in this very spot? It could not be a common occurrence. In fact, I knew of only the one in which I was the assailant. As much as I loathed to admit it, I was the brute to which they were referring.

They continued their back-and-forth exchange, speaking across my chest. "Her child was born sick, you know. I heard he was deformed, his legs warped and twisted."

A third woman joined in the discussion. "The family is destitute. Can't even afford a doctor. Such a shame."

"It's sickening." All three agreed wholeheartedly on this point.

I needed to learn the truth of the matter, despite my reluctance to engage with them.

"What is the woman's name?" I asked. "Where can I find her?"

One of the ladies, though not the one to whom I had addressed the question, sighed, exasperated at the apparent rudeness of my interruption. They were the ones whose manners needed improvement, in my opinion, chattering about another's misfortune from either side of an unwilling bystander. She did not ignore me, however, her affinity for gossip rendering her unable to stop herself from providing the information I requested.

"The family lives in Camden Town. I know that. But their name . . . ugh. I can't think of it." She tapped the jowls hanging on both sides of her face, as if the movement might dislodge the answer from the confines of her mouth. "It starts with a *c*, I think, but it was different, not Cooke or Clark." She leaned forward to look past my chest at her friend. "Do you remember?"

This lady sucked in air through her teeth. The tactic proved more helpful than the face tapping because a moment later she exclaimed, "I do. It's Cratchit. The woman's name is Emily Cratchit."

I nodded, and the ladies returned to their chattering. When the body was removed, the crowd resolved its own logjam, and movement on the street resumed. I ambled along with the herd of people, but my mind was absorbed with concern for the woman who had suffered as a result of my negligence. I needed to know whether the stories about her disabled child were true, and the first step in my plan was to find the Cratchits.

CHAPTER FORTY-FIVE
THE CRATCHITS

1839, Four Years before the Ghosts

With only the family name and a vastly exaggerated story of a pregnant woman injured by a brutish rich man to guide my search, it was surprisingly easy to locate the Cratchit family. It required two conversations with strangers and one small payment to an individual who was otherwise disinclined to share his insights with me, but I managed to glean the location of their home and some basic information.

The woman, Emily Cratchit, had indeed borne a child in the weeks after our violent, though accidental, encounter on the street. By all accounts, the boy was lame in some way, though the extent of the damage was unclear. The matter was made worse by the fact that the head of the household was unemployed and thus unable to support the child and his siblings.

I made my way down the steep slope of Cornhill to Cheapside and proceeded northwest until I reached Camden Town. The family's home on Bayham Street was nearly identical to the ones surrounding it, small and dilapidated. I did not intend to reveal myself, at least not until I discerned whether Emily Cratchit was the same woman I had run into several years before.

Endeavoring to be discreet, I hid behind a hovel at the top of a hill to watch the goings-on. The man of the house was nowhere to be seen, but the woman emerged right away, a basket of clothing propped on her hip. She dropped the heavy load and arched her back before bending to pick it up again and carried it the remaining distance to the drying line. I peered around the corner of the unsteady building I was using as cover, squinting to improve my vision.

This was an unnecessary exercise, an effort to forestall the inevitable, because by now I already knew the truth. I recognized her immediately, despite the brevity of our initial meeting. She was the woman I had knocked to the ground.

With this piece of the puzzle confirmed, my next objective was to see for myself the extent of the damage I had caused to her child. I did not have to wait long. As soon as the woman reached up to start hanging the laundered clothes, a parade of children came pouring out of the house, which was surely too tiny to hold them all. They commenced playing in the small patch of dirt that constituted the entirety of their plot, using sticks to draw on the soft ground and pretend sword fight, the same makeshift toy serving multiple purposes. They looked healthy enough to me, their raucous voices evidence of adequate breathing capacity, and their antics proof of their vigor. Not one was feeble or lame, and the weight of guilt upon my shoulders lightened.

The child I was searching for appeared next, however, and my temporary relief was promptly replaced with shame. A rickety wheelbarrow emerged from the house, pushed by the largest of the children I had seen thus far. The driver was a girl of nine or ten years, the occupant a much smaller boy who flailed his arms as the conveyance jostled him over the bumpy ground. The boy's top half looked to be intact, with no obvious deformities, but his legs were hidden inside the cart.

Perhaps the rumors of his lameness were untrue. Perhaps he rode in the wheelbarrow for fun rather than out of necessity. I would have to get closer to find out. Though I much preferred to remain at a distance, I left my hiding spot and walked down the hill toward the rowdy group. When the woman saw me, she froze. Whether she recognized me, or she was shocked by the appearance of a stranger dressed in business attire, I did not know. Either way, she dropped the pair of breeches she was holding and shouted for the children to go inside.

I shook my head, not out of disgust for her but for myself. I should have thought this through more carefully. My stealthy approach had frightened her and created additional hardship, for she would have to rewash the breeches, which were now lying in the dirt. The last thing I had meant was to add angst to her already arduous life. Her brood heeded the order immediately, dropping their sticks, running inside, and slamming the door shut behind them. Now the subject of my investigation was holed up with his siblings, shielded from my prying eyes.

The woman squared her shoulders in a way I had only seen men do before and planted her hands on her hips. There was no way to avoid a confrontation, so I mustered my courage and meager charm to introduce myself. She did the same, though I already knew her name. Her face was smooth and symmetrical, but her eyes were hard and her skin tone dull. Aside from the flatness of her belly, she looked the same as she had the first time I had seen her, lying in the street with her eyes squeezed shut against the rain.

"Do you remember me?"

"I certainly do," she said, her frowning face as steady as her stance.

"I wanted to ask . . . to see about the child." I stumbled over the words, not knowing which ones might soften the bluntness of my questioning and the callousness of waiting so long to do so, but I had to continue. "To see about his welfare. The child you were carrying when we . . . when we met."

"You mean when you struck me and left me breathless and broken on the street? That child?" She stared into my eyes, and the hatred emanating from her seeped into my soul.

"Yes," I replied, melting under the crushing force of her accusatory stare. Emily Cratchit was a formidable woman, and I lacked the skills necessary to defend myself against such a creature. "Tell me, is he sick? Is he lame? I have heard varying accounts and do not know which to believe."

"I had no idea I was the subject of an inquiry," she said, taking a small step toward me. I resisted the urge to move in the opposite direction. "Allow me to confirm the rumors. The child you speak of is indeed ill. His legs are unable to support his weight, and he has awful pains in his back. He is a beautiful boy, though, my sweet Timothy. He does not deserve to suffer this way."

Turning my eyes downward, I asked a question to which I did not want to know the answer. "Was our encounter the cause?"

She sighed, and though my eyes were focused on the ground in front of her feet, I saw her hands drop to her sides. "I have no way of knowing for certain. He was born not a week after 'our encounter,' as you call it. None of my other children have similar afflictions, so I assume you knocking me down and landing on top of me caused trauma to him."

I nodded. No longer able to ignore the consequences of my actions, I had to do right by this child. "Where is your husband?" I asked, taking the first step toward negotiating the details of how I would accomplish this.

"Bob is out looking for work," she said. "He has been at it for several months, and every day he comes home with no prospects and no money. By now, he must have visited every one of the businesses and warehouses in London."

I had heard of no such visitor to my own establishments; neither had I entertained a loan application from a man by that name. Perhaps Bob Cratchit was only half-heartedly pursuing employment, choosing to spend his time and what little money his family had at the pub or brothel. I hoped this was not the case, that this woman and her children were not reliant on a man prone to poor decisions and shirking of his responsibilities.

How on earth were they surviving with no income? I glanced around, this time seeing the situation under a new light. Emily Cratchit was the sole provider for the family, responsible to care for the children, maintain the household, and earn the money. She was juggling all these tasks at once and managing to hold everything together, albeit under the most tenuous of circumstances. The laundry she washed and hung to dry was not her own but someone else's. With the pittance she earned, the family was on the brink of starvation and homelessness. There was no way they could afford adequate medical care for the injured child.

An idea entered my mind, and I blurted it out at a volume louder than I had intended. "I will give you money." This was a viable solution for the predicament I was in, a way to make up for the suffering I had caused. "I am a business owner. I can do that at least. How much will do? One hundred pounds, maybe a bit more?" I was talking to myself now, more than to her. "That should provide food and medicine for the boy. That will fulfill my obligation."

Her eyes flitted side to side, up at me, and down again as she considered the merits of my proposal.

"No. That will not do at all," she said with a resolute shaking of her head. "Do not misinterpret, though. I am not absolving you of responsibility. You have a duty to compensate us for the harm you caused, and I am not above accepting charity when my children's lives are at stake. But a lump sum payment for the one child will only be a temporary fix. It will be gone in no time, either to repay our debts or to fund whatever it is my husband does all day."

She shifted her weight from one foot to the other, as if marching would help her think. It must have worked because her next idea was a brilliant one.

"You are a business owner, correct? You could hire my husband to work for you and pay him a reasonable wage, which will support all of the children. I will consider that fair compensation."

It was a better arrangement for the family, I conceded, as it had the benefit of ensuring the child would be provided for in the long term. I agreed to do precisely as she suggested, and we strategized about how she would convince her husband to inquire about the job. I could not understand why it would take any persuasion, since he had a family to feed and no income with which to do it, but she explained he was a carefree sort who did not take initiative on his own. She would tell him she had overheard talk about a position, and he should report to Scrooge and Marley's counting house that very afternoon. For my part, I would hire Bob Cratchit on the spot and provide a week's pay in advance to seal the deal.

With the plan in place, I wished her a good day with a tip of my hat. The very moment I did so, the children came running out of the house and resumed their raucous play. They surrounded me and made a game of racing to me, touching my leg, and rushing away again, giggling all the while. I lingered a bit longer than necessary, enjoying their infectious frivolity. Despite the seriousness of the contract to which I had agreed, I was content to know that I would not only be fulfilling my obligation but also improving the lives of the lot of them.

And there were a lot of them—six in all. I heard their shouted names that day and would eventually learn their places in the family. Martha was the eldest, and then Belinda. Peter, the oldest boy, thought himself the boss and heir to the family's nonexistent fortune, and the two smaller ones, twins, were Adelia and Fletcher. The youngest, my ward now, was a boy who would have been strong and healthy if not for me. They called him Tiny Tim.

CHAPTER FORTY-SIX

VIGIL

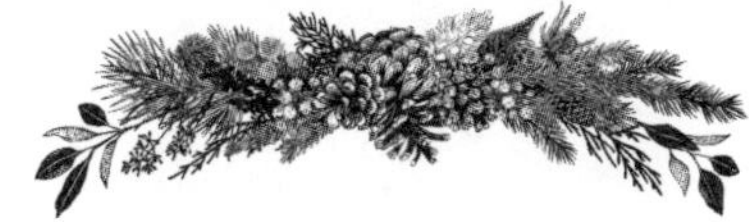

1850

The presence maintaining vigil at my deathbed is a comfort, but uncertainty and fears rise to the surface, nonetheless. Despite my best intentions, am I leaving this world a worse place than I found it? Did the ghosts' Christmas Eve revelations and the changes I implemented afterward come too late? Have I done enough to save myself from eternal punishment, or am I destined to suffer in limbo as Jacob does?

I wasted precious time hiding when I should have opened my heart to love and be loved in return. Because of my trepidation, I had only a few short years of a fulfilling life with Jacob. After his death, I squandered more opportunities for happiness, drowning in my heartache and closing myself off to those I cared about, whose lives I might have enriched. I should have been laughing and rejoicing and yes, even loving.

We mortals must not wait to start experiencing and giving joy. We must vanquish the insecurities that stand in the way of contentment and manage the grief caused by tragedies we have no power to prevent. We must accept with grace the burdens that fall upon our shoulders and not be crushed beneath them. The only way to truly survive loss is to persevere against the darkness.

I struggle to communicate this hard-earned wisdom to the devoted person at my bedside, but my efforts are frustratingly inadequate. My voice vibrates in my throat, but my lips do not cooperate to form the words, and the sounds I am straining to produce are merely moans.

I am grateful when my mouth is pressed open and a pungent liquid trickles in. I swallow purposefully, knowing this medicine will subdue the pain. It eases me back to where the phantom awaits, and I grip his outstretched hand.

CHAPTER FORTY-SEVEN

MISERLY BENEFACTOR

1841, Two Years before the Ghosts

Bob Cratchit was wholly unqualified to hold the position of clerk in a counting house. That much was clear from our first meeting. His employment at Scrooge and Marley was charity, pure and simple. Bob was a "good man," as people often said, who loved his children and did his level best. Unfortunately for him, for his family, and for me as well, his best was insufficient to meet their needs. His penmanship was atrocious, and his mathematical skills nonexistent. I concocted busywork for him, copying letters and such, which I most often threw into the charcoal stove at the end of each day, since they were more valuable as kindling than documentation.

He was late for work almost every day, a fact of which he thought I was unaware because I spent the morning hours at the warehouse. I did not cite him for his tardiness, however, deeming it a savings on my part because it meant I had less paper with his illegible scribblings on it to discard at the end of the day.

Though Jacob's desk sat empty beside mine, I could not bear to have another man sit in it, so I arranged a workspace for Bob in the tiny room where we had once stored our files. He complained about the accommodations at every opportunity. In summer, he moaned about the heat and lack of airflow, and in winter, he grumbled about the chill. There was nothing I could do about the high temperatures, but I thought the cold might be beneficial for his body and mind, as it had always been for me. Regrettably, I did not always treat him with respect, but I found it nearly impossible to do so considering his utter incompetence.

I wished I could have hired his wife as my employee instead. It was evident to me, and I suspected to anyone who knew the couple, that Emily was the cornerstone of the Cratchit family. She was superior to her husband in terms of intelligence, judgment, and every other asset necessary for success.

She never told Bob about the negotiation we had in front of their home, and she kept the subsequent ones secret as well.

Our second meeting came two years after the first—that is, if one did not consider our collision on the street a proper introduction, which I did not. This time, she came to me. She arrived at Fezziwig's Warehouse dressed in the same twice-turned gown she wore every day, though it was adorned with an excess of ribbons. The laborers ushered her into my office, but she refused to sit and did not remove her shawl or bonnet for the duration of her visit.

"I need more money," she said. "What Bob brings home is not enough to support me and the children. It is certainly not sufficient to hire a doctor for Timothy."

"But I pay him fifteen shillings a week," I said, "which is more than fair, considering . . . well, everything." I did not provide details about what I meant by "everything," but her nod made me think she understood my meaning exactly.

"I am not referring to what you give him," she explained, "though I thought it was much less than fifteen shillings." She shook her head and muttered under her breath words that, if I heard them correctly—and I hoped I did not—were not those of the Christian woman she purported to be.

"I am talking about the amount he gives to me," she continued. "You must understand Bob has not the mind for numbers and spends money we do not have to spare. At the end of each week, he comes home with sweets for the children and ribbons for me. He thinks it a kindness, but it would be better to spend those shillings on food and shoes instead."

I wondered how this intelligent woman had found herself married to such a foolish man as Bob Cratchit. Perhaps this was the plight of all women, but it was especially true for the poor who were forced to rely on men, no matter how inept, to provide for them. My knowledge of women in general, and of poor ones in particular, was minimal, a fact I demonstrated fully in my next question.

"Why do you have so many children when you cannot afford them? Having fewer mouths to feed would surely make your situation less precarious."

She pursed her lips. "There is not much I can do about that, is there?" Her tone seethed with contempt, which was well deserved.

Abandoning that ill-advised line of questioning, I steered the conversation toward a new path.

"I can increase Bob's pay," I offered, "though I fear the same problem will result."

"I thought of that, of course," she said, and I was not at all surprised to hear it. "You must give the money to me directly, so he cannot squander it. He will surely notice the additional funds, so we must have a way to explain it."

I thought she was giving Bob too much credit, but I judiciously kept that opinion to myself. Emily had already worked out the details of her plan. She would take in my laundry, as she did for others to supplement the family's meager resources. She would send her son Peter to my home each week to pick up my soiled linens and back again the next day to return them and collect payment. The amount represented a higher rate than was standard for such a service, but I agreed to the arrangement. She could have asked for more, and though I would not have been forced by either law or obligation to give it, I would have done so anyway.

Emily approached me on one other occasion. This time it was to provide for Tiny Tim directly, for treatment of the ailment I had caused, and so it was my moral duty to honor her request. A physician who serviced the poor in Camden Town had recommended leg braces for the boy, which were expensive by anyone's measure and surely beyond the capacity of the Cratchits to afford. I readily gave her the money to purchase them and prayed the devices would improve the boy's mobility.

Payments to the Cratchits were a manageable expense, but they were one of many obligations, both small and considerable, that together constituted a rather large burden.

For one, there was Mrs. Fezziwig, whose husband had taught me every skill essential to success and had been my mentor and the fatherly influence I had sorely needed. I was indebted to him and felt a responsibility to ensure the continued welfare of his family.

When he was alive, he had drawn a salary from the warehouse and took half the proceeds, with an equal share going to Jacob as partner. Upon Mr. Fezziwig's death, I was granted one-quarter ownership of the company, which meant his wife would receive one quarter of the profits and zero salary compensation—far less than when he was alive. The legal agreement had been based on the supposition that she would not live much beyond her husband, and her daughter would benefit from my position as a spouse. The theory turned out to be a faulty one because Mrs. Fezziwig remained very much alive and active in society two decades after his death, and her daughter was married to someone else.

The allotment was not enough to support her, as she had become accustomed to the lifestyle of a prominent family and enjoyed the amenities afforded by their relative wealth. She needed less, presumably, since she no longer had to provide for her youngest daughter. Still, if Mrs. Fezziwig's past behaviors were a reliable predictor of future ones, she would also be supplementing whatever Belle desired and her husband could not or would not provide.

Each month I made a deposit to the Fezziwig account in the amount of one-half the warehouse profits, though she was only entitled to one quarter. Since Jacob had been co-owner of the warehouse, his estate received the other half. Even Bob Cratchit could have done that calculation in his head—50 percent to Mrs. Fezziwig, plus 50 percent to Jacob's estate left zero for me. I ran the business, spending five mornings there every week, but I took no salary.

I did not know whether Mrs. Fezziwig was aware that she was receiving a greater portion than she was entitled. I was doing it out of respect for Mr. Fezziwig and in his honor, so acknowledgment of my generosity was not required.

It was out of respect for another deceased loved one that I continued to support my sweet nephew. His father, Samuel, had not asked for another "investment" from me, which was perhaps the first time he had honored a promise. I, in turn, remained at a distance as per my end of the bargain, but when Freddie had written to tell me his father was sending him to boarding school, I refused to stand by and do nothing. I would not allow my sister's child to suffer as I had, to be sent away from all he knew and made to feel abandoned and alone. Despite Samuel's threat to report my illegal romantic behaviors, I arrived at his front door unannounced and knocked forcefully upon it. He did not seem surprised by my appearance, and after a negotiation unfairly weighted in his favor, I agreed to pay for additional private tutors and the housemaid's salary so Freddie could receive his education in his own home.

My nephew's well-being was a burden I was content to bear, but there was another for which I was less enthusiastic. After Jacob's death, I discovered he had kept little in terms of savings. He carried no outstanding debt, but he had been living at the very edge of his means. The costs of maintaining his house were enormous, not the least of which was the small fortune in salaries he had paid the servants to keep the inside spotless and the gardens outside properly tended. Then there were the horses, the coach house to shelter them, and the groomsmen to keep both in working order.

In his will, Jacob had granted me ownership of the house, which I was grateful for since I did not want to live anywhere but in the place we had been happiest together. However, the benefit of that comfort came with the burden of those overhead expenses, which even after the servants had betrayed us and left their employment were substantial.

His wife, Rebecca, had conceded any stake she had in the house, but she insisted I continue to provide the stipend Jacob had promised her. How she had negotiated this arrangement was beyond my understanding, and I realized I was once again dealing with a woman more worldly and clever than I. The allowance was a generous sum, certainly more than one person required to maintain a comfortable lifestyle. In fact, it was many times more than the entire Cratchit family subsisted on. I supposed she, like Mrs. Fezziwig, had become accustomed to a lifestyle that entailed far more than was needed simply to survive. Rebecca shared her home with her servant, or friend, or perhaps something more significant, so the money likely supported that woman as well.

Jacob's portion of the warehouse and counting house profits, plus his other investments, which had become fewer and less diverse over the years before his death, covered the house expenses and the monthly payment to Rebecca, but only barely. This left half of the counting house income to cover my own obligations, including Freddie's care.

As I figured it, I was supporting thirteen people in all. Rebecca and her partner; Freddie and, at least partially, his father; Mrs. Fezziwig; and all eight of the Cratchits. It was fourteen if I included myself in the count, but there was little left over for me.

To fulfill my myriad financial commitments, I suppressed my own wants and poured every bit of my strength and energy into the pursuit of work. I streamlined the operations of the warehouse, letting go one employee and forcing the others to assume greater workloads. At Scrooge and Marley, I was stringent in evaluating loan applications and foreclosed on delinquent debts with a ruthlessness that would have made Jacob proud. I detested using these harsh tactics, but the way I saw it, I had no choice.

Some people accused me of being stingy—"miserly," I heard whispered between those I passed on the street. But necessity made me so. They could have called me "benefactor" instead, though people tended to be less generous with praise than they were with criticism. These two traits were rarely combined to describe one individual, but in my case, my proper title should have been "miserly benefactor."

CHAPTER FORTY-EIGHT

INESCAPABLE

1850

The dogged inevitability of death is undeniable, despite my efforts to delay it. It is cholera for me, but for others it was something different. For Fan, it was consumption, and for Jacob, it was a sudden end, the cause of which remains a mystery.

My ordeal continues under the phantom's patient supervision, though I am lucky to have devoted and caring attendants at my bedside. They encourage me to drink tonics to counteract the loss of fluids and wash my body and bed to keep me clean. When the spasms take hold, they whisper words of comfort in my ear, swab my forehead, and knead the muscles of my cramping legs.

The worst of it is over now, I think. I am too weak to move, my breaths so quick and shallow that the air does not reach the full depth of my lungs. I linger still, though my willingness to succumb grows with the passage of each memory.

CHAPTER FORTY-NINE
CHURCH BELLS

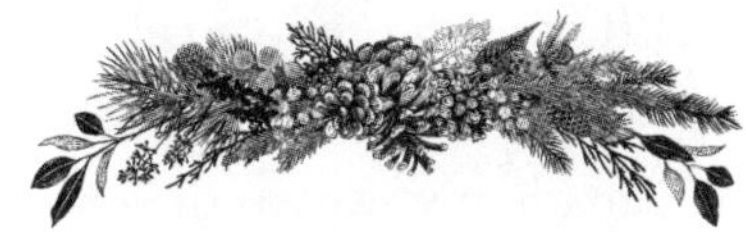

1843, Nine Months before the Ghosts

The wedding invitation arrived by courier. It was written by a young woman's hand, a conclusion I made based on the delicate penmanship and flourishes on the starting letters of each sentence. Freddie followed up with an appeal of his own, which he embedded within one of his regular correspondences.

"Please come, Uncle," he wrote. "It is important to me that you are part of this day. You will be my mother's only representative."

His plea filled my chest with a mixture of emotions, ranging from grief at my sister's absence to pride in my nephew's fortitude, and my shoulders curved inward to contain them. I swallowed hard to keep the sob from rising in full force. Yes. I would stand in my sister's place at Freddie's wedding, since he and I were all who were left to remember her.

My attendance would not indicate my approval of it, however, since

I thought it a most imprudent decision for him to marry at the age of twenty-two. He should wait until his late twenties at least, when he had a steady job and money in reserve. I told him as much in my reply, acknowledging the intensity of his feelings for the girl but offering the counterargument that if this was love and not simply a fleeting infatuation, they could wait a few years to be married. At the very least, they should delay until summer instead of holding the ceremony in early spring when the weather could be inhospitable.

I detailed my concerns, deeming it my duty as his uncle and benefactor to provide such advice. Alas, Freddie was very young indeed and had his father's propensity for impulsivity, so I knew he would carry on with the endeavor notwithstanding the rationality of my arguments against it. I finished my letter with, "If you choose to go ahead with the wedding, of course I will be there. As always, your loving uncle, Ebenezer Scrooge."

When the day came, I made my way to the church, bracing against a driving sleet that stung my face and the cold seeping through my coat. I sat in the pew farthest away from the altar to minimize any unwelcome attention. Regrettably, my seat choice had the opposite effect. Since the other guests crowded toward the front to be as close as possible to the couple, that left a dozen empty rows between me and the other guests, with nothing to shield me from view. It did not take long for me to realize the error in my logic, but by then it was too late to switch seats because doing so would have pulled curious gazes in my direction.

The only other wedding I had attended before this was my sister's, so I did not have abundant foresight about what to expect. Freddie's wedding included all the same components, though St. Paul's Cathedral was a more formal setting than the small country chapel where Fan's ceremony had been held.

One benefit of my calamitous seat choice was that I was able to see Freddie and his bride clearly when they made their grand exit at the conclusion of the ceremony. A broad toothy smile graced his face, and I dared say the young lady was as beautiful as he had described. Her skin seemed to glow, and her ash-blond hair glistened despite the gloominess of the day. She was a petite thing, pretty, though I was not usually inclined to appreciate such things. Catherine was her name. She smiled and waved to me, sending prickles down my spine, and I beamed back at her. Freddie slowed their progress momentarily and tipped his hat to me before continuing.

One detail of wedding etiquette, which I had not recalled, was that the church emptied from the front after the ceremony ended, with the guests following the newly married couple down the aisle, past those still seated in the rows farther back. For me in the rear of the church, this meant I was the last person to leave, and every single guest had to walk past me on their way out. When my brother-in-law paraded by, I turned away and leaned over, feigning the retrieval of a fallen item from the floor. After that, I focused my gaze on the back of the pew in front of me, but each time I looked up at the procession, there were eyes staring back. The other guests were probably wondering why an old man was sitting there alone, though I did not allow their judgments to wound me. Surely, I had as much right to be there as they did, if not more.

I remained in my seat long after everyone else had left, overcome with sentiments that were difficult to categorize. Part of what I felt was happiness for Freddie. In spite of the horrid weather and his ill preparedness for the financial responsibilities of marriage, he appeared blissfully and sincerely in love. What kept me frozen in place was the juxtaposition of this with the negative thoughts pushing their way to the forefront—sadness that my sister had missed this momentous event in the life of her son and emptiness at my reality of being alone in this world, without her or Jacob. The weight of my grief bore down as heavily as a yoke on my back. My chin resting against my chest, the ringing of the church bells muffled the sound of my sobs.

CHAPTER FIFTY

UNCLE

1850

I am aware of my surroundings, though I am unsure if this clarity is fleeting, or if it is the final step in my march toward death. The drawers beside my bed retain my most precious possessions, Fan's letters, which I have kept with me all these years.

What a treasure those letters were. They lifted my spirits when I first received them in boarding school and provided solace when I read them many years later while waiting for Jacob to return home from his nighttime dalliances. They buttressed me through my tears when I found myself alone again after he passed.

Now, the knowledge that they are close provides comfort. I last held them a day or two ago, or perhaps it has been a week or a month since I have been lying here on my deathbed. I wish I could hold them now, let them remind me in my final moments of the love I shared with my sister.

I reach for them, though the most I can accomplish is to raise my hands off the bed. Even if I could manage the feat, I would not be able to read them, as I cannot force my eyelids open.

A warm hand presses on mine and a voice, tender and reassuring, accompanies it.

"Uncle," it says. "Rest, Uncle."

"He does not have much time left," another, deeper voice remarks.

I have no fondness for the second speaker, so I focus on the first. This one calls me by a title used by only one person—Freddie, my sister's sweet son. I love him dearly and have done so since the day he was born. He must care for me as well, for he is here beside me in my final hours. I must have accomplished enough good in my life to warrant the presence of this magnificent soul as I approach the end.

His voice comes again, and his words accompany me as I recede one final time into the phantom's shroud.

"I am here with you, Uncle. You are not alone."

CHAPTER FIFTY-ONE
SIMILARITIES

1843, One Day before the Ghosts

My nephew never gave up on me, God bless him. I was not sure why, for my cowardice in complying with his father's demands to keep us apart had not earned me that steadfast loyalty. Perhaps he recalled his childhood when we had sat with his mother roasting chestnuts, or the hours we spent outside when he ran from tree to tree in the park. Perhaps it was my persistence in maintaining our written correspondence over the years.

Regardless, Freddie always remembered me, particularly at Christmas. That year, he sent a card, signed by himself and his new wife, and extended multiple invitations for me to join them in celebrations of the holiday. Of course, I could not attend because of Samuel, though the weight of his threats had diminished with each passing year after Jacob's death, as the evidence needed to bolster his accusations against me no longer existed.

I could not move past my grief or find my way through the void left by the loss of those I loved. I could not experience happiness without them, nor could I celebrate with Freddie, especially not at Christmas, since that holiday was the context of my saddest moments. The mere sight of a decorated evergreen or the sound of singing carolers moved me one precarious step closer to the same debilitating depression that had left me holed up in bed for weeks after Fan died, unable to face the world.

I was nearing such a state when my nephew arrived at Scrooge and Marley's counting house.

"A merry Christmas, Uncle. God save you." His ever-cheerful voice entered the room before he did. Though it was viciously cold outside, he maintained a smile, a twinkle in his eyes, and a rosiness in his cheeks.

"Bah." I could not afford the luxury of feeling anything at all on Christmas Eve, lest melancholy overtake me. "Humbug," I added for good measure.

"Humbug, Uncle?" Freddie protested. "You don't mean that."

"I do. What reason have you to be merry? You're poor enough." It was a cruel thing to say, but I was desperate for him to leave me alone and hoped my words would push him away.

"Well, then. If I should not be happy for being poor, what reason do you have to be morose when you are rich?"

His reply was at the same time witty and accurate. I did so love this boy. I had no clever retort of my own, so I again offered a pathetic "Bah, humbug." He waited, grinning, while I explained how the world was full of fools being jolly without money enough to warrant it. I finished my rant with, "Every idiot who goes about with 'Merry Christmas' on his lips should be boiled with his own pudding, and buried with a stake of holly through his heart."

"Uncle," he chided.

"Nephew, you keep Christmas in your own way, and let me keep it in mine." I was on the brink of crying and thought being stern a better alternative to breaking down into a slobbering buffoon.

"Keep it? But you don't keep it at all," he said.

"Let me leave it alone, then." I was begging now instead of arguing. "It has never done good for any of us."

"It has for me, Uncle, and for you as well. I remember a Christmas when you and Mama sat with me, watching me open gift after gift, some of which, if I recall correctly, you yourself had procured. What happened to you?"

"Your mother, my dear sister, died at Christmastime." I wanted to say this, but I did not. "And I found Jacob dead on Christmas morning. This holiday has brought me sadness, not joy. It is a time of memorials, not celebrations. Indeed, Christmas has not been good for me at all." I did not say this aloud either.

Since my response remained trapped in my own mind, Freddie continued. "You have no answer to my question, Uncle? I have no insight myself because you refuse to offer an explanation. Regardless of why you act as you do, I beg you to stop pushing me away and embrace the love I offer, if you would only choose to accept it. There is good within you, Uncle. I know it. Let it show itself, and you may find contentment, maybe even happiness. Christmas should be celebrated, and I say, 'God bless it.'"

Bob Cratchit had been listening to this exchange, a fact that came to my attention through his raucous applause at the end of Freddie's speech.

"If I hear another sound from you," I shouted over my shoulder, "you'll spend Christmas in distress, knowing you have no job to come back to." I could almost feel the poor man cowering in his chair, and I was grateful he had the good sense to keep his mouth shut after that.

"Come. Dine with us tomorrow," Freddie said. "I promise Catherine and I will welcome you with open arms. I dare say you might enjoy it. And if you do not, then know your presence at my table will make my holiday complete."

I loved this boy with every ounce of my being, and he was steadfast in his devotion to me. For a moment, I considered his proposal, for there was nothing I wanted more than for him to be happy. But no. I refused to celebrate the day that had brought me such sorrow, sentenced me to this lonely life. It was impossible for me to add to Freddie's happiness because I had none within me to share.

I shook my head, staring down at my desk rather than at him, and muttered a dismissing "Good afternoon."

"But why?" The catch in his voice plunged a dagger into my chest. "I want nothing from you except the company of my mother's kin. Why?"

As persuasive as his argument was and despite his sincerity, he could not convince me. "Good afternoon." I said it louder this time, hoping my forcefulness would drive him out before the tears escaped the confines of my eyelids.

"I am sorry, with all my heart, to find you so resolute," he said. "Just know my invitation is sincere. If you change your mind, please join us for dinner tomorrow. I wish you a merry Christmas, Uncle. And a happy New Year." He called out the final words as he bounded into the street.

"Good afternoon," I said again after the door slammed shut behind him.

It opened again almost immediately. I had no time to recover my emotions before two men sauntered in. They were both portly, their midsections as round as the wheels of a carriage, and their smiles painfully wide, showing the full height of their teeth.

"Scrooge and Marley now, yes. It has been a long day already," one of them said, hat held between his elbow and his belly while he ran his finger along a notebook page. "Have I the pleasure of addressing Mr. Scrooge or Mr. Marley?"

This was not a good beginning to the conversation. I did not take offense to being called Marley. Rather, it gave me comfort to hear his name spoken aloud. If this man had simply addressed me by one name or the other, I might have treated him with more decency, but his framing of the question in this way made it necessary for me to explain the reason for Jacob's absence. With a mixture of animosity at their intrusion and angst at the need for me to acknowledge this unfortunate fact, I answered, "Marley is dead. He died seven years ago, this very night."

The gentleman recovered from his gaffe with a seamless grace I could never have accomplished. "We have no doubt his generosity is well represented by his surviving partner," he said, holding up a paper I presumed to be the credentials of his charity.

I looked past it and glared at him. He offered no condolences, no recognition that one half of the partnership was gone. He had not even paused at the revelation of my loss but moved forward immediately to asking for money.

A flame of rage ignited within me, and I welcomed it as a reprieve from the ever-present heartache and the proximate regret at disappointing my nephew. Unleashing a disconcerting rant upon the men, I cited the availability of prisons and workhouses as solutions for the plight of the poor. I went so far as to suggest allowing people to starve or freeze to death as a righteous option for society, as it would decrease the surplus population and lessen the burden on businessmen like me.

I banished the petitioners with the same "good afternoon" I had used to dismiss my sweet nephew. I discharged my clerk in a not dissimilar manner at day's end, though not before chastising him for taking Christmas off from work, instructing him to return promptly the day after, and threatening dismissal from his job, for the second time that day, if he did not comply.

I had been a charitable man once, delivering food and gifts to orphanages at Christmastime and making donations to the church for the care of the destitute. But that was a pursuit I had long since abandoned, a time when I was not overburdened with responsibilities as I was now. Back when Jacob was alive.

I was a vastly different man than I had once been, and it was not a change for the good. I treated the charity seekers with the same contempt Jacob had employed when he denied loans to those who did not meet his impossibly high standards. My reaction to their philanthropic requests could have been quotes of his words. It was as if his spirit inhabited me, and I had lost all sense of who I was in my heart. Instead of embracing the parts of Jacob that had made me love him, I was channeling his negative traits and incorporating them as my own. It was a disservice to him and to everyone who had the misfortune of interacting with me.

CHAPTER FIFTY-TWO

THE GHOSTS

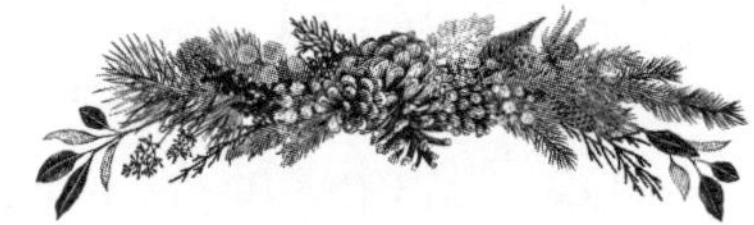

1843, The Night They Came

The ghosts came that night, after I turned away Freddie and insulted the charity seekers. The peculiarities started when I reached my front door. It was fitting that the knocker I had chosen, the one item I had contributed to the house, was where I first saw him. The metal transformed into Jacob's likeness and then smoothed back again. He fully materialized, chains and all, later that night and ushered in three spirits who taunted me, warned me, and frightened me, in turn.

The spirit of Jacob Marley, my partner in business, life, and love, must have paid a steep price in exchange for the visit. He did so to save me from the same tormented fate he suffered. He did it because he loved me.

I owed it to him to act on his warning and heed his advice, to ensure his sacrifice was not in vain. I needed to find myself again, to reclaim my penchant for compassion, which had once been at the core of my being, and to earn the blessings that came from a life of generosity and kindness.

I did so the very next day, surprising the Cratchit family and my nephew with visits and gifts. I left Jacob's cane at home that Christmas morning. I had never truly needed it anyway but had employed it as a shield to keep others away. Since I had feigned a limp to justify its use, the device had served as a literal impediment to forward progress.

The day after that, I put Jacob's house up for sale. I had no need for its four levels, multiple rooms, and expansive gardens. It was a monstrosity that kept me tied to the past, a waste of resources that could be better spent living well and doing good. It sold quickly and, though I had allowed it to fall into a state of disrepair in the years since Jacob's death, brought a high price. I sold the coach house behind it, along with the carriage I never used. I sold the furniture and the silverware, the china, pots, rugs, and draperies too. The only things I kept were our bed and the side table, which held my sister's letters. I took my books, which had traveled with me since boarding school, and the door knocker too, enlisting the help of a strong, and fortunately, handy passerby who helped me pry it off the front door before I left for the last time.

I would never stop missing Jacob, but I closed myself off from the all-encompassing grief I had wallowed in for too long. It was sad to let go of his things, but I traded the material reminders of him for the solace of my memories. They were enough to preserve his spirit in my heart throughout the remainder of my years on this earth, and I ventured they would remain with me after my mortal life ended.

The ample profit I received from the sale of the house was enough for me to live comfortably while providing generous charitable donations. Eventually, Mrs. Fezziwig joined her husband in eternity, and I sold the warehouse business, which gave me more resources to contribute to the community.

I gained a level of notoriety in London, as people delighted in the story of my sudden and extreme transformation from miser to philanthropist. Their versions included embellishments and often gross inaccuracies, but I tried not to care, so long as the essence of the narrative remained intact.

Samuel's threat to expose me posed no danger any longer. What was there for him to report? I was an old man who lived alone, smiled at everyone I passed on the street, albeit awkwardly, and gave generously to charities of all sorts. There was no evidence to support his accusations, and he would risk his own credibility if he chose to level them. It took too long for me to recognize his impotence, but I did in the end.

I brought Freddie into my counting house business and tried to be as effective and caring a mentor to him as Mr. Fezziwig had been to me. I moved to a small flat close to his house and embraced my role as uncle to him and his beautiful Catherine, who welcomed me into her family with genuine affection. I sat beside Freddie and comforted him while his wife labored to deliver his children, and I was one of the first to see his girls' pink angelic faces—so much like their grandmother's. I spent every Sunday with them, as I had with my sister when she was alive, and took the children on excursions, as I had done with Freddie.

I led a full life after the ghosts. A good life.

CHAPTER FIFTY-THREE

AT PEACE

1850

Jacob came to me seven years ago, and I believe he has been with me since, though I have no proof to substantiate it. He is standing beside the phantom now that the time has come for me to leave this world. If my fate is to join him in his interminable wandering, then I am content to walk beside him. If I have earned my place in a better eternity, I will endeavor to facilitate Jacob's passage there as well.

I lived a good life in the beginning, and again at the end. I hope it was enough to make up for the harsher years in the middle. Though I lost my way at times, I found it eventually, and redemption is itself a weighty achievement. I absorbed the lessons Jacob and his ghosts took pains to teach me—that life is precious and must be cherished; that loss is a normal part of human existence and the resulting grief cannot be allowed to engulf it; that satisfaction comes from sharing with others not only your monetary resources but also your energy, your heart, and your spirit; and that true joy is achieved only when we allow ourselves to receive those same gifts in return.

My breathing slows. Perhaps it has stopped already. The phantom has achieved his goal, and I mine. I have recounted the significant events of my life, all of them, from the happiest times I spent with Fan and Jacob to the worst days defined by anguish and loneliness. My journey has brought me to this moment, and I am finally at peace.

I changed the world for the better, altered the course of events as they may have otherwise played out. I am not dying alone and forgotten, as the spirits foretold. My nephew is here with me, and there are others. I have done enough, at least, to earn the honor of their presence with me at the end and to be remembered fondly when I am gone.

The ghosts were wrong in another prediction as well. The empty seat they showed me at the Cratchit family's table was very much occupied this year and every other since their Christmas Eve visit. I know this for certain when the sweet, strong voice of Timothy Cratchit reaches my ears.

"I am here with you, Mr. Scrooge. Your suffering is over."

Humankind is better off with Tiny Tim a part of it, and if I accomplished nothing more in my life than ensuring his survival, that single act makes my existence worthwhile. With the knowledge that this fine boy continues to light up the world with his kind heart and infectious smile, I am content to take my leave of it and accompany the phantom into the spirit realm.

"I am ready now, old friends," I say, holding Jacob's hand on one side and the phantom's on the other. "Let us travel together to the world beyond. God bless us, every one."

THE END

Acknowledgments

Writing this book was a labor of love. Though it often felt like a solitary endeavor, I could not have accomplished it without the unwavering support of my family, friends, and fellow writers. Please bear with me while I tell these people how much I appreciate them.

I'll start with those who provided tangible help to bring *Humbug* from a terrible first draft to the polished, beautifully designed book I am proud to claim as my own.

To my first readers, Mitchell, MaryBeth, and Brian, thank you for your honest and gentle feedback on my early drafts. This book is so much better because of your insights and recommendations.

I could not have asked for a better team than the one I found at Amplify Publishing and Mascot Books. To Jessica Cohn, thank you for believing in my story. Lauren Magnussen, thank you for your enthusiasm, expertise, and especially your patience throughout the production process. I felt supported through every step and am delighted with the final product.

To the talented members of my writers group, thank you for providing thoughtful feedback on my work. I leave every one of our meetings more inspired and motivated than when it started. Cheryl, Karen, Elissa, Constance, Becky, Patricia, and Stephanie, keep writing! I can't wait to read what you come up with next month.

To my fellow book-loving friends, I enjoy our discussions and the stories we share (the wine too, of course). To those who asked about my work and encouraged me over the years, thank you. It might not have seemed important, but you made a difference. My friends, I cherish you. Cheers to you and the many happy times ahead.

My family appears last on these pages, but they always come first in my life.

To Tom, my husband and partner in life, thank you for your companionship and love. We are in this together. It had to be you.

To my children, you are my everything. Mitchell, my sweet boy, every time I look at you, I see the greatest man I will ever know. I am honored to have played a role in guiding and protecting you as you grew up. I will always be your biggest fan. My beautiful Elise, I am so very proud to be your mom. Continue to forge your own path in this life and maintain your unapologetic commitment to always being your true self. I will be by your side whenever you need me, for as long as I live.

To my parents, I would be nothing without the foundation of love you provided. There is no stronger, closer family than the one you built. Mom, this much my spirit understands, our hearts are always holding hands. I know how much you sacrificed for me, and I am forever in awe at the depth and power of your love. Dad, we are alike in so many ways, which made us closer at times and distanced us at others. You taught me more about this world than anyone else.

To my siblings, I am happiest when we are together. Josh, I could not have wished for a better companion throughout childhood. You were my first friend, and I judge every other man against the precedent you set. Joseph, you are tough on the outside and compassionate on the inside, suffering alongside us during the hard times and celebrating with us through our joy. I strive to be more like you every day. Ruth, I honestly can't believe how lucky I am to have you as my sister, confidante, and ally. I count on you to be my voice of reason and continue to be amazed by your talent and commitment to the truth. Naomi, my baby sister who is now a devoted friend and quite simply the kindest, most amazing human being there is. Your mere presence, no matter where we are or what we're doing, always makes me smile.

To the people who, through questionable logic or perhaps temporary insanity, chose to marry into this family, I give you a ton of credit for putting up with our antics (not to mention my father's jokes). Jill, I am forever grateful for the positive force you have been in my children's lives. You are a treasured aunt and friend. Kevin and Nicole, thank you for adding to the fun on our many family adventures. Jared, I acknowledge your efforts.

To my nieces and nephews, Will, Kelsey, Claire, Aubrey, Emily, Drake, Christopher, Elizabeth, Connor, Waylon, and Paisley, I love you unconditionally.

To my in-laws, Mom and Dad, Bill and Missy, Julie and Noel, I am honored to be part of your family.

Finally, there is Catherine, who, though she is no longer part of this world, still manages to encourage and inspire me. I thought of her every time I sat down to write this book, determined to create a story she would have enjoyed. When self-doubt loomed and I considered giving up, when I wanted to do anything other than write, I did it anyway, for her.

Unlike Scrooge, **SARAH WHELAN** loves Christmas: the decorations, the music, the traditions—everything. She is humbled and excited to make her own contribution to the holiday with a new twist on Charles Dickens' classic tale. Sarah is a full-time professional writer, and her nonfiction has appeared in a variety of magazines. Her first novel, *The Struggle Within*, was published in 2018. She lives in Connecticut and loves spending time in her favorite city of Boston. You can reach her at **sarahwhelanwriter.com.**